To Joan —

My Life With Stella Kane

*Thank you for
being an inspiration.*

[signature]

Linda Morganstein

Regal Crest

Nederland, Texas

ISBN 978-1-935053-13-2
1-935053-13-2

First Printing 2009

9 8 7 6 5 4 3 2 1

Cover design by Donna Pawlowski

Published by:

Regal Crest Enterprises, LLC
4700 Highway 365, Suite A, PMB 210
Port Arthur, Texas 77642-8025

Find us on the World Wide Web at
http://www.regalcrest.biz

Printed in the United States of America

For Melanie, who helps me see the big picture

Everyone suspects himself of at least one of the cardinal virtues, and this is mine: I am one of the few honest people I have ever known.
~Nick Carraway, in **The Great Gatsby**

I think it goes back to the happy ending. If you want it badly enough, it will be the way it's supposed to be, in the movies.
~Cheryl Crane, daughter of Lana Turner

Prologue:

Nina Speaks Out, May 2003

I'M A LESBIAN. There, I've said it.

Some of you younger people might not understand why it's taken so long for me to admit this. Listen, I started in show business a long time ago, when people hid their sexuality.

Now the love of my life has passed away. On her deathbed, she asked me to tell about us. I will be the primary character in this story. I take full responsibility for portraying myself as a young woman.

I'm seventy-six now, but I don't feel old. Age, like sexual persuasion, is apparently more fluid these days. Looking back, I'm not ashamed about our decisions. Our life was too full for that kind of baloney. It wasn't always honest. How could it have been? I'm telling a Hollywood fable, after all.

This is a story of self-invention and drama. It's a story about the value and limitations of truth. Most of all, it's the story of the bond I shared with a woman and a legend. She was a star. She was the one I knew best and the one who will always remain a mystery to me.

Imagine a young woman hovering at the exit door of a train arriving at the Los Angeles station in the summer of 1948. That girl was me, Nina Weiss. This is where her story begins.

This is the story of my life with Stella Kane.

Chapter
One

The Arrival: June 1948

"NINA! NINA! OVER here!"

Elaine's cry pierced the air like a mighty siren's song. Nina hovered at the exit door of the Santa Fe Super Chief, amidst the clamor of brakes and the squealing of wheels, feeling dizzy from the engine fumes. She waved at her cousin. In that moment, hand raised in salute, she was struck by the foolishness of what she'd done. Four days of travel was the least of it. Now she'd arrived.

Of course, she had questioned her decision to come to Hollywood, but she'd staved off an attack of nerves by rereading Dante's *Inferno* on the trip. In Italian.

And then, too, she'd been blessed with distractions from the other first-class passengers, who'd felt the need to confess their life stories to her. There was a tense man with chapped lips named Wilson Purcell, a Mrs. Arberry who looked like a turtle and wore four different hats in four days, and a flirtatious Army Lieutenant with a missing leg whose name she'd already forgotten.

Nina adopted a cheerful façade as she stepped down to the platform. Her cousin barreled towards her, yanked via pink leash by a yapping poodle. Elaine wore a close-fitting white skirt and white box jacket with wide lapels. Underneath the jacket was a peach-colored silk blouse with a plunging neckline. She looked like a piece of ripe fruit bursting from gift-wrapping. The pooch strained at its jeweled collar, trying to scrabble up Nina's leg.

"No, no, Collette," Elaine reprimanded. She appeared to be drinking Nina in, scrutinizing every inch of her.

"I look dreadful," Nina blurted out. She was not blessed with a taste for fashion and it showed.

"You're marvelous," Elaine replied, reaching up to tap Nina's shoulder with a red-polished nail. "Just what the doctor ordered."

Nina glanced around at the people crowding the platform, dressed in bright outfits. She shuddered, thinking of what her suitcases contained. Dresses from Peck and Peck, button-down shirts from Brooks Brothers, penny loafers, knee socks, pleated slacks for more casual occasions. Conservative, practical clothes. She might as well have brought ice skates to Egypt. "I didn't bring the right clothes," she confessed.

"Come," Elaine said, "The limo's waiting and we have many, many things to discuss. You look fabulous. Very collegiate."

They proceeded to race through the station. They rushed through the exit. Outside, the sun was blinding, anchored in a relentlessly blue sky.

Elaine pulled out two pairs of sunglasses. "No one from New York thinks to bring these." They waited on the sidewalk as the limo driver loaded Nina's luggage into the trunk, then lifted Colette, who had stopped yapping and was licking the driver's cheek, into the front passenger seat.

Once in the limo, Elaine began rustling through her briefcase. For a time, they rode in silence, cruising west on Sunset Boulevard, whisking past cafés, nightclubs and elegant shops. The whole place seemed immaculate and weightless. "What a gorgeous day," Nina commented.

Elaine glanced out the glass. "It's always like this."

"How does anyone get anything done?"

"You'd be surprised." Elaine cleared her throat. "Speaking of getting things done, we were hoping you'd stay at least until September."

"I told you. I can only stay six weeks. I have plans with my fiancé and his parents."

"That's Bobby, isn't it?"

"Billy," Nina corrected. "Billy Waxman."

"The Waxmans. Aren't they related to the Guggenheims?"

"No. Billy's father is the Guggenheim family's urologist. He's Daddy's doctor, too. That's how Billy and I met."

Elaine yawned, then clamped her hand over her mouth. "Sorry. I've been burning lots of midnight oil lately." She smiled at Nina. "I'm surprised he let you go."

"He was upset. His parents were upset. My father was upset. Everyone was upset." Nina smiled ruefully. "Were you surprised that I let you convince me?"

"No. I was very persistent." Elaine returned the smile. "From the moment I met you at the funeral, I knew you'd be perfect for the project I have in mind." She wagged a finger at Nina. "Besides, I just had a hunch that you needed a change."

Nina felt a lump growing in her throat. When Elaine had approached her a few months before at their grandfather's funeral in upstate New York, she was not only introduced to a side of the family she'd never known, but she was offered a proposition that appeared at first irrational and ridiculous.

Her life was arranged quite nicely. When she graduated from college, she'd marry Billy Waxman and settle down to have perfect children. Any doubts were buried, although they occasionally surfaced as headaches between her eyebrows, in the region described as the all-knowing third eye.

Nina was jarred from her ruminations by the weight of a manuscript being dropped onto her lap.

"Read this script by tomorrow," Elaine said. "Just skim through it in bed before you go to sleep. That's what I do."

"I'm a very fast reader," Nina bragged. "Especially in English."

Elaine lifted her eyebrows in mock astonishment. "What else do you read in?"

"Oh," she replied, "Italian and French. A little Latin."

"Why, that's so impressive." Elaine pointed to the script. "It's called *The Threat From Within*. Do you remember *A Sister's Nightmare*?"

"I didn't see it," she said. "I don't usually go to Hollywood movies. Mostly, I've seen foreign films. I like the Italians, especially Visconti. I saw *Ossessione* a couple of years ago in Rome."

"Obscure foreign films. Oh, my." Elaine shuddered. "Harley Burton directed *A Sister's Nightmare* in the thirties. It was his only Academy Award nomination. Got beaten out by John Ford for *Grapes of Wrath* and he went downhill after that. Now we've dragged him from the drunken stupor he calls retirement to do a remake, only with Communists instead of gangsters."

"It's awful what they're accusing people of," Nina said.

Elaine held up a warning finger. "No politics at the studio."

Before Nina could ask how making a picture about the evils of Communism fit into this policy statement, Elaine held up a photograph she had also pulled from her case. "What do you think? Her name is Stella Kane."

"She's quite a dish." Nina tried to hand back the photo, but Elaine refused to take it.

"What is it about her?" Elaine persisted. "What do you see?"

By this time, they had crossed into Beverly Hills and turned north on Benedict Canyon Drive. The streets were spotless, with not a pedestrian in sight, the yards were the size of public parks. Nina took a deep breath. She studied the young woman in the photo. "Her eyes mock the world." They continued to climb up a steep, curved road lined with houses that grew even larger as their altitude rose. Up, up, they climbed. Nina studied the photograph with more attention. "It's hard to ignore her appeal, but she's a bit coarse."

Elaine lifted her sunglasses and stared at Nina. "That's very good."

"All my professors insist I have a gift for analysis," she replied.

Elaine let her sunglasses settle back onto the bridge of her nose. "White trash."

"Elaine!"

Elaine shrugged. "We've managed to knock off the crudest edges, but we have a tough road ahead. Our stunning hillbilly needs to be less crude without losing her effect."

"Like Pygmalion."

Elaine's face lit up. "Just like Pygmalion. Every studio in town wanted those rights. And MGM got that ogre Shaw to adapt his own play."

"Actually, I was thinking of the original tale by Ovid, *Metamorphoses*. Where Shaw got his inspiration."

Elaine smiled. "Honey, I didn't go to Barnard. You're going to have to enlighten me."

"A sculptor named Pygmalion carves his ideal woman from a piece of stone. He prays to the goddess Venus, who transforms the stone woman into flesh and blood. I was making an analogy about transformation. You want Stella Kane changed, but more alive than ever."

"I told them," Elaine murmured. "You're perfect."

Nina squinted at her cousin. "Where do I fit into this?"

Elaine placed a hand on Nina's lap. "You look very tired. We can discuss details later."

Nina leaned back against the snakeskin-soft leather seat and closed her eyes. She imagined a snake crawling from its casing. She imagined how tired that snake must be, shedding its old protection. "That girl could get under your skin," she whispered.

Elaine's voice floated towards her. "That's what we're banking on."

Stella Kane's lovely, defiant face floated into Nina's consciousness, as clearly as if she were looking at the photo. Not my skin, she thought to herself.

Chapter
Two

Big Dreams

NINA KNEW ABOUT big houses. She'd grown up in Scarsdale, after all. But her uncle's place was showy on another scale. When she and her cousin arrived at the top of a steep hill on a private drive off Benedict Canyon Drive, they were faced with a remarkable sight. The Villa was modeled on a palazzo in Tuscany. The main house had seventeen rooms, three verandas, twelve fireplaces, and a courtyard with three spouting fountains.

After a whirlwind tour, Elaine led her to The Cottage, a seven-room affair situated about a hundred yards from the larger building. "I'm staying there, too," Elaine said. "Just temporarily, until I sort out some details of my life." She paused. "Now, we can get to know each other. Like real families."

Real families. Nina smiled weakly and left for a much-needed nap.

That evening, Uncle Irwin and Aunt Nettie greeted Nina and Elaine with bear hugs and exclamations. Nina's father had never been a demonstrative man. This side of the family was different, apparently. Both her aunt and uncle were small people, but they radiated an energy equivalent to a large invading army.

"You can call me Poppa," her uncle informed her. "Everyone does, except my wife."

Although she was absolutely famished, Nina was led, at her uncle's insistence, to a glass room off the ballroom. As they entered, she gasped. Everywhere were tiny stunted trees in glazed ceramic vessels.

"My bonsai paradise." Poppa took her elbow. "This is a fairy tale forest. Over here is a rare species worth more than I want to say. See how it bends in the imaginary wind? I grew it that way. I learned this ancient art from my gardener Carl who spent the war in Okinawa."

"It's stunning. A beautiful miniature world."

"With movies, you have ambitious dumbbells to manage and greedy corporate bastards—excuse my language—to answer to.

Now politicians breathing down our necks, as though we're trying to destroy America. My god! We love America more than anybody." Poppa sighed. "Here, in this room, I am nature itself. I control it all." He glanced reflexively over his shoulder, as though he was afraid of being overheard, even in his private universe.

Their "light" supper took place in a dining room dominated by glowing crystal chandeliers, red velvet drapes, Italian Renaissance antiques and a wall of windows overlooking a valley of lights that was the city of Los Angeles. A starched butler served poached salmon and Waldorf salad and an array of meats accompanied by slices of baked bread and assorted crackers. Nina piled a generous selection onto her plate, under the watchful eyes of her relatives.

"She has an appetite," Poppa commented.

Aunt Nettie pinched the generous fold of skin dangling from her upper arm. "If I ate like that, I'd be as big as a house!"

"You like our place?" Poppa asked.

"It's marvelous," Nina replied.

Poppa inspected her. "Too gaudy for you. I know how you grew up. Tudor place on a maple-lined street, right?"

"American Colonial," she corrected.

"A white picket fence," Poppa continued. "I know my brother. Like he stepped out of an Andy Hardy movie. Living with the gentiles in Scarsdale. That's all right. Look, we both went through hell as kids. We lost our mother..." He paused, looking at Nina's face. "Whatsa matter?"

"Nothing," Nina sputtered.

Poppa's eyes grew teary. "I'm sorry, honey. You lost your mother, too. I kept track of you and your father, you know. Your father is a good man. He was always a good boy. A little bit of a stiff, maybe, but a good person. Our father, that's another story. A nasty gambler who did bad things. Both your father and I dropped him. I went to Hollywood, your father went to Harvard. Me, I didn't try to erase my past. Your father, he dropped all of us. But enough of the past." His face brightened. "Let's talk about you!"

"Irwin," Aunt Nettie said. "Leave her alone. She's tired."

"Elaine said you're engaged," Poppa said.

"His name is Billy Waxman. He's the son of Daddy's urologist."

"*Urologist?*" Poppa exclaimed. "I'll bet the son wants to be a urologist, too."

"As a matter of fact, yes. He's going into practice with his father when he finishes residency."

"The wife of a urologist." Poppa's eyes glowed. "If it was a movie, I'd have the girl coming to Hollywood just after the engagement." He paused dramatically. "But what happens to the girl? Nina, what happens to the girl?"

"Irwin," Aunt Nettie said. "Look at her face, you're upsetting her."

"I want to know her dreams. What are your dreams, honey?"

What were her dreams? Nina thought of Billy Waxman, of her vision of life with him. She felt a tear roll down her cheek.

"She's sad because she has no dreams," Poppa announced.

"She's sad because she has an uncle who's pestering her," Aunt Nettie said.

"You want something different," Poppa said. "That's why you came here."

"Irwin! I'm going to stuff a napkin in your mouth!" Aunt Nettie warned.

"If Shakespeare was alive today, this is where he'd be. He knew that the people need entertainment. There's nothing like it, you'll see. I know you think we're heathens, but you'll be surprised. You'll be surprised at how all this gets under your skin."

Under your skin. Nina shuddered. Poppa seemed like he was about to go on, but Aunt Nettie announced Nina should be sent to bed.

Nina and Elaine strolled back to The Cottage through a maze of flowerbeds in the magnificent gardens, under a magical sky. If possible, the star-filled night was even more enchanting than the day's sunny radiance.

"You were quiet tonight," Nina commented.

"I have a lot on my mind." Elaine cleared her throat. "Say, did you notice anything funny about Poppa?"

"Not really."

"Don't be polite."

"Nothing," Nina insisted. But she was fibbing. Poppa was obviously a man who felt hunted. He kept looking over his shoulder.

"Poppa is a genius. But ever since he had a mild stroke two years ago, he leans on an executive committee. And they're a pack of wolves. Not to mention the bunch of vultures he has to answer to at the corporate headquarters in New York." Elaine frowned, watching Nina's face. "Now that you're my assistant, you'll be learning a lot. I know you won't mention anything to anyone."

"Of course not," Nina replied, but she was barely listening. The air smelled of a hundred different exotic blooms. She could have dropped into a bed of flowers and dozed in their intoxicating fragrance.

"Nina?"

"Yes?"

"Tomorrow, it would be nice if you wore something very much

like you're wearing today."

Nina thought of her wardrobe. Everything she owned was very much like what she'd worn today.

Chapter
Three

The First Encounter

THE NEXT MORNING, an eager young woman in a French maid's uniform poured a cup of coffee for Nina. With an odd accent, she asked to be called Marie. Nina was reclining in a four-poster bed crowned with a silken canopy. The sun streamed through tall windows. Buried in the covers beside her was her crumpled copy of *The Threat From Within*. As Marie poured the coffee, Nina said, "*Je suis tres fatigue. Et vous? Ça va?*" The maid responded with a look of complete astonishment.

"I'm not French!" she exclaimed. "No one expects me to *speak* French!" She smiled at Nina's puzzled look. "I grew up in Nevada. But if you want the best job, you get on with the European Specialty Domestics Agency. They give you a name and what country you come from, then you take a training course, but who can remember all the words? No one cares. They don't talk to you anyway."

"What's your real name?" Nina asked.

"Betty. Betty Gretty. Isn't that for the birds? I like Marie better."

"I've spent some time in France. If you have any questions, I'd be happy to help," Nina offered.

Now that they were compatriots, Marie sat on the edge of Nina's bed. "Everybody at home in Winnemucca thinks I've got such a glamorous life, but there's always a price to pay. You'll see when you've been here long enough."

"I'm only here for six weeks."

"Sure." Marie winked at Nina. "We'll see. Anyway, I can't talk your ear off. Your cousin made me swear to get you out of bed lickety-split."

On this beautiful morning—maybe Elaine was right, maybe every day was beautiful—Nina put on a plaid skirt, a white cotton blouse, a green wool sweater and pumps with low heels. Elaine was at the breakfast table, sipping coffee and studying a copy of *Variety* when Nina arrived in the sunroom.

"You look terrific," Elaine commented. After Nina sat, she

pointed to a photo on the windowsill by the table. It was an eight by ten of Elaine and a familiar-looking older man.

"That's Eric Flint," Nina said. The whole world knew of Eric Flint. He was an aging icon still making swashbuckler movies. Even Nina knew of him.

"He's not here this morning but don't be surprised if he's here at breakfast sometimes." Elaine shrugged. "I was only nineteen when we got together. Poppa was livid. He would have fired Eric, but I wouldn't let him."

Marie brought soft-boiled eggs in ceramic cups, cottage cheese and dry toast. Elaine explained she was dieting. Nina wasn't. She took everything from the tray after Elaine had served herself and put it on her plate.

"Do you have any extra butter and jam?" Nina asked.

Elaine watched Nina tear into her food. "Do you always eat this way?"

"I guess."

"Lucky." Elaine pointed to the script Nina had brought along. "What do you think?"

"It was interesting."

"I didn't hire you to be polite, at least not to me. It's awful. But every studio in town is trying to find a way to make pictures that prove how American we are. Thank God we have the cast we do, and that's only because they were strong-armed. Every one of them deserves more than this script, including the director." She smiled. "I've known Harley Burton forever. I always called him Uncle Harley. Do you know that Uncle Harley pinched me on the rear end at my Sweet Sixteen party? Probably had six glasses of champagne, but that's no excuse."

"What did you do?" Nina asked.

"I announced it to the whole room."

"You didn't!"

"Of course I did," Elaine said. "I'd already learned not to get pushed around."

Nina looked at the set of Elaine's shoulders. At her strong jaw crunching on the dry toast. It was hard to imagine anyone pushing her around.

Elaine jumped up. "Yikes! Look at the time! We have to go!"

They rode to the studio in Elaine's powder blue Oldsmobile top-down convertible, their heads wrapped in silk scarves. At the gates of Lumina Pictures, the guard waved them past a line of waiting cars. They pulled into a parking spot labeled with Elaine's name.

Lumina loomed in front of them, a walled-in stronghold of stucco buildings capped with red tile roofs. Everywhere, people were rushing. In costumes, on bicycles, wheeling lights and bulging carts of mail. Everyone, down to the last person, wore a bigheaded expression, as though they were doing something earth-shattering. Elaine led Nina through the outdoor sets. A tenement street in Chicago, a Tahitian village of thatched huts, a pristine Anywhere America main street.

"They don't look at all real," Nina said.

"It's wonderful, isn't it? Let me show you what we do to make it real." Elaine pointed out where the costumes were sewn, where the props were stored, where the stars were made up and coiffed, where the writers typed.

Finally, they arrived at an imposing row of huge warehouse-like structures. Elaine pushed open the heavy metal door of Sound Stage 73. As they entered, Nina gasped. The place was as cavernous as an airplane hangar. It was filled with wires and lights and cameras and props and screens and walkways suspended across the heights, mysterious fixtures hanging from every corner. In the center of it all was the set, the absolute focal point, a square of dramatic setting about to come alive.

"Quiet!" a young man holding a clapboard called. "Quiet on the set!"

A hush fell.

"Cameras rolling," someone shouted.

"Action!" the director called.

From a side door, the girl from the photo entered the set.

"Robert?" Stella said, wiping fake snow from her shoulders. "It's awful out there." She approached a boy lying on a shabby couch. Nina was surprised at how deep and resonant the girl's voice was.

Elaine had briefed Nina on the cast as they'd made their way to the sound stage. The young man was a puckish aging chorus boy named Lance Lewis.

An older woman poked her head out from a door, gripping a potholder. Sybil Croft was an icon. But on this day, Sybil's aristocratic features were blunted with thick makeup, her hair dyed dull and gray.

"Oh, children," Sybil said. "I'm going to cook for you tonight. I really think I'm well again." She looked humiliated. Whether it was a piece of brilliant acting or true humiliation at the awful role she was playing, Nina wasn't so sure. Sybil disappeared behind the door.

Stella crossed to the couch. She fingered the lapels of Lance's overcoat. "You're in your winter clothes, my brother. Are you very cold?"

"No, I'm feverishly hot," Lance replied, bugging out his eyes.

"I'm too hot, sis. I got troubles, you know? Big troubles."

Nina thought she heard a muffled groan from one of two men standing nearby. His crony grimaced and poked his companion.

A knock at the door. Hollace Carter entered. He was also a household name, in a steady rivalry with Cary Grant. He was, in fact, taller and better built than Grant, with a more chiseled face and captivating hazel-colored eyes. He held up a federal agent's badge. "I was just in the neighborhood."

"Get out!" Lance cried. "I have done nothing wrong. You are hounding me for nothing. Nothing, nothing." He jumped up from the couch and stumbled to the door, fleeing into the storm. After a moment's hesitation, Hollace followed, looking puzzled.

"Robert!" Stella cried. She walked to the mantelpiece and picked up a photo, then set it down and stood center stage, staring into space.

Nina glanced around the set. Some of the waiting crew had paused, coffee cups in midair. "Help us," Stella said to the empty room. "My brother is a victim of evil. He is a pawn of terrible invaders trying to take away everything that is good in this country." Everything in Stella's delivery spoke of anguish rising from her heart. "Please help us. Someone please help us."

Nina felt tears forming in her eyes.

"CUT!" Harley Burton roared. "Print it."

The crew burst into applause. Stella bowed as they catcalled and clapped.

"Uncle Harley!" Elaine called.

Harley Burton took a few steps towards them, his arms outstretched. Harley was splotchy-skinned, with a veiny, bulbous nose and a bulging potbelly. Elaine and Nina began to slide backward, but they weren't quick enough. Harley squeezed Nina's torso against his. His shirt was damp. "This must be cousin Nina! Could she be a more perfect co-ed? I could use her in my next film, *College Night Out.*" Then he released her and gestured at Elaine. "But this one. She's a tiger!"

"Is everything going all right?" Elaine asked.

A vague look of dissatisfaction crossed Harley's face. "The script." He sighed. "Ah, the script is, well, challenging." Then, just as quickly, he adopted his former pep. "I've had worse," he proclaimed. "I can do this movie, for crying out loud. Look at that girl, Stella. She'll make it work. Where the hell did you find that kid? She's a gift from God."

"Sir!" An assistant rushed up, breathing hard. "He's coming."

A path opened and Poppa marched through, trailed by a gangly, hawk-nosed young man with dark circles under his eyes. "Girls!" Poppa cried when he spotted them. He turned to his gangly assistant, who was gripping a stack of papers. "Murray, this is Nina, my brilliant and attractive niece graduating from Vassar."

"Barnard," Nina said. "I'm a junior."

"This is Murray Lasky." Poppa leaned in to Nina and announced in a stage whisper: "We're having lunch at Hillcrest at one on Sunday. Be there. I want you and Murray to get to know each other."

Nina nodded. She didn't like the glow in her uncle's eyes. She turned back to the set. The entire crew was pretending to be busy.

"Attention!" Poppa shouted. He grabbed the wad of papers from Murray Lasky and marched up to the middle of the living room set. "Our government has become very concerned with Communists in the picture business. This movie will show where Lumina stands." He waved his batch of papers. "I have here a loyalty oath." A still photographer rushed over, ready to record the signings.

"Wait a minute!"

All eyes turned. A man hobbled towards them. Nina watched a look of dislike spread across Poppa's face. To Nina, the man's haughty look pegged him as an educated waspy type. She wondered how he'd found his way to Hollywood.

"Who's that?" she whispered.

"Dick Preston, the head producer on this picture," Elaine whispered back. "He's a stuck-up snob, if you want my opinion."

"Isn't this a bit unusual?" Dick Preston asked, limping up to the studio head. "Interrupting production?"

"Of course it is! Why do you think I'm doing it?"

Harley Burton coughed for attention, then piped in. "Preston's right. What's more important, a few signatures or this incredible film which is being at this moment delayed?"

"You can't be taking his side," Poppa said, eyes wide with disbelief.

Harley placed a hand on Poppa's shoulder. "Look, everyone knows Lumina doesn't employ Reds. Why call attention? Boy who cried wolf, know what I mean?"

Poppa paused. Everyone on the set paused. He looked around, frowning. "A leader knows when to retreat." He shook the wad of papers in his hand. "Forget it."

As soon as the executives were gone, the bustle began again, this time with a palpable air of reprieve.

"A close-up of Lance next," Harley called. "Stella, Sybil, Hollace, why don't you take a break? We'll call you when we need you."

"Stella!" Elaine called, as the actors began to leave the set. "I'd like you to meet my cousin."

Stella's eyes flitted from the tips of Nina's penny loafers to the top of her head. She held out a hand.

Nina squeezed Stella's hand firmly. For a moment, they stood there, hands locked. Then slowly Stella let go. "I don't think you got that squeeze from milking cows," she commented.

"Of course not. I got it from tennis. I'm captain of the varsity team at Barnard."

Stella grinned at her. "Maybe you can teach me your grip sometime. And I'll show you how to squeeze milk from a cow's udder."

Nina felt a rising exasperation. This low-class girl was teasing her and she didn't like it.

Elaine meanwhile was watching with an odd look on her face, and who knew what *she* was thinking? "Nina will be assisting me with your publicity. She's very near your age, you know." She looked back and forth between the two of them.

"I'm happy to help you," Nina offered. "I have a number of ideas."

"A number of ideas," Stella said. "I guess I'm pretty darned uncouth, aren't I? White trash. You're here to give me some lessons? Learn croquet? Speak like a college girl?"

"I do know *something* about what results from a good upbringing." Nina swallowed hard. "I'm sorry. I didn't mean anything insulting."

For a moment, Stella locked eyes with Nina. "I was kidding with you. I do that."

They watched her saunter away. Elaine took Nina's arm. "See? I told you she'd cooperate."

"That's cooperation?" Nina exclaimed.

" For a rising star, yes. Get used to dealing with celebrities. Do you know what makes a star? They're impossible to ignore. Don't question her powers to seduce you. Everyone feels it."

"I see," Nina replied, although she didn't see. Her brain wasn't working properly. Something about Stella had shaken her up.

Chapter
Four

The Meeting

"I TOLD POPPA that Murray Lasky was the last guy you'd date, even if you weren't engaged. He was a nothing little messenger boy. He thought up the idea of redoing Harley's old movie and let Dick Preston take the credit, so he was promoted to assistant." They were racing once again across the studio grounds.

Elaine frowned. "I'm a woman, they'd never let me run the studio. Poppa needs a successor. He's getting desperate enough to consider someone like Murray, whom he can at least groom into the position."

They hit a crossing in the road between two sound stages. Four men in bunny suits, a gorilla and an army of toy soldiers blocked their progress. "Poppa puts movie-making first." Elaine glanced at Nina as they stood waiting. "He seems boorish to you. And you think I'm pushy, too."

Nina started to object. Elaine held up her hand. "Poppa and I know how to make movies. He's looking for someone with the same devotion. Murray's the best bet so far. Poppa is trying to match-make something with you and Murray so he can keep it all in the family. Listen to me. You have a special place here. You're family, and who knows what will happen?"

"I'm only here for six weeks," Nina said. "How much can happen?"

"Oh, my," Elaine cried. "We're late." She raced into the crowd of costumes. Nina took a deep breath and raced after her, elbowing her way through the large bunnies.

They burst into the publicity department, burst past the secretaries, burst into the conference room. Murray Lasky was already seated at the conference table, along with three other men.

"You already met Murray this morning on the set," Elaine said. "Dick Preston's talented assistant."

Murray winked at Nina with conspiratorial familiarity. He had an air of sweet resignation. Nina had to agree with Elaine. He seemed like an unlikely studio head.

"This is our boss and head of publicity, Aaron Bermann." Elaine had already explained to Nina that they answered directly to Aaron, although Nina had gotten the distinct impression that Elaine, on some more ethereal level, answered to no one.

Aaron was tan, had close-cut, wiry silver hair and a barrel-chested wrestler's body. Some would consider him good-looking, but Nina found his overly self-conscious masculine appearance unappealing.

"And this is Shanahan," Elaine said. "Patrick Shanahan, although no one uses the first name. Just Shanahan. Isn't that right, Shanahan?" She didn't wait for an answer. "Shanahan answers to Aaron, too."

Aaron adopted a sneer that was supposed to be a smile. "What the hell did your mother call you, Shanahan? I've always wondered."

Shanahan could have been Spencer Tracy's bitter brother. He had rust-colored hair and gentle features offset by a hard-boiled scowl. He glanced challengingly at Aaron, and then went back to doodling on a pad of paper. Aaron's eyes narrowed, but he didn't pursue the topic.

"Last but not least," Elaine said, breaking into the silence with an unruffled tone, "this is Dick Preston. Head producer on our movie and also part of my father's executive committee."

"Very pleased to meet you again," Dick said, with a private school accent. Now it was his turn to give Nina a conspiratorial look. Just how many unspoken conspiracies were floating around this room?

"What the hell would I be doing watching a high school play in Ohio?" Murray Lasky said suddenly, in a loud, indignant voice. He waved a piece of paper, taking up an argument that had apparently started before Elaine and Nina entered.

"What the hell does it matter?" Aaron replied. "Nobody cares about you. It's all about the broad."

Dick Preston cleared his throat. Aaron looked over at Elaine and Nina. "Pardon my language," he said with utter lack of concern. "Elaine," he continued, "would you explain to this numbskull why we can't have this girl be some white trash number discovered in a gas station?"

"I understand the principle," Murray said, "I just don't see how I'd wind up watching a high school play in some podunk town in backwoods Ohio."

"Oh, brother," Aaron sighed. "Now *everyone* needs to have a *motivation*." He snatched the paper from Murray. His eyes settled on Nina. "You're the one going to some fancy college back east, right?"

"Barnard, actually."

Aaron held the paper out to her. "It's Stella Kane's biography. We're fixing it up. Murray kidnapped the bombshell from a garage on his drive out here from New York."

"I didn't kidnap her!" Murray said.

Nina could feel everyone's eyes boring down on her.

"Honey," Aaron offered, "the public needs an image. You saw that girl this morning. She's a knock-out, isn't she?"

Everyone was watching her. She studied the text. Then she handed the paper back to Aaron. "Her being the adopted daughter of a Presbyterian minister is good. And the part about her drama teacher isn't too far-fetched."

"See?" Aaron said to the rest of the group. "It works. I told you, it works."

"Couldn't you be a talent scout on your way to Hollywood via automobile?" Nina asked Murray. "You stop to visit an aunt and get invited to a neighbor kid's play, never suspecting to find such a gem."

Murray shrugged. "I'm a supposed talent agent discovering a supposed actress in a supposed play. Why not? What's the play?"

"Who cares?" Aaron said.

Dick Preston smiled condescendingly at Aaron. "Dottie Strong will ask. You know she hates ingénues. She'll tear Stella Kane apart if our beauty doesn't know the play she was supposed to be in."

"All goddamn right," Aaron said. "So, put in the name of a play."

"What play?" Dick persisted.

"What the hell does it matter?" Aaron roared. "What's that one we optioned last year? That guy from Tennessee."

"He isn't from Tennessee. His name is Tennessee," Dick said. "No, I don't think that any of his work will do. It's a little risqué." He was grinning wickedly at Nina. "What do you suggest?"

For a moment, Nina hesitated. Then she had an inspiration.

"Ibsen," she said. "*A Doll's House.* The *broad* could play the lead part, Nora." She glanced around the table.

"Hmmm," Aaron said. "Sounds classy."

"I've set up an interview for Stella with Dottie Strong next week," Elaine broke in. "We need to get straight on Stella's background and get the information to Stella right away so she can have it memorized." Elaine paused and looked around the table.

"The only one who knows about the play is Nina," Aaron said. "Let her fill Stella in."

"I don't think she'll listen to me," Nina objected.

"Whatever gave you that idea?" Elaine asked.

"I don't think she likes me," Nina said.

"She doesn't like any of us. That's the way they are. All we want is for you to explain what the play's about," Aaron said. "I mean, after all, you came out here to work. Not just to be Irwin Weiss's niece."

With that statement, everyone except Shanahan stared at her.

"All right," Nina said. "But just the play."

"Of course," Aaron said. He paused. No one spoke. "Well," he added, "if you should notice anything about her that we need to work on, you being acquainted with a classy way of life, you might mention it to us."

"You want me to spy?"

"Honey, this is America!" Aaron cried. "We don't spy. We observe."

"It's for her own good," Elaine said.

"You're giving the kid a break," Aaron cajoled. "Is that too much to ask? Helping a kid get what she wants?"

"I guess not."

"Then it's settled. Meeting adjourned." The entire group except Shanahan beamed at her.

Just as the meeting was wrapping up, Shanahan spoke. "What about Sybil Croft?"

There was a moment of heavy silence. Shanahan's lip curled as he looked around the table. "You bastards," he breathed out.

"I'm not going to say this again. Can the publicity for now. Nothing about Sybil Croft." Aaron glared at Shanahan.

"I won't let you turn this fine woman into a has-been," Shanahan said.

Aaron leaned towards Shanahan with an intent look. "I can turn you into a has-been."

Shanahan stared at his pad.

"All right," Aaron said. He, Dick and Murray rushed out. Elaine and Nina got up to go. Shanahan didn't move.

"Honestly," Elaine said, as they rushed past the secretaries, who were pulling lunch bags from their drawers, "that man is impossible."

"Which one?" Nina asked.

Elaine glanced over at Nina as though she was completely thickheaded. "Shanahan," she said.

"He seems very cynical," Nina observed.

"That's his one mood, except when he's drunk, then he's cynical and sarcastic. We wouldn't keep him, but he's the best head planter in Hollywood."

"Head planter?" Nina imagined Shanahan in a monstrous garden, shoveling dirt, with a pile of heads stacked beside him.

"The planters plant publicity items in the papers and

magazines. Shanahan is the best. He knows all the tricks and everyone in this town respects him. He used to be one of the best newspapermen in Chicago."

"Then what made him take this job?"

"I shouldn't be telling you this." Elaine peered around. "He used to be a priest. But he got kicked out of the church for stirring up trouble. Then he got himself kicked out of Chicago altogether for writing about corrupt politicians. I think he's punishing himself by working at a Hollywood studio. Like Catholic repentance or something."

They were back on the pathway now, headed to the commissary.

Nina stopped abruptly. "Oh, no."

"What's the matter?"

"I forgot my purse."

Elaine glanced at her watch. "Run back up. I'd never keep up with you. I'll wait."

Shanahan was still sitting in the same place, doodling on the same piece of paper. Nina could now see he was creating elaborate Catholic crosses. He pulled a flask from his jacket pocket and took a swig from it. "Lunch. Want some?"

She shook her head.

He took another swig from the flask. "Newly hired assistants don't usually get to come to these meetings. Nice to be the boss's niece."

She didn't know what to say. She certainly wasn't going to justify herself to this peculiar, rude man.

"Hey, sorry," he said with a rueful grin. "You didn't ask to be who you are, did you, kid? Well, welcome to Hollywood."

Chapter
Five

Discovery

MARIE BURST INTO the bedroom at eleven-thirty on Sunday, opening the curtains to the usual stream of sunshine. "Rise and shine, Mademoiselle. You'll be late."

"You don't have to call me Mademoiselle when we're alone." Nina yawned and stretched, accepting the coffee tray that Marie had carried in.

"Hey, who's in the uniform pouring coffee for who?" Marie replied cheerfully. "Anyway, I gotta stay in my role so as not to mess up in public. Now, better get a move on or it's my head gonna roll for not waking you up sooner."

After days of rushing from meeting to meeting, visits to the set and endless information, Nina had fallen into bed at ten o'clock that Saturday night. She'd left a note on the door begging to be allowed to sleep in. Now, she gulped down her coffee, then jumped from the bed and put on a nice pale green golf shirt and a matching golf skirt that highlighted her tanned legs. At twelve-thirty, she rushed out to the driveway where the cream-colored Buick roadster she'd been presented for the summer was waiting.

At the Hillcrest Country Club, she was led to Poppa's table. The Hillcrest, she had been informed, was the best country club in Los Angeles that allowed Jews. In fact, it had been built for Jews and was a haven for the wealthiest of them. Of course, this wasn't shocking information. Daddy was not allowed at the gentile Scarsdale clubs, having instead to join the Century Club in nearby Purchase. Daddy insisted that someday there would be many Jews in Scarsdale, but who knew if that was his idealistic side? Besides, Nina suspected he liked the comfort of living in a bastion of Protestant elitism, in their Andy Hardy house, eating pork chops with mashed potatoes and butter if they felt like it.

No one else had arrived, so she decided to review *A Doll's House*. She had just reached the fifteenth page of Act One when Elaine appeared. "I didn't know you were coming," Nina said, book-marking the page she'd just reviewed.

"I just finished nine frightening holes," Elaine said, plunking down into a chair.

"I thought you detested golf."

Elaine signaled to a waiter. "A vodka martini, please." She grimaced. "I detest all exercise. But it keeps me in touch with people I must schmooze with. Oh, here they come." Up trudged Poppa, Murray Lasky and Dick Preston. Poppa had a clod of turf stuck to his cap and Murray had a nasty purplish welt the size of an egg on his chin. Poppa shrugged. "I clobbered Murray with a pitching wedge. Goddamned thing flew right out of my hands."

Murray winced at the memory.

"Poppa," Elaine said, "you have a part of the fairway on your cap."

He grabbed the divot and threw it into a flowerbed. "Murray's the only guy in Los Angeles I can beat on the level."

"They didn't have golf where I grew up," Murray said.

"Who had golf where they grew up? It's a stupid game for rich people." Poppa pointed to Dick. "Even with the bum leg, Preston could beat me, but he pretends otherwise."

Dick shrugged. "I've been playing since I was a little boy."

"It's a stupid game for rich people," Poppa repeated.

Dick turned to Nina. "Do you play?"

She recognized the look. He was sizing her up, adding points for her classy outfit and deportment, deducting ones for her being a Jew.

"Since I was a little girl," she replied.

"We'll have to have a game sometime," he said.

"Yes, that would be nice," she replied politely. She knew they'd never bother. There was something about Dick that begged for veiled animosity and false promises.

The waiter brought Elaine's martini.

"That looks great," Murray commented.

"Give him one of these," Elaine said to the waiter. "It'll make that lump on your chin less painful," she explained to Murray.

"Oh, blast it! Forget lunch," Poppa cried. "What happened to the time? We have a screening at three." He jumped up. "Come on, Preston. Let's go. You kids have a good time." He clapped Murray on the shoulder. "I don't want to see you back at the studio today. Maybe Nina wants to go to a movie. Elaine, I want to see you in my office in forty-five minutes. Forget the lunch. Let these two have lunch together."

Elaine turned to Murray as soon as Poppa and Dick had gone.

"Did you talk to the one I mentioned?"

"Yeah."

"What did he say?"

"What do you think?"

"I thought so." Then they both sighed, apparently having come to an end to the conversation. As Elaine left, Nina watched Murray track her departure with a look of admiration. "She's something, isn't she?" he said.

Nina couldn't help taking a liking to Murray. "Poppa thinks that you and I—"

"Don't worry," he interrupted. "Just friends." He waved at a waiter. "I'm starved. How 'bout you?"

"Famished."

They both ordered full meals.

"I like a girl with a good appetite," Murray said after the waiter left. He held up his hand at the look on her face. "Just friends. Honest. I heard you were engaged. Who's the lucky guy?"

Nina didn't want to talk about her life. She wanted to talk about Stella. She held up the copy of *A Doll's House*. "I'm trying to get ready for my meeting with Stella Kane. Tell me about her."

Murray took a big sip from his martini. "Not much of a drinker, usually. Boy, I feel very relaxed. It's hard to relax in this town." He glanced at her companionably. "Can I tell you a little fairy tale?"

"Does it involve Stella Kane?"

"Yeah."

"Sure," she said.

Murray settled back in his chair. "Now listen." And then he told her his tale:

The summer of '44. I'm some punk discharged from the Navy and trying to figure out what to do. My family has Mob connections, but I can't stand that kind of work. It's not like I'm such a moral guy. I just like to avoid violence. So my brothers' boss, who knows someone in Hollywood, lines me up a job as a messenger boy. My big brother Hymie gives me a few bucks and an old jalopy he won in a card game. About seventy miles before Columbus, Ohio, the clunker starts smoking. I pull up to a great big shack surrounded by old junked cars. It's called KUBICEK'S AUTO REPAIR. A three-legged mutt comes howling out, followed by a gigantic man with hair so blond it's almost white. I swear to God, the ground shakes as the guy comes up to the car. We push the junker into a bay in the garage, while the little mutt nips at my heels. Then Kubicek starts pulling parts out and throwing them on the oily cement, while I stand around trying to make small talk, until he glares at me and says, "Go!"

I go to the cafe attached to the garage. The radio is playing an episode of The Shadow. *Standing in the middle of the room is a girl, maybe seventeen, interpreting the show in sign language to another kid, a coupla years younger. Both of 'em are bony and coulda washed their hair. Real hillbillies. But they were both knockouts. I go to the sticky counter, sit on a crummy stool and point to the menu.* "Double cheeseburger. Fries. Large Coke."

The older one wipes her hands on her apron and says, "We're outa hamburgers."

"Three hot dogs with the works," *I say.*

She shakes her head.

"What the hell do you have in this dump?"

"Eggs and toast. We didn't get any deliveries this week. We've got some spinach and carrots in the garden out back."

"I don't want no spinach and carrots." *I'm beginning to realize maybe not too many people come into this shack. The eggs probably come from the dusty chickens in the yard. Anyway, I'm not in any position to argue, so I say,* "Look, what's your name?"

"Stella."

"All right, Stella. Gimme three eggs, over easy. And a double order of toast and coffee. You got coffee, don't you?" *I reach over to stick the menu back between the sugar shaker and the napkin holder and wind up jumping nearly a foot into the air. That other kid, the younger one, is almost biting my neck. Snuck up like a ghost. The older one, Stella, makes a bunch of signs. The deaf one signs back, saying something like* screw you.

"Where you headed?" *Stella calls over, while she cracks the eggs into a pan of burning butter.*

"Hollywood," *I say. No reason to lie.*

Stella delivers the black, rubbery eggs to me. "Me and my sister are going to Hollywood."

Sure thing, I'm thinking. You and every other white trash girl from every gas station and feed store between the Atlantic and the Pacific.

"What's your daddy out there think about that?" *I ask.*

"He's not my daddy. He's my stepfather."

"Where's your mama?"

"She's dead."

"Hey, I'm sorry about your mama," *I say.* "Name's Murray Lasky. I can see you got talent, kid. You look me up when you get to Hollywood, you hear?"

The screen door pops open and Kubicek stomps in. "Fixed." *He tells me how much money I need and I almost puke.* "Gonna have to wire my brother in the morning."

Soon, it's three a.m. Kubicek has let me sleep on a fleabag mattress in the storeroom. I pray the guy was dumb enough to leave the keys in the car. I get to my jalopy. Who do you suppose is waiting, with two bundles hugged up against their chests? And the three-legged dog is there, too.

"Get out!" *I whisper. Meanwhile, the damned dog is starting to whine. "Get out or I'll pull you out."*

"I'll scream," Stella warns.

"Scream bloody murder. I'd rather have it out with that old man now than get nabbed for kidnapping tomorrow."

"I've got money." She waves this thick wad of dough at me.

"That won't do me no good in jail."

"He wants to get rid of us," she says. "Why do you think he left the keys in the car?"

"In that case, why would I want you?"

Now, Stella trains her eyes on me, suddenly silent. She reaches over to her little sister. Starts unbuttoning the kid's blouse.

"Stop it," I say. There on the poor kid's chest are these nasty bruises, raw and new, like handprints. Well, what the hell could I do, pardon my language. I started the car.

The waiter had brought their lunch at the beginning of the tale. He interrupted now, asking if everything was all right. Nina waved him away with a distracted thank you. "Then what happened?" she asked. Murray continued his story:

Those girls were driving me bananas. Thought the whole thing was some kinda vacation. I'd say to them, "As soon's we get to Hollywood, I'm dumping you on the first curb we see."

And Stella, each time she'd answer, "I'll take care of everything."

Somewhere in Arizona, outside of Flagstaff, I'm getting real tired. The last time we stopped for ice cream cones, they got my car all sticky feeding the dog.

"As soon's we get to Hollywood," I yell again, "I'm dumping you both on the first curb we see!"

"I'll take care of it."

I was fed up. "Oh, yeah? Look how good you took care of your sister back at that garage."

Stella gives me a look I'll never forget. Like a cat eyeballing a cornered mouse. She grabs a napkin and spits on it. Opens her sister's blouse and rubs, then holds the napkin under my nose, showing me the ink stains she's rubbed off. And the kid sister, she's got this look on her face, like ha ha.

"Why, you sneaky brats!" I shout.

Stella just slumps down on the seat and crosses her arms over her chest.

"I'm a fool," I announce to the desert air. But, you know, I had to appreciate her. That Stella, she was gonna take care of everything. And I don't care what they say about deaf people. The sister was no dope, either.

Murray took a deep breath.

"Boy," he said, "I'm getting a killer of a headache. Have to scram. Besides, gotta feed the dog."

"You mean—"

"Yeah. We kidnapped that ugly mutt, too. I named him Valentino."

With my own eyes I saw the Sybil of Cumae hanging in a bottle; and when the boys said to her: "Sybil, what do you want?" she replied, "I want to die."

~T.S. Elliot, in The *Waste Land*

Chapter
Six

Second Encounter

"OH, I HATE you! This will go straight to my hips." Elaine spooned the dripping remains of a three-scoop banana split into her mouth.

"It was your idea." Nina finished her butterscotch sundae with crushed peanuts. They were at CC Browns, home of legendary ice cream, across from the Roosevelt Hotel on Hollywood Boulevard. The cousins had been over to press agent Mark Minor's office on Melrose and had taken the decadent detour before heading back to the studio.

"I had to change your meeting location with Stella Kane," Elaine said. "She doesn't want to meet at Chasen's. She wants to meet at Sybil Croft's place. Stella is living with Sybil Croft now. The press will catch on soon and then you'll have to make up some nonsense, as I'm sure the truth is not appropriate, whatever it might be."

Nina set down her spoon and wiped butterscotch from her lips. "Stella's sister Abbie got into trouble with the landlady's grandson where they were before. They had to move."

"You've been gossiping with the planters again."

"Isn't that what I'm supposed to do?"

"Yes, of course. But I'd hoped you'd spend more of your time with Stella."

"In the last week, I've chaperoned Stella on I don't know how many dates with that list of heartthrobs you gave me. I've supervised her publicity shots, I've supervised practically everything she's done with her waking hours."

"But have you spent *time* with her?" Elaine persisted.

"Not alone." In fact, if anything, Nina avoided spending time alone with Stella.

Elaine removed her napkin from her lap and stood. "I could have hired anyone to *supervise* Stella. Come, use my office while I'm out and about. You'll need the privacy to get ready for your meeting without being distracted by all the people who want to spill their guts to you."

Once she'd settled down in Elaine's office, Nina reviewed the synopsis of *A Doll's House* that she'd written. She reworked Stella's invented biography. She wrote more notes. She still had forty-five minutes left to go, so she went for a cup of coffee. Who should she find holding the percolator but Shanahan. He glanced over her with a tight look, then shrugged and poured her a cup. "Learning a lot?"

"That you're the best head planter in town."

"Don't go trying to butter me up. Use the débutante act on the gullible."

"This *is* me."

"If you say so." He slurped at his coffee.

"Anyway, who are you to talk? I'm supposed to think the drunken sourpuss with the lousy vocabulary is you."

Shanahan managed a smile. "You bet." Just as quickly, the smile disappeared. "What a louse I'm being. When I landed in this town, everybody treated me like I'm treating you, with one exception."

"Sybil Croft," she ventured.

"Who told you that?"

"I figured that one out on my own."

"So what else have you figured out about me?" He hesitated. "Someone told you I was a priest."

"Someone did."

He leaned in close enough so she could smell the coffee on his breath. Strangely, she didn't feel the need to back up. There was nothing even mildly threatening or repellent about his closeness. "God didn't cooperate."

"Do you still believe in God?" She held up her hand when she saw he was about to laugh. "It's a legitimate question."

"The Old Testament one who sent Job to the dust."

"Maybe we can discuss Job sometime. I wrote a paper for a Bible as Literature seminar. I came up with a very novel interpretation."

To her surprise, he let out a burst of genuine laughter. "You bet. That'd be very enlightening."

"I'm off to a meeting," she said.

"Let me know if you need someone to dust off your shoulders when get back." Shanahan looked almost agreeable as he watched her go.

AT FOUR, NINA approached Sybil Croft's place off Sunset Plaza, north of Sunset Boulevard. By Hollywood standards, the estate was modest, all of eight or ten rooms on a quarter-acre or so, a pale beige stucco with a brown-tiled roof and tall windows, surrounded by well-tended flower gardens and fragrant citrus trees. At the door, a stiff-shouldered, balding butler with a British accent introduced himself as Alfred.

Impulsively, Nina asked, "Do you know Marie? She works for my uncle."

"Yes," he replied cautiously.

"It's okay," she assured him. "Marie knows I keep details under my hat."

He studied her face. Then, apparently satisfied, he said, "Actually, she's my niece."

"What a small world. Your accent is very convincing."

"Thank you. Miss Croft, she often tells me, 'Drop the phony accent, Alfred.' But I've been at this too long. My own wife wouldn't know me. Miss Croft, however, why she wouldn't care if I drawled like the cowboy I once was."

"She seems to be a very special person."

Alfred regarded her with narrowed eyes. "I would not like to hear *anything* said against her." There was a harsh undertone to his words, perhaps a vestige of his rough-and-tumble cowpoke past. They had crossed a large sitting room whose French doors opened to a screened porch that faced out onto a lush garden. Seated at a glass-topped table were Stella, Sybil and a teenaged girl who very much resembled Stella. They were drinking tea from china cups and eating tiny cookies and cucumber sandwiches with the crusts cut off. In a huge metal cage nearby were two African Grey parrots.

"Scram! It's the cops!" one of the parrots screeched. *"Party's over! Party's over!"* screeched the other parrot. *"Watch out for that dame! She's trouble!"*

"Sorry. They used to belong to a director of bad crime movies." Sybil waved Nina to the table. "Abbie and I will stay just long enough to finish our tea. Then we'll let you and Stella get to your business."

Nina suddenly realized she'd been too nervous to eat anything that day but the butterscotch sundae. She grabbed a cucumber sandwich. It slipped out of her fingers and dropped onto her lap. For a dumbfounded moment, she sat staring at the soggy cucumber slices, and then Stella's sister burst out laughing. Nina glanced at Stella, who was trying *not* to laugh. Looking at the two sisters, Nina realized how much the studio had already done to refine Stella. They had lightened her hair, scrubbed and toned her skin, pared and cleaned her nails. Abbie was much coarser looking, although equally gorgeous. Then Stella was laughing, too. The both of them were *laughing* at her. She tried to be angry, but they were both so beautiful and artlessly delighted, Nina couldn't be as indignant as she probably should have been. What a pair. Their magnetism was a little frightening. Alfred, who had been hovering near the doorway, rushed over with a moistened napkin. Nina cleared her throat. "This is a lovely tea."

"Alfred's doing." Sybil smiled at Alfred. "Must have learned when he was a young man in England."

Alfred rolled his eyes. "Madam is too kind."

Like the two sisters, Sybil Croft radiated sensuality, but of a more refined nature. She reminded Nina of Katherine Hepburn. She was angular and somewhat androgynous with intelligent, penetrating eyes. Her expression was fondly teasing, but Nina sensed a certain unspoken weightiness of spirit beneath it.

By the time Alfred had whisked away Nina's mess, Abbie had stuffed two cucumber sandwiches into her mouth and was reaching for a cookie. Stella began moving her hands while shaking her head and frowning. Abbie grabbed the cookie from the plate and took a large bite from it. Stella signed more emphatically.

"Maybe you should let her be," Sybil said to Stella. She raised her hand and blocked her face from Abbie. "She might be feeling just a little jealous."

Abbie glared at Sybil.

"Don't hide your face from her," Stella said to Sybil gently. "That's showing disrespect."

"I'm sorry." Sybil signed something to Abbie, who scowled haughtily at the gestures. The Kubicek girls had that in common, Nina thought, that mocking attitude.

"I didn't get that right, did I?" Sybil asked.

"Watch me." Stella signed slowly and deliberately, while her features adopted an apologetic cast. "You meant it, now show it. Move your hands and arms, show it in the way you look. Sign is a language about what you feel and show."

Sybil tried again.

"Very good," Stella said.

Abbie signed to Sybil.

"I feel so ignorant," Sybil moaned. "What did she say?"

"She says you have a lot to learn."

"Isn't that the truth?" Sybil turned to Nina. "Sign is a language more beautiful and complex in many ways than our spoken words. I don't think most people realize how much they reveal in their faces and in the way they move their bodies. As actors, we do. But learning sign has made me even more aware."

"It's a story in the air. There are things you can tell that words can't say." Stella smiled slyly. "And hearing people don't know how much they can't hide." As Stella spoke, she signed the conversation to Abbie. "Mama was deaf. I learned to sign the same time I learned to speak. I know how beautiful it is. But most deaf people are ashamed. In public, they make tiny signs so they won't be noticed. People think the deaf are stupid."

"Stella has a special gift," Sybil interjected. "She's an expert in a language of visual expression, a great bequest for an actress who works with the camera. Think of the close-up! Imagine how her ability to express her character with the most complex of expressions, how the camera loves that. Stella will be great. She has the talent and the determination." Sybil smiled. "And a bit of ruthlessness. She needs that. Of course she needs to learn all the silly things about being a leading lady."

Stella grinned. "Not without a fight."

"But you won't fight too much, will you, dear?" Sybil said.

"Just enough," Stella replied.

Sybil laughed. "You walk the fine line, not afraid of the complications. Once, I did the same. Now, some of my complications are catching up with me."

"It *don't* have to be that way," Stella drawled, emphasizing the non-grammatical word.

Nina flinched. She knew Stella was seeing Mildred, Lumina's diction coach. It had to be stubbornness on Stella's part, talking like that. Her attention was drawn back to Sybil when the older actress sighed, a pained look on her face. "Acting is all I've ever done. It is all my family has ever done." Then her tone grew philosophical. "People are ridiculous about death in this culture."

Nina bent towards her briefcase. She didn't like talk about death. She pulled out her papers and spread them on the table. Abbie reached for another cookie and knocked her cup over. The tea from Abbie's cup splattered Nina's papers. The words were blurs of blue ink. Stella reached over with a napkin and blotted at the top page, then held the ink-stained cloth up to her sister, gesturing angrily. Abbie responded with a sign that even Nina could tell was off-color, then leapt from the table, grabbed a handful of pastries and ran from the room.

"I can wait—" Nina started to say.

"No," Sybil interrupted. "We were about to go anyway."

When they'd left, Stella turned to Nina. "She's mad at me." She gestured at Nina's notes. "Has this ruined our meeting?"

Nina cleared her throat. "The ones on the top that got wet are just notes in case I forgot anything. I was a little nervous."

Stella settled back in her chair. The way she sits, Nina noted. She's going to have to learn how to sit properly, without slumping like a man, with those knees spread out like that.

"Are you surprised I live here?" Stella asked.

"I suppose I am." Nina thought it might be best not to reveal how much she knew.

"Sybil's been helping us." Stella smiled. "She's got a generosity I'll never have. She's got sense I'll never have neither."

"Either," Nina corrected. "That was a double negative." She grimaced. "Sorry. But I'm supposed to be getting you ready for your interview and you wouldn't want to be using double negatives..." Nina's voice trailed off as she watched the smile fade from Stella's face.

"A *double* negative. Lordy." Stella raised an eyebrow. "Sybil's got sense I'll never have *either*," she said, very deliberately. "Okay? What did they tell you about me?"

"Mostly the official biography."

"Did Murray Lasky tell you anything about finding me?"

"No."

"You don't lie much."

"What?"

"The face is the window to the insides. And that was a big, fat lie."

"I think maybe we should just get down to business."

"I am getting down to business." Stella had a gleam in her eyes. "How can you invent who I'm going to be if you don't know who I am?"

"I'm here to brief you on the play."

"Look at that face." Stella pulled her chair closer to Nina's. On this day, she wore no perfume, but smelled like Ivory soap. Nina's heart, which had never completely calmed down since she arrived in Hollywood, pounded faster in her chest.

"You've probably never had to lie much. Not the kind poor people have to tell."

"Well, you certainly learned how to lie."

"I knew it. You heard Murray's story, didn't you?"

"Murray did tell me something about how you came here."

"Well, he didn't tell you everything. He knows Mama died. He doesn't know how I felt stuck in that hellhole with Kubicek. Working in that damned café and taking care of Abbie." Stella smiled, a faraway look in her eyes. "Mama played the radio. She wanted me to hear a lot of voices. By the time I was seven or eight, I was acting out the shows." Stella shrugged. "At least that old coot let me go to school after Mama died, but I never could do anything but rush home as soon as the last bell rang."

"My mother died, too. When I was born." A lump formed in Nina's throat. Why had she blurted that out?

"I'm sorry," Stella said. "Died in childbirth. It's the child that gets the burden." She narrowed her eyes. "Your face. I can see you had troubles."

"My mother's parents were the worst. Daddy worked in Grandfather's law firm. My grandparents were very wealthy. Even before my mother died, they thought of my father as a social climber. When my mother died, Daddy stayed with the firm. My grandparents always appeared to be okay with us, but I grew up with the awful feeling that I was somehow responsible for my mother's death." Nina began fumbling with her papers. "I don't know why I'm telling you this. I'm usually the one that people confess to." She looked up to find Stella staring at her. "I want to get back to you."

"You already heard about me."

"You're not kidding."

Stella cocked an eyebrow at Nina. "You think I was bad, tricking Murray like that with the ink stains on Abbie's chest?"

"Of course not."

"You're screwing up that face again, Pinocchio. Watch, your nose is going to grow. Oh, this is rich. A publicist who can't lie."

"I can lie. Everybody lies. They just don't have someone like you inspecting their faces so closely."

"Get used to it. I wouldn't know how to do otherwise."

Nina threw up her hands in frustration, not even caring anymore how childish the gesture must look. "I don't want to talk about this anymore."

"Then what do you want to talk about?"

"*A Doll's House.*"

"Oh, the play." For a moment, Stella's hands flew, composing her thoughts in the air. "What did you think about that final confrontation scene with the husband? I know exactly how I'd play that scene."

"You don't have to worry about the details." Nina held out her synopsis.

Stella stopped abruptly. She reached over for the paper and studied the paragraphs, reading them over several times.

"I'm very good at that sort of thing," Nina explained. "I have this way of being able to summarize anything, to find the theme and put it in a short, but—"

As Nina spoke, Stella tore up the synopsis and let the shreds scatter onto the tiled floor. "Do you think white trash can't read a whole play?"

"I never thought that," Nina objected. What was her face saying, though? Never in her life had she ever been so nervous about what her expressions revealed.

"Then maybe you believe white trash can't figure out themes."

"I thought you'd be relieved. You're so busy with other things."

"I think we need to end this meeting. I'm fretting about my sister."

"If that's what you want." Nina gathered up her notes. "Dottie Strong will ask about the play. If you had a brief synopsis, you'd be fine."

"Now I might have to use my own thoughts."

"Stella, I was only trying to do my job."

"Start by assuming poor people are blessed with brains even if they didn't go to college."

"I never thought otherwise," Nina said stiffly. She held out a tea-stained copy of Stella's biography. "The interview is two days from now. This is the biography we arranged for you. You probably don't want to *discuss* it either. I'll assume you'll be prepared."

Stella paused, then reached out and accepted the biography. She scanned it, then looked up at Nina.

"Did you write this?"

"I improved it." What was the point in fibbing, with this girl inspecting her like she did?

"By the time of the interview, I will be this person." Stella folded the paper in half. "It's good. You're very creative."

"You think so?"

"Would I lie?" Stella grinned.

"How would I know?" Nina let a small giggle escape.

Stella's face grew serious. "I will work with you, but I'd like your respect."

"I respect you."

"Not really. Not yet." Stella laughed. "Doesn't matter. I was dramatizing. I don't know what gets into me."

"You want respect. I want the facts. How can I work with someone when I don't know what's dramatizing and what's real?"

"I hardly know myself," Stella replied, with a little shrug.

Nina sighed. "All right. I'll let myself out. Go look after your sister."

"*The jig is up!*" one of the parrots screeched, as Nina left from the sunroom.

"*It's all over!*" screeched the other parrot. "*Weapons down and surrender!*"

Chapter
Seven

The Interview

STELLA'S INTERVIEW WITH one of Hollywood's most influential columnists was scheduled for 1:00 p.m. at the Brown Derby. At 1:45 p.m., no one had shown up yet but Elaine and Nina. Elaine ordered her vodka martini and Nina had her iced tea with two slices of lemon.

"Remember," Elaine said, "we have to clear any alcohol off the tables before the photographer takes any shots." Elaine spotted Bette Davis sitting three tables away and grabbed Nina's arm. "Bette Davis," she whispered. "Bette! Bette!" she called. The great lady looked up from her Caesar salad and nodded absently. Elaine whispered through her teeth, "She's been a trial at Warner's. Seven thousand a week and demanding control over her pictures, when none of her films has grossed anything near what she did before the War." Elaine sighed. "Crawford, Davis, Sybil Croft. Living legends. But we have to change with the times. And we can't tolerate difficult people."

Elaine, Nina now understood, evaluated humanity based on relative degrees of cooperation. Good people cooperated; bad people did not cooperate. Elaine tapped Nina's arm. "About Dottie Strong. She's not predictable, she doesn't always cooperate *one hundred per cent*. The only way to guarantee total cooperation is to make her completely happy."

"What makes her completely happy?"

"Booze and exclusives."

The dining room smelled of Hollandaise sauce and warm bread. As usual, Nina was hungry. Her stomach growled. She wondered when the rest would show up.

"And don't," Elaine added, "even think of mentioning Lolly Cooper."

"The *Modern Screen* writer? Why not?"

Before Elaine could explain, Shanahan came strolling up, a bit unsteadily. He paused at their table. "Looks good," he commented, nodding at Elaine's cocktail. "Mind if I join you gals?"

Elaine glared at him. "Don't you have work to do?"

"Take it easy. Meeting with the guy from the *Philadelphia Enquirer*. Gonna give him a fabricated scoop on his hometown boy, Troy Baker. What brings you out today?"

"An interview," Nina said. "Stella Kane, with Dottie Strong."

"Hoo-boy, that's right!" Shanahan hit his palm to his forehead. "Just make sure you don't mention Lolly Cooper," he stage-whispered to Nina.

"Shhh," Elaine said. "Keep your voice down."

"The Wicked Witches of the East and West," Shanahan stage-whispered. "Lolly Cooper gushes sweet drivel for the fan mags and Dottie Strong writes in her hoity-toity column the dirt that Lolly can't dish out. They're quite a pair. Sisters, ain't that just something?"

"They haven't talked to each other in years," Elaine added.

"Those ladies are the eyes of God," Shanahan chanted. "They see from behind. They see from below." He made a swipe at his shoulder, as though brushing away Job's dust. Before Shanahan could go, Dottie Strong marched up. She was a small, wiry woman with a masculine face and sharp, bright eyes.

"Shanahan," she boomed with a baritone, cigarette-raspy voice. "How the hell are ya?" She pointed to Nina. "*This* is Stella Kane?" she asked, sounding horrified.

Nina blinked rapidly, but kept her mouth shut. All right, she wasn't much of a glamour puss, but really.

"This is Nina Weiss, my assistant," Elaine assured Dottie.

"Weiss?" Dottie said.

"She's my cousin."

"Nepotism," Dottie intoned, and waved at the passing waiter. "Double bourbon on the rocks." She shook her head with an air of moralistic grandeur. "Nepotism," she repeated. "Bette!" she called across the room.

Bette Davis looked up from her salad and waved at Dottie with a tired, regal gesture. Dottie turned to Shanahan. "What's up with Sybil Croft? I've gotten word to ignore her. No publicity. *Nada*."

Shanahan shrugged, trying to look nonchalant, but his left eyelid was twitching. Elaine glared at him. "Gotta go," he said, and rushed off.

"Well, my goodness," Elaine said to Dottie. "What a question. Why, you'd think Lumina wasn't cooperating fully with you." She narrowed her eyes. "I know you understand how much we rely on you to handle our exclusives."

Dottie glanced at Elaine's empty glass. "Looks like you could use a refill," she said. The waiter arrived with her bourbon and she gestured to Elaine's glass. "Bring my colleague another." She pointed with a repulsed look to Nina's half-filled iced tea glass. "And another of *that*."

"There she is," Nina said, her voice squeaking. Stella was stunning. She'd arrived late, as requested, in a tweed woolen suit, with a silk blouse and a string of pearls around her neck. The costume department had tailored the skirt, nipped at the jacket, so the outfit was marvelously sexy without losing its decorum. Stella was reserved, mysterious, everything anybody could desire. And, judging from the way all eyes were turned to her, the entire crowd in the packed dining room thought so, too, as the *maitre d'* led her across the length of the room. Stella swayed seductively, without appearing to notice any of the attention riveted on her.

"This," Elaine said, as Stella arrived at their table, "is Stella Kane."

"What a parcel," Dottie Strong admitted. "Sit by me, kid. Let's see if you hold up once you open your mouth."

Stella slid in beside Dottie, radiating earthy dignity. She was cooperative and charming, without a trace of the defiance Nina had feared she'd display. She recounted her progress to Hollywood, including her early years with her invented parents and her invented youthful attempts at theater. Nina listened, fascinated, as though she hadn't written nearly the whole thing. Which brought them to *A Doll's House*.

By this time, Dottie had downed two double bourbons and ordered a third. She paused at the mention of Ibsen's masterpiece, her eyes sparkling. "Great play, as I remember. Been years since I saw it." She glanced sharply at Stella. "Can you remind me what it's about?"

Stella stared at the table. Then, she looked up and recited the synopsis Nina had written. The one that she'd torn up after reading briefly. Nina's jaw dropped. She took a gulp of tea to hide her expression. Stella glanced briefly at Nina. It was subtle, just a flicker of her mocking eyes. "But that's just a dry lifeless old summary the studio gave me in case I couldn't remember," she said. Her voice grew passionate.

"I *know* that play. No *damned* summary can get at its heart. Here's a woman escaping her little dollhouse, because she's going to find her life, no matter what. That play's about becoming a human being, doing what you have to do to become a human being with a life. What are lies? What is doing exactly what you need to do to *live*?"

At Stella's use of the word 'damned,' Elaine's face whitened. It was a cardinal rule in Hollywood that actresses didn't use offensive language of any sort. But Dottie Strong wasn't bothered. Not hardly.

"Kid, you're the real thing!" Dottie crowed, raising up her glass in salute. "I haven't been so impressed since Marlene Dietrich came to town. Go out and conquer the world."

Stella's expression was still serious. "I will," she said quietly.

Dottie turned to Elaine. "My advice, don't ruin her. Give her a little leeway, don't tame her too much." She turned back to Stella. "And you. Watch it. It's a tightrope over a very deep cliff." A few moments later, Dottie wrapped up and ambled over to Bette Davis's table. As soon as Dottie's back was turned, Elaine made a show of applauding.

"That was brilliant. I knew you'd think of something, but I admit I didn't believe you were capable of such a lovely bit of work just yet. So complicated, with its twists and turns. The synopsis. The rebuttal of the synopsis. Beautiful, just terrific." Elaine paused. "Although we really must avoid profane language and be aware of our deportment. Still, it worked, that's what's important. And Nina, you thought of it! You did come up with this, didn't you?"

"Of course she did," Stella broke in. "Every last bit of it."

Before Nina could say anything, Elaine continued, "You're a whiz kid! Well, you have a few more weeks here. If you can conquer Dottie Strong, you can win over America. I want you to be Stella's shadow. No, I want you to be her Pygmalion." She turned to Stella. "Do you know who that is? Probably not."

Nina expected Stella to explode, or at least to snap back. Instead, Stella nodded. "As a matter of fact, I do know all about Pygmalion."

Elaine slid from the booth. "Nina must have told you. She's such an encyclopedia."

"No," Nina started to protest, but stopped when Stella laid a hand on hers.

"Nina has been helpful," Stella said. "Very, very helpful."

"Are you coming?" Elaine asked Nina.

"Yes, but can I meet you in the car?" Nina asked.

Elaine looked at Nina quizzically.

"I wanted to talk to Stella for a minute." Nina could see her cousin's expression deepening into suspicion, then Elaine's face brightened.

"Oh, yes. You want to *talk*. Marvelous. I can't wait to find out what you two are up to next. Just marvelous."

"I suppose I should thank you," Nina said to Stella, as soon as Elaine had gone. "All the credit."

"Hasn't everyone been telling you I'd cooperate?" Stella replied.

"But it has to be on your terms, doesn't it?"

Stella slid a few inches closer. "I got this far on my own terms and I will never do otherwise. But I'm not dumb enough to think I don't need help."

"You're not dumb," Nina said. "You're smart. Maybe even smarter than me. You're right, I was judging you based on stereotypes."

Stella squeezed Nina's hand. An electric charge ran up Nina's spine. "There's a lot I know," Stella said. "One thing is that I need you."

Nina gulped down the lump in her throat. "Whatever for?"

Stella smiled. "Some other time. The words will get in the way. At least right now."

Chapter
Eight

Like Pygmalion, Maybe

IF NINA EVER imagined that budding actresses lived glamorous lives, she learned otherwise quickly. On the Monday following the Dottie Strong interview, she reported to the studio at seven-fifteen, only to be informed that Stella had already arrived and was with Phil Pope, Lumina's top make-up artist.

"I emphasize the cheekbones," Phil explained to Nina, as he hovered over Stella, who, for her part, was looking bored—but who knew if that was real or posturing?

"We're going to tone down this cleft in the chin, too strong." Phil shuddered. "Like a man."

Stella yawned.

Next, Mark Handley sprayed Stella's hair into a flawless crown. Then off to Meredith Foote, who dressed her in the working-girl outfit of her character from *Threat From Within*.

"Ah, perfect." Meredith turned to Nina. "Drab, but *never* too drab, *never* too tired, *never* ugly, never ever ugly, not even if she's on her death bed." She pointed to Stella. "This one, I don't know if we could make her ugly. She's a goddess, isn't she?"

"Yes," Nina sputtered.

Meredith didn't notice Nina's reaction. She was eternally in her own sphere of design. "I'll be creating originals for this young lady, mark my words." She reached over and adjusted the lapel on Stella's coat. "But, dear, please. A little softer, the posture, the demeanor."

Stella shrugged, causing Meredith to sigh. "They start out this way, but they learn."

As Nina and Stella rushed to Sound Stage 73, Nina remarked, "This is quite something, how you spend your time."

"At least we're making a movie. When I first signed my contract, it was dancing lessons, acting lessons, diction classes, publicity shots in little bathing suits, publicity shots in nightgowns, publicity shots in more bathing suits." Stella struck a coy, sultry pose.

Nina couldn't help laughing, aware of the amused glances from the rest of the foot traffic in the lane. "We'd better get going."

Stella swayed up the walk, glancing seductively over her shoulder. "Come on, then," she whispered breathily, then of all things, moistened her lips with her tongue.

Nina frowned. "Stop it."

Now it was Stella's turn to frown. "It's cheap, but they wanted it. Then they found out I could act. Now they want more class. That's why you're here."

"Watch." Nina headed towards Stella, doing her best to appear demure yet sensual, repressed yet exuding secrets. "Like this. It's all suggestion." Absorbed in her demonstration, Nina approached Stella, gradually becoming aware of Stella's frown. "What's wrong?"

Stella turned, heading to the sound stage.

"What's wrong?" Nina repeated, hurrying to catch up with her.

Stella's face was a mask. "I can't explain," she said. "Don't ask me again."

THE REST OF the day was spent in endless takes, long periods of waiting, more takes, more waiting. For her part, Stella had warmed up, was good-humored despite the waiting and the hot lights and the wet, sticky air of that humid day. She was pleasant to Nina. Too pleasant, Nina thought. She felt pushed away.

And so went the rest of the week. Stella was cooperative, but distant. After the day's shooting, there were the dailies at 6:00 p.m., so that by the time Nina had arrived home to the Cottage in the evening, all she could do was spoon the meal Marie had left for her into her mouth, then fall into bed and sleep like the dead.

In the meantime, Nina had set about helping to create not only Stella the actress, but Stella the rising star. Elaine had provided her with a list of publicity possibilities, from which she was to choose the most promising.

And so, at Nina's request, on the Saturday afternoon of her third week in Hollywood, fan magazine hack writer and the sister of Dottie Strong, one Lolly Cooper, appeared at Sybil Croft's estate.

The day of the interview, Nina arrived early with a Saks shopping bag. Stella and Abbie accepted its contents and went into the cabana near the pool. When they emerged, Nina clapped with delight. "You both look wonderful." She felt sure the sisters could both pass on the tennis courts of any country club—provided they kept their behavior in check, of course. Abbie came prancing over in her new outfit and grabbed one of the tennis rackets Nina had brought. She waved at fantasy balls, looking very taken with herself.

Stella, on the other hand, looked vexed. "I don't like it."

"At least these aren't little bathing suits," Nina replied. "They're tasteful sports outfits designed to play a game."

"I don't like games. They're for rich people."

"Tennis is a beautiful game. I've played since I was five. You appreciate skill, I know you do. Besides, is stardom for poor people? I think stardom is for rich people." Nina grinned at Stella. "And how about me? I could be considered a rich person."

Stella shrugged. "When you grow up like me, you pick up a natural resentment of rich people. Now show me." She reached over and took one of the rackets.

"You don't really have to know how to play," Nina said.

Stella froze.

Uh oh. Nina knew she was on fragile ground once again. To avoid a repeat of the *A Doll's House* fiasco, she began burbling banalities. "It takes years to be good," she explained, watching the scowl form on Stella's face. "The whole thing is arranged. The photographer will pose you. It's all taken care of. Nobody cares, you know that."

"Show me," Stella said, slowly and deliberately.

"I'll show you some basics. If you insist."

"I'll beat your pants off," Stella replied.

"Fat chance." For once, Nina knew she held the upper hand. She led Stella onto Sybil's tennis court. From the other side of the wire fencing, they could see Abbie prancing around the lawn, absorbed in a fanciful game of her own.

"Should I get Abbie?" Nina asked. "Do you want her to learn these strokes, too?"

"Let her be. She'll do fine."

Nina showed Stella a forehand grip and a backhand, the correct stances and explained a few of the rules. "Above all, keep your eye on the ball."

"I can do that." Stella watched Nina with a disconcerting intensity.

Nina went over to the other side of the court and gently hit a ball over to Stella. Stella's first return went into the net.

"I'll do another," Nina called. "Go easy. Be gentle." They hit a few balls back and forth. Stella returned each shot with surprising accuracy, as Nina sent her a sixth and seventh shot. On the eighth return, her shot went into the net.

"Damn," Stella cried.

"See? It takes time, Stella." On the other side of the net, she could see Stella gripping the racket, lost in thought. Then her body seemed to swell, as if she was mustering every ounce of determination she possessed. "Go ahead," she called. "Don't hold back, just slam it over."

It was *Stella's* challenge, not Nina's. Nina threw the ball up and delivered one of her most devastating serves, a cannonball. She charged the net in the unlikely event that Stella could muster a pathetic return. Gripping the racket entirely wrong, with the poorest of form, Stella attacked Nina's shot like a madwoman, sending the ball over Nina's head. It landed just within bounds.

"Is that the idea?" Stella called over sweetly.

"Beginner's luck," Nina called back. She walked up to the net, shaking her head. "You wouldn't hold up in a game."

"Of course not," Stella said. "You're very good, aren't you?"

"Yes, I am."

"I like that. You're my kind of woman."

Much to her chagrin, Nina's mouth fell open. Aware of Stella's penetrating eyes, she turned away. Miraculously, she was saved by a cry from across the lawn.

"Halloo!" someone trilled loudly. Trudging up the walkway were three figures. Alfred led the way, followed by a young man yoked with a camera and a bulging camera bag. "Halloo!" the third figure trilled again. It was, Nina knew from ungenerous publicity department descriptions, Lolly Cooper, voluminous writer for *Modern Screen*. Lolly Cooper was as massive as her sister Dottie was pint-sized. She rumbled up the path in a billowing muumuu festooned with tropical blossoms. When the party of three arrived at the court, Lolly broke from the others and marched up.

"Where's Elaine?" she asked in a syrupy voice. As her sister Dottie's guttural bellow was surprising from her little wiry frame, equally as strange was Lolly's little-girl voice rising from her imposing form. But the sisters shared one thing, the piercing look in their eyes.

"I'm her assistant," Nina explained, watching the displeasure appear in those piercing eyes.

"Oh, her *assistant*," Lolly repeated sweetly. "I usually don't work with *assistants*."

It was time to resort to nepotism. "Actually, I'm Irwin Weiss's niece."

That seemed to satisfy Lolly. Her eyes now began a search of the nearby premises. Abbie was still prancing on the lawn in the distance, waving her racket. Stella waited nearby, posing.

"Is this," Lolly said in a bored tone, "the standard let's-pretend-we-know-how-to-play-tennis routine?"

"I suppose you could say that," Nina answered.

"Then let's get going. Is the ballerina over there supposed to be in the story? If so, get her over here." Alfred was dispatched to retrieve Abbie, while the photographer, whose name was Nils, set up at the court. The photographer was strikingly handsome. In addition to their vivid accounts of Lolly's physique, the office gossips had also informed Nina that Lolly only worked with photographers who had the appearance of male gods.

"I typed up a few suggestions for your photo essay," Nina said to Lolly, who had taken to a nearby bench.

"Blah, blah, blah," Lolly muttered. "Put it in my bag over there." She unwrapped a mint she'd dug from the pocket of her muumuu and slipped it into her mouth. "Blah, blah, blah," she murmured to herself.

"I'll see how things are going," Nina said hesitantly. She slipped away and approached Nils.

"Is she always like this?" she whispered to the photographer.

Nils shrugged. "Only when she thinks there isn't any dirt to make things interesting." He inspected the lens of the camera he'd brought, then looked up and his jaw dropped. Abbie had apparently noticed the handsome man with the camera as well. She sashayed toward the photographer.

"Well, let's get started," Nina announced nervously. Abbie continued her seductive assault, until she was facing the nearly drooling photographer.

"What's *your* name?" Nils breathed out.

Abbie signed her name. "She's deaf," Nina said. Abbie was running a finger along the lapel of the photographer's suit jacket. Nearby, Nina could see Lolly Cooper perking up. She rose from her bench and lumbered over. "The sister's *deaf?*"

Stella marched over to the group. "I don't want you to use that."

"What do you mean?" Lolly Cooper said, dropping her little-girl tone. "This is at least *interesting.*"

"Stella, what's the harm?" Nina asked.

"No, no mention of this," Stella insisted. "Now, let's take the pictures and be done with it."

"Well, for pity's sake." Lolly turned to Nina. "This makes the story *interesting.* This makes a good *cover story.* We don't often do *cover stories* on unknowns."

Nina felt a very large lump forming in her throat. "Stella—" she began.

"No!" Stella interrupted. "No, no and no."

"I guess it's no," Nina said to Lolly.

"All right then." Lolly's tone returned to its previous sweetness. But her eyes reflected a sense of scorn, directed at Nina, whom she clearly considered to be an ineffectual lackey. Nils spent the next hour or so shooting adorable shots of the two sisters in winning tennis poses, while Lolly and Nina watched silently.

When it was all finished, Alfred brought refreshments to the pool area. The entire group sat gloomily, loading up on pastries and punch. All except for Abbie, who was flirting happily and outrageously with Nils. Nina watched Stella trying to get Abbie under control, but Abbie would have none of it. Finally, she was practically sitting in the man's lap. He, for the most part, was not helping matters, barely feigning decency.

"Interesting," Lolly murmured, her eyes bright.

Stop it! Stella signed to Abbie. Abbie shrugged, mouth set in a defiant teenage grimace. Stella stood up, signing something that anyone could tell was threatening.

Abbie backed away from Nils. She searched the area, then ran to the table near the cabana and picked up the camera bag filled with the day's film. Hugging it to her chest, she ran to the edge of the pool and held the bag over the water.

"Interesting," Lolly murmured. "Very interesting."

Abbie stood challengingly, bag perched over the water, while Stella continued to sign. For a few minutes, there was a standoff.

"Can I help?" Nina called over.

"No," Stella said calmly. "I didn't want to have to resort to this." She signed something to Abbie.

Abbie stared, her expression transforming from defiance to alarm. Slowly, she retreated from the water's edge. She went over to the photographer and handed him the bag. She spun around and ran off, in the direction of the house.

"I guess that's it for today." Lolly heaved herself from the chair casually, as though nothing out of the ordinary had just occurred. "Yes, well, I think we'll be shuffling along."

When they were out of hearing, Nina turned to Stella. "I'm sorry."

"What are *you* apologizing for?"

Truthfully, Nina wasn't sure. She just felt bad about the whole thing. "What did you say to Abbie? At the end, when she got so frightened?"

"I told her I'd send her to an institution, but I was just burned up."

"Stella," Nina began, "Abbie seems like she might need some kind of help. Not an institution, of course. But maybe to spend some time with other people like herself."

"I will not have you or anyone from the studio telling me what Abbie needs or doesn't need. *I'll* do what you want. But you let me take care of my sister. Is that clear?"

Nina didn't think it would work to apologize again and she

didn't want to. "I guess we're done. I'll go."

"Wait." Stella came up close to Nina. So close Nina could smell the sweet-acrid smell of exertion that clung to her. It was an enticing odor, like ripe tropical fruit.

"You're stuck with me. Rude, cross, everything, it's not meant to push you away. We're a team."

"At least for a few more weeks," Nina replied.

"A few more weeks?"

"I can't believe no one told you. I'm only here for six weeks. It's half over. I *must* have mentioned it."

"I thought it was open to change."

"Considering how much I annoy you, I wonder why you want me to stay."

"Annoy me?" Stella looked truly startled. "Whatever gave you that idea?"

"Nothing. Never mind. I'd rather not discuss it." Coward, Nina admonished herself as she turned quickly and rushed off, calling over her shoulder: "I'll see you on Monday. Let's just start fresh then, okay?"

"Isn't that how it should be?" Stella called back. "Each day new, bury the past."

Nina made her way to a phone. When Elaine answered, she explained the afternoon's antics.

"Not a problem," Elaine said.

"What?"

"Lolly Cooper knows exactly what she can print and what she can't. She cooperates."

"But she saw all these terrible things."

"I'll give her a little call and thank her for her enthusiasm and generosity portraying our rising stars, but it's only a formality. Lolly knows the routine." Elaine sighed. "Still, see if you can keep things a little more under control in the future."

"I will," Nina replied, with what she hoped sounded like conviction.

Chapter
Nine

Just The Summer

NINA'S HOLLYWOOD SUMMER felt like a whirlwind, slipping by faster than she could ever have imagined. She was confused. On the one hand, she just wanted it all to be over. On the other, she felt like she'd only just begun to understand how challenging publicity was, a fascinating game of make-believe. Poppa was right. If Shakespeare were alive today, he'd probably be in Hollywood. Shakespeare understood invention. He understood how to please the people.

The Sunday following the tennis incident was Stella's twenty-first birthday, or at least the date they'd decided would work best in her biography. Aaron Bermann and his wife were hosting a brunch in Stella's honor at their place on Coldwater Canyon Drive, complete with the press and a crowd of up-and-coming celebrities. At first, Stella would have none of it. "Why would I want to spend my birthday with Aaron and his awful wife and a bunch of guests who've been forced to attend?"

"It isn't your real birthday. It's great publicity."

Stella sighed. "All right. I'll ask Sybil to watch over Abbie at the party so there's no trouble."

Nina cleared her throat. Now came the dreaded hitch. At a meeting the previous week with Elaine and Aaron, Aaron had supplied Nina with the invitations. There were two significant omissions from the list: Sybil and Abbie.

"Stella won't agree," Nina had protested.

Aaron let his jaw drop in an exaggerated gesture of disbelief. "Nina, did I just hear you say you don't know how to do your job?"

"No."

"That's funny," Aaron said. "Because I heard you admitting you was a bust at your job."

"Aaron, you know Stella. We can't exclude her best friend and her sister."

Aaron turned to Elaine. "Maybe we need to put Nina on something less complicated and let a pro take over."

Elaine shrugged. That, apparently, was going to be her only comment, so Aaron ranted on. "She can have her own party on her real goddamned birthday and invite five male geishas and the janitor for all I care, as long as she does it hush-hush. But this is *my* party and she'll come and she'll be a good girl."

NOW, NINA WAS confronting Stella with the situation. With an odd regret, she knew Stella would attend her false birthday party. So they argued and Stella stomped off, and a few days later she agreed.

The morning of the brunch, Nina arrived to pick Stella up. At first, no one answered the bell. Finally, Alfred pulled open the door, looking distraught.

"What's wrong?" Nina asked.

"Miss Stella is expecting you."

Nina stepped in and touched his jacket sleeve. "Is something wrong? Please. I'm not just anybody."

"Yes, well, one would have thought that," he replied, eyes narrowed. "Miss Stella is in the sun room."

Stella was pacing in front of the glass wall that faced out onto the garden. The parrots were agitated, too. They slid back and forth along their perches, squawking, heads bobbing, feathers ruffled.

"Don't shoot! I give up! Don't shoot!"

"I can't go. You'll have to make excuses."

"I'm not going anywhere until you tell me what's wrong!" Nina hadn't intended to speak so loudly.

Stella looked taken aback. Nina spoke quietly now, but urgently. "I thought we were in this together."

"Abbie and Sybil are gone. I was waiting to tell you that I couldn't go before I went looking for them."

"I'll help."

"Don't bother. I still won't go."

"Let me help. I don't care if you go or not." Before Stella could speak, Nina threw out: "I know. That's a lie. But let me help anyway. I won't *make* you go."

Stella shrugged. "I think I know where they are."

Nina followed Stella out the glass doors onto the patio. They went to a gate at the far edge of the property, then through the gate into a meadow of dried golden grass. After at least a hundred yards, the path disappeared into a scraggly thicket of trees that reminded Nina of a large version of one of Poppa's tortured bonsai fairy-tale forests. They entered the ethereal woods. A small clearing appeared. In the middle of the clearing was a wooden bench. On that bench, Sybil sat, with Abbie's head resting in her lap. Sybil watched them approach, not looking particularly surprised. "You should have gone to your party. We would have come back."

"I know," Stella answered.

"Then why didn't you go off to your birthday, or your supposed birthday?" Sybil asked.

"Damn them for making me go without you."

Sybil Croft addressed her next words to Nina. "Stella needs to understand the tragedy of when a person has no life. Abbie has no life right now. I'm on the verge of losing mine. We are commiserating in this lovely spot, that's all. Stella should have gone to the birthday."

"The both of you are feeling sorry for yourselves," Stella interjected. "I told you. I'll take care of you."

"I can't talk to her," Sybil sighed, hugging Abbie to her. "She can't listen."

"Of course she can," Nina began, and then took a good look at the expression on Stella's face. Stella's eyes were veiled, her features were rigid, and she clearly couldn't listen.

"Stella must go to her birthday brunch," Sybil said. "I insist."

"Stella?" Nina said.

Stella, wordless, turned and headed out of the thicket.

"I am very fond of her," Sybil said. "You know that, don't you?"

"Yes," Nina said. "Yes, I know."

"And I know *you* are, too," Sybil said, in a tone that inspired a sudden blush up Nina's neck. "I wish you the best, I really do. It will never, ever be uncomplicated. Remember I told you that. Now go to her."

Nina caught up with Stella just before the pool. They walked silently until they reached the garden, then Stella said: "Everyone thinks I should send Abbie away, but they can go to hell. I'm all she has."

Nina took a deep breath. "Maybe that's because you haven't let her have anything else."

Stella's face remained perfectly calm, but a tremor ran through her body. "You can go to hell, too."

"I know you don't mean that."

"Yes I do."

"You don't."

They glared at each other.

"I don't think you understand my situation," Stella said.

Nina couldn't disguise the frustration in her voice. "You make it nearly impossible. How could a person ever understand your situation?"

Stella searched Nina's face. "Good thing you're only here for the summer."

When Nina started to speak, Stella held a finger up to her lips. "No, it's over. Let's discuss the birthday. I need to know how I'm supposed to be. Here's your chance. Make me what you want me to be."

AT THE BRUNCH, Stella outdid herself. She was classy and gracious, vivacious but reserved. She still had an almost masculine brashness to her gait and posture, which Nina wasn't convinced would ever be tamed, but she was too captivating for it to matter. The party took place in the ranch-sized backyard of the Bermann estate, populated with reporters, photographers and publicity-seekers whirling around in clouds of self-interest, bringing their inverted absorption into the birthday song, which sounded like the narcissistic cries of selfish songbirds. Nina felt a burst of admiration for Stella, who listened to the unsettling tune with her head held high.

Near the end of the event, Elaine sidled over. Nina was standing under a tall potted palm, enjoying a brief moment of solitude.

"I like it," Elaine commented, glancing around to make sure there were no nosy eavesdroppers in the vicinity. "Not a Greer Garson, mind you, but more like Lauren Bacall, a tempest under wraps." She held her glass up to Nina. "Definitely not white trash, to your credit." Elaine shrugged. "She still throws her shoulders around like a rodeo cowboy, but we'll work on it." She touched Nina lightly on the arm. "Everything you reported to me I've been able to use. And, best of all, I think she likes and trusts you. Honestly, I don't know what we're going to do when you leave." Elaine halted abruptly. "What's the matter?"

A single very mortifying tear was rolling down Nina's cheek. "Nothing. I don't know." She backed away from Elaine. "I'd better go. I see Dottie Strong headed over to Stella."

Chapter
Ten

A World Of Mirrors

STELLA'S PUBLICITY CAMPAIGN was going better every day. Dottie Strong had made mention of Stella three times in three weeks and all three bits had been glowing. Now the fan magazines and the trades were gloriously pestering them.

Nina knew there was trouble at Sybil's place, had witnessed Abbie's rebellions and Sybil's lurking depression, but Stella insisted she would take care of it. No one was inclined to interfere. Most of all, Nina wanted to avoid any complications that would prevent her from finishing up her summer in a way everyone would pronounce as excellent. Then beat a hasty retreat. The closer the time came to leaving, the more she felt compelled to push any lingering doubts away. She was going, and that was that. It was 7:30 p.m. on Monday of Nina's fifth week in Hollywood. She and Stella had just left the dailies, headed out to the parking lot.

"What'd you think of that dialogue?" Stella asked, grimacing. "Sometimes, I feel like the parrots."

Nina stopped and pointed. "That's Cary Grant. What he's doing here? I thought he was tied up in contract."

Stella grinned at Nina. "A short time ago, you wouldn't have cared much about Cary Grant's comings and goings."

"I don't care. Not really."

"I want you to come somewhere with me this Thursday night."

"After another day like this? Where would we go this late and how will we keep our eyes open?"

"I'm going to a reunion with my drama teacher."

"Rhonda Stills is your drama teacher."

"At the studio. This is different. This is Edith Bernstein."

Nina knew very well about Edith Bernstein. Elaine had found several occasions to complain about the venerable matriarch and her teaching methods, which contributed heavily to actors sliding into that worst of states, being uncooperative. "Why were you working with *her*?"

"When I first got here, I worked as a waitress in a lousy place, not much better than Kubicek's dump. One of the other girls there, she was an actress. She dragged me to Edith for the first time."

"A waitress? They told me that Murray Lasky got you a screen test."

Stella smiled. "He didn't dump us off on the first curb and desert us. But it took him a bit of time, a few months, to convince the studio to test me, and god knows how he managed that, he won't say. I had to get by. I sure knew how to be a waitress. I had to leave Abbie alone more than I wanted. That's when things started to go wrong with us. Anyway, Edith is having a reunion event for my class and I want you to come. I'll make it worth your while. I'll go with Tony Pascal to Ciro's."

No one had thought Nina would be able to get Stella to go out with Tony Pascal. He *was* a slimy drip, but that never counted for much in show business. He was also the hottest ticket in town.

So Nina went to acting school.

THE OFFICIAL TITLE of the acting school was BERNSTEIN'S WORKSHOP FOR ACTORS, but the sign on the landing of the stairwell in the shabby building on Santa Monica Boulevard read WORKSHOP—FOURTH FLOOR. The elevator was broken, so they took to the stairs. On the third floor landing, Nina halted, breathing hard, not from the exertion, but from a jolt of panic. "I won't have to do anything, will I?"

"Nothing you don't want to do."

"I can't act. It's the only thing I wasn't good at in high school."

"You weren't good at something?" Stella replied in mock astonishment.

"They asked me to work backstage after one scene in my senior drama class."

"Don't fret." Stella took to the last flight of stairs before Nina could extract any more reassurances from her.

Edith was already poised in front of a semi-circle of actors when they arrived. She acknowledged their arrival with a slight nod of her beautifully coiffed head, and then turned back to her disciples. Stella pointed to a corner from where Nina could watch and took her place in the semi-circle. There were three good-looking boys and three good-looking girls dressed in black.

"In your advanced class," Edith intoned, "you were all good. This is a class of natural ability." She paused. Her students waited. "Some of you are working now. Professionally." A few heads turned furtively in Stella's direction, and then turned quickly back to Edith. "I will say this again and again. Acting is a lifelong commitment to discipline and to uncovering something deep inside yourself that you can draw from." There were a few murmurs, heads nodded in rapture. "I asked you back here to review where you've been and to ponder where you are going." Edith's hands rose up into the air in a posture of submission to the sublime. "In lies, we find truth. In truth, we find lies. Now line up facing one another. We're going to do the very first exercise you ever did with me. You must always be beginners."

The actors leapt to their feet and formed a double line. They were one person short. Nina's stomach flip-flopped. Edith turned to Nina, who was beginning to feel light-headed. "Lend us a hand."

Nina shook her head. "I'm just watching."

"Maybe it's time for you to participate." The matriarch approached her. "There are no mistakes if you keep an open mind."

Responding to the potency of Edith's voice, Nina grasped Edith's hand. The actors clapped. Nina took her place across from Stella, feeling a bit sick.

"The mirror exercise," Edith announced. "One of you is looking into a mirror. The other one is the mirror image. Your motions are simultaneous. Start slowly. Make every gesture as deeply felt as you can. You are one person." The actors in Nina's line began to move. The actors facing them began to mirror their movements. After a moment's hesitation, Nina began to make some simple motions. Stella copied them so quickly that Nina's mouth fell open. Stella dropped her mouth open. Nina's gaze fell. Stella's gaze fell.

"Look into each other's eyes," Edith commanded gently. "Don't look away. What are you feeling? How does it show in your face, your body? Mirrors, are you feeling it?"

Nina looked up. Stella looked up. They locked eyes. In almost no time, Nina was lost in the absolute perfection of Stella's mimicry. No matter what Nina did, Stella's reactions were immediate, exact, until Nina had the strangest feeling that they *were* one person.

It wasn't as though she was lost, exactly. But she was in some way. She was losing something to Stella's complete engulfment of her. Nina stopped finally when she became aware of the entire group watching them. They had all stopped and were staring. On their faces were undisguised looks of reverence. Except for Edith, whose look was impenetrable.

"And now trade," Edith ordered. "Make it smooth. I shouldn't see any change."

The actors opposite Nina's line began to lead. The switch was seamless. Except for Nina. She stood stock still as Stella gestured in front of her. "Move," Stella whispered. "Mirror me."

"No whispering," Edith commanded.

Nina tried her best, tried to match Stella's sensuous movements, tried to see deep into her gestures. But she felt she was just going through the motions. As she moved, Nina could hear Edith's voice in the background, in what sounded like poetry:

"You are unhappy, you look at yourself in the mirror, you see your sadness.

"You are what you see in the mirror.

"Isn't that what love is?

"Do you love another or what you see of yourself in them?

"Give yourself up to your mirror.

"It may be your only chance to understand the selfish nature of passion.

"With that knowledge, you will understand the craft of acting."

When the exercise ended, Nina broke from the group and fled back to her original corner.

"Wait," Edith said, approaching her, with Stella trailing along. "That was fine."

Edith turned to Stella. "Practice together. It'll be good for both of you."

"I understand," Stella replied.

"What on earth were you and that woman talking about?" Nina burst out, when Stella and she were back on the street, headed to Nina's Buick.

"Never mind. You're leaving so soon, it hardly matters."

"I feel left in the dark and I don't like it."

"I can't explain and it really doesn't matter."

Nina knew that, when Stella adopted that tone of voice, the subject was closed. They rode silently back to Sybil Croft's place. Just as Stella was getting out from the car, Nina spoke. "We were like one person."

Stella stared at her, leaning back into the car.

"You make me feel—" Nina stopped, searching for the right words, but she couldn't find them.

"I know," Stella said.

"How can you know? If I don't."

"You know, too. Don't worry so much about the words. Hearing people worry too much about the words." Stella shut the car door. From the other side of the glass, she signed something Nina couldn't understand.

At least not in words.

Chapter
Eleven

Slimy Drip

CIRO'S ON SUNSET Drive was the place to be. Stars on stage and stars in the audience, crammed at closely spaced tables in the rococo room, attended by bustling waiters and cigarette girls in black net hose. When Nina informed everyone that Stella would be there, hanging on Tony Pascal's arm, the reaction was even better than she expected.

"How the hell did you get her to do that?" Aaron Bermann crowed.

"Good work," Elaine said. "I knew I was right to bring you out here."

Even Shanahan put in his two cents. "That musta been a tough nut to crack."

To all of this, Nina just nodded modestly.

Elaine and Nina spent Monday planning the event and set Shanahan to notifying the press. Elaine, in her superior wisdom, had embellished on Nina's plan. She decided to arrange two tables of phony dates, involving some of the major players connected to *Threat From Within*. The one exclusion was Sybil Croft. Everyone was too cowardly to disobey Aaron's edict to shun Sybil.

Herman Hover led the Lumina group to their tables that night. The proprietor who'd revived Ciro's was an unmistakable figure, balding, with a long nose and sporting a cravat hand-painted with tropical birds. "You're all so beautiful," he cried, upon their arrival. And he was right. What a party they were. The couples were enticing:

Hollace Carter, fresh from a painful breakup with a fiery redheaded actress, was dating Loretta Mars, known more for her supporting roles, but a striking beauty nevertheless. Lance Lewis and Terri Baxter made a perky couple, two aging ingénues still popular with audiences. Elaine chose to drag Murray along, not wanting to risk any complications regarding her semi-scandalous, semi-secret dalliance with Eric Flint. The one real couple of the evening was Dick Preston and his actual wife, Annabelle. As for

Nina, she came alone.

Oh, and of course, there was the couple of the evening. They were splendid, glowing with the aura of rising fame. The majority of eyes in the room were on Stella and Tony Pascal. She clung to Tony's muscular arm. The air was thick with the intoxication of glamour. Still, Nina felt a twinge of misapprehension.

After belting down a double whiskey, Tony propelled Stella to the dance floor. Stella's dance lessons had paid off. She was the perfect partner. No one could take their eyes off the pair as their torsos swayed rhythmically together. Elaine was drooling with delight. She made triumph gestures at Nina, which Nina returned, although the little devil of misapprehension was beginning to grow. A tap on the arm interrupted her conflicted emotions.

"I'm going to miss you," said Lance Lewis, sitting to her left.

Nina liked Lance. He had always been nice to her, taking time for light conversation, even when she first arrived. He was also one of the cutest men she'd ever met, cuter in her opinion than Mickey Rooney. Nina knew he and Hollace Carter shared a bachelor pad in Santa Monica, and she could certainly see how Hollace would enjoy Lance's companionship, regardless of his minor status in comparison to Hollace's established fame.

"Thank you," she replied. "Where's Terri?"

"Crying in the ladies room. Her real boyfriend is over there with a dame and *that* wasn't arranged."

"Oh, no."

"Don't worry. Terri's no dumbbell. No one will see teardrops." Lance took a sip of his drink and let his eyes settle on the other Lumina table. "I feel so sorry for him."

"Who?"

"Dick Preston."

"Why on earth?"

"For exactly the reason I hear in your voice. Everyone hates him. Can you tell me you have any reason, other than his arrogance, which is like having fingers and toes in Hollywood?"

"He sends out this peculiar energy. As though he expects to be hated."

Lance bent closer. "His father is one of the richest men in the universe and the entire family came over on the Mayflower. The father's a big shot at a bank that backs Lumina Pictures. Dick is the bad-luck son. He broke his leg playing lacrosse, that's why he limps. He dropped out of college and went to work for the father and lost some big account. So what does the father do? Get him a job at Lumina. Daddy backs the studio with big bucks, but only if Dick can't be fired. Funny thing is, he's doing fine, but I'm afraid he'll find a way to screw up."

"How do you know him so well?" Nina asked.

"I don't." Lance's face clouded over. "These are just some things I heard. I shouldn't be telling you, but you're easy to talk to." Dottie Strong was weaving towards them, cocktail in hand. "Oh, brother, I hope Terri gets back from the powder room soon."

Dottie barged up to the table and wagged her finger at Hollace Carter. "Bad boy, Hollie," Dottie chided. Hollie was the nickname Hollace went by with his intimates, among whom Dottie must have counted herself. "I give you credit for calling me about the terrible breakup with Mona Wade, but not letting me know you're dating again?"

Hollie adopted an appropriate look of remorse.

"It's not his fault," Loretta Mars piped in. "We just started seeing each other. But *please* feel free to let the world know."

Just then Terri Baxter bounced up to the table and slipped in next to Lance. "Hi, honey," she chirped, then winked at Dottie.

"Good," Dottie murmured. "It works. People will love it." She threw up her hand as Lance started to speak. "Don't bother. I'm only going to throw in a line at the most on you two. I don't need details. Let's get the drinks off the table and take a few glamour shots."

Dottie rested her gaze on Stella Kane and Tony Pascal. She wagged her finger at Stella. "I hope it's a set-up, because *you* could do better." She gestured to her photographer. The table was quickly cleared of alcohol and the ashtrays were emptied. The couples leaned together and manufactured cheerful faces. "Aren't we all on cloud nine?" the photographer commented.

After a last round of inspection and a baleful shake of her head in Tony and Stella's direction, Dottie meandered off, intent on interrogating Franchot Tone, seated at a nearby table.

"That woman is a witch," Tony Pascal exploded, as soon as Dottie was out of earshot. "And I'd use a 'b' instead of 'w' if I wasn't in mixed company." He lit a cigarette and waved to a passing waiter for another double whiskey.

"He's had enough," Elaine said to the waiter. Before Tony could protest, she added, "Go out on the dance floor. I think that's gotten the best results so far. And don't converse."

"She doesn't have anything to say, anyway," Tony groused. "C'mon, baby," he said to Stella, whose face remained agreeable. He lifted his well-built body from the chair, grunting at the effort brought on by his alcoholic consumption. As Stella left, she made a sign to Nina. A bent 'V' hand shape that waved down and forward from her mouth. Nina dropped her head and took a gulp of air, trying not to giggle. Abbie had shown her that sign. It meant 'snake.'

As soon as they'd left, Elaine sighed. "I'm sorry, Nina. This was not one of your brightest ideas. He's a — a — "

"Snake?" Nina offered.

Elaine tried to keep a straight face, but her mouth struggled. "Anyway, I wish you'd given this particular match-up a little more thought."

It was useless to remind Elaine that the pairing was her idea, that the entire publicity department had pressured Nina about "this particular match-up." Oh, well. Pass the buck was not an unusual game around these parts. Another reason to go back to her real life. She glanced at the dance floor. Tony was pushing his strapping body against Stella's, clutching her bare back, rubbing a sweaty palm on her skin.

"Stella has been so cooperative lately," Elaine said, her voice growing as apprehensive as Nina felt inside. "But if his hands go any lower, I don't know what she'll do and I don't know if I'd blame her, frankly." They watched as Tony's right hand began a slow, weaving descent along Stella's spine. "Listen to me." Elaine whispered in Nina's ear.

"What?"

"You heard me."

Nina inched out of her seat. "Faster," Elaine hissed. "She'll slug him."

As Nina approached, Stella twisted away from Tony's pressing hulk and glared at Nina. He gripped harder, beginning to nuzzle his lips near her ear. Nina tapped Tony's shoulder. He lifted his head and stared, lips wet, eyes glazed. "May I?" she said brightly, holding out her arms.

"I don't want to dance with *you*," he spat out.

"I wasn't asking *you*," she replied sweetly.

"What the hell do you think, two dames dancing?"

Stella pulled away, eyes lit up with amusement. "Scram, you loser."

"Beat it, Tony," Nina added.

Every head in the place was turned their way. Stella stepped into Nina's arms. For a very brief moment, they danced. Just long enough to distract from the ugly scene with Tony.

"Make it seem like a lark," Nina whispered.

"Don't worry, I know," Stella whispered back.

Nina didn't think the crowd really knew what to make of it, other than appreciating the spontaneous effort to make light of a potentially ugly incident. Besides, who couldn't appreciate two beautiful women dancing together? When they stopped, there was a scatter of applause. And no one paid much attention to Tony Pascal skulking off the floor. When they arrived back at their table,

Nina nodded at Elaine. Elaine shrugged, but her voice was tired when she whispered to Nina: "I'm going to have to call in a few prized favors to keep this out of the papers tomorrow."

What Nina remembered most from that evening was not her gratitude to Elaine for making the most of an awkward situation. What she remembered was what it felt like to be in Stella's arms, with their bodies pressed together.

Chapter
Twelve

It's A Wrap

NINA'S STAY WAS almost over. Production wrapped on *The Threat From Within*. Right on schedule and on budget. The old-timers on the set marveled at how Harley Burton cranked out footage with minimal retakes. The only unfortunate small delay was a change in the final scene. In Nina's opinion, the original scene was the best in the movie. It had an ambiguity usually only found in foreign films. Like a real tail pinned on a paper donkey.

And what became of that ending? The front office ordered it reshot. And so Nina learned another thing about Hollywood. Communists were nothing compared to ambiguity.

What else did she learn in Hollywood? She learned how romances were arranged, how pasts were doctored, how spontaneous events were carefully scripted to create the publicity which no one and everyone believed. She learned how all of this hoopla was planted to gossip columnists, magazine writers, to all the journalists across their great country and throughout the world, who broadcast to a public hungry for dreams.

Nina had learned to invent lives. She had passed through stages of doubt and hesitation, and had thrown herself into lies with this rationale: It was only for the summer. Besides, one indisputable truth was constantly impressed on her. Publicity was for everyone's good. No one lost, everyone gained.

She was due to leave Hollywood in a few days. Poppa's overblown wrap party was scheduled for the Beverly Hills Hotel, the palatial pink landmark of all that signified royalty, Hollywood-style. The event was designed to get maximum publicity. Everyone agreed *The Threat From Within* needed all the help it could get.

In keeping with the patriotic theme of the movie, the publicity department chose a Revolutionary War motif complete with soldiers on horses lining the entryway of the hotel and a party staff decked out in colonial costumes. The bartenders were bare-chested Indians in buckskin and feathers, the cocktail waitresses wore wigs and gowns and the waiters wore battle uniforms of the rebellious colonists. The kitchen roasted turkeys, steamed corn and baked pumpkin pies. In an anachronistic but grand statement, a gigantic ice replica of Mount Rushmore was carved and mounted at the head of the ballroom. Nina threw herself into a frenzy of planning that final week. She was leaving forever and she would go out in glory. Of course, Elaine had hinted that she would always be welcomed back.

Poppa was less subtle: "Honey, you don't want to be a urologist's wife! What kind of life is that for a girl with your creative genius! Look what you've done while you were here! You'll be back, mark my words."

Oh, no. No, she wouldn't. No matter how much she was fascinated by it all. It was an interlude. A person could probably live her whole life here and have it be an interlude. What kind of a life was that?

On the evening of the party, the sky over the Beverly Hills Hotel blazed with fireworks and cannons boomed. The thrilled crowd screamed at the arrival of Sybil Croft, Hollace Carter, and Lance Lewis, parading down the red carpet, past the soldiers on horseback.

Then the crowd descended into a hush as Stella, in a tight white dress and silver heels, emerged from a limousine. Elaine and Nina were standing near the entrance of the hotel. Like the fans, their breaths, too, caught short. What had they made? It was incredible. Stella walked towards them, head held high. She was stunning. Her swagger was no longer brutish; it was daunting. The crowd remained hushed as she swept past them.

As she came near them, Stella looked right at Nina. It was a quick, private look. Then she was gone. Nina felt dizzy.

"Come," Elaine said. "The reporters will be all over her."

"You go," Nina said. "I'll be right there." It took her several seconds to gather herself back together. Both Elaine and Stella had disappeared into the swelling crowd by the time she went in. Nina took a deep breath and made a promise to herself. She was leaving in two days and this was her final big event. She wasn't going to think about anything. She was going to have a good time.

As the ice Presidents melted at the head of the room, the revelers mingled, the known and the less known, infected with the spirit of grandiosity. Nina wove through the crowd, picking up bits of the talk that made this life what it was:

" – He's been called up to some hotel room three times now. They're asking him who he knows who joined the Party – "

" – Say, it's not like I'm asking for a favor. I deserve this picture. Look at my record, three hits – "

" – She's a has-been – "

" — Attendance is down. It keeps going down — "
" — Anti-trust! It's not anti-trust, it's judicial murder — "
" — Look over there. You see who's got his arm around — "
" — This whole place is going to hell! I know it's been said before — "

The place was so packed, she managed to avoid any of the cast from the picture, which suited her fine. But she wasn't having a good time. She was drifting on her flimsy patronizing raft, mentally criticizing the inanity of the surrounding sea of conversation. Conveniently forgetting how much she'd come to participate in the brouhaha. At around 10:00 p.m., she was standing in a corner, when someone approached her from behind. She jumped, and then turned to face Dick Preston.

"I didn't mean to frighten you."

The usual sense of discomfort she felt around Dick crept up on her. She remembered Lance Lewis's expression of sympathy. She knew Dick had let Harley direct his movie without interference, and even championed for the ambiguous ending. But she couldn't shake her negativity.

"You don't like me, do you?" Dick asked. "That's all right. I'm not a likable fellow, am I? But I have one redeeming thing to say in my own behalf. Are you interested?"

He seemed genuinely concerned, so she nodded.

"I wish I was a man of principle," he announced.

"You set Poppa straight about the loyalty oaths. I heard you defended some writers in front of the House on UnAmerican Activities Committee," she said consolingly.

"That's nothing. In the big picture."

"What do you mean?"

"Let's just say I wish I could be a really brave man." He smiled at her puzzled expression. "Are you wondering why I'm not if I want to be?"

"I'm sure most people wish they had more honor and principle than they do."

"And you?"

For a moment, she honestly couldn't think of an answer. Then she smiled up at Dick's arrogant, troubled face. "The truth is, I don't think I've been properly tested."

Dick's eyes widened, then he laughed. "You are an interesting girl. I'm sorry you're leaving. I'd love to talk to you after you've been properly tested." He held his drink up in salute. "Good luck and good-bye."

Nina pushed her way through the thick crowd, listening once again to the deals and loud complaints, the harsh laughter and drunken arguments. The crowd was getting a trifle pugnacious. No matter. It was still a magnificent night. Even Shanahan, who had

obviously taken full advantage of the free champagne, came
staggering up to her around eleven, looking less discontent.
Probably because, miraculously, Sybil Croft had been allowed to
attend.

"What a soirée," Shanahan observed.

Nina surveyed the room. "Every reporter in town is here."

"And drunk as skunks. We love free refreshments. Do you
think they had oysters in the seventeen hundreds? I don't care. I
love oysters."

"I'm going to miss all this, Shanahan. Even you."

"Same to you."

"Will you do me a favor?"

"What might that be?"

Nina hesitated, then blurted out: "Watch out for Stella."

"I don't think that dame needs anyone."

"That's what she'd like everyone to believe. Will you do it?"

Before he could answer, a wave parted in the crowd. Through
it marched Stella, heading straight towards them. She halted right
in front of Nina. "I want to talk to you." Then she turned and
walked away.

"Whew," Shanahan said, wiping his brow.

She started to follow Stella. Before she could leave, Shanahan
grabbed her elbow.

"There's someone you should meet. I think you'll find this an
eye-opener."

Approaching them was a man about Poppa's age. He was
stuffed into a tight, ill-fitting tuxedo. He had a beaked nose and a
high forehead, giving him the appearance of a predatory bird.
"Shanahan," the man said.

"Moe Mink," Shanahan replied. "How'd you get in here?"

"The old man thinks he's God. But I'm still a person in this
town."

Shanahan gestured at Nina. "Moe, this is the old man's niece."

Moe barely nodded at her. He glanced around. "What
bullshit."

"Watch your language, Moe, there's a lady present."

Moe shrugged. "I'm starting a magazine."

"That's what the rumors say," Shanahan replied.

"Gonna call it *The Tinseltown Insider.* Gonna print all the dirt
that all the goddamned studios are covering up. All the dirt that
little two-faced coward Dottie Strong threatens to print, then only
hints at. You know who really gives her most of the dirt? That fat
sister of hers. They pretend they don't talk to each other." He
leaned closer to Shanahan. "See? I know almost everything. And
you know the rest." He seemed to notice Nina for the first time.

"You know what you can tell your uncle?"

Nina peered at Moe as though he was a particularly lowly creature on the evolutionary scale, but he didn't care. "You can tell him I know every fag and Commie and starlet-chaser under his studio roof."

"Okay, okay," Shanahan said. "We'll talk about this some other time."

"And you know them, too, Shanahan," Moe said, but Shanahan had taken Nina's elbow and was leading her away.

"When your uncle came to Hollywood, he came with three kids he grew up with. Aaron Bermann, Harley Burton, and Moe Mink. Irwin, Aaron, and Harley, they had something that pays off in this town. Big egos. Now, Moe, he has an ego, too. But his is a sad kind. I'll bet you a dime his old man used to beat him up when he was a chubby, sensitive kid and called him a pansy. Anyway, Moe worked at the studio, but he couldn't produce a moneymaker to save his life. He got replaced by Dick Preston, which wasn't easy for Irwin to do. Moe knows a lot about Lumina. He's right, between him and me, we know a lot of the dirt."

"You wouldn't work for him, would you?" she asked.

"Now, that'd be jumping from the frying pan into the fire," he replied.

Nina didn't like the tone of his voice, not from a man who liked to punish himself. She spotted Stella standing near a doorway, her gaze trained on Nina. Stella disappeared through the doorway.

"Go," Shanahan said. "Your lady friend awaits you."

"Don't make too much of this."

"Hey, I'm the last one you'll ever need to worry about. You heard Moe. I know all the dirt there is to know. But I'm not a man of judgment. At least not anymore."

She headed for the door through which Stella had disappeared. The portal led to a hallway ending in an exit that led to a pathway that wound in twists and turns until it opened onto a patio. It was like a maze leading to a core of privacy, into which Nina stepped.

Stella's back was to Nina. She leaned on a stone pillar attached to a low stone rail at the far end of the patio. The night air was warm and quiet, shielded from the party that was only a muffled throb in the distance. Her lightened hair had a silvery quality in the moonlight. Nina marched to the stone railing and placed herself upon it, where Stella couldn't help but see her.

"What do you think becomes of Nora?" Stella asked.

"In *A Doll's House*? I suppose she goes out and struggles and tries to become an accomplished person, but it wasn't easy for women in those days."

"It isn't easy for women in these days," Stella said.

"So we still resort to deception," Nina said.

"You mean me."

"I mean both of us."

"Is that why you're leaving?"

"I was always leaving. Is that why you asked me out here, to discuss philosophy?"

"No, although that's a part of it. I wanted you to come out here because I want you to stay." Stella pulled her white satin wrap over her shoulders. "Stay here with me. I want you." Stella's face grew concerned. "What's the matter?"

"No one has ever said that to me before."

"That they want you? What about your Billy? Doesn't he want you?"

"I think he assumes he's got me."

"Lucky Billy. Well, I need you. Abbie needs you. Sybil needs you. You're the only one on the inside of that upper circle who we trust."

A strange, conflicted emotion rumbled in Nina's middle. "That's what you meant."

"It's part of what I meant. Look at me!"

"You're perfect."

"You created me."

"I made suggestions."

"You certainly did. I knew you were blabbing everything to the big honchos. I didn't care. I trusted you and I still do. Somehow, you've found a way to be honest and tricky at the same time. That's why I want you. Please stay."

"I can't."

"You like me, don't you?"

"I like you. But that doesn't change anything. I have to leave."

"Why?"

"Stella, don't. I can't go any deeper. I have to go back to my old life."

"Where it's safe?"

"If you must know, yes. Back to my cage. I'm not Nora! I'm not brave, all right? Isn't that what you're thinking?"

"I'm thinking how much I feel for you."

"Stop!" Nina bent her head and put her hands over her ears like a child. When she looked up, Stella was smiling at her.

"You belong here," Stella said.

"I don't! What kind of life is this? It's all a big delusion." She was almost sputtering. "Honestly, I can't see anything that would make a *real* life here. Besides, I think you've misinterpreted my affection for you. I wanted us to be friends." Nina was aware that she had turned her face away from Stella. She didn't want Stella peering into her eyes.

Stella sighed. "You'll be back."

"No. I won't."

"You can't go back to what you were. You can't." Stella turned and headed to the door.

Two days later, Nina was on the Sante Fe Super Chief. Headed 2,985 miles in four days. Home. This time she would tackle Dante's *Paradise*, although she had to admit she'd always found the great author's vision of the heavenly rewards a bit boring, compared to his anguished and extraordinary visions of hell...

PART TWO:

THE SECRET OF CALLIE YOUNG (1949)
DIRECTOR: DEWEY STARKE

"...Meaningless fluff, but what terrific fluff. In The Secret of Callie Young, Stella Kane plays a motherless tomboy growing up on an isolated ranch. One dreadful night, Indians massacre Callie's father and Callie is captured. The savages teach her Indian skills and let her dress as a young warrior. When the right time comes, she escapes.

Coming into a town, disguised as a boy, Callie encounters a traveling show. Displaying her incredible skills to the handsome owner (Hollace Carter), she's taken on. And, speaking of attraction, the handsome owner finds himself unaccountably attracted to his new young performer. Funny and touching confusion follows. A delightful romp that won't stay with you, but will keep you amused all the while you're in the theater..."

—Review in the Los Angeles Times. July 10, 1950

"...The subversion of the film is woven within a genial veil of meaninglessness that masks unconscious fear and a fixation on homoerotic craving. The trope is one of gender confusion; the mask is fragile but complete, a disguised representation of the convoluted simplicity of the time's zeitgeist. Viewer becomes forbidden in a postmodern morality play of subcultural innuendo..."

—Camille Campton, "Gender Subversion in Films of the Nineteen-Fifties." Feminist Film Studies. July, 1990

Chapter
Thirteen

New York, New York

STELLA WAS RIGHT. Upon returning to her old life, Nina was not the same. Suddenly, English Lit seminars seemed dreary. Her senior thesis on Milton bored her nearly to death. Secretly, she imagined the Hollywood musical version of *Paradise Lost*. In the worst of developments, she went from being a slightly hesitant fiancée to an awful one.

It shouldn't have come as a surprise, then, that Billy Waxman dumped her for a cheerful girl named Bunny Steingarten whom he met at the annual Foreign Orphans Charity Ball at the Ritz-Carlton. Bunny was a cultured insider with an impressive lineage, including Lehmans, Seligmans and Warburgs. Bunny and Billy were two peas in a pod.

On some unconscious level, Nina was relieved at Billy's desertion. But she had to grieve with the melodramatic angst of youth, becoming even more grumpy and difficult as she passed through her final fall semester at Barnard. During the Christmas holiday break from school, in an effort to make herself more miserable, she accepted an invitation from her maternal grandparents to spend a few days in Manhattan, at their brownstone on East 73rd Street. Now she could revel in the torment of Grandpa Avery and Grandmother Esther's lavish attention veiling their hidden resentments at Nina's existence and its role in their daughter's loss of life.

Unsurprisingly, her grandparents declined an invitation to attend the New York premiere of *The Threat from Within*, to be held at Lumina Picture's flagship theatre on 42nd Street, The Empress, just two days before Christmas Eve. Nina had received the invitation from Elaine a few weeks before. Elaine informed her that the opening, though splashy, would not include anyone from the West Coast. That was a bad sign, Nina knew.

The movie began to applause, but soon the claps gave way to silence, then a few groans. *The Threat from Within* was a threat to film appreciation. The middle-aged couple next to Nina left halfway through. Nina, however, was mesmerized. The first time Stella appeared on the screen, Nina's heart began to race and it continued its rapid beat through the entire course of the confused, butchered tale, hacked to near insensibility by the executive committee, despite all efforts, Nina was sure, by Dick Preston and Harley Burton to salvage some sort of coherence. Stella, however, was magnificent. In close-up, she drew audible sighs from the audience, desperate for something to like. And, for Nina, it wasn't just Stella. Seeing her compatriots on the screen, Hollie, Sybil, Lance, remembering the seductiveness of their work together, she was hit by a profound longing. She left the theatre in a state of euphoria and despair, emerging into a joyful crowd strolling Times Square. Snowflakes fell, chestnuts roasted over hot coals and carolers warbled from doorways. As she trudged through the depressingly festive scene, she heard someone calling: "Nina! Nina!"

Polly Van Sant rushed towards her. Polly was a rich gentile girl with porcelain skin who'd lived in Nina's dorm for two years. They'd never been close. The old-money types didn't tend to associate much with the Jewish girls. But they all knew the details of one another's lives, family origins and romances included. Polly was dressed entirely in bohemian black, including a jaunty black beret. Even more remarkable was her warm, familiar greeting. Nina soon found out why. Polly was dating a Jew.

"He's a director," Polly gushed, "A little theatre in Greenwich Village. My parents are livid! But he's marvelous, wonderful, a genius..." she paused. "Are you still engaged to that medical student?"

"No."

"Oh, I'm so sorry," Polly breathed out with appropriate sympathy, and then she immediately perked up. "Bernard and I are going to a friend's opening tonight. Come. I absolutely insist."

Nina started to protest, then envisioned another evening with Grandpa Avery and Grandmother Esther playing pinochle, and saw very little reason not to go. That evening, she took a taxi to the theatre, running late, and joined Polly and her boyfriend barely minutes before curtain time.

After the opening, Polly and her genius, a scowling, bearded iconoclast named Bernard Cohen, insisted Nina attend an after-theater party on the Upper West Side. As they raced uptown in a wildly driven cab, Polly and Bernard enthused about the play, a piece of existentialism in which the lead actor was chained to a lamppost by his mother. Before Hollywood, Nina might have shared Polly and Bernard's enthusiasm. This night, she'd watched impatiently, surrounded by the rapt audience. If possible, the play made *Threat from Within* seem almost intelligible.

When they reached the party, at a lavish penthouse apartment on Central Park West, a woman named Sue Edelman greeted them at the door. Sue was extremely striking, with short black hair and olive skin, perhaps in her early thirties. She wore black silk slacks and a black silk vest over a cowl-necked silk blouse. Her dangling earrings looked Egyptian.

Polly and Bernard had raved to Nina on the hazardous ride from the theater about Sue, about her insightful, provocative reviews, her marvelous taste, her connections in the theater and art world. Nina fully expected Sue to be an unbearable snob. Imagine her surprise, then, when the woman greeted them warmly. Sue was as compelling as Stella, but in a way that was completely different from Stella. Sue Edelman had not a remote sign of coarseness. Everything about her radiated sophistication. There was something she and Stella had in common, though. They both had that ironic look in their eyes. Just as with Stella, Nina watched Sue appraise her, the slightest hint of a smile forming. Then she took Nina's arm. "Let me show you to the bar. You're of drinking age, I hope."

"Why, of course," Nina replied, somewhat affronted. Who ever paid attention to those silly rules, anyway, at private events?

Sue squeezed Nina's arm. "I was joking. You'll have to pardon me. I have a tendency to tease people I'm drawn to."

Another thing Sue and Stella had in common, Nina thought. Teasing. It disturbed her that Stella was so much on her mind all of a sudden. She tried to bring her attention back to the crowded room. A cluster of guests blocked their way. The guests took obvious note of Sue's arm wrapped around Nina's. Sue announced Nina's name, then paused. "What was it you're doing?"

"I'm just finishing up at Barnard." Then she added, "But this summer I worked in publicity in Hollywood. My uncle runs Lumina Pictures."

"How amusing that must have been," a bald man with a pipe commented. The rest nodded, sending signals of disdain, and stepped back to let the two women pass.

After securing drinks for them, a gin martini for herself and a glass of Chardonnay for Nina, Sue excused herself to greet new arrivals, leaving Nina to wander through the throngs. The huge main room of the penthouse was lined with tall windows overlooking the park, furnished in understated modern eclecticism. She wound up in front of a huge, bizarre canvas hung prominently on a wall at the far end of the room, a mass of thick brush strokes in a palate of fleshy pinks, dried-blood reds and muddy browns resembling animal entrails.

"Do you like it?" Sue Edelman was standing next to her.

"Honestly?"

"If we're to become friends, I'd hope you'd always be honest with me," Sue said, her eyes searching Nina's face. "I'm a critic, you know. I feel I have an obligation to be honest and I expect the same from my friends."

"Then, I don't think I like it. It's very disturbing."

"I'm not sure I like it either." Sue gazed at the painting with an appraising eye. "It *is* very disturbing. But each time I look at it, it's disturbing in a different way. That's why I bought it. It was done by a friend, Philip Guston. Come with me." As they made their way through the partygoers, Nina noted the admiring glances cast in Sue's direction. Sue obviously had that in common with Stella too. She was a star. "So you worked at Lumina Pictures. I haven't been able to bring myself to see that hideous piece of artless propaganda they just released, *The Threat From Within*. You didn't have anything to do with that abysmal project, did you?"

"Well, yes, I did. I had a lot to do with it."

"Oh, I'm sorry, how rude of me. We critics can't help being terrible snobs. We can't justify our existence otherwise. Tell me about Stella Kane. I saw her in her very first picture. It was a tiny, non-speaking role, but I was quite struck by her."

"She's not like anyone else I've ever known. She's complicated and impossible. She's beautiful and unpredictable and unfathomable, and you never know when she's real and when she's acting."

"Your Stella sounds thrilling and perilous."

When they reached the other side of the room, they stared for a few moments at another canvas, this one consisting of serene rectangles of color floating over one another. "This was done by Mark Rothko, who will be very, very famous one day. But I don't buy things for that reason. I like how each of my paintings affects me. I have a relationship with each one. My heart and mind are at one with the piece. I may be a snob, Nina, but I do feel. I feel profoundly for what I experience in the arts."

Nina nodded. She was intrigued.

"You know," Sue said, "we're in an amazing period in New York right now. A Renaissance. Not only in art, but in all the disciplines. We live in a time that's both disturbing and yet so alive in many ways. A time depressingly conventional, fearful, blind, and yet fermenting with creation. Someday, this smoldering creative volcano is going to explode and we will see a whole new era of freedom and possibility."

Sue Edelman's enthusiasm was infectious. Nina felt a shaft of light forming above her, above the deep well of moroseness she'd sunk into.

"What did you think of the play tonight?" Sue asked.

Driven with a touch of her old bloated, enthusiastic intellectuality, Nina launched into a detailed analysis of the evening's play. Eventually, she stopped to get some air, then said: "I thought, to summarize, that the play evokes the idea that we're in danger of losing our individual identities in today's world. Don't you agree?"

"That's the playwright over there. Let's ask him." Much to Nina's horror, Sue called over a glaring young man with greasy hair and thick glasses, wearing a baggy wool sweater. He clearly came from the same school of scowling intellectuals as Bernard Cohen, Polly's Jewish genius.

"Paul, Nina just summarized the point of your play and we were wondering how accurate she was," Sue said. Nina hadn't been wondering any such thing. While Paul glowered, Sue repeated Nina's summary. When she finished, the playwright turned to Nina ferociously.

"Exactly," he growled, "just what I meant." Then he stalked away.

"You're marvelous, you know," Sue said, as soon as he'd left. "You exude a wonderful freshness. A nice intellect. Whatever compelled you to go to Hollywood?"

How could Nina explain? "It was..." she began, and then let her voice trail off.

She glanced around the room at the marvelous paintings and sculpture, at the throngs of animated guests, all engrossed in brilliant conversation, and she was at a loss. The weight of New York's self-conscious superiority was impossible to fight, especially with Sue standing near to her. Someone was waving frantically at Sue from across the room. Sue took her arm once again. "What are you going to do when you graduate from Barnard?"

"I don't know." In her grumpy fog, with her marriage plans nixed, she'd stopped thinking about her future.

"You will need to think about your new life," Sue said gently. "A person needs to have goals."

"You sound like my father," Nina blurted out.

Sue's look was subtle. "Hardly my intention. Promise me you'll give me a call before you graduate. We can discuss the possibilities."

Nina called Sue in April. They met at the Palm Court in the Plaza Hotel on a blustery, sleet-driven day. The warmth and splendor of the dining room had a settling effect on people's spirits. The well-dressed crowd hummed. Nina, however, was still youthful enough to be capable of harboring wretchedness among the comforting palms, the golden hues, and the plates of fabulous food.

"You look simply forlorn," Sue commented, when she arrived at the table where Nina was already seated. "I'm sorry I'm late, I had to drop off a review before deadline."

"Do I really look that miserable?"

"You do."

"Well, how marvelous. I hoped I was better at hiding it."

They ordered the grand tea. When the waiter left, Sue continued her pleasant-toned inquisition. "What is it? You can tell me. I know we've only recently met, but I feel a certain...affinity for you."

"I feel the same."

"Then talk to me." Sue put a hand over Nina's.

Nina shivered at her touch. "I was just wishing it was something other than tea we'd arranged. I'm sorry, it just reminds me..."

"Of what?"

"Of another tea. In Hollywood. With Stella Kane, Sybil Croft, and Stella's sister Abbie." The waiter arrived with their in-the-moment tea, served in delicate china, smelling wonderfully of bergamot.

Sue poured cups of steaming liquid for them both. "You called me because you want to go back and need some sort of permission or encouragement."

"No," Nina said. But she knew Sue was right.

"Before just now, I misinterpreted your intention for calling me."

"Did you think I was going to ask you to find me a position here in Manhattan?"

"Perhaps that, perhaps a gesture of...fledgling camaraderie. But you don't want that." Sue waved her hand in the air, as though brushing away gnats. "What a ridiculous beginning to a lovely afternoon. Let's start over. Tell me what you've been up to, tell me what you're planning to do."

Nina opened her mouth, but nothing came out.

"I *would* help you," Sue insisted. "I'd love for you to live in New York. Don't worry. I will never demand anything of you that disturbs you in any way."

Much to Nina's horror, she felt tears forming. One mortifying drop slid down her cheek. The waiter had arrived with a tray of delicate, almost sculptural little sandwiches and another of sensual-smelling warm scones with butter and jam. He set the trays on the table with polished reserve and left quickly. "You're one of the most *interesting* people I've met lately and I thought...well, maybe I thought about living in Manhattan, but in another way I wasn't sure."

"It's Stella Kane, isn't it?" Sue asked.

"No!" Nina cried, arousing the startled looks of a pair of fragile matrons nearby. "No!" she repeated, in a whisper.

"I can see this is something with which I can't compete." Sue held the plate of tiny sandwiches out to Nina. "You're a very engaging young woman, probably more so because of your contradictions. You provoke pursuit, without conscious intention to do so. I suggest you go back to Hollywood. You can always call me if you decide to return."

Nina couldn't think of a response, but Sue didn't seem to need one. She steered the conversation to a recent gallery opening and from there they engaged in an hour or so of stimulating conversation from which they departed with a brief hug. "I'll let you know what I've decided."

"You've already decided," Sue responded. "Don't forget me, if you ever decide to come back East."

Chapter Fourteen

Return

AND SO, IN June of 1949, Nina descended once again from the train into Elaine's arms, while Collette yapped and scrabbled at her nylons.

"Get down, Collette," Elaine said. "You're glad to see your Auntie Nina, aren't you?"

Elaine had gained a few pounds. In her kiwi-colored skirt and matching jacket, she looked more than ever like a piece of ripe fruit. She held Nina at arm's length.

"Look at you. As trim as ever. Come, I've got so much to tell you." They raced through Union Station into the eternal sunshine. This time, Nina had brought sunglasses. She slipped them on as the driver loaded her bags into the trunk of the limousine. As soon as they'd settled into the soft leather seats, Elaine pulled a magazine from her briefcase. "Have you seen this?"

The magazine's heading:

THE TINSELTOWN INSIDER

Below, the headline:

"Film Idol Nabbed with Underage Floozy"

A foggy photo showed an ectoplasm getting hustled into a police station by two beefy blurs. Elaine tore the magazine open to reveal a much clearer photo of the ectoplasm in better days.

"Oh, no," Nina said. "I'm so sorry."

Elaine read:

    Last month in Las Vegas, Eric Flint was
    hauled to the pokie. The next morning he was let
    off the hook, all very hush-hush. Informed
    sources report the old swashbuckler, lately known
    as much for his naughty escapades as for his
    screen performances, was found snuggling with a
    teenage strumpet in a sleazy club in the wrong
    part of town.

"Do you know what kind of problems this is causing? We had

the whole thing covered up and this rag went and uncovered it!" Elaine threw the magazine. It flew over the front seat and hit the windshield, startling the chauffeur. Collette put her front paws on the top of the seat and yapped at them. "Sorry," Elaine called, and then continued. "Moe Mink bought me a pony when I was five. When the first issue came out a couple of months ago, my father called Moe. The traitor refused to talk to Poppa!"

"How can he print these kinds of things?" Nina asked.

"He has his victims followed. His lackeys go through trashcans, they find witnesses, they have spies in the studios. You must understand why this is so terrible."

Nina couldn't help breaking out in a grim smile. "Because it's true."

Elaine nodded glumly. "However, every cloud has a silver lining."

"Even this cloud?"

"Poor Eric cooked his own goose. And I see you wincing at my clichés, you little stuffed shirt, you. Anyway, I was getting tired of his shenanigans and this was a perfectly good final straw to justify breaking things off." She adopted a pained expression. "I have a terrible confession."

"Oh?"

"Murray Lasky and I are dating. I know you and he became close last summer."

"Murray and I were just friends. He must have told you that."

"He told me how *he* felt. However, I could tell you were in love last summer. I assumed it was Murray. And, of course, when you decided to come back, I thought—"

"Murray? Heavens! No, it wasn't Murray at all."

"Then who was it?"

"I wasn't in love." The very last thing Nina wanted to be talking about was personal romance. She was a spurned fiancée at best, with no prospects in sight. She wasn't even sure if she wanted any prospects.

"Was it Hollie Carter? If it was, I wouldn't get my hopes up."

"It wasn't anyone."

"I see," Elaine said, with a dubious expression. "Please don't mention anything I've said. I don't want my father to know Murray and I are dating, at least yet. He has too much on his mind." She sighed. "I seem to have an appetite for weak men." Then she pulled a script from her briefcase. "This is our latest project, *The Secret of Callie Young*. We brought in Ben and Cookie Heller to write this script. They were appalled at doing a *western*, until we mentioned the fee."

Nina was grateful for the change in conversation. "I love Ben and Cookie Heller. They entertain and still retain intellectual integrity. *Moon Over Rockaway* is one of my favorite Broadway musicals."

"We have to drag them out here to write scripts. We have to make all sorts of changes to tone down their antics. They argue, then run back to New York and insist they'll never come again." Elaine's face clouded over. "There's a lot of talk about them lately. We're choosing to ignore it. But I don't know how long that can last."

Ben and Cookie Heller's opinions on free speech had been aired in all the New York papers. Nina didn't think mentioning her admiration of their courage would be appropriate at the moment.

Elaine leaned towards Nina. "It'll be a miracle if we pull off this picture. Hollie is not the absolute guaranteed draw he was a few years ago. Then the Hellers and their politics, although we won't speak about that. Finally, there's the director, Dewey Starke. He's British. You should see what he does with these simple little scripts we give him. Ranting about Homer and Shakespeare and mythic dimensions."

"He sounds intriguing."

"He's a little kooky, but his movies make money." Elaine brightened. "We're all very excited to have you back. Among other things, you're so good with Stella, another area of difficulty, I must confess."

They were climbing Benedict Canyon Drive, nearly to the Villa. Elaine casually inspected her long red nails. "She doesn't know you're back."

"No one told her?"

Elaine shrugged, looking casually reflective. "The only ones who know are my parents, the staff at the Villa and the executive committee. We thought it'd be a nice surprise for everyone else."

As the limo pulled up to the Villa, the tall wrought iron gates swung open majestically. Nina shrugged, trying to match her cousin's casual manner. "Stella and I parted on equivocal terms."

"Equivocal terms? That sounds awful. We're counting on you to help us with her. *I'll* give her a piece of my mind, if I have to."

"No!" Nina cried, knocking the script onto the floor.

"Nina, what on earth's the matter?"

"I'm just bushed from the trip. My head aches like the dickens."

Elaine patted Nina's hand. "Of course. You're exhausted. I'm sure you read the entire Bible in Hebrew and listened to the sad stories of eight first-class passengers on your trip. Take a nap before supper."

When Nina arrived in her room in The Cottage, her phony

French maid Marie was waiting. Marie catapulted into Nina's arms. "Hey! I missed you."

"I missed you too," Nina replied, wrapped in a Winnemuccan-style bear hug.

"Uncle Alfred swore you'd be back," Marie crowed, disengaging herself from Nina.

Nina's stomach lurched. "You told him? Did he tell Sybil? Who else did you two tell?"

Marie's face arranged itself into a mask of offended dignity. "I swear, it was only him and he's never told an employer's personal affairs to anyone in his entire life. That's what he's like. And I learned that from him."

Nina slumped onto her bed. "I don't mind if Alfred knows."

Marie sighed with relief. Then she leaned over and whispered in Nina's ear: "Uncle Alfred said you'd come back. He said he thought you had something to learn here."

"I certainly can't imagine what he's talking about."

"That's all right." Marie straightened her uniform. "Uncle Alfred says time has a way of taking care of things. He says he's an optimistic fatalist, whatever that means."

Nina's flight to Hollywood had not erased her depressive New York outlook. "I thought time just made you old."

"You have to look at the big picture," Marie explained patiently. "Hey, where would evolution be with that kind of attitude?" She saw Nina's cross look and hesitated. "I better go."

"Wait." Nina hesitated. "I was wondering how things are, you know, with Sybil, with Stella and Abbie."

Marie started to speak, stopped, then looked earnestly at Nina. "Like I said, my uncle and I wouldn't let out a peep about our employers' lives. I will say, it's a good thing you're back." She turned and fled before Nina could say another word.

Supper at the Villa was superb, as usual. But the cheese trays and caviar and mouth-watering French onion soup topped with buttery fried toast could not completely ease the evening's uneasy tone. Everything had started out hunky-dory, with big hugs from Poppa and kisses on the cheek from Aunt Nettie.

"We all knew you'd be back," Poppa announced, after swallowing a cracker mounded with beluga caviar. He turned to his wife. "We knew she wouldn't become a urologist's wife."

"Don't start," Aunt Nettie admonished.

"Start what?" He motioned a knife at Nina. "Eat some of this Camembert cheese. Take some caviar. Here, eat."

Nina, in an unusual moment, was not very hungry. She was stirring around her soup, but its intense aroma was oddly unappealing. Like the buttery toast points, she felt like she was floating aimlessly on a thick soup, but hers was a soup of doubt and uncertainty. Oh no, she thought. I've been here only a few hours and my similes are getting trite. Now that she'd left New York, she was already mourning the loss of possibilities, the promises extended by Sue Edelman of a glorious intellectual life.

"What does your father think of all this?" Poppa asked, interrupting Nina's reverie with more disturbing questions.

"Irwin, please. Leave her alone," Aunt Nettie warned again with a resigned tone.

"He wasn't terribly thrilled." In fact, Daddy had been about as upset as he ever allowed himself to be. Now here she was, questioning her own decision on the eve of her arrival. Elaine, too, seemed less than elated. She was pushing the morsels of food around on her plate.

"Look at you both!" Poppa said, but as soon as the words were out of his mouth, he too adopted a glum look. "It's a jungle out there." He stabbed a fork in Elaine's direction. "I know you're going out with Murray. Don't know what I was thinking. My successor, ha! Remember, you're the one who's going to suffer when some jackass takes over Lumina, and at least you could find a strong man to marry. Am I asking too much?" Without waiting for an answer, he turned to Nina. "All is not wine and roses. I'm getting heat from the parent corporation back east. I'm getting heat from politicians. I'm not going to say there's a blacklist, but I have some people who might be on some kind of a list which we won't talk about." His face grew from red to deep crimson. "And then there's that obscene publication put out by the traitor Moe Mink."

"Irwin, relax," Aunt Nettie admonished. "You're going to give yourself another stroke."

"Poppa, we're working on all this," Elaine added with terse brightness. "And now Nina's back to help!"

The toast points were sinking into her soup. Nina let her spoon drop against her bowl, wiped her lips with her linen napkin, and jumped to her feet.

"What's the matter?" Poppa exclaimed.

"I didn't realize how terrible things have gotten. If I'd known—"

"Oh, heavens," Poppa said, spreading out his arms. "Sit down, enjoy your meal. I thought since you'd been here before, you'd understand. We're just blowing steam. It's always like this here. That's what makes it so exciting."

Nina hesitated, and then sat back down. She reached for the caviar and the crackers. Actually, she was rather hungry.

Poppa watched her load her plate with satisfaction. "That's my girl. Eat. You'll need the energy. We have a lot to do. Big plans. Big dreams. What's a little adversity?"

On their way back to the Cottage, Nina breathed in the fragrant aromas of the garden and sighed. "There isn't anything like this smell back East. It's like a potion. Maybe that's what I need. A magic potion to make me feel like I've done the right thing."

"Are you sorry you came?"

"I don't know. Maybe."

Elaine took in a deep breath and her face grew surprisingly vulnerable. "Thank you for coming. I sincerely hope it was the right thing."

"Me too." She smiled gamely at Elaine. "I'll read *The Secret of Callie Young* in bed tonight. In the morning, I'll be ready for anything."

Chapter
Fifteen

Mythic Dimensions

NINA HAD A copy of *The Secret of Callie Young* tucked under her arm the next morning, as she and Elaine headed to the set. "I wonder what mythic dimensions Dewey Starke will bring to this one. It's already loaded with latent meaning."

"Let's not even discuss it. I think Dewey's been conspiring with Ben and Cookie on this particular lollapalooza."

They arrived at the sound studio between takes. Set dressers scurried around, putting finishing touches on a frontier hotel bedroom. The lighting crew was fiddling with some technicalities, complaining loudly to one another about shadows. Stooped in his director's chair, Dewey Starke was scribbling notations on a battered script. With his delicate, pale features and horned-rim glasses, he looked more like a scholarly elf than a director.

"Mr. Starke!" Elaine called. "So sorry to interrupt you."

Dewey stared absent-mindedly, his pencil poised in the air. "Excuse me?"

"Elaine Weiss? From publicity."

"Publicity person," Dewey said, rubbing the eraser end of the pencil along his jaw. His eyes settled on Nina. "And you?"

"My cousin Nina," Elaine said. "Just graduated from Barnard."

Dewey's face lit up. "Barnard. A former classmate from Cambridge teaches literature there. James Whitney."

"What a coincidence. Dr. Whitney taught my Milton seminar. He was on my senior thesis committee."

"Oh, heavens be praised. They've suckered another intellectual into our midst."

Nina shrugged modestly.

"We must have lunch together," Dewey said.

"Nina would be delighted to have lunch with you." Elaine had that gleam in her eyes.

Dewey motioned Nina closer and pointed to the script. "A classic romance. Boy meets girl. But here girl is disguised as boy. It's an age-old gender twist." He took her arm. "The audiences want westerns. They want romance. But underneath they want to be moved in some fundamental way."

Elaine turned so Dewey couldn't see her face and rolled her eyes at Nina. But Nina exclaimed: "I detected the hidden gender complications and yet was taken up with the action."

"Precisely! Explore the mythology without betraying the mundane plot." Dewey leaped from his chair. "I must confer with my set designer. Visuals are essential."

When he was out of earshot, Elaine sighed. "You see?"

"He's delightful."

"I'm sure the two of you will be delighted exploring all the hidden meanings." Elaine paused. "And, of course, you'll be delighted to let me know *everything*."

That was why they wanted her back. To spy. Oh, well. It was for everyone's benefit. No use thinking much about it. She was a little distracted, anyway. The set had no actors. That was about to change.

Nina and Elaine waited while the cinematographer fooled with a tricky tracking situation. One of the assistants went to get the actors. Hollie Carter appeared first. He wore a plaid shirt, leather vest, pointy cowboy boots and tight blue jeans. Looking terribly rugged, he acknowledged the admiring gesture from the script girl. Then he noticed Nina and waved, with a look of surprise and delight.

And then Stella appeared, swaggering onto the set. Nina gasped. Stella's hair was cropped into a boyish cut. She wore a buckskin outfit that somehow disguised her femininity and yet hinted at it, too. One of the grips whistled. Stella bowed to him. As she did, she noticed Nina. After a moment's hesitation, she smiled. It was Stella's mysterious smile.

Nina felt the old confusion rushing in. What did that smile mean? What kind of a response had she expected? The most frustrating thing was how much she, Nina, cared. Frankly, she didn't want to puzzle so emotionally about Stella's every gesture.

Dewey gathered his actors for a run-through of the scene. He waved his pencil in the air like a baton. Stella and Hollie huddled next to each other, nodding at Dewey's pontifications. Hollie draped an arm around Stella's shoulder, and she leaned against him. "Look at them," Elaine whispered. "If I didn't know better, I'd swear they were an item. You know, you put two people into a romantic picture and things start to boil. This time, though, we know it can't happen."

"How do you know that?" Nina watched Hollie's hand circle around Stella's shoulder blades.

Elaine glanced at Nina quizzically. "I thought you were privy to all the hush-hush, especially with those two."

"Apparently not."

"Get ready, folks!" the assistant director called. "Quiet on the set!"

Hollie took his place on the bed in the frontier hotel bedroom.

"Take one, scene thirty-seven," cried the assistant director.

"Rolling," said the cameraman.

"Action!" Dewey cried.

A knock at the bedroom door.

"Come in," Hollie called.

Stella shuffled in, shifting from one foot to another. Hollie jumped up from the bed.

"Didn't mean to disturb you," Stella said huskily.

"It's fine, Cal. What's the matter?" Hollie edged away from the bed.

Stella held out a wrist.

Hollie took it gently. "Boy, you got a nasty sprain." He stroked Stella's wrist. "You need a doctor."

"No!" Stella cried, pulling her wrist away. "My daddy always said doctors were as like to kill you as cure you."

"Ain't many doctors can kill you treating a sprained wrist."

"You won't throw me out of the show?" Stella moaned.

"Because you're hurt?" Hollie threw his arm around Stella's shoulder. "You're my star attraction." Stella leaned into Hollie's chest. Their faces moved together. Then, violently, Hollie jumped away. Stella fell back, just catching herself before she fell.

Nina jumped too. So did Dewey, Elaine and half the crew.

"But I'll fire you on the spot, next time you hide getting hurt from me!" Hollie yelled and marched from the room. Stella tiptoed around, touching her thwarted lover's things. She completed her private invasion with a guilty look, her gaze lingering on the bed.

Nice bit of business, Nina thought.

"Cut!" Dewey Starke yelled. "Beautiful! Print it! One take, my lord. I love you two."

The crew clapped.

"Actors! Take a break," Dewey called.

The actors stepped off the set. Stella, after a moment's hesitation, headed towards Elaine and Nina.

"Look who's back," Elaine said to her.

"Visiting?" Stella asked.

"Working," Elaine proclaimed.

"I see." Stella adopted her inscrutable look.

"Now you two can take up just where you left off."

"Just let me know what I have to do," Stella said. With that familiar line, she turned and headed towards her dressing room.

"Young lady!" Dewey Starke gestured at Nina.

"What did you think about that scene?"

"They were very good," Nina said.

"I don't want drivel, I want objective analysis." Dewey stared at Nina like one of her most demanding instructors. "We still need something."

Nina ran the scene through her mind again. "These characters fear that they're violating a strong moral code. Let their confusion be even more tantalizing, but submerged."

"Ah, yes," Dewey sighed. "I begin to see some solutions."

"I hate to interrupt," Elaine interjected. "But Nina and I have an important meeting."

"She's a treasure," Dewey said to Elaine.

"We think so, too," Elaine replied, taking Nina's arm and leading her off the set.

Elaine and Nina charged into the familiar meeting room and rushed to their places. No one in the room acknowledged Nina with any particular fanfare. She might have returned either from the dead or a trip to the powder room.

"Sybil Croft is nothing but trouble," Aaron Bermann cried.

"Sybil's the most talented and beautiful actress we have on contract," Shanahan shot back. He glanced over at Nina, eyes registering the mildest surprise, and then gave her an almost imperceptible nod of joyful greeting.

Aaron glanced over his shoulder as though there might be a microphone in the flower arrangement on the side table near the window. "She's trouble. The petitions, the causes, the soirées with every pinko in town invited. It's a miracle she hasn't been called before the Committee. Probably family influence."

Dick Preston tapped his gold fountain pen on a pad of paper. "I agree with Shanahan. We're wasting our resources if we don't use Sybil Croft."

"She thinks she's not like everyone else. We give her an excellent part and she refuses it," Aaron complained.

"A charwoman?" Shanahan slapped his palm on the table. "What about the heiress in that one in development with Sterling Hayden? Isn't Dick producing?"

"How'd you hear about that?" Aaron said and turned to Dick. "I thought you were getting Crawford for that one."

"Jack Warner won't let Crawford out of three pictures he has planned for her. He's got her tied up 'til 1951."

"What about Stanwyck?"

"Same problem," Dick said. "Studios are getting stingy about loaning out their big names."

"Look," Aaron said. "Sybil hasn't had any real box office since before the Japs bombed Pearl Harbor. I know box office poison when I see it. Besides, the woman is almost *forty-five*."

Shanahan looked from face to face. "She's still a fine actress."

"Shanahan, face the music," Aaron said. "She's trouble and she's old. And she's not making us enough money to be either."

Shanahan grabbed the pencil he'd had stuck behind his ear and threw it onto the table. "To hell with you." He slammed out of the room.

"That man is testing my limits," Aaron said, and turned to Dick once again. "Get Bette Davis."

"I'll try," Dick replied. "But if I can't, I'm going to cast Sybil Croft and that's that."

"All right, all right," Aaron moaned. "If you can't get *anyone else*, cast her. Let's talk about Stella Kane."

Everyone glanced at Nina.

"Here's the deal," Aaron said. "Stella's hot property, but something's still not just right." Aaron fixed his gaze on the ceiling, searching for divine guidance.

"What's the image I'm looking for?" he pondered. Ever so slowly, he lowered his gaze. "She's gorgeous and sexy, but she's too independent." Aaron glared.

"You," he said, jabbing his finger in Nina's direction, "will fix the problem."

When Nina started to speak, he jabbed his finger at her again. "Fix it."

"I'll try," Nina stuttered.

"You will do it, you won't just try." Aaron's face took on a meditative façade of peace for a moment, and then clouded over. He jabbed a finger at Dick. "You put that goddamned fairy in a war movie. If he can play a soldier then I can play Scarlett O'Hara."

The image of Aaron as Scarlett O'Hara brought a few suppressed smiles to the group.

"I cast Lance Lewis because we needed a weak character," Dick protested. "He's *supposed* to be a bad soldier."

"Honey," Aaron said, turning to Nina. "You saw *Threat From Within*?"

Nina nodded, not specifying how many times she'd returned to the Empress to stare at the screen in the nearly empty theatre, watching the awful potboiler over and over.

"What'd you think of Lance Lewis?"

"His acting *did* fit the role." Nina knew exactly what Aaron meant. Lance wasn't very good. However, she wasn't about to slander him for Aaron's sake.

Aaron threw up his hands. "No one's gonna give me the answers I expect today." He pounded a fist on the table. "We're fighting a battle here. Get going! Think up some angles! All of you!"

As they all stood to leave, Aaron called out, "Nina!"

"Yes?"

"Welcome back," Aaron said. He sounded like he meant it

Chapter
Sixteen

Injecting Freud Into It All

TWO DAYS LATER, Dewey Starke and Nina were in the Lumina commissary. A waitress named Irma had just delivered Nina's chicken potpie. Dewey had a tuna and tomato salad, which he nibbled while Nina dug into her entrée They were seated along the western wall of the large dining room, at the section of small tables reserved for those who intended to meet "intimately." The rest of the room bustled with large parties around tables for six, eight and ten, served by pink-uniformed women lugging hefty trays. Nina could see the cast for *Callie Young* enjoying a boisterous meal in the middle of the room. Hollie was telling a story, waving one arm, the other arm hooked on the back of Stella's chair.

Forty-eight hours had passed since she'd arrived back in Hollywood. Nina hadn't contacted Stella yet. She had to have a plan. To avoid confusion. Dewey followed Nina's gaze to the lively cast table. "I haven't worked with this much talent since I left London. I must thank Dick Preston. A bit snooty, but you Americans, the wealthy ones, you can be that way, as though your entire nation didn't come over on stinking boats full of criminals and religious fanatics and persecuted souls." Dewey winked at Nina with conspiratorial, gossipy amusement. "Dick Preston is a throbbing volcano. Is he a good man or a bad man? He can't make up his mind. But, in the meantime, he'll keep trying to do the right thing. Which means allowing me to make pictures as I see fit, despite the blockheads and witch-hunters and puritanical fanatics in the front office."

Dewey raised a delicate eyebrow at Nina's mildly shocked expression. "I won't suppress my observations and I expect the same from you. You're a prize."

"You're overestimating me."

"You're underestimating yourself." He placed a small piece of tomato in his mouth and chewed meditatively. "The young swing erratically between egotism and self-deprecation." Before Nina could answer, he called out, "Waitress! Waitress!"

Irma paused, tray in hand.

"Would you mind going over to that table and telling the cast they have ten minutes before they're expected on the set?"

A cloud gathered on Irma's face. "I'm a waitress, not an errand girl."

Dewey smiled placatingly. "I remember your last picture, *The Sheik's Revenge*. I saw it in London many years ago. Quite well done. I admire the old silents very much."

Irma shrugged. "That's more than I can say about your last picture, *Blast the Enemy*."

"That film was based loosely on King Richard III."

"I don't care what it was based on. It was a stinker."

As Irma marched away, Dewey laughed. "She's right. But it did make money. And I learn every day. Listen: 'Then I looked up, and saw the morning rays/Mantle its shoulder from that planet bright/Which guides men's feet aright on all their ways.' "

"The first canto of *The Inferno*," she said.

Dewey regarded her seriously. "There's an art to getting things between the lines. Who reads between the lines?"

"People who know to look."

"The rest of the population is content with catharsis. They go to their destinies kicking and screaming, dragged by the devil of catharsis."

Irma approached their table, in time to catch the last of Dewey's comments. She snorted under her breath and began clearing their plates. "Dessert?"

"I'll have a raspberry tart," Nina said.

"And you, Mr. Starke?" Irma asked. "Would some dessert be *cathartic*?"

"Do you have a dessert particularly for that?" Dewey asked.

"I'd say the tart. It's both cathartic *and* divine, if you order the whipped cream."

"I think I'll skip it," Dewey said. "Divine and cathartic might be too much in one day."

Across the room, Nina could see the cast from *Callie Young* preparing to leave. She knows I'm here, Nina thought. She's ignoring me.

Dewey followed her gaze again. "Filled with secrets. Forbidden romance. Kicking and screaming your way to your own destiny. Think about these things. I must go."

Irma came up as Nina finished her tart.

"Some advice?" Irma asked. Parties from a few tables were waving in her direction. She ignored them. "I'll be frank. I like that girl in Dewey's picture, I've been watching her. She's got real spirit. And talent, much more than most of these newcomers."

"Stella?"

Irma nodded. "In my time, she'd have been fine. The only way she'll thrive, the way the world is these days, is if she seems tamed."

Nina groaned. "I thought we'd tamed her about as far as we could."

"You need to hook her up with a man," Irma explained patiently. "Look at Bogart and Bacall."

ELAINE WAS WAITING for Nina when she returned to publicity. "And so?"

"We talked about catharsis."

"Is that something I should worry about?"

"If I remember my Freud, it's only an issue when it becomes conscious."

"Oh, heavens. He's not injecting *Freud* into all of this?"

"I don't think you inject Freud into a romance about sexual disguise," Nina replied. "I think he comes with the territory."

"I want you monitoring this as much as possible. Call it The Freud Alert." Elaine grinned at her own witticism.

"I'll start tomorrow." Nina cleared her throat. "Hollie and Stella seem like they're getting close."

"It would never happen."

"Why? After Hollie's last breakup with that Mona Purcell, even if *that* was invented, then what about—"

"Nina," Elaine interrupted. "I'm trying to be discreet. We'll talk about this another time."

The next afternoon, Nina was on the set with Marty Gramm, one of the still photographers. Marty was a gentle giant, six-five, with the forbearance of a saint. He was one of the best photographers in Hollywood. His subjects felt comforted when he aimed a camera at them. Marty and Nina had arrived intending to take a series of publicity shots of Dewey and the primary actors in action. They'd just arrived when all hell broke loose.

It was, Nina found out later, the seventh take of Stella in close-up. The master shot of the same scene had been filmed successfully that morning, along with a two-shot. Now, in this crucial moment concentrating on Stella's face, something was wrong.

"Cut!" Dewey jumped away from his spot next to the camera, clutching his hands to his head. "No! No! No!"

He ran to Stella. "I want to see your insides torn apart! You love this man and you can't even show him you're the right sex!"

"Go to hell!" Stella cried and stormed off the set.

Everyone froze, mouths gaping.

"Oh my God, what have I done?" Dewey cried. "Someone, go talk to her."

There was an embarrassed silence.

"She's a gifted performer." Dewey glanced mournfully around the room. "Someone go tell her I apologize."

No one moved.

"Hollace—" Dewey began, but Hollie Carter held up his hand. Then Dewey looked at Nina.

"No," she said. "Why would she listen to me?"

"You're the only one," Dewey said. "I have a feeling about this."

"COME IN!"

Stella sat at a makeup table when Nina opened the door of the dressing room. She was studying a page of script with intense concentration.

"They sent me to calm you down, but you don't seem upset."

"Why else would a person walk off the set?"

"Beats me."

"Dewey's right," Stella said, rising and going over to a tiny sofa. She patted the place next to her. "In a close-up the camera's like God. I wasn't expressing an inner truth."

Nina didn't move. "I don't understand actors. Or acting, for that matter. It's all a lie and yet there's all this talk about truth."

"It's not something you understand with your mind. Come over here."

"What do you want me to do?"

"First of all, sit by me."

"You aren't upset at all," Nina said, not moving from the doorway. "That was completely an act."

"Not completely. Now come over."

Nina moved away from the door and inched across the room. It was over-heated, despite a rackety fan.

"Sit," Stella commanded.

Once Nina sat, Stella settled back against the pillows and closed her eyes. Nina knew this much about Stella and her associations with the deaf. By closing her eyes, she was distancing herself even more than the average person. "I was *somewhat* upset, but not about the scene, although I wasn't happy about that either."

"Was it about me coming back?"

"I knew you were coming back."

"You couldn't have known. I didn't know myself." Nina paused, feeling how close Stella was to her on the loveseat. "If it wasn't me, then what were you upset about?"

Stella opened her eyes and sat up. "*Somewhat* upset."

"Okay, what were you *somewhat* upset about?"

The look in Stella's usually ironic eyes darkened. "Things are not good, right now. I tried to send Abbie to a deaf day school, but she wouldn't go. And Sybil, she's got me worried, too. She's dragging around, spouting off about death and reincarnation. And all the damned publicity people keep ragging on me to make changes, but the changes don't make sense." Stella paused and inspected Nina's face. "I'm glad you're back. You bring sense to all this."

Nina was touched by Stella's words. So she put her foot in her mouth. "You and Hollie are getting cozy. Let him help you."

Stella looked pained. "That was low."

Nina took a deep breath. "I missed you," she said.

"I missed you too, honey," Stella replied.

There was a loud knock at the door.

"Good," Stella said. "I'm ready for that scene now."

"What!" Nina exclaimed.

Stella looked at her, puzzled.

"Did you get me in here just to get motivated for a *scene*?"

"Yes and no." Stella headed to the door, leaving Nina to leap from the couch and scurry after her.

When they got back to the set, Stella aced her close-up in one take.

"What on Earth did you say to Stella?" Dewey asked Nina later, after the actors had cleared the set. "It was magical. She had the passion I was looking for."

"I can't say," Nina replied mysteriously.

"I respect your reticence and I'll be humble enough to learn from your astonishing effect on actors." Dewey bowed from the waist.

In the week that followed, Nina haunted the set of *Callie Young*, accompanying press and visitors. She watched the dailies in the early evenings when the rest of her work was finished. Under Elaine's supervision, she wrote copy and arranged interviews. Most importantly, she thought about Stella. Whether on the set or during publicity events, she never tired of watching her. Still, she began to see what Aaron and Irma meant about Stella. She had an unapproachable quality that, while compelling, was a bit too daunting.

NINA NEEDED TO talk to Stella alone, despite her anxiety about their perplexing conversations. The next morning, she waited until Stella had finished a long scene and went to her dressing room for a break. Stella opened the door to her knock. "What a nice surprise." She motioned Nina in.

"I need to talk to you."

"Look at that face. What on earth could you be asking me that's so dreadful?"

"Don't. I'm going to leave if this gets all twisted up."

"What did you want to ask?"

Nina fidgeted in the tiny space by the doorway. "Do you have a boyfriend?"

She expected a flippant response. Instead, Stella grew serious. "Why?"

"You said don't go inventing your life without knowing something about it."

"Oh. It's business."

"What did you think?"

"I don't. Have a boyfriend, that is." Before Nina could respond, she added: "I haven't been close to *anyone*." She looked at Nina pointedly. "Except you."

"I'll take that as a compliment."

"Take it how you want. It's the truth."

"Stella, I'm going to be frank with you. I'm not sure what truth means to you."

"I'm not sure what truth means to *you*." Stella went over to the door and held it open. "Make up your schemes. Reinvent me. But don't rap my knuckles about truth and lies."

"I have a plan." Nina paused, feeling her throat constrict. "I needed to know if you were romantically involved for real."

Stella reached out and touched Nina's chin. "Officially, no."

Nina was startled by her gesture and flinched without meaning to. "Unofficially?"

"For now, 'no' to that one, too."

"Good. I'll get to work on my plan."

"I'm in your hands."

Later that day Nina approached Elaine in her office.

"Stella tells me," Nina began, trying to sound casual, "that she doesn't have a real boyfriend."

"Is she telling the truth?"

"I think so. But she can be so hidden."

Elaine's eyes lit up. "Hidden? Do you have any new information?"

"No. I've been in a bind about Stella. We still don't have the right angle for her."

"Isn't that a fact?" Elaine sighed. "Tell me your plan."

"Not yet. Let me work on it a little longer."

Chapter Seventeen

Kindred Souls

THE NEXT WEEK, Nina chanced on Shanahan in the break room.

"Shanahan, we haven't had a chance to talk alone."

"Avoiding me? Scared of my unseemly ways?"

"No, I've got your number. An ogre with a heart of gold. Or a believer with a cynic's façade. Or a former priest who pretends to be a drunk. Take your pick."

Shanahan held up both arms. "Whoa, girlie. Come out swinging, why don'tcha? I don't know if I can take that kind of brutal candor."

Nina shrugged. "It's your fault. You're one of the few people I know who I can just be myself around."

Shanahan whistled softly, then made a deep and reverent bow. "For that compliment, I am truly honored. I hope I can live up to that estimation."

"You will. I did you a favor today."

"I hope it was a good plant."

"It was. I bumped into Hank Sweeney from *Variety* at Chasen's. He promised to hint that Sybil Croft got the part in Dick Preston's picture. That might help her to get it for real. I don't care if Aaron kills me. I don't understand why he's being so awful about Sybil."

Shanahan whistled softly. "You're a doll."

"Don't worry about it."

"No, I owe you one. You'll hear from me."

Nina heard from Shanahan sooner than expected. It was midnight that evening.

"Come down to the Hollywood Sheriff's Station. Don't go in the front. Find the east alley and knock at the door marked No Entry."

The phone went dead.

At the sheriff's station, a sour-faced deputy let Nina in through the door marked No Entry. She followed him down a dim corridor that smelled of cigarette smoke and disinfectant. They arrived at another door, this one of thick metal with a small window of barred glass. The deputy paused.

"Where's that Elaine broad?"

"I'm Elaine's cousin."

The detective sneered. "All in the family. Isn't that nice?"

Before Nina could say anything, someone called up the echoing hallway. "Mike, you harassing the young lady?"

"No," the deputy replied. "Heck, I'm not stupid. I leave the family members of the old man alone. How old is this one anyway? Looks sixteen."

"She's all right," Shanahan replied. "Anyway, let's get down to business."

The interrogation room décor consisted of a thick wooden table surrounded by four ugly wooden chairs. The bare walls were painted mustard yellow and the linoleum floor was a nauseous green. In one of the chairs was Abbie, disheveled and looking very defiant.

"She won't speak," the deputy said. "She's pretending she doesn't hear me."

"She's deaf," Nina said.

"Damn," the deputy said, and then shook his head. "Excuse the language."

"What's the scoop here?" Shanahan asked.

"The kid plowed a nice Lincoln Continental into a tree, miracle she's hardly scratched or bruised. No ID on her. Buggy belongs to Sybil Croft, so I called you."

From her crouched, defensive position on her chair, Abbie let out a whimper. Nina mimed an ironic shrug and rolled her eyes. Abbie giggled.

"Nothing funny here," the deputy barked.

"Give the kid a break," Shanahan interjected. "She's nervous. Besides, she's got an impairment."

"I don't care if she's deaf. This is stupid delinquent behavior, in my book. This little girl would be in trouble if it wasn't for her connections." He shook his finger at Shanahan. "Make sure someone keeps this kid under control. I can only do so many favors, you know that. Make my life easier, take my time for the important predicaments."

"You got it, Mike," Shanahan said, standing. "Let's scram, girls."

Abbie and Nina followed Shanahan down the dingy hallway and out to the back parking lot.

"Stella and Sybil are waiting at Sybil's place," Shanahan said. "Want me to take her?"

Abbie was clinging to Nina's arm. She pointed rapidly at Nina. *You. You. You.*

"I'll take her," Nina said.

As they turned to leave, Shanahan called: "Hey! You know, Moe Mink would love to get his hands on Stella or anybody at Lumina for that matter. We're gonna have to do something about this girl, excuse my bluntness, before she does something really bad."

"I know. But I'm not sure what to do."

"Let me work on it," he said.

Nina hesitated. "This is one thing Stella may not be willing to listen to anyone about. Don't count on using your connections in this situation."

He held up a hand. "Let me work on it."

Sybil and Stella came rushing up as Abbie and Nina pulled into the driveway. The car had barely stopped before Abbie leapt out and threw herself into Stella's arms. She started to sob in great gulps against Stella's chest.

Sybil stopped squarely in front of Nina. "Is everything taken care of?"

"Thanks to Shanahan."

"God bless Shanahan," Sybil breathed out.

"He's a good man."

"He's a very good man."

"He says you helped him out when he first came here," Nina said.

"We helped each other. But that's another story. For now, at least Abbie's not hurt."

"What on earth happened?"

"Let's go inside," Sybil replied.

While Stella put Abbie to bed, Sybil made tea in the kitchen. "I don't know what we're going to do." Sybil poured boiling water into the teapot. The scent of chamomile and mint infused the room. "Abbie is a bright and troubled young lady who happens to be deaf. She needs more challenge than Stella is willing to let her have. And more discipline."

Before Nina had a chance to reply, Stella came in. "What are you two whispering about?"

"Is Abbie all right?" Sybil asked.

"Good enough, considering. Don't go changing the subject." Before Sybil could reply, Stella said: "I know. She's too smart and she's too used to having her own way."

"Why don't you sit?" Sybil said gently. "Have a nice cup of tea."

Stella sank into the chair next to Nina at the kitchen table. "I'm at wit's end. Never thought I'd say that."

"Let me help." Both Stella and Sybil stared at her. "I'll find a way." On her way to her car, Nina mulled over her promise. She had absolutely no idea how she was going to keep it. It was Shanahan who came to her rescue. True to his word, he provided her with the solution, after some very busy work among his contacts.

Chapter
Eighteen

One Of Us

ON THE FIRST Saturday in July, Nina drove to Sybil Croft's place. Alfred loaded Abbie's things into the trunk, and then they all, including Alfred, had a good cry before Stella, Abbie and Nina took off.

So far, all Nina knew of California was Hollywood and the movie business. It was something of a shock to leave the urbanity of Los Angeles. In no time, they were in farmland, vast acres of orchards, hundreds and hundreds of trees laid out in neat rows along narrow roads with a backdrop of low hills blanketed with dried golden grass.

Nina drove, Abbie beside her, with Stella in the back seat. They sat silently for nearly the entire hour-long trip. "I think we're almost there," Nina said brightly. "It's not very far at all. Shanahan was right. It's actually very close. Easy to come and visit any time." Her remarks were met with more silence.

They were driving through an expanse of orange trees now, raising dust from the road and bouncing through ruts that rattled the car's frame. They soon came to a sign reading SNIPES ORANGE RANCH.

"Here we are!" Nina cried. They rattled down the lane, veering briefly to avoid an oncoming truck laden with oranges. She parked near a white ranch house surrounded by outbuildings and farm machinery. Scattered across the property were huge wooden crates piled with what appeared to be a million oranges.

A man in a straw hat who'd been crossing the yard waved to them. He was wiry and graceful, with a deeply tanned, weathered face. As he got closer, he began to sign. Stella jumped from the car and signed back. For several minutes, they carried on a conversation, Stella gesturing at Abbie, who was following the silent discussion closely. Then, she too jumped out of the car, signing rapidly as she approached the pair.

For another moment, Nina sat and watched from the driver's seat. Stella was grilling the man, while Abbie, too, interjected demands. For his part, the man seemed to be holding his own. His face never appeared anything but calm and gently amused. Then, after a particularly boisterous interchange, they all three paused. Stella gestured at Nina to come out. As she approached, the man tipped his hat and spoke. "How do you do?"

"Oh," Nina said.

"Yes, I speak, and I'm hearing, too. I'm Hiram, the ranch foreman. I grew up with a deaf mother, just like these Kane girls."

"Where are the Snipes? Shanahan said they were expecting us."

"Out back. They're very much expecting you."

They followed Hiram around the side of the ranch house. A stand of tall trees shaded the yard. The intense sun laced through the branches, creating a pattern of dappled light over picnic tables covered with blue-checked tablecloths. They stood, the four of them, mesmerized by the beauty of the scene. The tables were piled high with bowls of potato and macaroni salads and plates of fried chicken and bowls of baked beans, but no one was eating yet. They were signing.

In the near silence, punctuated by calls of the birds in the trees and occasional bursts of laughter and excited sounds from the mouths of the picnickers, by occasional slaps of the hands and a whooshing sound as arms brushed together, the joy of the moment was conveyed through hands and bodies moving.

A woman with grey hair massed in a knot at her neck stood and signed to them. When Nina didn't sign, she nodded hello.

"This is Annie Snipes," Hiram said. "The owner's wife."

Nina could see Annie watching her lips as she introduced herself.

They approached the picnic tables. Nina was aware of the unself-conscious stares from the group. It was a though she was coming upon an entire group of Stellas, reaching inside her through her expression and body movements.

Hiram pointed to a bear-sized man with dark brown eyes. "Carl, Annie's husband, doesn't read lips."

Carl signed something. He had obviously just read Hiram's lips.

"He says he *can* read lips when he wants to, but he doesn't want to. Something about when he was a kid," Hiram informed Nina.

"That's Patty," Hiram said, pointing to a young woman. "Carl and Annie's daughter."

"I'm sixteen today," Patty said. She was a thin, pretty girl with a blond braid trailing down her back. As she spoke, she signed. "I'm usually the interpreter for the hearing visitors," she informed

Nina. "Sit next to me, I'll help you." Patty pointed to the young man who was seated across from her, who looked to be Abbie's age. "This is my cousin, Tex. He's from Arizona. Just got here last week. He reads lips."

Tex was a lanky boy with a ruddy tan and high cheekbones. He began signing rapidly, looking at Stella, then at Abbie, then at his cousin. Everyone burst out laughing and Tex grinned bashfully.

"He said he's never met a movie star before. He says he thought they always wore fancy clothes, but instead you're wearing them."

Nina looked down, suddenly self-conscious at her sweater set and skirt. Stella and Abbie had worn slacks and plaid shirts.

Patty signed at Tex, and then smiled at Nina. "I told him you're important, too."

Nina turned to Tex. "Why do they call you Tex if you're from Arizona?" He signed something back. Everyone burst into laughter.

"He says because Arizona would be a silly name," Patty interpreted. She patted the place next to her. Nina went over and sat. "You'll have to pardon us. We make a lot of jokes. It's part of being with the deaf."

Now that Nina was seated, hands flew as Stella and Abbie met everyone. Abbie took a seat next to Tex, while Stella sat near Patty's mother, with Hiram on her other side.

"I was expecting more inmates...no, that's terrible. Lodgers?" Nina said to Patty.

"We don't call them either. They come here to work and are part of the family. To be somewhere where it's not odd to be deaf. To be somewhere that's not a school. The schools can be good, but they're not for everyone." She held up her hand as though Nina were going to protest, although Nina hadn't planned on it. "Some young people need something else, at least for awhile. Right now it's only Tex and Abbie. But that's unusual."

Soon, their plates were piled high with food. In no time, everyone was eating and signing, all very animated, including Abbie, who was the most spirited Nina had ever seen her. She rivaled Stella at her most glowing. Nina watched, fascinated, as Abbie relayed a story that had the group mesmerized.

When Abbie had finished, Carl Snipes signaled Nina's attention by tapping her shoulder and signed.

"What did he say?" she asked Patty.

"He saw you staring at Abbie. He wants you to know she's a very creative signer. He thinks she could have been an actress if the movies had never discovered sound."

"I never thought much about it. Abbie *is* a natural talent."

Carl, without waiting for an interpretation, made a thumbs up sign at Nina.

"Oh, Daddy." Patty sighed. "He reads lips at his own whims. You never know what he's up to."

Carl grinned and signed to his daughter.

"What did he say?" Nina asked.

"He said he hopes as his child that I learn something from that."

The afternoon was filled with talk and signing and laughter, until Nina's nervousness disappeared and, in truth, she was happier and more relaxed than she'd been in a long time. Tex got a good deal of ribbing over his awe of Hollywood, which he took in good stride. Patty patiently relayed the jokes and teasing and amiable arguments that went on in sign. Nina noticed, however, when Patty tried to sign and interpret in spoken English at the same time, she appeared more awkward. When everyone forgot Nina was there, their signing took on a much more fluid quality.

I am truly an outsider here, Nina thought, but the realization wasn't as upsetting as she would have imagined. It was more like being in a fascinating foreign country than among what she had always thought of—she had to admit—as damaged people.

Patty must have read her mind. She tapped Nina's knee and leaned into her. "Don't think we're that different from anyone else. Don't romanticize. We have the same problems, believe me."

"But you seem to be able to read each other's emotions so much more clearly than hearing people. And the language is so expressive," Nina said.

Patty shrugged. "Reading emotions is one thing. Relationships, that's another."

Nearly three hours into the afternoon, things began to wind down. Suddenly, there was an awkward pause in the activity. Stella turned to Nina and began to sign, then shook her head, reminding herself that Nina was a hearing person.

"It's late," Stella said, with a pained look on her face.

"I'm sorry, we don't know how to end a party," Patty said. "Just a little longer. It's time for the cake."

Annie Snipes went into the house and returned with an orange-shaped cake topped with sixteen candles. Patty beamed with pleasure, as the group signed and sang her a birthday song. Now it was clear that the party was over. Stella began signing to Abbie, who turned away. Stella repositioned herself so Abbie could see her. Abbie signed, her face defiant.

She ran across the yard, and into the kitchen of the ranch house, slamming the door behind her. Annie came over and signed to Stella. Stella shrugged. Annie signed again and Stella signed back, looking insistent. Annie picked up the empty birthday cake plate scattered with melted candles, and headed to the house. Stella came up to Nina. "Would you go with Hiram and get Abbie's things from the car?"

There was a flurry of good-byes, both words and sign. Carl Snipes signed something to Nina.

"He says deaf people don't like to say good-bye," Patty said. "It takes forever to get away."

When Hiram and Nina returned, Stella was waiting for Nina on the porch. She wore her most inscrutable look. Annie and Carl were standing off to one side, arms around one another. Before Nina could climb the stairs to the porch, Stella descended.

"Let's go. I can't draw this out," Stella said.

Just then, Abbie came barreling out of the house. She ran up to Stella and for a few moments they clung to one another, until Stella pulled herself away. Abbie glanced at Nina. After a moment's hesitation, she threw her arms around Nina. The she signed something. Nina looked at Stella, who said: "We have to go."

Carl Snipes walked them to the car. He held the door for Nina, and then went around to do the same for Stella, but she had popped inside the Buick before he had the chance.

He bent at the waist, so Stella could see him through the window. He signed something through the glass. Stella nodded, but didn't reply. Carl tapped the glass and left.

"What'd he say?" Nina asked, as they pulled away.

"He said that I'm just like deaf, which was very nice. He warned me about—can you guess why Abbie ran from me?"

"I assumed she didn't want to stay."

"No. She *did* want to stay."

"If you're like deaf," Nina said, fixing her gaze to the road ahead, "I suppose you'd understand what it's like to find your own people."

"I don't see how you'd understand. Have you ever *been* an outsider?"

"Don't push me away. I know what this must be like for you."

"Pull over," Stella said.

Nina steered the car to the side of the long drive. They were completely alone except for the orange trees as far as the eye could see and the rolling hills beyond.

"You know this is the best thing for Abbie," Nina said.

"I need to be quiet. This is a kind of pain there aren't words for." Stella wrapped her arms around herself, curling up in an almost fetal position. "Don't talk."

Nina's heart did a flip-flop. Don't talk? How could she make things better, if she couldn't talk? Impulsively, she slid over and reached out. Stella was in her arms. It was an awkward embrace, on the constricted car seat. It wasn't until she felt Stella squirming that she realized how hard she was squeezing.

"I can hardly breathe."

"I'm sorry!"

"No, I like it. Hold as tight as you can."

Nina held Stella tightly for another few seconds. She released her hold and slid back to the driver's side, embarrassed and confused. She had just meant to comfort Stella, but the feeling of having Stella pressed against her had brought a rush of sensation, the kind she knew wasn't comfort at all. She could still feel it, a tingling in places that had nothing to do with consolation.

"Don't fret," Stella said. "I can't fret anymore today and I don't want you to, either. Just drive."

THEY PULLED UP to the front entry of Sybil's estate as the sun was beginning to set. The reddening light reflected from the many-paned windows of Sybil's lovely place, giving the world an otherworldly glow.

"Nina? Want to know what Abbie signed to you at the Snipes Ranch?"

"Of course."

She said you're a part of us now." Stella watched the struggle on Nina's face. "What did you think would happen? You came back." Stella got out of the car and closed her door. As Nina pulled out of the driveway, she could see Stella, still standing by the entryway.

When she got back to the Villa, Nina sat in the Buick, not budging. Then, with the weight of the day on her, she leaned against the steering wheel and sobbed. She didn't know what was more upsetting, the day itself or her shame at feeling so selfishly befuddled when it was Stella and Abbie who should have been the ones who were distraught.

Chapter
Nineteen

Bachelors At Home

THE FIRST WEEK of July was reasonably tranquil. Shooting went well, with no more outbursts. Stella, in fact, was calmer than Nina had ever seen her. Nina, for her part, was still working on her plan. She'd decided to take Stella's advice and not think too much. In any case, other disturbing situations were brewing that demanded attention.

On Thursday that first week of July, Elaine called Nina into her office. "Look at this," she said, handing Nina the *Los Angeles Times* turned to Dottie Strong's column, with a paragraph circled. It read:

> Everyone and his brother are so concerned about Communists and their fellow travelers infiltrating our business. But what about the other threat? The one we're ashamed to talk about. I mean, the twisted perverts who hide behind "normal" façades, all the while practicing their ugly, depraved acts behind closed doors. I've lately been a party to some insinuating gossip about some major personages and their immoral ways, which I decline to print until the facts are verified. But when they are...take cover, boys.

"I didn't know we had a problem," Nina said. "Besides, it's all threats with Dottie. She'd never print anything that would actually hurt the studio."

"No one said there was a problem," Elaine replied evenly. "But if there was one, this would be a bad sign. Things are getting very frightening these days, with the *Tinseltown Insider* creating problems where there weren't any before." She sighed at Nina's confused look. "Lance Lewis and Hollie. It's not good, those two living together."

"Why?"

"Honey, there are rumors when two men live together." Elaine made an effeminate gesture with her hands.

"That's ridiculous," Nina said, thinking of Hollie. He was one of the most masculine men that Nina knew. It wasn't like she was so innocent that she hadn't met any homosexual men before, but they weren't anything like Hollie.

"Less ridiculous than you think." Elaine held up a hand as Nina started to speak.

"I was hoping you could think of something. I'm proud of you. You're learning so much. We love having you here, really we do."

"I have an idea."

"Good." Elaine tapped a pencil rhythmically on her desk. Tap, tap, tap. It was an edgy sound. "If I've learned anything, it's that the best—the *only*—position to be in is one step ahead. Please, give us a plan that puts us one step ahead."

TWO WEEKS LATER, on a Sunday morning, Elaine and Nina headed to West Hollywood. After turning onto a pretty, tree-lined street, they parked near a tall wrought iron gate, on the other side of which was a driveway leading to a two-story white clapboard house with green shutters. Before they had a chance to get out, Elaine said, "Isn't that Dick Preston?" Indeed, there was the producer, slipping into a black Pontiac parked at the curb across the street. "I wonder what he's doing here?"

From behind the house, two Afghan Hounds came barking down the driveway. Hollie emerged from the house and unlocked the gate. He was wearing swimming trunks. His muscular chest peeked from beneath a loosely belted terry cloth robe. Nina had instructed the guys that they wear something virile and revealing. Hollie's attire fit the bill. He struck a manly pose and growled: "How about it?"

"Very appealing." Elaine's tone was analytical, without a trace of carnal appreciation.

Hollie turned to Nina and gestured toward his home. "Like our place?"

"It's lovely." She meant it. The front porch was laced with flowering vines, and had an inviting swing and a hummingbird feeder, around which several hummingbirds now hovered. Hollie's place was really a largish cottage, a pleasant change from the castles and faux plantations she'd been around lately.

Hollie grinned his trademark grin at her. "I want to thank you for your efforts on our behalf."

Without thinking, Nina took a quarter-step towards him, pulled in by his magnetism. What made a star? They were all different and, yet, in some crucial way, they were all alike. There were the friendly ones and the morose, arrogant ones. A person didn't have to like or even respect a star, but a person couldn't disregard one. Hollie was a star. There was something irresistible yet unattainable about him. He took Nina's elbow and began leading her around the side of the house, leaving Elaine to follow.

"Where's Lance?" Elaine asked.

"Changing for the interview."

They proceeded to the pool area behind the house, where they found Lance spread across a lounge chair.

"Oh, no," Elaine cried.

Lance looked up. "What's wrong?"

Nina couldn't help but giggle. Hollie was grinning widely, but he quickly arranged his face into a frown. "Lance, what on earth?" he said mock-sternly.

"Don't you like it?" Lance was wearing a pink swimsuit and pink plastic slippers. He had a pink feathery boa around his neck.

"This isn't amusing," Elaine said. "I am not here to be a party to practical jokes."

"You have no sense of humor." Lance got up and sighed. "I've got another outfit in the pool house."

"Then go put it on immediately. Lolly Cooper will be here any minute."

"All right, all right." Lance trudged in the direction of the pool house. As soon as he was out of earshot, Elaine turned to Hollie. "What if Lolly Cooper arrived early?"

Hollie shrugged. "Lance can't help himself. He's got a little devil inside." He turned to Nina. "A lot of us have secret devils inside, don't you think?"

"Probably a lot of us do," she replied.

"I'm not worried about inner devils," Elaine said. "I'm worried about what the world sees. We don't like this whole situation. Hollie, you have more to lose than Lance does. Much more."

They all knew, including Lance himself, that Lance was hardly what a person could call a star. Lance was charming and adorable. With his guileless blue eyes, he could still pass for nineteen, if the lighting was good and he was made up heavily. Lance was just past thirty. *The Threat from Within* was the first role he'd played where he wasn't a chorus boy or college undergraduate. Dick Preston had insisted on giving Lance the part. The recollection of that particular detail reminded Nina that they had just seen the producer rushing to his car. It must have stirred Elaine's curiosity, too.

"Was that Dick Preston leaving just now?" Elaine asked.

Hollie appeared taken aback. "He was delivering some script changes."

"Home delivery," Elaine murmured. "Interesting."

Lance emerged from the pool house, looking very handsome in dark green swim trunks, a towel wrapped jauntily around his neck. "Better?" he called in a deep baritone. Before anyone could answer, a loud buzzer sounded.

"It's the press," Hollie said. "I'll bring them around."

"Now remember," Elaine said to Nina, "Whatever you do, don't mention Dottie Strong."

THE PRESS CONSISTED of Lolly Cooper and another handsome photographer who'd replaced Lolly's previous photographer, Nils. Lolly was in one of her more jovial moods. Nina swallowed hard. She'd heard that Lolly was usually most cheerful when she was feeling the most predatory.

"Hello, my loves," Lolly cried, rumbling up the path to the pool area. "What a charming place. So inviting! And look at the two of you. So handsome. I can't understand why you haven't been snatched up by some lucky women."

"Let's do a tour," Elaine cried. She began racing everyone from room to room. They went from poolside to garden to the drive outside the garage, where the boys posed against their imported sports cars, chests bared and legs draped over the fenders.

Lolly lumbered after Elaine, exclaiming at the quaintness of everything. She marveled and chirped, instructing the grumpy photographer to take shots of the boys together at the piano, mixing drinks at the bar, making a mess in the kitchen. "You two have all you need," she oozed. "I can see how there wouldn't be any room for girls in your life. Are you dating, or are you happy just being together?" Her tone was truly frightening, a mixture of cheer and insinuation.

Hollie and Lance explained how they each were dating, but not seriously. They were waiting for just the right girl to come around.

"What would that girl be like?" Lolly asked. "My goodness, she'd have to be quite something to tear you away from each other."

"Tell your readers we're always looking," Lance said sweetly, reciting the scripted remarks Nina had written. "It's not easy finding the right girl here in Hollywood." Then he winked. "Real girls are the ones who read your magazine. I wish I knew more of them."

Lolly beamed, but her eyes were cat-like. "Are you sure there aren't any secret romances? I've heard some rumors."

"Well, look at the time!" Elaine exclaimed. "Lance, don't you have to sign autographs at that skating rink in Pasadena?"

"Wait," Lolly said. "Tell me, boys. What exactly are the

qualities of these real girls you're looking for? I'm sure my readers would love to know if they qualify."

In response, the boys recited an inventory intended to spark hope in the hearts of fans. The boys wanted hometown girls without airs, regular girls who knew how to cook, sew, were sensible, and yet had dreams. They wanted girls who were passionate, yet demure, sensible and devoted.

"What a nice little list," Lolly said sourly. All the bases were covered. She couldn't dig enough to get at dirt she couldn't print anyhow.

Looking at her quivering jowls, Nina couldn't help feeling a little sorry for Lolly. She seemed swollen with untellable tales, a simpering journalist of pap wallowing in her impossible restraints.

Elaine escorted the press to the gate. Hollie, Lance and Nina watched from the porch.

"That *was* quite a checklist," Hollie commented. "Have you ever known a girl like that?" He was grinning seductively at her, but Nina felt no actual heat emanating from him.

"Never. Why, she'd be insufferable."

Lance raked his fingers through his blond hair. "I have at least two-thirds of the qualities, don't you think, Hollie?" Then he batted his eyelashes at them.

"Cut it out, Lance," Hollie said. "For God's sake, just can it for a little while."

For a brief moment, Nina thought she saw a glimmer of fear pass over Hollie's face.

"He's just kidding," he said to Nina. "He's going to get us in hot water someday, with that kidding." He continued to stare at Nina. She felt as though he was trying to evaluate her with some perplexing sort of criteria. He walked Nina to the front gate where Elaine was waiting. Before Elaine was in earshot, he said, "Thanks, I think Lolly ate up the whole bachelor thing."

"Well, it was easy. It's not like there was really anything to worry about."

She was surprised at Hollie's response.

"You're either very innocent or very tricky. Either way, I like working with you."

"WANNA GO ON a trip?" Shanahan asked Nina a few days later.

"With you?"

"Nah, with Tinkerbell."

The next thing she knew, Nina was clinging to her seat in Shanahan's dented jalopy as they careened down Santa Monica

Boulevard, racing through yellow lights and veering around pedestrians. "Are we in a hurry?"

"I always drive like this."

They nearly sideswiped a silver Rolls Royce that had turned onto the Boulevard from Bundy Drive. "Can you at least tell me where we're going?"

"To the Santa Monica pier."

She couldn't imagine what business they'd have on the pier, but she suspected it was no use asking. "I heard Dick cast Sybil as the heiress in that Sterling Hayden project."

"That bit you planted in Hank Sweeney's column topped the cake." A look of satisfaction spread across Shanahan's face. "Aaron nearly blew his top. Thought I did it. Fact of the matter, wish I did."

"Sybil's funny, don't you think? Odd funny."

"What's so odd?"

"She has odd philosophies."

"Odd philosophies? Sybil's got real intelligence. You don't know beans about her."

"She's a great lady. But she's troubled, then acts like it doesn't matter, because of reincarnation."

As they approached the sleepy beach town of Santa Monica, Nina detected the smell of salt air. She loved the ocean. She felt a sense of calm, which broke at Shanahan's next words.

"I don't want you digging around for Sybil's secrets!"

She was going to protest, but something told Nina to remain silent.

"Remember I said one or two people gave me a break when I was new in this town?"

"I remember. That was awfully nice of Sybil."

"Nice?" Shanahan glanced at Nina witheringly. "She was a famous Broadway actress when she came out here."

"I know."

"Came from the Croft family."

"Her parents are some of the finest stage performers I've ever seen."

"Then you know her father is a man of principle, always getting in trouble for spouting off about this cause or that. And her mother was a suffragette or something."

"Why did she come here?"

"Family was too dominating, I think. So when Aaron Bermann went east to raid Broadway for talent and made an offer — well, she headed west to make her own way." He shook his head bitterly.

"Is Sybil in trouble?"

He took a deep breath. "Maybe."

"How?"

They had reached Santa Monica. Shanahan paused to let a gaggle of tourists clutching beach chairs and picnic baskets cross the road. The salt smell was strong in the air now. He parked the car. They crossed the street to the sidewalk that led to the pier. Shanahan pointed to the ocean, which was glowing under the bright, cloudless sky. "Who needs death to go to heaven? Go to the ocean."

"Sybil says death is only a passing to another phase," she said.

"Well, I'll grant you one thing. Sybil does have uncommon philosophies. You want a hot dog? I'll buy."

"In that case, okay."

He bought them each two, with everything, including onions. They ate them at the railing near the merry-go-round, while the oompah music blared and the children whirled in circles.

"Were Aaron and Sybil involved?"

Shanahan nearly dropped his hot dog. "Who told you that?"

"I have eyes and ears." Nina shuddered. "I can't imagine what she'd see in him."

"A statement of rebellion if a person's family was snobby. But that's just hypothesis, you understand."

"I understand."

"Let's go." Shanahan wiped mustard from his mouth with a paper napkin. "We got business to attend to."

At the end of the pier, past the amusements and the food stands, past the fishermen and the tourists on this weekday afternoon, a man sat on a bench, facing the water. As they approached, he turned abruptly so Nina couldn't see his face, which was already hidden by dark glasses, a hat, and an upturned collar. "I told you to come alone."

"This is my assistant," Shanahan called back.

"Since when did you acquire an assistant?"

"When I found one I could trust." Shanahan said this with a completely straight face. Nina had to gaze out to the ocean to hide her surprise. A curious sea gull on the railing watched her. "*Caaawwww!*" it screeched, staring with taunting eyes.

"Well this isn't for a young girl's ears," the man said, "no matter whether she can keep quiet or not."

"Take a hike," Shanahan said to Nina. "Go wait by the merry-go-round."

"But—"

"You heard me."

The gull flapped after her, watching intently for any morsels she might possess. "Sorry," she said to the gull. "I ate it all."

"*Caaawwww!*" it replied.

Despite the sunny sky and the sounds of play, the cry sounded Edgar Allen Poe-like. Something dark and ugly was lurking.

Shanahan was back in ten minutes.

"Who was that?" Nina asked, as they headed back to the car.

"Can't say."

"Then what was it about?"

"The lousy creep was right. It wasn't for your ears."

"I'm getting awfully tired of what you can't say to me."

"Don't go beating your brains out. This information isn't for anyone's ears. This is the kind of information gets to the fewest ears possible."

"I hoped to learn something from this trip."

"Kid, pay attention. Read between the lines."

"I need some lines to read between."

"My job is to get the scoop from blackmailing bums, then make sure no one else gets it." Shanahan rubbed his fingers together in the universal sign for money. "If bribes don't work, we have to be more clever. They always want something."

"Won't you tell me what he said?"

"No. But I will tell you it involves a friend of yours."

"Stella?" She tried to keep her voice casual.

"No." He glanced at her curiously. "You got something on her?"

"Of course not. Then who?"

"Her big-shot leading man."

"Hollie?"

"Now you're in business." He shook his head. "Someday the studio isn't going to be as invested in covering his bottom."

"What do you mean?"

"No, no." Shanahan held a finger to his lips. "Let's get another hot dog. I'm still hungry."

"Me too," Nina said. It must have been the salt air.

Chapter Twenty

The Plan

A COUPLE OF days later, Nina met up with Stella at a makeup session before the day's shoot. Nina loved to watch Stella's transformations. The metamorphosis for *Callie Young* was especially intriguing, watching Phil Pope mold Stella into a disguised boy. That day, Nina had good news. The well-connected Hollywood correspondent for the *Chicago Tribune* was going to interview Stella on the set, in full costume and makeup. When Nina arrived, Phil was already doing Stella's face, choosing from among jars and trays on the crowded table, while Stella sat placidly in her chair.

"She never complains," Phil announced.

"It's relaxing," Stella replied. "There aren't many places I feel so restful."

"Some of your more important personalities are *very* impatient," Phil said. "A few are swell, like you. That leading man of yours is another one." He laughed. "He adores makeup."

"What do you mean?" Nina asked.

Phil's look darkened. "Just flapping my trap."

"She's all right," Stella interjected. "Don't worry about Nina."

Phil sighed. "Live and let live, that's my motto. Also, let he without sin cast the first stone, get my drift?"

Nina was reluctant to drift too closely to those particular shores. "Stella looks fabulous," she said, standing. "Is she done?"

Phil stepped back and inspected Stella. "Go knock 'em dead, gorgeous."

Nina motioned to Stella. "I can tell you about the interview on the way." As they rushed to the costume department, Nina briefed Stella on the fabricated details. She stopped when she noticed Stella grinning wickedly at her.

"I thought I was still trying to make up with Hamilton Evers after our spat."

"It didn't work out, as you very well know," Nina replied with a touch of agitation. "Honestly, Stella. Couldn't you have tried harder? You are a gifted performer. But no one in their right mind believed you and Hamilton had anything going together, the way you acted with him."

"Nina, I can do most anything. But being cozy with Hamilton Evers was like necking with a weasel. Worse than Tony Pascal. Remember Tony?"

Nina shuddered. "Got booted out of town, didn't he?"

"I think he went to prison," Stella said, grinning.

"Good riddance. But let's not get off the subject. Stella, you need to be, well, a little more enthusiastic about your love life."

They had arrived outside of Meredith Foote's costume sanctuary. Stella paused before going in. "I told you and I keep telling you. I'm yours." Stella winked at Nina and opened the door. "Fix it for me."

"I HAVE IT." Nina was standing in the doorway of Elaine's office. Elaine lifted an eyebrow. "It solves several problems at once." And then Nina explained her plan.

She had taken Elaine's advice to heart. When the critical time came, she was one step ahead. After filling in Elaine on the details, they arranged a meeting to get Aaron's approval. Nina insisted that they arrive early.

"Early?" Elaine cried, as though Nina was suggesting they arrive without clothing.

"Trust me."

The men arrived to find Elaine and Nina in their seats with their materials and cups of coffee laid out before them. Nina glanced at her watch, then over at Elaine, who raised an eyebrow appreciatively. "I was just briefing Elaine on my plan."

"We came from another meeting," Aaron said. "Look, who knew it would run over half an hour. Sorry, girls."

"Shall I start again?" Nina asked.

"Please do," Aaron said, frowning.

And then Nina explained her plan.

Aaron whistled softly. "Nothing like two dames scheming."

"It's good," Murray said. "But will they go for it?" That statement caused a round of chuckles from all attending. What choice did they have?

Shanahan didn't say anything, but his look was only moderately skeptical. Nina knew that Shanahan understood very well the pressing need for an immediate and inspired bit of diversionary publicity, after the disturbing incident at the Santa Monica pier.

Dick Preston's response was the most puzzling. He looked

genuinely amused, but when he spoke, there was an edge of sarcasm to his tone of voice. "Given the ones we've been fixing them up with lately, this should come as a relief. They're safe with each other." He looked around the room, as though challenging the group to make him elaborate. But it was understood that nobody would.

Nina started with Hollie. They arranged a nice lunch at Chasen's and, as Nina imagined, he was not hard to convince. He was still raving about Nina's brilliant interview arrangement with Lolly Cooper. Over bowls of chili, they discussed Nina's latest plan, Hollie nodding with enthusiasm. "Anything," he said, turning away from a stuttering adolescent for whom he'd just signed an autograph. "I trust you." Hollie grinned at her. "You *understand.*" He held up his hand when Nina started to speak. "Everything's safe. As long as we're all in this together."

Nina left the meeting both excited and perturbed. Her next meeting made matters more bewildering.

FOR THEIR RENDEZVOUS, Stella insisted on Bublichki, a Russian place on Sunset. Nina arrived at the odd little restaurant and was seated at a table in a corner of the dining room. A mottled gray cat strolled up and rubbed against her legs. Ten minutes passed, then a "gypsy" came out from behind a curtain and approached her table. The "gypsy" had a sharp-featured, inquisitive face and long silver hair. She wore bangles on her wrists and a scarf around her head.

"I'm Madam Liana. Can I look into your future?"

Nina detected a heavy dose of the Bronx in Madame Liana's vaguely exotic accent. "No, thank you."

"My dear," Madam Liana replied, "the joint is empty. I'll do it for nothing. My intuition tells me you need some prognostication."

"I'm not sure I want to know the future. Even for free."

"Everyone wants to know." Madam Liana plunked herself down next to Nina. "C'mon, honey. Stick out your palm."

Nina reluctantly extended her hand and let the fortune-teller study it.

"In time," Madame Liana intoned, "what scares you is what you'll become."

"Excuse me?"

"Hang on, girlie," the fortune-teller said, folding Nina's palm into a fist and placing it onto the table. "You've got quite a ride coming."

"This is nonsense. I'm a rationalist," Nina said huffily. She paused, and then blurted out, "I don't understand."

Madame Lianna took her palm once again. "To be more specific, you will be mixed up with a headstrong woman. That relationship could last a long time." Madam Liana squeezed Nina's hand and said, "No pussy-footing around, dearie. I tell what I see." She stood up. "Some paying customers may have arrived."

Stella showed up not a minute after the "gypsy" left, almost as though on cue.

"Sorry. Got a call. From Hiram at the Snipes Ranch."

"Is everything okay?"

Stella frowned. "I feel almost worse that Abbie's doing okay than if she was miserable. She doesn't miss me."

A waiter came by and attempted to pull out a chair for Stella, but she shooed him away and pulled the chair out herself.

"Stella, that's not good etiquette."

"Oh, go on. There's no one here except that moldy old couple by the window and I don't think they're reporters. Let me be tonight. I'm feeling touchy."

"I just had my palm read by that supposed gypsy over there nagging the moldy old couple. Do you believe in that?"

"My mama had a knack for prophesy. I have dreams that come true. Just before Murray came to the café, I dreamed that Abbie and I were rescued."

"I've had too much education to believe in backwoods superstition." Nina stopped at the expression on Stella's face. "I'm being an awful snob again, aren't I?"

"You are. What was your fortune?"

Nina picked up the menu. "I'm starving. Let's talk about food. What's good here?" She looked up to find Stella staring at her.

"I have a question."

Nina had the distinct feeling that the course of the conversation was about to steer in yet another bumpy direction. "Did you want to order some wine?" she asked.

The whole restaurant seemed to be operating on some weird plane of existence. As soon as the words were out of Nina's mouth, the waiter appeared with two wine glasses and a carafe of ruby red wine.

After the waiter retreated, Stella asked, "Nina, do you like me?"

"You know I like you."

"Then why are you avoiding me?"

"We see each other day and night."

"You know what I mean."

"No, I don't."

"Yes, you do."

"I *don't!*" Nina whispered explosively, aware of the waiter hovering nearby.

"I think you do."

Nina pushed back her chair from the table and stood up. "We should have met at the studio. I think you're riled up about Abbie and it's not a good time to be meeting."

"Sit down," Stella said.

Nina backed a couple of steps from the table.

At that moment, Stella looked very serious and very beautiful. "Please don't go."

"I'm not sure what you want from me. Whatever it is, I may not be able to give it to you." Nina said. She took another step backwards. But she didn't go. She waited.

"I want you in my life. For a long, long time," Stella said.

Nina hesitated, then sat.

"I love the blintzes," Stella said, pointing to the menu. "There was a time I wouldn't have known a blintz from a piston rod." She ordered several dishes, enough so the waiter looked mildly surprised. "We're hungry," she informed him. The room was beginning to fill. A violinist strolled between the tables playing romantic ballads. The odor of melting butter, cream and spices wafted from the kitchen.

The blintzes were heavenly.

Nina sighed at the first bite. She took several, then put down her fork. "The reason I asked to meet with you—" she began.

"Don't," Stella interrupted.

"Don't what?"

"Let's enjoy this for a while. I'll listen to your scheme, but let's just enjoy the food for a little while." She pointed to the last blintz. "Do you want to share this?"

"I can't resist."

"No need to resist." Stella scooped half the rich delicacy onto Nina's plate. "Maybe you'd like to visit Abbie with me sometime."

"I'd like that."

Stella studied her face.

"Don't you believe me?" Nina asked.

"Of course. Why do you think I don't?"

"The way you're looking at me."

"I have to look at you that way. I need to see you to get past your words."

The waiter delivered two plates of delicate broiled lamb chops and a potato gratin.

"Mmm," Stella sighed.

"Delicious," Nina murmured.

For several minutes, they ate, savoring every bite.

"Sybil told me about this place," Stella said. "I've always

enjoyed it, but now you're here."

"Are things better with Sybil now that she has the part in Dick's picture?"

"It's more complicated than that." Nina waited for Stella to go on, but Stella pointed her fork at Nina's plate. "Eat. You know, sometimes I have to slow down, remember I can have the same thing tomorrow if I want to. Let's just talk. What's your favorite play?"

"I've read so many plays, novels, poems. I can tell you how they're structured, what the themes are. I think I squeeze the life out of everything I read."

"You don't feel any pleasure?"

Nina tapped her head. "In here."

"Any movies? That made you feel something below the head, I mean."

Nina shrugged.

"How about me? You've seen me in movies."

Nina could feel herself blushing. "What about you? What's your favorite play?"

"Probably *The Taming of the Shrew*."

Nina burst out laughing, causing Stella to frown.

"Is there something wrong with that?"

"No, it's perfect. You seem to have read a lot of plays."

"As many as I could find in my awful little hometown library. The librarian took pity on me. She somehow was always finding more when I ran out."

"That's charming. Why wasn't that in your biography?"

Stella shrugged. "No one asked me. I guess it was easier for you all to make it up. You're staring at me. Why?"

"Do you have to ask? You're always reading what's going on inside me from my face."

Stella's look darkened. "Don't find me *too* fascinating."

"You don't want anyone to know who you really are. You don't want to be idolized for who you profess to be. What *do* you want?" She immediately regretted her words, as it was Stella's turn to jump up from the table.

"Sit down. People are watching."

Stella remained standing, looking defiant.

"Please sit down. I want you to stay."

Stella sat. She accepted the dessert menu from the waiter. "I was thinking Hollie and I should get involved."

Nina's mouth fell open.

Stella grinned wickedly. "I meant, for the publicity."

"That's *my* plan."

"Oh, is it now? Tell me."

And so, Nina presented her scheme.

"Yes, it's perfect," Stella said. "What's wrong?"

"I expected a fight."

"Because I always fight a little to show I'm not completely a prisoner of some kind?" Stella opened the dessert menu. "Of course, there's one condition. That you be the publicist."

"Why do you think I came up with this plan? I have to take charge if we want it to work. But I need you and Hollie to *cooperate*." Nina felt an inner quake at her own use of Elaine's favorite word. And now she was tossing it around.

"We'll make a marvelous threesome," Stella said. "Now let's have dessert."

"I couldn't eat a bite more."

"Let me order. You have to let me have my way in some things."

"At least the dessert."

Stella ordered a concoction of chocolate and whipped cream and sponge cake, dripping and sweet. They ate every bite.

"Feel good?" Stella asked.

"Yes."

"Because I agreed to your plan or because of our evening together?"

"Both. I haven't had many dates with men that were as nice as this." Now it was Nina's turn to detect the subtle expression on Stella's face. "But don't make too much of what I just said," Nina warned her.

"I'll try not to."

As they were leaving, they passed Madame Liana, who was bent over a puzzled-looking couple with a bouquet of anniversary roses on their table. She beamed at Stella, and then waved.

"What was that about?" Nina asked.

Stella took Nina's elbow and guided her to the door. "She's a friend of mine."

As they went out the door, Nina glanced back. The waiter and the "gypsy" and the *maitre d'* and even the cat seemed to be watching their exit as though it was the end of a well-scripted scene.

Chapter
Twenty-One

A Mean Turn Of Events

IN HOLLYWOOD, PEOPLE don't just go out. Celebration is a critical affair.

Two Fridays after Bublichki's, the Crystal Room of the Beverly Wilshire Hotel was abuzz. Three hundred and sixty-five of Hollywood's most influential were packed at crowded tables under brilliant chandeliers. They were gathered for a party honoring a detested executive at Paramount. Sy Kern had been forced into retirement due to a pronounced mean streak that had metastasized into terrible production blunders. Nevertheless, Sy was one of Zukor's cronies, had been at Paramount since the twenties. The farewell party radiated a dark euphoria, like a wake for an evil uncle sent off with grief-cloaked glee.

In the sanctimonious elegance of the evening, the over-stuffed room smelled apprehensive. Many of the attendees felt the hatchet hanging not too far from their own necks. In July of 1949, there were too many rumors, too many box-office failures and too many secret lists.

Nina's escort for the evening was Walter Bermann, a planter from the studio who happened to be the nephew of her boss, Aaron. Nina didn't have much room to criticize nepotism, but she, like most of her coworkers, felt a little leery of Walter simply because of his genetic link to Aaron. However, Walter couldn't have been more unlike his uncle. He had such a forgettable demeanor that people tended to introduce him repeatedly to one another. He was dull in all respects, except for one priceless talent: he mentally recorded important conversations, like a human bugging device. Walter's blandness suited Nina fine. After Billy Waxman, she wasn't interested in getting involved with anyone.

The reception area outside the Crystal Room was already crowded when Nina and Walter arrived. They plunged into the din. Shortly thereafter, Shanahan arrived, wearing an ugly brown suit and a fruit-bowl patterned tie.

"Hi, boss," Walter said.

Shanahan circled his arm around Walter's shoulder. "You know what you're supposed to do tonight, my little man?"

"Yeah," said Walter, squirming under Shanahan's grip.

"Good, then trot along," Shanahan said.

"Are you okay?" Nina asked as soon Walter left. The antics were already so loud, she had to raise her voice.

"You'll have to excuse me," Shanahan said. "I'm plastered."

"I can see that."

"I remember things better when I'm tanked up. That's why I drink. Most people drink to forget. Not me."

"Happy to hear you don't have the same sorry reasons as most people." Nina glanced around. She was beginning to wonder where the rest of their Lumina party was.

"Let's have a toast." He held up his glass. "You're not just the boss's niece. Here. Here." He drained the glass. "Reason I drink so much is so I can say what I think."

"I thought it was so you could remember everything."

"Don't humor me."

"You're pretending to be intoxicated and are dressed like a used car salesman. What do you expect?"

"This is what people expect from a fallen Man of God. Besides, it works." He fingered his ugly fruit tie. "Maybe I did go a little overboard." He glanced around. "Is Sybil Croft coming?"

"No, due to Aaron. Gosh, he seems to have his fingers in an awful lot of pies."

Shanahan snorted. "More than you know."

From across the room, Nina spotted a reprehensible attendee. "Look over there. Moe Mink. I'm shocked he got invited."

"He comes anyway, invited or not. Everyone's afraid to kick him out."

"What do you think of that story last week about Anita Wells and Ralph Kelly?" The *Tinseltown Insider* had reported the couple's hanky-panky during a production at RKO. Unfortunately, each of them was married to someone else.

"I'm wondering how long some of our pals are gonna dodge the mighty noose of Moe Mink," Shanahan said.

Just then a rustle ran through the crowd. The people parted like the Red Sea. Down the magical pathway came Hollie and Stella, glowing, wrapped arm in arm. At the same moment, Dottie Strong appeared from nowhere beside Nina and Shanahan. She was wearing a hat marbled with tiny papier-mâché fruits. "What's with *those two*?"

Nina arranged her face into a mask of dismay. "It's an approved date. Because of the movie." She leaned closer to Dottie's boozy, masculine face. "Lumina would discourage any romantic situations, if they were real. If you promise not to print anything just yet, I can give you some interesting hints as to the future."

"Hey, watch what you say," Shanahan interrupted. "You know this broad has a poison pen."

Dottie glared at him. "You need a new tie."

"You need a new hat," he shot back. The two reporters grinned at each other in mutual satisfaction.

Nina sighed. "We feel Hollie's a little mature for a relationship with a girl Stella's age. But please don't print that. At least, leave out the names."

Dottie's brain was calculating. Her eyes narrowed. Then she was gone as quickly as she had appeared.

"You're a work of art," Shanahan commented.

"Thank you."

"I mean it. You really got the old snoop fired up. She can't figure what you're trying to get her to do or not do. Even I was baffled."

"I myself didn't understand a word I said," she joked gleefully.

"That's what makes you so good." Shanahan tipped his drink at Nina. "Let's toast the magic of bamboozling."

IN THE CRYSTAL Room, Lumina had three VIP tables near the podium. Although Sybil Croft was banished, another actress of her generation was there. May Evans had been popular in the thirties, playing aristocratic women. She was small, with quick, nervous gestures and a delicate, birdlike beauty. After the War, she floundered until the studio moved her into character roles as scatter-brained matrons.

May was with her husband, Jason Noland, a fading leading man. Jason gave Nina an odd glance when she arrived at the table. He was currently under contract at Universal, cast opposite younger women in awful B melodramas. Recently, Lumina had borrowed Jason for a big-budget production.

When they had settled in their seats, Nina said rhetorically, "Everyone knows one another, don't they?" They were Jason and May, Stella and Hollie, Lance Lewis and Terri Baxter, Elaine and a producer from the studio named Ed Jacobs, and Nina, along with Walter.

"We've all met. Although some of us know each other better than others," Jason Noland said in a sly voice.

Nina sat next to Walter, with Stella on her other side. Stella wore a strapless rose-colored satin evening gown. Mark Handley, that genius of a hairdresser, had left Stella's short hair simple and slightly boyish, a startling contrast to her revealing dress.

As planned, Stella and Hollie began fawning over each other, whispering and giggling, fingers intertwined, creating an envelope of sensuality. Everyone at the table noticed. Much of the room noticed. They were following the plan, but Nina felt irritated, then impatient with herself for such an unreasonable reaction.

When Elaine asked Nina to go and give Dottie Strong some background information on *Callie Young,* she was relieved to get away. On the way to Dottie's table, she bumped into Shanahan again.

"Quite the couple, those two," he said.

"Hit of the evening," she replied.

"She's really something, isn't she?"

"She still seems a little unpolished to me."

"Don't give me that baloney. I see the way you look at her."

Nina knew she was blushing.

"Watch your step, kid. She's trouble. She can't help it. It's in her nature."

"I have no idea what you're talking about."

Shanahan shrugged. "Don't worry about me. I don't make judgments."

Nina was about to protest again when Walter Bermann came sauntering up.

"What's up, pal?" Shanahan asked. "You're looking like the bird who ate the canary."

"I parked myself next to Dottie Strong for ten minutes in the lobby, while the old girl grilled the first assistant director. You know, I've met that dame seven times and she still doesn't recognize me." Walter was perpetually mystified by his own anonymity.

"Was the guy spilling his guts?" Shanahan asked.

Walter beamed. "Like a POW with needles under his fingernails. All this tripe about secret rendezvous and so on."

"Marvelous," Nina said. "Now some icing on the cake." She headed in the direction of Dottie Strong's table. She had a number of confusing innuendos up her sleeve. When she got back to the Lumina table, Hollie and Jason Noland had disappeared.

"The boys have gone to see a man about a horse," May called to Nina in her comic-nervous voice and laughed at Nina's puzzled expression.

"Why don't you sit back down?" Elaine asked, patting Nina's chair. Once Nina sat, Elaine whispered: "It's an expression. It means going to the rest room."

"We've known Hollie forever," May said to Nina from across the table. Nina seemed to be acting as the focus for May's larger conversational agenda. "He's dear to us both. No one in Hollywood knows him better. Except Lance."

Lance glared at May. May laughed in a bittersweet way. "We're delighted Hollie's doing so well." She pointed to Stella. "We just love what this young woman's done for his career so far and now look at this little romance I see developing. Isn't it a shame I couldn't do that for Jason." May's eyes were glazed. "Jason and I have been married since we were eighteen. We're one of the most enduring couples in Hollywood. Do you know why?" No one responded. "We accept one another, and I mean everything!" She pointed again to Stella. "I wonder if this young woman will do the same with Hollie. Accept *everything*."

Stella, who was sipping a glass of soda water, watched May with no indication of what she was thinking about May's comments.

May paused, seemingly in need of breath. Elaine spoke up. "May, I'd like you to come with me and tell about your new movie to Bob Sanders from *The New York Post*."

May tittered. "Am I being a bad girl?"

Elaine looked at May with a face of deadly calm.

"Oh, all right," May said.

When Elaine and May left, there was a silence, and then people at the table turned to one another, beginning private conversations. Stella and Nina, with empty chairs on either side of them, were momentarily alone.

"That was tough," Nina said.

"It's sad," Stella said. "She's feeling real sorry for herself." But her mind clearly was on something else. "We're going to start filming on location in Arizona. Why aren't you coming?"

"Aaron gave me some important jobs here. We have Page Larson on it." The truth was, she wasn't sure she wanted to go on location. Already, she felt like she was creating a monster and was finding it hard to watch her creation grow.

Elaine was suddenly standing over them. "Did I hear something about Arizona?"

"I was going to speak to you about Nina coming on location," Stella said. "I think we really need her." She stroked Nina's forearm. A small inarticulate sound escaped from Nina's lips. She was saved by the return of Hollie and Jason Noland.

"Sorry," Jason said. "Hollie and I were catching up on old times." A look of what appeared to be genuine concern formed on his face. "Where's May?"

"She's talking with *The New York Post*," Elaine said. "Don't worry, I have someone watching her. She's good."

Jason eased back into his seat. Meanwhile, Hollie had come up behind Stella and put his large hands on her bare shoulders, giving them an affectionate squeeze.

"I was just stomping my foot about Nina being the location publicist in Arizona," Stella said to Hollie.

"I can't imagine anyone I'd like more," Hollie replied.

"We insist. Don't we, Hollie? Nina's the only one."

"The only one," Hollie echoed. "How else would we handle our situation?"

"We'll have to discuss it with Aaron," Elaine said. But Nina saw that familiar gleam in her eyes.

An eternity later, as the Lumina group was preparing to leave the party, exhausted by the insincere tributes to Sy Kern and the rest of the night's shenanigans, Nina chanced upon Jason Noland, sitting in a chair in the lobby, staring off into the distance. He looked up at Nina and then turned away, pulling his jacket collar up around his neck. Where had she glimpsed that distinctive profile and protective gesture? Then Nina knew. She flew across the lobby. "Shanahan!"

"Where's your boyfriend Walter?" Shanahan asked.

"Out getting his car. He's not my boyfriend. Do you remember going to the Santa Monica pier?

"Like it was yesterday."

"I've put two and two together."

"That so? And what'd it add up to?"

"Jason Noland is blackmailing Hollie. They must have been—" Nina paused, searching for a discreet word, "—involved. The studio paid Jason off by borrowing him for Dick's French Revolution project. He'd never have gotten that role otherwise."

Shanahan bowed. "Thank you, Miss Nancy Drew."

"Car's ready!" Walter Bermann was crossing the lobby, headed their way. "Hey, boss, you stealing my girl again?"

"Trying to, but she's not interested," Shanahan said.

"Good night, Shanahan," Nina said. "You know, I'd like it if I could be just a little more informed. I think I've earned it now."

Shanahan shrugged. "Just keep those ears and eyes open."

Two days later, the following item appeared in Dottie Strong's column:

"...Well, dear readers, once again it's love versus business in our lovely Tinseltown. I'm sworn to secrecy, so let's just say that a budding amour between an eligible bachelor and his gorgeous leading lady is a no-no, as far as their studio is concerned. Seems a matter of age, as though many of those same studio execs don't

have pretty younger wives or, dare I say, little
starlets on the side. Question: Will the power of
love win out? This columnist must confess to
being a romantic deep down..."

The power of love. It would win out. At least until *The Secret of
Callie Young* was released.

Chapter
Twenty-Two

A Party Of A Different Stripe

TEN DAYS BEFORE the trip to Arizona, Nina was invited to one of Sybil Croft's notorious Sunday brunches, this one in honor of Ben and Cookie Heller's twenty-fifth anniversary. Nina wasn't sure it was a wise idea to attend. But what the heck? She was tired of avoiding anything the least bit risky regarding politics and free thought.

The day of the brunch, Nina overslept. The night before, she'd attended a premiere of an MGM musical at the Egyptian Theater, accompanied by Walter Bermann and two Lumina contract players they were promoting. The whole group went to Ciro's afterwards and she'd fallen into bed at three. All night, she'd dreamt of synchronized swimming in a pool with no exit ladders, and never heard the alarm. She climbed from her Buick in Sybil's driveway nearly an hour late. Alfred was there to greet her.

"Alfred," she said. "I heard you prophesied my return."

"What a babbler my niece is. What else did she tell you?"

"You declared that I had some questions to answer in Hollywood."

"I will admit to perhaps saying something of that sort. No disrespect intended."

"Of course not." She followed Alfred's straight back through the house. "What are they?"

"They?"

"The answers I need."

"Miss, some men very much wiser than myself have insisted that asking the right questions must precede getting the right answers."

"Maybe I'm not asking the right questions?"

"To admit being at a loss is the first step to true knowledge."

Nina charged ahead of Alfred and blocked his path. "Are you really a butler?"

With a perfectly straight face, Alfred replied, "You bet I am." They advanced through the patio doors of the sunroom. The parrots danced with delight on their perches.

One of them called, *"The dame's got a gun! I give up!"*

"They remember you," Alfred commented dryly.

On the patio, they passed a banquet table laden with silver serving trays of scrambled eggs and sausage and waffles. Another table held bowls of fruit salad, carved pineapples, baskets of rolls and muffins. Nearby, a handsome would-be actor in a red waistcoat tended bar. The guests were seated on the lawn, on lounging chairs grouped in circles. Sybil rose from one of the chairs and flowed to Nina, her multi-colored silken caftan wavering in the slight, warm breeze. "Welcome. Come meet some of my comrades — no, that's a nasty word these days. I mean friends." She led Nina to a circle of lounges on the lawn.

Nina was introduced to a middle-aged couple. The balding man had protruding ears. His wife had frizzy hair and wore lipstick that veered slightly over the borders of her thin lips. They were the distinguished writers, Ben and Cookie Heller.

In addition to the Hellers, there were two directors (Wasnowski and Kyovsky from Eastern Europe), two comedians (Leo Bergen and Misha Yonchenko), and a novelist named Augie de LaRose, whose wife was with the Los Angeles symphony. All of the introduced had been subject to rumors as to their political persuasions.

Besides the strangers, Stella, Hollie, and Lance Lewis were also in the circle. Nina felt a wave of misgiving. She probably shouldn't have come and she was sure the studio would not be thrilled with Lance, Stella, and Hollie being there, either. As she was led among the circle, Nina could sense Stella's attention directed at her. Finally, Stella rose from her chair. "I'll take you to the buffet," she said.

Sybil squeezed Nina's elbow. "Go. Take a big plate. There's always too much."

Stella tailed Nina while she loaded a plate from the two serving tables. When Nina couldn't fit any more on her plate, she turned to head back to the party. Stella shifted so her back was to the guests. "Now don't get upset if anyone makes comments about your connections."

"That I'm a relative of Irwin Weiss? Does that make me abominable?"

"Abominable." Stella let the word roll from her lips, clearly enjoying the sound. "What does that mean?"

"You don't know what that means, after all your play reading? It means vile, despicable, loathsome. I was asking if nepotism made me so vile."

"Nepotism?"

"Giving favors to your relatives."

"You're a member of the Weiss family. A lot of these people are scared they're on some blacklist or about to be on one. Anyone who seems a part of the studio system, well, you can see their point of view."

"Then why did Sybil invite me?"

"I had her invite you."

"Why?"

"Because I like to be around you. Screw people's opinions."

"I'm certain that comment was meant for my ears only."

Stella's smile was invitingly conspiratorial. "Only you."

"So, you're the niece?" Cookie Heller asked when they'd returned, in a loud, Bronx-accented voice. "You look too intelligent to be the niece."

"Cookie!" Ben scolded. He turned to Nina with an apologetic grin on his comical face. "She'll never go to hell for lying."

"That's what I miss about the old days," Cookie said. "When Ben and I were in the vaudeville circuit, we said anything we wanted and nobody cared."

Sybil signaled a passing waiter and picked a champagne glass off his tray. She pointed him in Nina's direction. "No. Thank you," she said. Drinking early in the day made her sleepy.

"C'mon," Lance Lewis slurred. "We're celebrating. Don't be a wet blanket." He appeared to have been doing a bit of celebrating already.

After a brief hesitation, Nina took a glass. She took a very large sip. Then a few more. The early afternoon began to take on a hazy, pleasant glow. She drained her glass. The croquet-players on the lawn looked like flamingos.

"I thought the Jews didn't believe in Hell," Sybil was saying.

It took Nina a minute to retrace the conversation. She accepted another glass of champagne from the waiter's tray. From the corner of her eye, she could see Stella watching her with a look of amusement. She cleared her throat. "In the strictest sense, they don't. Afterlife has been controversial in Judaism. Some Israelites posited the existence of a place called Sheol. Later, the Cabbalists saw a kind of hell and a heaven, but entry into either place wasn't so strict as the Christian version."

"She's adorable," Cookie announced. "Even if she is the niece."

Lance drained a full glass of champagne and signaled for another. "What's the answer? Do the Jews believe in hell or not?"

"Didn't you hear the young lady?" Ben said. "They can't make up their minds." His face grew dark. "What Jews worry about is hell on earth. Extermination. Worse, the extermination of ideas."

"He says *I* talk too much," Cookie commented.

"My view is more like the Hindu belief," Sybil interjected. "We endure certain lessons and pay the price for foolishness and mistakes, or suffer the same things again in the next life. I see that now in my own life."

"Sybil, please," Hollie said. "Things are looking up."

"Tell us about *A Secret Affair*," Cookie added. "Larry Fleischman had a hand in the writing. I'm sure it's a good script."

"Yes, a good script. One any actress would die for." Sybil lifted her chin. "I'll pay for this part. I'll play a charwoman or a psychotic fading actress. And who knows, after that?"

A somber cloud drifted over the group.

"Look how serious you all look," Sybil said. "Why is everyone so afraid of finality? If anything should happen to me, I expect no one to mourn. If the time comes where things are too bankrupt, I *want* to die. I will not wind up a withered crone surrounded by mementos I'm too blind to see."

"Oh my lord," Lance said, draining yet another glass of champagne. "People will always love you."

"Your admirers despise you for having the audacity to grow old. I will not become a caricature of myself. Now let's focus on why we came. To celebrate our friends, the Hellers."

"We need a toast," Lance said. "To the Hellers! Twenty-five years together. I'm envious."

"We're the only ones loony enough to tolerate each other. That's the secret of marital longevity," Cookie crowed.

A playful look returned to Ben's face. "We started out hoofing together and joke-telling. We fell in love, learned about life, and before you know it we're writing musicals that intellectuals admire. Well, both my grandfather and father were rabbis. Maybe it rubbed off."

The atmosphere had taken on a translucent glow. Nina was overcome by a wash of exhilaration. "Congratulations," she cried. "You're an inspiration."

"I don't know about the rest of you," Stella said. "But I think we're in heaven right here. At least compared to where I came from."

"It's the sunshine," Hollie said.

"That's a euphemism for money," Cookie Heller informed everyone.

"No, it's a euphemism for pretending," Lance said. His face grew dark. "I'll tell you what hell is. Not getting to be with the one you love." Tears began to roll down his cheeks.

"Lance, my dear," Sybil said, "I believe you're a bit in the cups."

"Hiding," Lance persisted. "Living with secrets. That's hell."

He signaled for more champagne, but Sybil gestured the waiter away. "Don't mother me," Lance said, his voice growing petulant. He jumped up and chased after the waiter, grabbed a glass, and staggered back to his chair.

Sybil went over to him, holding out her hand. "Lance, please. You've had enough. We'll have the chauffeur drive you home."

"Don't baby me!" Lance cried.

"You're acting like a child," Sybil replied.

"I'm acting like a drunken man hiding his real self."

Hollie was shaking his head and Stella was frowning at him, but Lance persisted.

"But you know about secrets, don't you, Sybil?"

Sybil took a step backward.

"You have things to hide, things to regret," Lance continued.

Sybil's look was wary.

"How about giving away your own *baby?*" Lance cried with a childish satisfaction. "How's that for a secret?"

There was a stunned silence.

"I'm sorry," Lance said. "I didn't mean to say that."

"No one heard a thing," Ben interjected. He turned to the group. "Did we?"

They all shook their heads. "What about Wyler's latest release? I say it's overrated," Ben said, glancing around at the group with stern insistence.

The conversation turned to William Wyler as everyone obediently developed amnesia.

The next thing Nina knew, she was opening her eyes. The catering crew was dismantling the banquet tables, while the bartender packed his liquor bottles. Stella reclined next to her. "How long has the party been over?" Nina asked.

"How're you feeling?"

"I have a headache. Were you waiting for me to wake up?"

"I was."

"You must think I'm a complete nincompoop."

"I enjoy you."

"You enjoy me passing out at parties?"

"Yes, I do."

"Oh, brother." Nina sat up and rubbed her eyes. "What other terrific qualities do you enjoy about me?"

"A lot of things."

"Name some. I dare you. Big mouth. Can't hold her liquor. Oh, and pretentious. But we established that one from the beginning."

"Everything about the way you are," Stella said.

Nina jumped up. "Where's Sybil?"

Stella rose and held out her hand. Nina hesitated.

"Take it," Stella said. "I won't bite. At least not yet."

"Sometimes you say the strangest things." Nina placed both hands behind her back. She knew that she was acting coy, but her mind told her she was just bamboozled by Stella's odd ways. "I'd like to apologize to Sybil," she said.

"Sybil hates apologies." Stella walked right up and wrapped an arm around Nina's waist, then led her in the direction of the main house. The handsome bartender/actor gave Stella an appreciative stare. She seemed oblivious.

"Can you drive?" she asked.

"I can now, after my snooze."

They were nearly to the house when Stella turned to face Nina.

"I think it's becoming clear how everyone here needs your help. But we never talk about what you need."

"I don't need anything. Not in the way I think you're alluding to." Nina heard the severity in her voice. It came from a deep place, like Lance's outburst. Then Nina felt a small crack in her shield. "But don't give up on me," she said quickly, almost inaudibly.

Chapter
Twenty-Three

Then There Was The Word

NINA LEFT FOR Tucson a few days after the cast and crew. On the train, she spent most of her time concocting scenarios and publicity plot lines. She arrived late Monday, checked into the hotel, and fell into bed, her mind still buzzing with schemes. All night she tossed and turned, dreaming that her intricate plans were upset by disasters of biblical proportions. Locusts, plagues, floods, everything but the smiting of the first-born son, and that might have found its way into the mix if the alarm clock hadn't jolted her awake.

She drove a rental car out to the location site, a ranch about three miles from town. It was already beastly hot, ninety degrees by midmorning. The road cut through red, parched flats of desert riddled with green cactus. She rattled up the bumpy driveway, her throat parched and the skin tightening on her face from the dehydrated air. When she arrived at the ranch location, she found Marty Gramm, the gentle still photographer, smoking a cigarette and pacing near a corral, while an animal handler stood by with a saddled palomino.

"What's up, Marty?"

Marty tossed his cigarette into the dust and ground it out with his heel. "Stella's in her dressing room. We were supposed to be done by ten. I been waiting here for twenty-five minutes."

"Has anyone asked her what's wrong?"

"Nina, spare me! We've sent over everyone but the President. I've worked with Garbo. I've worked with Dietrich, Davis, Harlow. I've worked with every precious star in the business. This is what happens. They start out great, cooperative, then a little taste of fame and look out."

Nina thought back to the previous night and her nightmares of the ten plagues and sighed. As she headed away, Marty called to her: "Someday I'm going back to Schenectady and opening a little studio doing graduation portraits of pimpled teenagers and weddings of ugly people."

"Sounds tranquil, Marty," Nina called back.

"WHO IS IT?"

"Nina."

The door swung open and there stood Stella, dressed as Cal. Nina felt her usual surge of pleasure/confusion seeing her again, but Stella didn't seem pleased to see Nina.

"What do you want?"

"What do you think I want?" Nina replied. She felt miffed by Stella's abrupt tone.

"I'm sorry." Stella stepped away from the entry and gestured to a loveseat crammed into a corner opposite a makeup table. Nina sat on its edge. The tiny dressing room trailer was nearly bare of Stella's personal effects, except for a framed picture on the makeup table. Nina had never seen the picture before. Stella noticed Nina looking at it and brought it over. "I brought this with me for luck. I usually have it next to my bed."

"Is that your mother?"

"Yes."

"She's beautiful. Well, naturally."

"What do you mean?"

Nina blushed. "Well, you."

"You think I'm beautiful," Stella said. It was a statement, not a question. She sank onto the couch next to Nina and slumped back against the cushions. "And difficult?"

"Stella, what's the problem?" Nina asked. "We've already established our personal negative attributes. I need to know why you're not getting photographed by Marty Gramm right now."

Stella went back to the makeup table and carefully set the photograph in its place. She came back to the couch and settled back down next to Nina, then was silent for several moments. Finally, she said, "I'm scared of horses."

"Why didn't you say something?" Nina asked. She tried not to smile.

"You're laughing at me," Stella said.

"Don't like it when the tables are turned?"

"This is different."

"I'm laughing because I thought you weren't afraid of anything. It's sort of a relief."

"You can't tell anyone."

"I have to," Nina exclaimed. "There are ways we can work around this, but not if no one knows."

"No one but you!" Stella said. "We'll work it out together."

"How are we going to do that?"

"How do *you* feel about horses?"

"I think they're wonderful creatures. I used to ride when I was younger. Took quite a few lessons, actually."

"I should have known."

"Stella, don't use that tone."

"What tone?"

"The one that denigrates me for being privileged."

"I got bitten by a sorry old mule when I was six years old. I can't stand mules and I don't like horses neither. And don't correct me. I like the double negative, it expresses how I feel better than just one negative."

"You could learn to like horses. You like beauty and grace and strength. The horses I rode were magnificent creatures, impossible not to appreciate."

"Wait," Stella interrupted. "Look at me. Let me watch you. Tell me about horses."

"They're powerful, quite capable of hurting a person. You see, they agree to be in a relationship with us. They can feel when you climb on them how well you can ride, all sorts of things about you. You need to approach them knowing they can tell what you're like. You know how sign language is about expression. Horses are creatures of deep expression. They feel your energy."

"Tell me how it feels to be on top of a creature like that," Stella asked.

"You feel the strength beneath you, you move together in harmony." For some reason, the room seemed to be growing exceptionally warm. "It's hot in here," Nina commented.

"Tell me more," Stella said.

"I hope you don't think this is terrible. With men and horses, it's often about control and power. With women, especially little girls, it's their first secret longing, straddling that kind of living creature. How can I put it? It feels...good." She felt herself blushing. "Does that help?"

"Mmm," Stella murmured. "Whenever there's a horse involved, I want you there. And I want you to give me a few lessons."

"If it's anything like tennis, you'll be fine in no time."

Stella smiled slyly at Nina. "Honey, it sounds a lot more interesting than tennis. Now let's go do those publicity shots."

"Will you be all right?"

"As long as the horse doesn't go anywhere. At least this first time. And as long as you're there. Don't take your eyes from me, understand?"

"I understand."

Stella smiled. "Thank you, my mirror."

A very short time later, Stella sat on the placid stationary palomino out in the corral, while Marty Gramm circled around her, snapping photos from various angles. Every few minutes, she glanced over at Nina. Nina, as promised, never took her eyes from

Stella. In any case, Stella looked splendid, as natural and confident as a born cowgirl. As for the horse, he too seemed to find Stella fascinating. He was gentle, but responsive, glancing back occasionally, ears alert.

SHANAHAN HAD A buddy at the *Tucson Herald* named Tom Kirby, who was thrilled to be their stooge. A few days into the filming, Nina arranged to have lunch on the set with Stella and Hollie to discuss a little encounter she had in mind involving Kirby.

That morning, Stella had a scene on horseback. Nina arrived on the set, as agreed, to supervise. It was a cloudless day, the sky a deep shade of blue. Klaus Vilmer, the cinematographer, was not entranced with the brilliant sky. They waited for an eternity while Klaus' crew set up the screens that took the natural light and altered it so it would appear real on film.

After what seemed like an interminable time, Stella and Hollie were called out from their dressing rooms. As Stella came onto the set, Nina could see Stella looking for her. The scene began on horseback. Nina watched proudly as Cal/Stella and her mount trotted into the corral. Pico, Stella's palomino, had fallen in love with her. He whinnied happily whenever she came into sight. On this day of shooting, everything went beautifully. A master shot of the scene was perfect. Tense, sensual. Cal and his frustrated boss climbed from their horses and bickered, trying to fight off their mutual attraction.

The entire crew knew they had a winner. Everything seemed to go right. Later, after the scene had been reshot in close-ups, Nina found Hollie and Stella under a canopy, at one of a long row of folding tables set up by the catering crew for lunch. They were obviously pleased with themselves and with the world in general, and beamed at Nina when she arrived.

"What a great morning," Nina said.

"Who'd have thought?" Hollie exclaimed. "A western!" He reached his arm around Stella's shoulder and bent his head affectionately towards her. "We *do* make a great pair."

"We do, that's for sure," Stella replied, leaning her head on his shoulder.

Nina plunked down into a wooden folding chair. "Honestly, the way you two act, I almost believe your romance."

"In some other world," Hollie said.

"In some very different world," Stella echoed.

"Never mind, I was kidding." Nina pulled her notebook out of her briefcase and handed them each a sheet of dialogue. "This is for Sunday."

"Perfect," Hollie said. "I must say, I've never enjoyed any of my invented romances so thoroughly." He took Stella's chin in his hands. "Darling, maybe someday we'll get past these obstacles." He glanced over at Nina. "Won't we?"

"Absolutely," Nina said. "Well, on paper, anyway."

"What a relief," Hollie sighed and turned to Stella. "Who wants to grow old alone?"

Stella stood abruptly. "Oh, for crissakes," she said and turned away, heading out towards the trailers. "I can't bear that kind of talk."

"Sweetheart," Hollie called, "have we upset you?"

"Go to hell," Stella called back.

As soon as she was out of hearing distance, Hollie turned to Nina. "She's fine. She's in her role. Frustrated in love. You understand."

"I do," she said. What she didn't understand was his complicit look, but she chose to ignore it.

"She's really got what it takes," he said. Now he rose and looked at Nina with utter seriousness. "Our futures are riding on that, aren't they?"

On Sunday morning, Nina met Tom Kirby outside the hotel. He appeared to be in his late thirties, but had an eager schoolboy look that some men sustain forever. Kirby had a right to feel eager. Shanahan and Nina were giving him a huge break.

Kirby entered the dining room, camera in hand. Hollie and Stella were seated in an intimate corner. Kirby glanced around melodramatically. A number of heads turned in his direction. Pantomiming satisfaction, he pranced in the direction of the intimate couple. "Ah ha!" he cried. "Caught you!" Nina could see Stella and Hollie suppressing a giggle. Kirby raised his camera. As soon as the flash bulb popped, Hollie leapt from his seat. All eyes turned to the trio.

"Say," Kirby called, "looks like you two are up to something racy. Spent the night together, huh?"

Hollie advanced threateningly. "Beat it, buster, before I make you regret it." Stella leapt from her chair and took him by the arm. She held him back while Kirby relentlessly snapped shots.

"Please," Stella pleaded with Hollie, "leave him alone. He's not worth it." While Kirby tailed them, snapping shots, they stomped from the dining room of rapt voyeurs.

The scoop ran in Monday's *Tucson Herald* and was picked up the next day by Dottie Strong. Then, as they'd hoped, the incident went from coast to coast. The public loved it. Nothing like a little hanky-panky on location to get the people aroused. Much to everyone's delight, the couple was being pestered for interviews and dodging persistent reporters. On the next to last day of shooting, Nina sought out Stella during a break. "About the *LIFE* interview. I have some changes."

"Fine," Stella said. Her eyes were far away.

"I wanted to explain a few very important points," Nina insisted.

"All right," Stella said.

Nina explained each point to Stella with growing frustration. "You aren't listening!"

Stella cocked an eyebrow at Nina, then repeated Nina's latest fabrications with candor and charm. "Okay?"

"I'm sorry, you just seemed distracted."

"Something bad has happened," Stella replied.

"Everything's going marvelously."

"Remember? There's prophesy in my family." Stella shivered, then straightened up. "I just have a feeling. Anyway, I need your help."

"With the horses? You're doing fine."

"Not with the horses."

"Then with what?"

"With the scene we're shooting tomorrow."

"Your scenes have been fabulous."

"Come to my room tonight."

"To do what?"

"To read some lines."

"You know what an acting dunce I am."

"It doesn't matter."

"You want me to come to your room and read lines with you? If you were a man, I'd think this was fishy."

"If I were a man, I wouldn't be so obvious. Look, here comes Hollie." Stella grinned and waved, but the grin faded as he grew closer. "Oh, no," she whispered.

Hollie was holding a rolled-up magazine. When they'd found a remote corner, he unrolled it so they could see the front cover.

The headline blared:

HOLLYWOOD QUEEN'S SECRET LOVE CHILD!!!!

What followed was an elated expose of Sybil Burton's secret indiscretion.

"Will everyone think I blabbed this to the studio?" Nina said. "I swear I never did."

"Oh, Nina," Hollie said, "Most of Hollywood knew. It was assumed no one would speak of it. Say, we'll be back in a few days. Maybe you girls can do something. You seem to be pretty good at fixing things." Hollie's look was not optimistic.

"I WAS ABOUT to give up on you." Stella's face was scrubbed clean of makeup. She looked very young and appealing, with her tousled, short hair and bare feet. She smelled slightly lemony.

"Did you call Sybil?" Nina asked, hesitating on the threshold.

"Alfred answered. He said she's all right, but didn't want to talk to anyone. We can try again in the morning."

Stella's room was very much like Nina's. Braided rugs, pine furniture, wood-paneled walls decorated with cattle paintings and leather horse tack. Stella motioned Nina in, then shut the door and leaned back against it. "If I were a man, I guess you'd be nervous right now."

"I'm nervous anyway."

"Let's just play our parts. It helps to block out the real world's troubles." There was a heavily marked script on the bed. Stella got it and handed it to Nina.

"I'll be terrible, I promise."

"You sound so grim." Stella walked to the middle of the room and shook her shoulders, rolled her neck. Like a chameleon, she transformed into Cal in all his/her awkward sensuality. "I love the desert at sunset," she said. "So full of mystery and secrets."

Nina could see her lines on the page, but nothing came from her lips.

"Just read," Stella said. She repeated: "I love the desert at sunset. So full of mystery and secrets."

"You're a boy who likes mysteries and secrets," Nina said in a faux-husky, jittery voice.

Stella burst out laughing.

"I told you!"

"Look at me," Stella said. "Listen carefully to me right now."

Nina felt like she was hanging from a cliff and her hands were slipping slowly from their grip on the edge.

"You've never felt this way about anyone before." Stella smiled slyly. "Pretend you're riding a horse if you have to."

"Okay," Nina said weakly. She let herself sink into reverie.

"Breathe," Stella coached. "Forget everything but us together in the beautiful desert night. Forget everything but right now."

Nina closed her eyes, and then opened them.

"You're a kid who likes mysteries and secrets," she said gruffly.

Stella's eyes flashed a small acknowledgment. "There are some secrets a person just can't tell."

"Not to anybody?"

"Not to anybody."

"That's a lonely thing." Nina was, amazingly, starting to immerse herself. She could feel the warm desert air and smell the intoxicating blooming cactus.

Stella kicked at a rock, raising desert dust. She turned her back to Nina. "I have a hidden secret."

"If someone were to tell me their most hidden secret," Nina announced, "I would carry it to my grave."

"Promise?" Stella whispered.

"Promise."

Stella turned to face Nina. "I love you."

Nina dropped the script.

"Pick it up," Stella said.

Nina stood, frozen. "I don't need to. I know what the script says."

"What does it say?"

"I can't."

Stella set her script down. She went up to Nina and circled her arms around Nina's waist. She slid her hands against the small of Nina's back so that their bodies pressed together.

"All right," Stella whispered. "Now try."

Nina took a deep breath. She let her torso push against Stella's, feeling Stella's firm body pressing against her. That's funny, she thought. It *is* like riding a horse. Better. Slowly, she brought her face close to Stella's face. Then she let her lips press against Stella's. It was much, much better. She sank into the kiss, an involuntary moan escaping from her throat. She wasn't sure how long it went on. Long enough so that her knees wobbled. She pulled away. "I can't do this."

Stella touched her cheek, then leaned in and kissed it lightly. "Why not?" she whispered.

"I can't." Nina backed up. "That was low. The way you got me to come up here. It was a big cliché and I fell for it."

"You didn't have to come. Why did you?"

"I don't know. I wish I hadn't." Nina fled from the room.

AS SHE LAY awake that night, she thought of the finale of the scene she and Stella had been rehearsing. The boss jumps on his horse and flees after the forbidden kiss. Only a short while later Callie reveals herself as a woman. Then came the happy ending. Oh, wasn't that swell? It was fine, in the movies.

THE PHONE RANG at 2:30 a.m. It was Shanahan. She knew what it was about. Before he spoke a word, Nina knew.

Chapter
Twenty-four

The Flight Of The Soul

SYBIL CROFT WAS a very special person. She spoke her mind. She believed she would return in another form. Alfred found her, submerged in her bathtub, electrocuted by a radio whose dial she'd been tuning. The coroner's report ruled it a tragic accident.

The funeral was elaborate even by Hollywood standards, the whole bill footed by Lumina Pictures. Poppa's limousine led the motorcade. The long procession wound up the hill to Forest Lawn Cemetery, while fans, now apparently forgiving of her sin, lined the streets. The graveside flowers alone could have filled a conservatory.

A reception was held at the Roosevelt Hotel. Limo after limo pulled up, disgorging mourners. Sybil's father, the great Lawrence Croft, was there to bury his daughter and to greet Hollywood's renowned — people he had scorned all his life. His ancient hawk-like features were molded into a serene mask as he shook the hands of those who, in his words, were destroying the high art of acting and culture in general. Beside him stood his partner on stage and in life, Sybil's mother Helen. They were awesomely composed. Every inch of their demeanor spoke of a dignity buttressed by self-righteousness.

Abbie came from the ranch, accompanied by the Snipes. She wailed too loudly, but no one stopped her. Stella was exceptionally controlled. Nina couldn't stand looking at her, knowing what she was probably going through inside. They hadn't really spoken alone since the hotel room encounter in Arizona. Nina circulated in a daze of misery and regret, avoiding the one person she wanted to share comfort with.

The gathering grew in size and intensity, fed with loss and guilt. Sybil was denied her most fervent request, that her death not be mourned. Everyone ate too much, they drank everything in sight, they hurt inside. Of course, Nina overheard a few deals being made, but that was to be expected.

Sometime after eight o'clock, she was standing with Hollie and

Lance when Dick and Annabelle Preston appeared. Annabelle was one of those women whose entire world revolves around her man. It was difficult to make eye contact with her for long. She spent most of her time looking at Dick. You could imagine her when Dick wasn't at home, waiting for him by the door like an eager pet. This particular evening, however, Annabelle had something on her mind. "I insisted on coming over here," she announced. Dick was glowering. "I know you were her best friends."

Both of Nina's companions looked terribly uncomfortable.

"Dick thought she was the most talented actress at Lumina," Annabelle said. "Honestly, I was almost suspicious. You know what they say about Hollywood producers." Annabelle paused, taking in the peculiar expressions on the faces of her audience.

Lance, particularly, had developed a peculiar twitch in his left eye. His voice seemed to burst from an expanding pipe. "You should kneel down and pray for what you've got in this man."

Dick stared at his shoes. Annabelle looked confused. "I just wanted to pay my respects," she said shakily. Slowly, her puzzled look transformed, as though an unbidden spark was kindling. "Dick likes me to stay buried away from all of this. But I might want to know more about the rest of his life. I'd like to share more of it with him."

Dick's mouth fell open.

"We should go," Annabelle said. "I don't know what got into me."

As Dick and Annabelle disappeared, Nina felt another vapor surrounding the remaining threesome. At a different time and place, she might have asked: "What was that all about?" But now, she remained silent. After all that had happened recently, she wasn't sure she wanted to know.

THE ALARM CLOCK read 3:17 a.m.

"Get your clothes on."

"Oh, no. Shanahan, I can't take any more."

"Come down to the Hollywood Sheriff's Station. Go in the same way you did last time." The phone went dead.

The same sour-faced detective who'd fixed the Abbie situation let Nina in. Without a word, he led her down the same dim corridor to the same locked room. Just before he turned the key in the lock, he turned to Nina with a sneer. "Fairies make me sick." Then he unlocked the door.

Lance sat in a chair. Shanahan stood in a corner nearby. Lance's shirt was torn, one of his cheeks was bruised, and he was missing a shoe. The detective cleared his throat as if he was going to spit on the floor. "Disgusting," he said.

"They didn't have to beat me up," Lance replied.

"Our friend got picked up by a vice cop in Griffith Park behind a nice big bush," Shanahan informed Nina.

"Oops," Lance piped up.

"Don't be a smart-alec," the detective snarled. "I don't know what's worse, Shanahan, what this homo was up to or you sticking up for him."

"Can it!" Shanahan said. "Go read your Bible about casting stones."

"I'm ashamed of you, bringing up the Bible like that," the deputy said. "Now, get that pervert outa here."

Shanahan lifted Lance up with surprising strength. Before they were out the door, the detective called out: "Ask the fag about the one that got away. Have him tell his pal that we saw who he was and we got his number, too."

As soon as they were in the alleyway, Shanahan turned to Lance. "What the hell were you trying to pull?"

Lance shrugged. "Don't you ever get horny?"

"That's swell. You go tomcatting on the night of the funeral of a great lady who's your friend, because you're horny? Not to mention your unnamed pal. Did he even look back when they dragged you off?"

Lance shrugged again.

"What exactly is happening?" Nina asked.

The two men glanced at her. Not unkindly. Not even particularly condescendingly. Just glanced, as though they had suddenly realized she was around.

"I believe," Shanahan said, "our friend here is protecting someone."

"They say actors are pretty immature," Lance added helpfully. "This might be a case of school yard loyalty."

"I'm sorry," Nina said. "I really don't understand."

"Now, listen to me," Shanahan said patiently. "This's all gonna be covered up. Right?"

"Yes, as always," she replied.

"Well, I'd say some friend of ours was feeling very angry about what happened to Sybil. So he goes flirting with disaster and brings his pal Lance with him, knowing no fear because the studio will cover for them. Then he chickens out and deserts his pal."

Shanahan paused and took a deep breath. "Look, my friends, nobody's more down about Sybil than me." For a moment, he allowed the pain to show on his face, and then hardened his features.

Lance looked grave and angry. "Maybe some people like my

friend just got sick of how it is."

Shanahan sighed. "Whatever you or that person meant, it's over. It never happened." He turned to Nina. "Take him to a motel. I don't want him to go home tonight."

The first thing Lance did when they climbed into Nina's Buick was burst into tears. Nina dug a handkerchief out of her purse and handed it to him.

"I'm sorry," he said. "This was a really big mistake. Do you think I'm a degenerate?"

For a moment, Nina didn't reply. She wasn't avoiding an admission. She was thinking. She'd only known a few homosexuals. There was a curator at the Guggenheim. There was the interior designer her grandmother hired—but these were men whose effeminate ways were tolerated, as though their professions absolved them. "I don't know," she said quite honestly. Although her throat felt constricted, she asked, "You and Hollie are together?"

"We came from New York together in '34. I was nineteen when we met, he was twenty-nine and already a leading man on Broadway. Lumina gave him a screen test. Anyone could see he was a star. I just started following him around like a puppy. I followed him here. Knew he'd get tired of me, though."

"But you live together."

"Oh, honey, we're just friends now. Besides, Hollie only got involved with me because I resemble this boy Paul. I think he's the only one Hollie ever really loved. It's a terribly sad little fairy tale. Paul was a rich boy, Hollie was the chauffeur's son. They were inseparable until Paul went off to college. Then Paul got hit by lightning on a golf course in the middle of his sophomore year at Yale. Electrocuted. Hollie never recovered."

A terrible thought occurred to Nina. Before she could say anything, Lance spoke.

"It's a horrible coincidence. Hollie went a little crazy after Sybil—the whole thing about electrocution, it's very odd. He's normally the most careful person. I hardly know anyone more discreet." Lance hesitated. "Going to the park—"

"You don't have to tell me—" Nina interrupted.

For the first time that evening, Lance seemed his old self. He giggled. "No details. Well, it *was* all Hollie's idea. I knew it was stupid, but I love him, so I went along."

"Then he ran away?"

"I'm not blaming him," Lance said vehemently. "That's not why I'm telling you. I want you to watch out for him. He's always been so discreet. I wonder about his state of mind."

They had been cruising along lower Sunset Boulevard, past a

series of motels whose signs flickered VACANCY. Nina pulled up to The Seven Seas, a tropical joint that looked decent despite its Malibu lights, artificial grass-thatched roof and volcano water fountain spouting outside the front office.

"I'll go in," she said.

"How will you register?" he asked.

"Mr. and Mrs. Gatsby." Nina winked at him.

When she returned with the keys, Lance was slumped against the seat. "Will you come in with me for a little while?"

The dawn was beginning to break, a great burst of pink and orange in the eastern sky. The flame-colored light reflected in the water of the tiny swimming pool beside the parking lot. A new day. Nina thought of all she had to do at the studio.

"Please," Lance said.

Room 17 was a small Polynesian box with cheap oil paintings of the sea on its wood-paneled walls. Lance went into the bathroom to clean up. Nina grabbed a copy of the *Tinseltown Insider* someone had left lying face-down on the nightstand and settled into a bamboo chair. A chill ran through her when she saw the cover. It was the issue that featured Sybil's love-child transgression.

Lance emerged from the bathroom smelling soapy, his cheeks scrubbed pink. He plunked onto the squeaky bed. "I have to tell someone."

It'd been an awful day. Nina didn't know if she could stand another confession.

"How do you feel about Dick Preston?" he asked.

"Well, I think he's a bit of a snoot. But who am I to cast stones?"

Lance smiled sadly. "People don't know how much he suffers."

A tiny bulb began to glow in Nina's thick skull. "You mean," she said, "you and Dick Preston? But he's married."

"Oh, honey," Lance said, "you'd think you'd been raised in backwoods Missouri like me. Say, this mattress belongs in a flop house." He arranged the pillows on the bed and tried to get comfortable, the bedsprings protesting each move he made. "Dick will always be married. Annabelle's like a tattoo. But many men through history have had mistresses or whatever."

Nina suddenly felt the weight of the entire day and evening crashing on her. She was exhausted, to the tips of her toes. This night had brought too many revelations and she had no energy reserves left to sort out this latest one.

"I can't stay," she said. She was so tired.

"I know I can trust you not to tell," Lance said, his look betraying a certain anxiety. "I don't know what it is about you,

Nina. Have you considered espionage as a career?"

"Not complicated enough," Nina replied.

It was all she could do to get up from the bamboo chair and go to her car.

Chapter
Twenty-Five

Misadventures And Secrets

WHATEVER HOLLIE'S SHENANIGANS had been meant to express, he left them behind in the weeks that followed. At Dewey's insistence, a week of retakes was added. Those extra days of production went marvelously, though, despite the upsets and tragedies. Maybe because of them. And Nina became devoted more than ever to inventing Hollie and Stella's romance. Much of her waking time, she was thinking about Hollie and Stella, about the imaginary complications of their story: How they felt about one another, their spats and their reconciliations. What a difficult and fascinating couple they were! Volatile, passionate, yet capable of deep affection! And, always, the hint of a burning sexuality. She went to sleep at night thinking of Hollie and Stella. She woke up from dreams about them, and then thought about them all day. Her magnificent obsession was working, too. Stella and Hollie were the talk of Hollywood.

The couple appeared together at premieres, nightclubs, parties and award ceremonies. Through all the whirlwind of publicity, Nina expected Stella to confront her. But since the incident in Arizona and the funeral that followed, Stella seemed remote. Nina should have been relieved, but she wasn't.

SHOOTING WRAPPED THE third week of August, ten days over schedule, but no one complained. They all knew they had a hit on their hands. Now what the studio needed was another winning script for Stella and Hollie. In the third week of July, Murray Lasky thrust a script at Nina. "Gimme your opinion," he said.

The Right Man was a romantic mystery-comedy along the lines of *The Thin Man* series, clever and nuanced. Nina could imagine what Dewey Starke would spout about its subversive possibilities, but she didn't say anything of this to Murray, of course. To Murray, she said, "Definitely big box-office."

Murray scratched his chin. "Dick Preston is crazy about it.

Seems he once read a mystery by this guy Bender, about a rich guy's son who gets nabbed for killing some rival. Turns out the poor guy's father framed the poor schnook. The whole thing is creepy, far as I'm concerned. But Dick was hot to go with it, so he had Poppy Kahn write a treatment that Irwin hated. Couldn't stand how evil the father was."

Murray cocked an eyebrow at Nina. "Hey, I know what you're thinking. Dick is obsessed with his father and now he's got hold of this plot. There's a word for it—"

"Oedipal," she said.

"Yeah, anyway," Murray said, "Dick wouldn't give up. So, they sent the treatment to Joe Breen and he hated it, too. That shoulda been the end of that masterpiece."

Censorship couldn't be ignored in Hollywood, ever since the thirties, when Will Hays became president of an agency designed to enforce the Production Code, a litany of ethics written by a Jesuit priest and a Catholic publisher. Joe Breen was Hay's successor. The agency became the Production Code Administration or the "Breen office." Lumina had had relatively little trouble with Breen compared to some of the other studios.

Breen wasn't favorable towards crime flicks that violated the Code's demand that "the sympathy of the audience should never be thrown to the side of the crime, wrongdoing, evil, or sin." An Oedipal script sympathetic to an accused murderer was a problem, not to mention the slandering of a capitalist father figure.

"But that wasn't the end of it at all, was it?" she asked.

"Dick's possessed," Murray said, shaking his head. "Since we need some hot property for Stella and Hollie, he gives the treatment to Ben and Cookie Heller and tells 'em to doctor it up."

"They did a bang-up job. I love the script. And I love the Hellers."

Murray shrugged. "I'm not gonna beat around the bush. We been getting some pressure about the Hellers." He glanced over his shoulder. "I did some things in my youth a lot worse than what they ever did." He shook his head sadly. "I'm just lucky it's Commies they're after. It's—" He looked at her.

"Ironic?" she said.

"Yeah. It's very ironic. The whole damned world is ironic these days."

"The project might work," Nina said. "Hollie and Stella as the private eye team draw attention away from the murder plot."

"Yeah, but then there's the private eye stealing his brother's fiancée."

"What did Breen say about that?"

"Hasn't seen the new script yet. We're deciding whether to submit."

"I'd send it on," she said.

"Thought you'd say that. Elaine said it, too." Murray tapped his temple. "I appreciate women's intuition. When you're in a pickle, talk to a woman."

"That's what I like about you," Nina said.

"Hey, don't go making me blush." Murray came around from his desk and put his hand on Nina's shoulder. "I want you to start thinking up the publicity angles pronto."

She'd already started. As soon as she'd read the script, she'd had visions of what to do. She felt on track, she felt energized.

AS POSTPRODUCTION ON *Callie Young* moved along, plans for the publicity campaign were hatched. The word was out. They had something big. Then, in the middle of everything, another disaster.

Aaron, Shanahan, Elaine and Nina were in a meeting when Poppa burst in, waving a copy of the *Tinseltown Insider*. "What's this?" he roared. It took a few minutes for the copy to get passed around. They did it silently, while Poppa glowered.

"FADING LUMINA CHORUS BOY DISCOVERED IN HOMOSEXUAL NIGHTSPOT!!!

"First Commies, then Sybil Croft, now homosexuals," Poppa roared.

Aaron shook his head. "We had no idea."

Poppa's face was a disturbing shade of purplish-red. A vein bulged in his forehead. "Oh, please, Aaron. You know we don't care about the facts. But don't give me any *drek* about what you know and don't know. Explain to me, instead, how you're not preventing these smears from getting out."

"Poppa," Elaine said. "Maybe you should sit down."

"Maybe I should fire all of you!" Poppa cried. "What's next?" He turned to Nina. "Who will you be having an affair with?"

Nina's face turned nearly the same shade of purplish-red as her uncle's.

"I'm sorry," Poppa said, noting her response. "I was only making an example." He sank into a chair. "All right," he said, looking at Aaron. "Take care of it."

SHANAHAN AND NINA drove Lance to Union Station. They

saw him off on the Super Chief. Just before he was to board, Shanahan handed him his ticket.

"This is one-way," Lance said. "Everyone said it was just until things blew over."

"Yeah, well, some people thought you might just stay in New York," Shanahan said miserably.

"They can't..." Lance said, but he didn't finish.

Of course they could.

Tears welled in Lance's eyes. "Okay. I don't blame you. I love you both. Oh my god, I can't believe this."

On the way back to the car, Shanahan straightened his tacky tie and brushed the lint from the sleeve of his cheap suit. "Don't think I'm getting paid enough for this. I might need a change of scenery."

"What do you mean?" Nina asked, a premonitory sense of dread hitting her.

"Nothing."

Very soon after, Shanahan quit. Nina came in to work and he was gone. He'd cleaned out his office in the middle of the night. A week later, she ran into him at The Brown Derby. He was at a table with a cheap-looking pipsqueak. Nina approached her former colleague and his companion. "How could you?"

"This is Harry Merton," Shanahan said, indicating his creepy pal. " We're at the *Tinseltown Insider* together. But I guess you heard."

"I hoped it was a nasty rumor."

Shanahan wiped ketchup from his mouth with his napkin. "Life's complicated, kiddo."

"Why?" She felt like she might cry. People watched from surrounding tables. The two men began picking at their food, ignoring her. This bit of rudeness was too much. She walked away. But she felt very sad. Good-bye, Shanahan, she thought. She was going to miss that man. She didn't expect to hear from him again, but she was wrong.

The clock on her nightstand read 1:30 a.m.

"Guess you think I jumped from the frying pan into the fire."

"I hardly think I should be talking to you, you were so rude at the restaurant."

"I'm only this rude to the ones I care about. Now, listen to me. A guy finds a place that tells the truth, even if it's an ugly truth. All right, maybe they don't have the best motivations, but they don't pretend to."

"I don't believe you."

"Oh, boy."

"It's about Sybil."

"Now, don't go barging—"

"Whose baby was it, Shanahan? Was it Aaron's? Or was it yours?"

"I don't know. Nobody knows, because she wouldn't say. She was too independent. Not willing to take help from anyone or get too involved—" He broke off, as though his throat had closed up. Then he began again. "Look, no love lost between me and Aaron Bermann. If I hadn't quit, he would have found a way to can me eventually."

"I'm very sorry," she said.

"No more sorry than me," he replied, voice still thick. "I should have done more for her."

"Still, to punish yourself this much, going over to that dirty rag, that's going too far."

"Don't make assumptions."

"Then tell me the truth."

"Let's just say I'll keep in touch."

Before she could respond, he hung up.

Later that morning, Nina dragged herself to the studio. Stella was in her dressing room. Nina pummeled the door, which Stella opened warily. She barged in, fists clenched. "Do you still like me?" she said, without thinking. That was what Stella did to her. Short-circuited her wiring.

"More than ever."

"Then why haven't you..." she stopped.

"Why haven't I been pursuing you?"

"No. Yes. I don't know."

"I'm waiting for your head to catch up with the rest of you."

"You knew about Lance and Dick. You knew about Hollie. Why didn't you tell me?"

"Did you really want to know?"

"Of course I did," Nina said, but she sounded unconvincing, even to herself.

"You can see why we need you," Stella said. "Maybe not knowing everything helped you come up with answers. No need to bother with the questions."

Nina smiled. "Some philosophers, including Alfred the butler, believe that you have to ask the right questions in order to get the correct answers."

Stella shrugged. "A wise woman once said everything's revealed at the proper time. Until then, we live in the dark. Maybe answers come before questions sometimes."

"The wise woman was Sybil, wasn't it?"

"And look what that piece of wisdom did for her."

"Sybil's life ended like she told us itwas going to," Nina replied.

Stella walked over to a small makeup table and slid onto an upholstered seat, facing the three-paneled mirror. "Come here."

Nina hesitated. "I've had enough mirror games."

"It's not a game."

When she was standing behind Stella, facing their two images, Stella said: "I once heard that God is like a mirror. The mirror never changes, but everyone who looks in it sees something different."

Nina watched Stella's mirror image challenging her.

"What do you see?" Stella asked.

"Just the two of us."

"What about us?"

"Nothing. I don't understand."

Stella sighed. "It doesn't matter. Just keep making your plans."

"As a matter of fact, I have come up with another installment," Nina said.

"It wouldn't be that me and Hollie get engaged, would it?"

"Can't you ever let me be a step ahead of you?"

"When I'm ahead, I can wait for you. Like I've said, I'm good at waiting."

"Don't!" Nina could feel tears of frustration welling up. "I don't know what you're waiting for."

Stella just lifted an eyebrow.

"This is all new to me," Nina said. "I'm not making judgments, but I need to figure out how I feel about all this. And..."

Stella waited.

"Please, don't keep me in the dark. Let me know what's happening."

"Honey, I'll be straight with you. You're not ready. Let's just take things a few steps at a time. Deal?"

Nina hesitated. "Deal. After all, why do we have to go so fast all the time?"

PART THREE:

THE RIGHT MAN (1950)
DIRECTOR: DEWEY STARKE

"Movie Reviews" *Modern Screen*, **December 1950:**

I doubt if there will be a more charming film released this year than The Right Man, a marvelous blend of comedy, mystery and romance that recalls The Thin Man series. The team of Stella Kane and Hollace Carter light up the screen. Hollace plays the black sheep brother of a stuffy young stockbroker (Brad Black) engaged—much to his parent's horror—to a Macy's sales clerk (Stella Kane). Just before the wedding, the stockbroker's brother—a private eye—shows up to investigate a murder (an inconsequential but entertaining subplot that simply provides a mystery to solve). The detective-for-hire needs female assistance and enlists the aid of his brother's fiancée. Kane and Carter are a wonderful, bantering duo. One thing leads to another...I won't say more, as I insist all of you race down to your local movie house and delight in all the zany entanglements that ensue. I, for one, would be thrilled to see a series in the making. It's hard to imagine this couple apart.

Chapter
Twenty-Seven

A Time Of Condemnations

POSTPRODUCTION OF *CALLIE Young* continued through the fall. In late October, the completed cut previewed in Encino. Audiences cheered well into the credits. On November 22, *Callie* had her grand premiere at The Empress on Times Square. This time the cast was sent out to attend the opening. The critics went bananas. *Box Office Digest* hailed Dewey Starke as a genius, crediting him with "guiding the western into the realm of the classics."

With obsessive zeal, Dick Preston convinced Irwin to assign Hollie and Stella to *The Right Man*. He demanded a top-notch production, with a budget of $1.6 million, a 54-day shooting schedule and Dewey Starke at the helm. But the studio was still having problems getting the script past Joe Breen and his censorship authority. Throughout the fall, there were rewrites and tortured meetings and resubmissions. Winter arrived with the project still on hold.

Ten years earlier, Stella and Hollie would have been rushed through another picture, until *The Right Man* was a go. But in 1949, profits were down. Like many of the studios, Lumina had cut down on production. So people waited as the end of the decade came upon them.

On New Year's Eve, Poppa and Aunt Nettie hosted a *sayonara* party to the forties. It was a jittery bye-bye. Nina had decided that it was her night to coast. She was a little frazzled. And, besides, it was the beginning of a new decade, why not throw in the towel and just celebrate? She assigned Betty Allsop, an eager publicity newcomer, to tail Stella and Hollie.

In addition to opening the entire main floor of the Villa to the revelers, Poppa had rented two huge white tents. In each, there was a band, one for slow dancing and the other a lively big band ensemble. The guest list was a litany of Hollywood royalty.

The weather was unseasonably warm, mild and cloudless. The contented crowd circulated in and out of the tents. They wandered through the maze of gardens, glasses in hand, as music from the two bands mingled in a discordant yet oddly pleasant way.

Nina had bought a new dress for the affair, a strapless blue satin gown with a full skirt. She spent the early part of the evening mingling among the guests, trying not to think too deeply. She sipped champagne and eavesdropped, avoiding personal conversation as much as possible. It was a relief to just drift, without plans or obsessions. Something was nagging at her, however. Halfway through the evening, Elaine approached her and asked, "Is something wrong?"

"What do you mean?"

"I thought you might be in pain, the way you're hunching over like that."

Nina came right to the point. "Are my shoulders too muscular for this dress?"

Elaine appraised Nina's appearance. "There are some who might avoid the strapless look." Then she reached out and hugged Nina. "Oh, sweetie. You didn't want me to fib, did you?"

"We fib every day," Nina replied.

"Never when it comes to attire," Elaine admonished, with mock gravity.

"I wish you'd been at the boutique when I tried this on."

"Which boutique?"

"Mitzi's Precious Occasions."

"Precious Occasions," Elaine spat out. "Don't ever go there again. Mitzi has no taste. And neither do her sales ladies." She patted Nina's cheek. "Now, straighten up. A person never wants to accentuate a mistake by trying to hide it."

Nina could see the conversation was beginning to bore Elaine, who surveyed the room. "Oh, here come Dick and Annabelle. The man has gone absolutely berserk. If he brings up *The Right Man* again, I'll hit the ceiling."

As the Preston's closed in, the band began to play "Stormy Weather."

"How appropriate," Elaine commented.

Dick Preston's first words were: "I must have Lawrence Wycoff for *The Right Man*."

"Dick," Annabelle interjected, "couldn't we at least say 'Happy New Year'?"

Dick bowed. "I apologize. Happy New Year, ladies."

"Lawrence Wycoff is an uncooperative stuffed shirt," Elaine said. "He should stick to *King Lear*. Everything else is apparently beneath him."

"He's guaranteed class," Dick said.

Annabelle hiccupped. "I've had two glasses of champagne. I'm feeling festive. We're entering a new decade!" She held up her glass. "To a new world!"

Dick ignored his wife's rosy salute. "Wycoff is perfect, Elaine. He *is* the father for this movie."

"He might be," Elaine admitted, "but why bother me? I don't have anything to do with casting."

Dick raised one eyebrow. "Let me hear it from your lips. He's perfect."

Elaine shrugged, and then nodded.

"From your *lips*," Dick insisted.

"He's perfect," Elaine said.

"All right then," Dick said with obvious relief. "I just wanted to hear it from your lips. Now I know it'll work out."

The band's rendition of "Stormy Weather" ended to enthusiastic clapping. Annabelle picked up another glass of champagne. "I know why my husband is so bully over Lawrence Wycoff." Dick attempted to remove the glass from Annabelle's hand, but she shrugged away from him and leaned in towards Elaine and Nina with a conspiratorial expression. "Wycoff *very much resembles* someone." She looked over at Dick, who was glowering at her. "Oops. I'm blabbering."

Dick took Annabelle's elbow. "I think it's time for us to go."

As they pushed through the crowd, arm in arm, Dick limping on his cane and Annabelle swerving tipsily, Nina said, "That was creepy."

Elaine sighed. "It's a pity some women can't just say what they mean." She glanced at her watch. "I've got to find Murray. Hate to abandon you. Oh, look who's coming."

Making their way through the crowd were Ben and Cookie Heller. The Hellers launched into an enthusiastic tirade about their latest script as soon as they arrived. "It's our tour-de-force," Ben exclaimed. "Funny, romantic, a mystery, but oh, boy." He glanced around. "The censors are going crazy. Not only do we encourage a look at capitalism —"

"Ben!" Cookie stage-whispered.

"On top of it all, we built in Oedipal conflict," Ben said. "Still, they can't pin anything down and it's driving them crazy."

"Now if that Dick Preston doesn't ruin it!" Cookie cried.

"I can't understand," Ben said. "He's usually so supportive. Now this thing about the father's part. I worked with Lawrence Wycoff in New York. He's impossible."

Cookie winked at Nina. "It's Freudian with Dick Preston. When it's Freudian, there's no stopping it."

The band had just begun to play again.

"Would you honor me with a dance?" Ben asked Nina.

"He's a klutz," Cookie cautioned.

"I'll consider myself forewarned." Nina let Ben lead her onto the dance floor.

"Ouch!"

"Sorry," Ben said.

"It's all right," Nina moaned softly. Cookie watched from the sidelines, grinning.

Despite his genial expression, there was a glistening of sweat beaded at Ben's temples. "I know there are rumors about us," he whispered. "Everyone says there's no list, but that's rubbish and we all know it. We should go back to New York and forget this place, but I'm putting a son through Brandeis and Cookie has a sick mother." He gave Nina an imploring look.

Ben and Cookie had to know their public proclamations were a big part of the problem. In fact, everything about them — their smart writing, their irreverence, their honesty — was a problem. Nina felt a pang of sorrow. "Just try to be careful." They both understood how completely hollow her response was. Ben smiled sadly and shrugged as the song ended.

A familiar rustle went through the crowd. Stella and Hollie had swept into the tent. Once again, the band began to play. To Nina's horror, Ben seemed ready to take her up in his arms for another round. She was saved by the arrival of her couple on the dance floor. "Where's Betty Alsop?" she asked.

"Drank too much champagne," Hollie replied, smirking. "She's asleep on a couch in the ballroom in the Villa. Don't worry. Stella and I are doing very well by ourselves. We decided no spats this evening."

"Nice dress," Stella commented. "Nice shoulders."

"Don't tease me," Nina protested.

Stella turned to Hollie. "She has nice shoulders, doesn't she?"

Hollie made a show of assessing Nina's attributes. "Nice shoulders. Athletic, I would say." He smiled his glorious, dimpled smile at Nina. "Care to dance?"

"You two dance," Stella said. "Ben and I will go talk to Cookie."

For a few moments, Hollie and Nina just danced. Hollie was skilled in a relaxed, comforting way. In addition, her recent understanding of his "secret persuasion" made Nina feel safe. She found herself leaning against his strong chest, only to glance up finally at his amused expression.

"Watch out. Who knows what gossip we'll arouse."

"No one on earth would think I could steal you away from Stella."

"You underestimate yourself."

"Thank you, I suppose," she replied. She glanced over at the sidelines. Stella was surrounded by a group of men in tuxedoes. "Should we rescue her?"

"In a minute. She's quite capable, as you know." Hollie cleared his throat. "Stella and I went to see Abbie last Sunday."

"Without telling anyone? Whose idea was that?" Nina tried to fight off a feeling something very much like jealousy.

"Nina, am I telling you anything you don't know? Stella and I are truly fond of one another." He wore an odd expression, a mixture of amusement, self-mockery and regret. "I almost wish the whole thing was true. She's the most interesting woman I've ever known."

"You don't mean — "

"Don't worry." He smiled. "It just isn't possible."

"I wasn't worried." Nina faltered. "It's not like — like — " She couldn't finish.

Hollie tilted her chin gently up to his. The same gesture, Nina recalled, he'd made a few years back in *Come To Me*, the blockbuster he'd made with Ann Sheridan. One of the few American movies Nina had seen as a teenager. "How is Abbie?" she asked.

"She's becoming a person on her own. That's hard for Stella."

Nina let the warmth and safety of Hollie's embrace lull her into confession. "Why does she have to be so complicated? I want to help her, but I'm never sure how she's going to react to my ideas."

"She appreciates you. You know that. Of course you do." Hollie pulled Nina a little tighter. She could feel the muscles of his chest through his tuxedo. "It'll work out. Just keep planning for us. We count on you." He led Nina off the dance floor. As they got closer to Stella and her throng of admirers, a look of relief and affection appeared on her face. It was a look of intimacy, one that the three of them knew was directed at both Hollie and Nina.

Chapter
Twenty-Seven

A Good Shove

IN MID-JANUARY, JOE Breen granted approval of *The Right Man*:

> "...Although the subplot of false accusations still weighs on my mind, I think you have altered the story enough for me to give my tentative go ahead. I am not happy, however, with what I perceive as certain innuendoes, both of a moral and political nature..."

Poor Breen. He was powerful, but a realist. He had to placate the studio monarchs who were his bread and butter. For the role of the greedy industrialist father, Dick Preston won his campaign to hire the prima donna Lawrence Wycoff. He pressured and persisted, argued and wheedled, and eventually wore everyone out. May Evans was chosen to play Wycoff's wife. When Nina heard the news, she couldn't help recalling May's strange behavior a few months before, at Sy Kern's retirement party. She wondered how May felt playing Hollie's mother-in-law. May was, after all, only nine years older than Hollie. Not to mention the hidden relationship between Hollie and May's husband, Jason Noland.

Given the complications, Nina felt uneasy even before production began. Shooting started in mid-February. From day one, Dick Preston began to haunt the set. Things went well for two weeks, despite Dick's shadowy presence. The consummate director, Dewey Starke was averaging twelve set-ups and over two minutes of footage per day. Nina kept busy sending out promo material and arranging romantic encounters for Stella and Hollie. For whatever reasons, their romance had struck a nerve with the public. The pairing, like a number squared, had astronomically increased the public's adoration and curiosity. They ate up every detail of Hollie and Stella's outings on the town, their breakups, their inevitable reconciliations.

Then, in the third week, Dick Preston began making suggestions. First in memo form, addressed to Dewey:

"...I don't believe the role of the father is being given quite the slant intended by the script or the novel from which it arose. I suggest..."

In the fourth week, the suggestions began on the set. One day that week, Nina arrived at around eleven, after a series of meetings. Larry Evans, one of her favorite fellow publicists, appeared at her side, smirking. "You gotta see this. It's classic. That fella knows every trick in the book."

"What do you mean?"

"There's all sorts of ways for an actor to steal a scene. Wycoff has 'em all mastered."

On the set, Hollie, Stella and Wycoff stood in a bank lobby.

"Watch," Larry said.

"Scene forty-two, take seven!"

"Rolling."

"Action!"

"Mr. Bigley," Hollie said, "your son thinks someone is framing him."

"Mr. Wright," Wycoff replied, with cool malevolence, "I've already told you, until I know who hired you for this case, I will insist on giving all my information to the police." He paused and lifted an eyebrow at Stella. "And who is your lovely companion?"

"This is my brother's fiancée," Hollie said. "She's assisting me."

As Hollie spoke, Nina noticed Wycoff sidling off his mark, so that Hollie had to turn away from the camera to speak to him.

"I see," Wycoff said. "The two of you seem awfully companionable."

"Cut!" Dewey cried. He marched onto the set, looking uneasy.

"Mr. Wycoff," he said, with deference.

"Mr. Starke," Wycoff replied.

"Perhaps once you hit your mark, you could stay in place during that last line, as we discussed."

Wycoff puffed out his chest, like a proud peacock. "I cannot work under these intolerable circumstances."

Then who should come scurrying up but Dick Preston. He pulled Dewey aside.

"Ten to one Preston's telling Dewey that Wycoff has been acting for thirty-five years and knows what he's doing," Larry

Evans whispered to Nina. We watched Dewey's fist clench. Dewey
shook his head and marched away from Dick.

"All right," Dewey cried. "Let's do it again."

"Scene forty-two, take eight!"

"Rolling."

"Action!"

And, Lord be praised if Wycoff didn't do it again. Only this
time, Hollie began sidling with him, which caused Wycoff to
scream: "I cannot tolerate this."

"Cut!" Dewey cried.

"This aging male pin-up is overstepping his bounds," Wycoff
bellowed.

"Hey, sir," Hollie said, touching Wycoff's sleeve, "I was just..."

"Take your hands off me," Wycoff said.

"I was just trying to get across that we're all in this together,"
Hollie soothed.

"You and I are not in anything together. You and I are not in
the same league and I want you to remember that," Wycoff said.

All this time, Stella had been quite placid. Now, Nina saw a
certain look cross her face. Nina whispered to Larry Evans, "I think
we're about to see a new twist."

Larry had worked with Stella before. He whistled softly. "You
betcha."

"Mr. Wycoff," Stella said. "Let's try it one more time. Please? I
have a solution."

Wycoff lifted an eyebrow. "All right," he said cautiously, but
with decided curiosity.

Once again, the scene began.

Amazingly, at the very same line, Wycoff began his
grandstanding slither. At that moment, although it was not
anywhere in the script, Stella walked over to the great and
venerable Wycoff. Without saying a word, she gave him a vigorous
nudge, sending him back to his mark. Then she calmly spoke her
next line: "I just want to make sure justice is done." And the shove
appeared as a perfect bit of business.

"Cut!" Dewey cried.

Everyone froze. Stella stared at Wycoff. Wycoff stared back.
Then, Wycoff started laughing. "What a little hellion!" He bowed to
Stella and pointed to where his feet were planted on his mark. "Is
this where I'm supposed to be?"

"Move from there again and I'll shove you again," Stella
replied.

Wycoff threw up his arms. "Heavens, no!"

"I mean it," Stella said.

"I know you do," Wycoff said with pleasure. "In fact, the

shove is perfect. You may shove me again." Wycoff signaled to Dewey. "If that's all right with you."

"Fine," Dewey sighed. "Let's get this scene."

"She is one piece of work," Larry Evans breathed out.

"I'll say," Nina replied.

"All right," Wycoff called over. "Let's do it again. This will be the last one, I promise." He winked at Stella.

The next take went marvelously, but after it was done, Dick Preston came rushing up, face afire, and bellowed at Stella, "I will not have you acting so unprofessionally on one of my sets."

"Wait one moment," Lawrence Wycoff interjected, placing an arm around Stella. "This young woman knows how to make an old dog jump through his hoops. And besides, Mr. Preston, I am growing weary of your obsequiousness and interruptions." Dick's face blanched. But his good upper-class training prevailed and he managed to nod respectfully and limp away with as much dignity as he could muster.

That evening, Nina was heading across the parking lot when she heard her name being called. It was Dewey. "Can we sit in your car?" he asked. As soon as they'd climbed in, he said, "I want that man off my set. Tell your cousin."

"Elaine has no control over the producers," Nina protested weakly.

Dewey shrugged, responding to Nina's tone, not her words. "My dear, who runs the world, but women?"

"CAN WE TALK about something private?" Nina asked. Elaine was at her desk.

"Shut the door."

Nina did so and relayed Dewey's request.

"Nina, I have nothing to do with how the executive producers run their projects."

"That's what I told Dewey."

"What did he say?"

"Something about women running the world."

"Isn't that man a character?"

The next morning, Dick Preston was absent from the set. He never appeared again without first asking permission.

Things went smoothly again after that, for a while. Then, at the end of March, Klaus Vilmer collapsed. One minute the cinematographer was sitting in Greenblatt's Deli enjoying a pastrami on rye, the next he keeled over into a plate of kosher dill pickles. Klaus was diagnosed with a mild angina complicated by nerves. The production was held up for three weeks, much to the front office's horror. Smack dab in the middle of all the brouhaha, at one of their meetings, Aaron brandished a letter from the governor of Ohio, requesting Stella's presence at a patriotic gala dubbed "OHIO CELEBRATES AMERICA!" "It's a great idea," Aaron crowed. "We have a break in the shooting. It's perfect timing."

"What about the plays she never acted in? The adopted parents she doesn't have?" Nina protested.

"Oh, my God!" Aaron roared. "I need aspirin. Someone get me aspirin!"

Walter Bermann jumped up. The rest waited while Aaron moaned and clutched his head. Walter came running back with the aspirin and a glass of water. Aaron swallowed the pills and laid his head on the table. Everyone waited. After a full minute, he lifted his head and wiped his brow with a handkerchief. "Nina's just keeping us on our toes," he announced, stuffing the handkerchief back in his pocket.

"Honey," he said. "Those are just details. Look, those people don't care what the actual facts are. You'll go out there with her. Have her sit in the nice limousine and wave at the crowd. Give a nice interview, go visit some sick children at a charity hospital, then leave. Just avoid any situations."

"I—I—"

"Honey, Nina," Aaron interrupted. "They want her. The rest is what?"

Nina fixed her gaze stubbornly at the table.

"What, what?" Aaron prompted. "What is it?"

Nina wiggled in her chair. He was right, of course.

"Details," Nina said. "The rest is details."

"That's my girl," Aaron crooned. "Besides," he added heartily, "I know for a fact Irwin is acquainted with the publisher of *The Columbus Evening Dispatch*, not to mention the governor. A nice phone call or two, there's nothing to worry about."

"I SWORE I'D never go back," Stella said.

"It's not *exactly* going back. At least not to your home town."

"Close enough."

"The whole thing'll be over in two days."

"That's two days too much."

"I promise, I'll supervise everything, no surprises."

"Just the two of us are going?" Stella asked.

"Well, yes."

"I see." Stella fingered a script that lay on the table in front of her. "Let me think about it."

That afternoon, Stella approached Nina on the set between takes. "I'll go. But I need something."

"As always," Nina said with mock consternation. "And what is that?"

"A car. I want to take a little drive."

Chapter
Twenty-Eight

Two Peas In A Pod

TEN DAYS LATER, Nina and Stella were on a flight to Columbus, Ohio. Stella seemed very much herself, graciously signing autographs for the stewardesses, the pilot, the co-pilot, and several passengers. She threw herself into their scheming and rehearsals.

"What do you think?" Nina asked, watching Stella read a set of responses to anticipated questions from a list she'd prepared.

"I always wondered why I love acting so much," Stella said.

"It's just a suggestion."

"It's good." Stella looked over the response again. "You know, honey, I think *you* are in my head. You put my thoughts in words I couldn't."

"Say it."

Stella reread the response a couple of times. Then she folded the paper and closed her eyes briefly. Nina loved to watch her do this. Stella's eyes opened and her face took on a look of absolute modesty, sincerity and charm. She repeated Nina's words, but they were now something much more special.

"You're incredible."

"Thank you," Stella said. She was still wearing her modest face.

"No, I mean it," Nina said. "Come back. Be yourself."

"I am being myself."

"No," Nina said, a bit shakily. "I mean it. Be you."

"This is me," Stella said. "It's a me that you invented on this paper." Slowly, Stella's face transformed. She watched Nina throughout the transformation as closely as Nina was watching her. "Is this the face you were looking for?" she asked.

Nina shivered. She could see Stella still watching her.

"Come on," Stella said. "Let's do some more responses. They're fun. Don't worry so much."

They spent most of the rest of the flight rehearsing for all possibilities. Just before they were about to land, however, Stella seemed to withdraw. They wound up arguing about a minor point in one of the last responses. Even when Nina relented, Stella didn't perk up.

An awestruck deputy mayor and his secretary met them at the Columbus airport. It was nearly midnight. Stella and Nina had adjoining rooms at the Deshler-Wallick Hotel downtown. The deputy mayor and his secretary followed them on the elevator. They escorted them to their rooms. Nina thought the pair was going to unpack the luggage, but after a few more reverent compliments, they finally left.

A few minutes later, there was a knock at the door that separated Nina's room from Stella's. Nina unlatched the bolt. Stella leaned against the doorframe. "Night cap? We can order from room service. I love room service."

"I'm awfully tired," Nina sighed. She waited expectantly.

Stella stepped backwards into her own room. "Only asking," she said. Her tone lacked enthusiasm.

"It's that I'm so exhausted," Nina offered, but she let *her* tone suggest possibilities.

"Forget it." Stella shut the door.

"Stella?" Nina called through the door. Stella didn't answer.

"Stella?"

Nothing.

Nina left the latch unbolted and went to bed.

The next morning, Stella poked her head through the door. "Wake up. We've got a drive ahead of us. Let's get room service. I'll order."

The waiter arrived with a fully laden cart. Stella watched with delight as he lifted silver liners from the china plates and bowls. Scrambled eggs, buttered toast, bacon, fried potatoes, fruit salad, coffee and orange juice. They devoured everything, enough for two six-foot traveling salesmen.

Despite her pleasures in room service, Stella remained jumpy and distracted. After their meal, she slipped back into her room and came back straight-jacketed into a beige trench coat, buttoned to the collar and clenched at the waist with a tight belt.

"Are you expecting stormy weather?" Nina asked. The sky outside was cloudless.

"Maybe," she replied. "Let's go."

When the elevator doors opened, they could see a gaggle of reporters near the entryway of the lobby. They slipped through a service door. The car Nina had prearranged was parked outside the delivery entrance to the kitchen. They left Columbus and headed east. Nina liked the way Stella drove. She piloted the car with one hand dangling on the steering wheel, elbow on the doorframe. They passed the city limits and emerged into farmland and woods. "Stella, you seem different here."

"I've got a few things on my mind this morning."

Just outside of Zanesville, they turned onto a side road and then they were there.

The place was exactly as Nina imagined it would be. An ugly mutt came howling out of the garage. Dusty chickens scattered in fright. A few seconds later, a large, pale man lumbered out of one of the repair bays, wiping his greasy hands on a dirty rag. Kubicek, Stella's stepfather, approached with composed yet charged expression, like a plain pine box with a bomb inside.

Nina turned to Stella, shocked. Something in Kubicek's powerful coolness, that was a part of Stella. When Kubicek was almost ten feet from the car, Stella opened the door and climbed out. "Wait in here," she said.

Nina was already out the door. She stayed on her side of the car. The old man stopped about five feet from Stella. The dog ran up growling, stopped abruptly and sniffed at Stella's trench coat.

"You got a new one," Stella said, bending down to scratch the mutt's tattered ear.

"He's not as good as the one you stole," Kubicek replied.

"Good boy," Stella murmured. The dog licked her hand and wagged its matted tail.

"Smells family," the old man commented. He had adopted an ironic smile. Stella's smile.

"We're not family," Stella said, glancing up at Kubicek. "We're people who got stuck in the same place."

Kubicek raised an eyebrow. "In your eyes. Mine eyes see family."

Stella pulled a wad of cash from her coat pocket.

"Don't want your money," Kubicek said.

"This is just what I took from you."

"I'd a wished you'd brought back the dog you took instead."

"I couldn't bring him, so take this."

Kubicek crossed his arms over his coveralls. Stella tossed the wad of cash at his feet. The old man lifted a grimy boot and kicked the money across the dirt to Stella's feet. She refused to pick it up. Finally, the mutt snatched up the dough and scooted into a rusted car, chewing greedily as it went. Both Stella and Kubicek watched. Then Stella said, in a flat voice, "Your other dog's fine. He's got a good life."

The old man nodded. Then: "How's about your sister?"

"Fine." Stella's face mirrored the old man's, a map of stubbornness. "Living with a deaf family."

Kubicek said nothing.

"I took care of it," Stella said. These were words Nina had heard so many times from Stella's mouth. Only today, there was a shakiness she'd never heard before.

"So you gave her away," Kubicek said with a satisfied smirk.

"Don't mess with me, old man."

Nina felt like she was watching a chess match that Stella seemed to be losing. Kubicek scratched his ear. He shifted slowly from one foot to the other. He rearranged his features. "I wish your mama was alive. She woulda liked seeing you looking like that."

"Don't talk about my mama," Stella said in a low, angry voice. "She was never really yours. She was mine until the day she died."

Kubicek shook his head. "Same as always. You gotta own everything." He turned to Nina, as though she had suddenly appeared from the ether. "Takes whatever she can get. Gives it away when she don't want it no more."

"Leave her out of this," Stella warned.

"Is she yours, too?" Kubicek shot back.

"No—" Nina began.

"Don't get into this," Stella interrupted.

There was a silence. Kubicek turned to Nina again. "Watch your step with her. She can't control it, she can't love it."

"What do you know about love?" Stella spat out.

"Who's gonna love her?" Kubicek taunted. "Who's not just getting snared up in her? But that's okay. She'll take care of everything."

"Shut up!" Stella cried. "Shut up! Shut up!" She clenched her fists and pressed them against her ears. Nina stared at Stella, open-mouthed.

Kubicek's pale eyes lit up, a sniper aiming for the heart.

"She can't control it, she can't love it," he repeated very slowly, so that each word was like a bullet. "Takes what she wants. Gives it away when she don't want it no more." He turned and lumbered towards the garage.

Stella watched him leave, her arms now dangling at her side. On the seat of the rusted car carcass, Kubicek's new mutt was finishing up his snack of cash. From inside the repair bay, they could hear Kubicek starting up a generator. Its high-pitched, squealing roar pierced into the yard.

"I have to get out of here," Stella said.

They barreled down the main road, Stella's foot pressed hard on the accelerator, whizzing past startled farmers in battered pickup trucks. The day had become unseasonably warm. Stella was still wrapped from neck to knee in her trench coat. A stream of sweat trickled down her temple. After twenty or thirty miles, Nina said, "Stella, pull over." There was a side road coming up. Nina pointed to it.

When they'd stopped, Nina opened her door. The only things close by were a dilapidated brown farmhouse beside a dilapidated brown barn, surrounded by flat, open fields. A stiff, humid breeze blew. Nina walked out to the front of the car and motioned to Stella. Stella's hair was pasted in wet clumps against her neck, across her forehead. Her face was mottled. She stepped out of the car and approached Nina warily.

"Take off that coat or you'll be in the hospital in an hour," Nina said. She began unbuttoning Stella's coat, starting at the collar. When the buttons were undone, she peeled the coat off. "It's over." Stella's clothes were completely soaked. She was staring at Nina with defiance. But Nina wasn't fazed. She'd just had a realization. "With you it's always a scene. But this scene backfired, didn't it?"

Stella turned her back to Nina. In the distance, a cow mooed plaintively. Nina walked up to Stella's hunched body and wrapped herself around Stella, her breasts against Stella's back. She held on for what seemed like a very long time, until Stella had stopped shivering. When they finally pulled apart, Nina's clothes were soaked too. "I saw you." A strange, overwhelming feeling was welling up in her.

Stella broke away, charging to the driver's side of the car. "Let's *go*."

When they were driving again, Nina stared at Stella. Before, she had always found Stella beautiful, stunning and intriguing. But this was different. Now, Nina *had seen* her. The feeling she felt was huge, like she had acquired the keys to the gate of a magical secret fortress.

"Don't," Stella said.

"Don't what, honey?" Nina asked. At that moment, Nina wanted nothing more than for Stella to acknowledge Nina's entry, however back-door, into Stella's private world. But Stella wouldn't answer. In fact, she wouldn't speak. They spent the rest of the trip back to the hotel in silence. But Nina wasn't fazed by Stella's stony resistance. Her senses felt alive, just being near Stella, whom she'd *seen*.

STELLA WAS, OF course, the hit of the Columbus, Ohio celebration. She posed outside of the Ohio Statehouse for shots with the governor, mayor, deputy mayor and every fervent patriot in town. She lunched with the wives and visited an orphans' home. Nina trailed along, watching for situations, but everyone was too dazzled to initiate any.

That evening, Nina used special care in getting ready for the fund-raising dinner. She felt like a high-school girl, breathless and giddy. When Stella knocked at the door between their rooms, Nina's heart leapt in her chest.

"Is this what you wanted?" Stella asked, looking down at her subdued navy blue taffeta dress with its covered arms, button-down bodice and full skirt.

"You look lovely," Nina said. "But proper."

Stella nodded. "Let's get this over with."

"Well?" Nina asked.

"Well, what?"

"How do I look?" It was as though Nina had been struck with a sudden virus, that's how fast and unexplainable this was, this overwhelming need for Stella's admiration. She'd chosen a dark green silk dress for that evening, something she thought Stella would like her in.

"You look fine," Stella answered indifferently.

Stella's remark was devastating. Nina felt utterly foolish, yet incapable of stopping the longing. She was as possessed as the most besotted fan, agonizing over Stella's unattainable desirability. But her agony was greater than any fan's, because she had *seen* Stella. And now Stella was pushing her away.

Nina made it through the evening half-listening to the beer-bellied boor seated next to her. While he related his life story, involving the takeover of his father-in-law's car dealership, Nina watched Stella, mesmerized, in glorious pain, absorbed in excruciating desire.

At the end of the gala, she threaded her way through the throngs to get to Stella. Stella was signing autographs. Nina stood at the edge of the crowd, feeling impatient and restless. When Stella broke away, she headed not for Nina, but to the exit from the ballroom. Nina tailed after her.

"Look," Stella said, when Nina had managed to catch her, "I'm very tired tonight."

"That's all right," Nina said, trying to keep up, as Stella rushed to the elevator.

Stella pushed the elevator button and stood tapping her foot near to the door. When they reached their floor, she charged out. Nina paddled after her, too addle-brained to even be embarrassed. When Stella reached her room, she said "Good night," then disappeared behind her door.

Nina stood, dazed, in the brightly lit hallway. After a while, she unlocked her room, shed her heels, and paced the carpet, charged with energy. Probably five minutes passed, although it seemed like an hour. Nina marched to the door that joined their rooms and pounded on it. Enough time passed so that she began to wonder if Stella was going to ignore her.

"What is it?" Stella asked finally, cracking open the door.

"You said you wanted me before," Nina burst out. She must have looked pathetic.

Stella's expression thawed. She smiled her most ironic smile. "Don't believe everything I say. I'm just warning you."

"I don't need to be warned."

"Before, you didn't. Now, you do."

"Why?"

"Now you've fallen for me. Like everyone else."

"Fallen for you?" It was ridiculous to protest. Nina wanted Stella more than anything she'd ever wanted before. Suddenly she didn't care about other people's opinions, about anything. Not because she was like everyone else. Because she'd *seen* Stella. For the second time that day, she put her arms around Stella. "It doesn't matter. None of it matters." She kissed Stella lightly on the lips. She pulled Stella tighter, her breath quickening. She felt a great dam breaking inside herself. "Come into my room." As she spoke, Stella stiffened in her arms.

"Don't beg," Stella said.

"I wasn't begging," Nina replied, and she hadn't been. But Stella's tone made her feel ashamed. She looked into Stella's face, wanting Stella to help her get out of the shame, to make what they were doing seem all right. But Stella's face was a powerful blank, the cold Kubicek look Nina had witnessed that morning.

"I have to be alone tonight," Stella said, stepping back and closing the door.

ON THE RETURN flight, they remained in awkward silence for perhaps thirty minutes. Nina broke the hush. "I don't know what came over me."

"Let's forget it," Stella said.

"I'm not..." Nina said, and then hesitated.

"Not what?" Stella asked. She was looking at Nina's tortured face.

"One of those kind of women," Nina said, her face growing red. "I mean, look at us. We don't wear men's clothes...or...or..."

"Smoke cigars?" Stella suggested, a playful tone creeping into her voice.

"It's not funny," Nina said.

"No, I suppose not," Stella said, but she was still smiling.

"I just wanted you to know it wasn't what you think. I want to help you. But we have to concentrate on what's important. We can't get distracted from what's important."

Stella leaned back and closed her eyes.

"So I was thinking we should just forget what happened last night. Just be friends."

"Okay," Stella replied.

"All right," Nina said, trying to sound final. She would ignore any remnants of the ache she'd felt yesterday. She would squash any pathetic adoration, look condescendingly upon the miserable part of herself who was as bad as any Iowa schoolgirl or pimpled adolescent boy. And that was that. Most of all, she would forget she'd *seen* Stella. It was a brief glimpse into unknown territory, probably best left unexplored.

Chapter
Twenty-Nine

With Or Without Evidence

SOON AFTER THE Ohio trip, production resumed on *The Right Man*. That same spring, a congressman sent a Mr. Jackson to Hollywood to investigate its morals. Although Mr. Jackson went back to Washington without hard evidence, hard evidence was not required to taint reputations.

Hollywood, let's face it, was not a place built solidly on a foundation of moral values. That spring, Judy Garland attempted suicide. Ingrid Bergman ran off to Italy with her Italian director. Not to mention Errol Flynn and Rita Hayworth. But Hollywood understood very well the importance of giving lip service to those values.

In April, May Evans' blackmailing husband, Jason Noland, called a press conference at the Beverly Wilshire Hotel to announce his plan: the formation of a Decency Committee, which would define proper values for all of the Hollywood community. A fury of debate ensued. But those who opposed the idea were not in the majority and it was not a time to protest any support of decency too loudly.

A few nights after Jason's announcement, Nina got one of her late-night calls.

"Don't worry. Won't talk your ear off. Just had a little bit of a tip-off for you."

"Shanahan, it's been a while. I'm still mad at you, but I miss you."

"Aw, go on. Now, open your ears."

"They're open."

"As you know, that crumb Jason Noland has as much decency as a wolf with rabies. But Noland's feeling the heat. My employer has been gathering up a real pile of dirt on him. The two-faced palooka figures he'll divert attention. Decency Committee. Ain't that a hoot? Well, if and when he goes down, he might drag whoever he can with him. And that means Hollie."

"What should I do?"

"Just make sure you're protecting your boy. Hey, and make sure your cousin knows. You scheme up something and take it to Elaine. You're real good at plotting together."

"That's a compliment, I suppose."

"Like hell it is. See ya around."

The phone clicked dead. Nina cradled the receiver in her hand. She imagined Shanahan in his shabby apartment on Western Avenue, slumped in a lumpy armchair, playing guardian angel on his very own Decency Committee of one.

The next morning, Nina went straight to Elaine. "Got a minute?"

"For you, always." Elaine carefully closed a folder she'd been perusing and gestured to the chair in front of her desk.

Nina remained standing. "This won't take long."

Elaine's eyes narrowed. "You only stand when there's trouble."

Nina adopted a scandalized look. "Someone once said to me that there's never *trouble*. Only situations. And what do we do with situations?"

Elaine smiled. "You tell me."

Nina told her cousin, without revealing the source, the information Shanahan had conveyed, leaving the details about Jason Noland somewhat vague. About halfway through the revelation, Elaine took up a pencil, which she rapped against the closed file in front of her, tap tapping in a staccato drumbeat. At the end of the sad tale, she shrugged wearily.

"Yes," she said. "Well, this is quite a situation. Let me know when you come up with the resolution." She winked at Nina. "I know you can handle it."

WITH PRODUCTION IN full swing, Nina became absorbed in demanding publicity situations for the next few days, leaving the Jason Noland situation a nagging ache relegated to the back of her mind. Since the shoving incident, Lawrence Wycoff and Stella had become great buddies. They spent their breaks huddled in corners, discussing who knew what with great intensity. Something about Stella had inspired the great thespian to display his highest self. He was even pleasant to Hollie. When the latest fiasco blew, it wasn't Wycoff who detonated. Since her husband's announcement of his Decency Committee and the resulting controversy, May Evans had become unusually jittery. At first, she only missed a few lines. Then she missed an entire afternoon due to a migraine. Six days later, the shooting schedule called for a critical scene, a revealing encounter between the industrialist's wife and Hollie's private eye character.

Nina was on the set that morning. She noticed uneasily that May twitched and shivered through the blocking and first run-through, fleeing to her dressing room while her stand-in worked with the lighting crew. Nina, with the rest of the crew, watched with trepidation as May twitched and shivered back onto the set.

On the first take, May blew her third line. Again on take two. Three, four. Seven takes later, she had not gotten past line six. Dewey Starke was a model of patience. On the eighteenth take, however, he screamed: "Cut! Cut! Cut!" He stalked up to May, who was wringing her hands. "May, May," he crooned. "Just say the lines. Let me get the master shot. We'll worry about the rest later."

May jerked her head in a kind of demented nod. Hollie, who had been flawless in each take, took a step towards May. "May, if there's anything I can do to help..."

May's face crumpled. "Help?" she screeched.

That last line was delivered loud enough to reach the ears of all fifty-three people inside the sound stage. The electricians peered down from their perches on the walkway. The script girl raised her eyes from the script. Cameramen peeked from around their cameras. The second assistant director scratched the bald spot on the top of his head.

Slowly, May gathered together a force so venomous that it had the physical energy of a wind draft. Hollie raised both hands and held them out.

"How long will they protect you?" May shouted at him. "What makes you think you can get away with everything?" She glanced around wildly. "You think my husband is a hypocrite? How many hypocrites are in this room?"

"Let's take a break," Dewey Starke announced.

"Someone ask him what I'm talking about," May Evans shouted, pointing to Hollie.

Hollie's face was unusually pale. He stood, frozen, while May pointed at him. "He thinks he's protected because he such a special star. But he'll see."

Dewey gestured to Phil Perkins, May's makeup man, who rushed up and took her elbow. "It isn't fair, Phil," May said.

"It sure ain't, honey," Phil crooned.

"We're not terrible people. We're just trying to survive."

"Like everybody," Phil said tenderly. "C'mon, let's go to your dressing room and I'll fix you up. Make you all better."

May let herself be led away.

Nina prayed a silent thank you that she hadn't brought any press along that day. She glanced around the sound stage. Fifty-plus individuals. That meant fifty-plus potential gabbers. The probability of complete censorship was probably zilch. At least

May's accusations had been tremendously nebulous. She looked up to find Hollie standing beside her.

"This isn't good," he said.

"That's an understatement."

"We need to do something."

"I'll work on it," Nina promised.

Stella had just appeared on the set. She was conferring with Dewey out of earshot. "I know you will," he said and gestured towards Stella. "So will Stella and I."

"No!" Nina said. "Let me take care of it." She shook a finger at him. "I don't want any more surprises." What she wanted, of course, was control of a crowd of iron-willed people. Fat chance.

A couple of days later, speaking of iron wills, Nina had Dottie Strong on her hands. Nina had arranged for yet another romantic adventure for Hollie and Stella, involving a yacht and an invented cute anniversary of some sort, to be reported to the world in an exclusive by Dottie. Early in the event, Dottie interrupted Nina's publicity babbling to announce: "Look, why don't I just skedaddle and make up some text. I'm wasting my time and all the pictures are in the can." It would have been easy for Dottie to skedaddle. The yacht had never left its moorings at the Los Angeles Yacht Club. All of Hollywood knew that Dottie experienced notorious seasickness and never sailed forth into ocean waters.

"Wait," Stella called over. "You may not want to leave just yet." She and Hollie had been cuddling up on the bow, adorable in matching yachting ensembles.

Nina recognized the look on Stella's face. To make matters worse, Hollie's look was just the same. Dottie was assessing everyone's faces. Nina waited, unable to protest without revealing her ignorance.

"Tell me," Dottie said. "It better be good."

"Oh, it's good," Stella replied. "Better than good."

Nina's heart did a flip-flop.

"Tell me," Dottie repeated, her eyes gleaming.

"Only if you promise to say it's a rumor," Stella warned. "Nothing's set yet."

THE "RUMOR" APPEARED in the next edition of Dottie's column. Elaine called Nina into her office within seconds of receiving her copy. "What is this? Why wasn't I consulted? Nina, did you go over my head? Did you bring this to Aaron?"

"I didn't bring it to anyone," Nina admitted.

A look of revelation grew on Elaine's face. "It was the two of them, wasn't it?"

Nina nodded.

"How can you possibly look so morose?" Elaine cried. "It's wonderful! I want you to start arranging everything as soon as possible."

"I don't know if I can be a part of this," Nina objected.

"Why on earth not?"

"They didn't even consult me."

Elaine shrugged. "Well, we know it's not sex. Excuse me, but I just want to get down to brass tacks, honey. This is big." She squinted at Nina. "Are you sure you weren't part of this?"

"No. They plotted the whole thing themselves."

Elaine pulled a pad from her desk and began jotting down some notes, then handed the pad to Nina.

"Here are some numbers to call for arrangements." She paused. "Maybe you should start thinking a little about your own personal life. I wouldn't be saying this, but I'm family. It wouldn't hurt for you to go on a little date or two yourself."

Nina folded her list of numbers. "I'll take care of it," she said and left without addressing Elaine's comments any further.

Chapter
Thirty

Celebrations

WHEN SHANAHAN QUIT the year before, Walter Bermann replaced him as head planter. Everyone knew Walter was no Shanahan, but no one expected him to be. Walter's blandness was ideal for the changing times. He managed to get a lot communicated without anyone feeling threatened. Walter and Nina had continued to "date" at necessary functions, to their mutual satisfaction. They didn't discuss their personal lives. Walter was discreet and Nina didn't have much of a personal life to discuss. Nina knew Walter lived with a guy who designed sets at MGM. In April, she ran into Walter and his roommate at Barney's Beanery. Barney's had a wood-burned sign on the wall that read "Faggots Keep Out." She was with Murray Lasky. They'd decided to grab a couple of burgers for old time's sake. Walter introduced them to the man he lived with, and then hustled out as fast as he could.

"I like Walter," Nina said. "He's sweet. I can't believe he's related to Aaron."

Murray winked at Nina. "Are you two dating?"

"Oh, no. It's arranged."

"You want cheese on your burger?"

"Double cheese. Bacon and avocado."

"What a gal." Murray gave the waitress their order, and then sighed. "Elaine is the best thing that ever happened in my life. I only wish you could be as happy as me in a love situation."

"Fat chance."

"Why not? In my eyes, you're a real dish. Any man could see that you're hot to trot when you find the right horse." Murray grimaced. "Hey, sorry. I'm just a vulgar dumb son-of-a-gun."

"Don't worry about it." Nina returned to Murray's favorite topic. "Elaine is incredible. She could run the studio, if they let her."

"Elaine could be President, if they'd elect a woman," Murray replied. "Thanks, honey," he said to the waitress, who'd brought two frosted mugs of root beer. He raised his mug. "Here's to my girl." It was a little stomach-turning, how smitten Murray was. Nina clinked mugs with him and took a deep swallow of root beer.

Murray bent in to her. "Between you and me, I'm not liking what I see around here these days. Irwin, he's from the old school and he's stubborn as hell. I don't know how long the boys in New York are gonna let him do things the old ways. Plus, there's the vultures circling around, his executive committee. They're making decisions behind his back. Don't ever repeat that."

Murray clammed up as the waitress arrived with their burgers. When she'd left, he brightened up. "Hey, let's not spoil a good time." He took a huge bite of his burger. After several bites, he set the sloppy burger down and wiped ketchup from his mouth. "Say, what's the scoop with Stella and Hollie getting married? Ain't that carrying things a little too far? Maybe I'm old-fashioned, but I believe there has to be love. Say, there isn't anything going on between them? You know what I mean? It's a funny world. Things change." Murray cleared his throat. Nina watched his face struggle as he collected his thoughts. "Now, I wouldn't be saying what I'm gonna say if we weren't almost like family."

"Murray," Nina interjected, "I know you've been talking to Elaine. Please. I can't hear it again. I *do not* want to discuss my personal life or lack thereof. As you just said, let's not spoil a good time."

"No offense intended."

"No offense taken. Let's just change the subject."

Murray spent the rest of the evening raving about Elaine's attributes and attractions. Nina was glad to get home. She had a lot of planning to do. On May 5th, Dick and Annabelle Preston were to celebrate their twentieth wedding anniversary. At first, Dick wasn't too happy with having his anniversary transformed into a public spectacle, but he'd been getting some heat lately. A few weeks earlier, at a meeting of executives from the major studios, he'd praised freedom of expression and wound up facing some snide comments in Dottie Strong's column. Poppa and Aaron convinced him of the wisdom of some good press for a change.

THE PRESTON ANNIVERSARY celebration took place in the Grand Ballroom of the Beverly Hills Hotel. In a burst of inspiration, Nina crafted the surprise announcement that would cap the evening. Walter Bermann had his planters leak rumors to the press and they all showed up.

Mr. Emmett Preston III was seated at the table of honor with his elegant wife, June. Nina led them to their places, feeling a bit of a shock at meeting Dick's father. He *was* a dead ringer for Lawrence

Wycoff, just as Annabelle had hinted. Mrs. Preston was an aging dyed-blond beauty with porcelain skin, patrician features, and vacant eyes. Dick and Annabelle had been due to arrive much earlier, but there was no sign of them, so Nina reluctantly decided to babysit the elder Prestons for a polite interval.

As soon as they sat, Mr. Preston ordered a scotch on the rocks for himself, a vodka martini for his wife and a ginger ale for Nina. Mr. Preston was in the category of men who didn't believe women existed in their own right; they were simply free-floating appendages to men. He began a venomous tirade against Alger Hiss—to the air, since only women were present. About ten minutes into the lecture, his face took on a look of naked distaste. Nina turned around. Standing behind her were Dick and Annabelle.

"Hello, Father," Dick said.

"Late to your own wedding anniversary."

"It was my fault," Annabelle piped up. "I broke a heel."

Dick's father looked through Annabelle. "Forty-five minutes to change shoes?" he wondered aloud.

"Why don't you sit," Nina chirped diplomatically.

The anniversary couple ordered apple juice for Annabelle, bourbon for him. "My tongue gets too loose when I drink alcohol," Annabelle cheerfully informed the table. "Don't want to let any cats out the bag, do we?" She laughed, and then glanced around at the stony faces. "That was meant to be entertaining," she said. She might as well have been speaking to a party of the deaf. No one spoke for a dreadfully long time. Just let me get through the next few minutes, Nina prayed, and then I'll make my escape. A hand tapped Nina's shoulder. It was Bernard Geller, from *The New York Post*. Bernard was one of Nina's favorite reporters, a pleasantly ugly short guy with bushy eyebrows and a Columbia School of Journalism education.

"Hello, Bernard," Mr. Preston intoned.

"Nice to see you again, sir," Bernard replied. "How's the land deal in Brazil going?"

"Quite well."

Nina had just spotted Stella and Hollie across the room. Stella was wearing a tight, strapless coral pink gown. Hollie had his arm draped over her bare shoulders. They were surrounded by a coterie of hungry press. She had a brief moment of panic, thinking they might be trapped. Then she noticed that Elaine was mingling among the reporters. She brought her attention back to the table, in time to hear Emmett Preston III finishing a thought:

"...no, he was simply not capable."

A waiter brought the elder Preston another scotch, which he

hoisted in the air. "Here's to my son. He was a decent athlete, but he got himself crippled. He graduated near the bottom of his class. He came into my business and lost me half a million in six months. That's my son. Give him an opportunity and he finds a way to squander it."

While his father spoke, Dick Preston drummed his fingers rhythmically on the linen tablecloth, a blank expression on his cultured face. Dick's mother continued to smile her empty smile, gazing pleasantly off into the unfocused distance. Annabelle, God bless her, looked like she was going to protest, until Mr. Preston turned in her direction and flicked his hand, as though shooing a fly. Nina felt a sudden wave of sympathy for Annabelle. With enough silencing, she would no doubt be wearing Dick's mother's vacant stare in twenty years.

Bernard Geller, looking very grave, backed away from the table. "Well, thank you," he said.

"I'm not done yet," Mr. Preston said. "Aren't you taking notes?"

"It's in my head, sir," Bernard replied.

"Write it down," Mr. Preston ordered.

Bernard resisted heroically for several moments, fidgeting.

"Perhaps you want to be reporting in Hackensack, New Jersey?" Mr. Preston said. "I could arrange that in a matter of hours."

Bernard put his pencil to his pad and scribbled.

"My son is a liberal, you know. He sympathizes with reformers and intellectuals who would like to see America become a socialist state. I think he's just trying to defy me with all this treason. Bite the hand that feeds him. His evil father, the capitalist."

Mr. Preston watched Bernard scribble. "Hmmm," he muttered. "Have I left anything out?" He turned to his son. "Son, have I left anything out?"

"Father, you've had your fun," Dick said. "Don't you think that's enough?"

Mr. Preston sighed. "Yes, I think so." He tipped his drink at Nina, coming close to acknowledging her. But she wasn't pleased at his attentions — she was chilled by the look in his eyes. He chuckled in a malevolent way. "I'm a close acquaintance of the publisher of Bernard's newspaper. Bernard will write up a perfectly decent interview. He will tear up what he's written, if he wrote anything at all, which I doubt. He will phone my secretary in the morning, who will provide him with the drivel he'll need." He glanced at Bernard, who was trying very hard to maintain his respectful mask. "Won't you, Bernard?"

"Yes, sir, Mr. Preston."

"Do I detect a bit of hostility in your tone, Bernard?"

"No, sir. Absolutely not."

"Fine. Then have your photographer take his pictures and then you may go."

Nina stood. "I must go as well."

Mr. Preston turned to her, courteous and gracious. "You are a charming young lady. While I do wish you could stay with us for the evening, I understand that duty calls."

Nina performed a curtsy and fled.

Later that evening, she listened to a tribute paid by Emmett Preston to his son and his son's wife on their anniversary. It was the worst mockery in a round of false tributes.

At around 10:30, she was in a quiet corner, preparing for the surprise announcement, when Dick appeared out of nowhere.

"I have something to ask you," he whispered. His hair was mussed, as though he'd been running his hands obsessively through it. "I've lost track of Lance Lewis. I need his address. I have some business dealings I need to discuss with him."

Nina knew Lance had been strictly forbidden to contact Dick or to let Dick know where he was. "I don't have his most current address."

"You can get it," he said.

"Would Lance want you to contact him?"

"Yes, he would. In fact, I'm sure he would be very upset if he knew you withheld this information from me."

"Aaron will blow a gasket if he finds out."

"Aaron?" Dick spat out. "What right does that man have to make judgments? What about Sybil Croft? Look, you were her friend. Aaron was a vindictive monster who bled her career dry because she spurned him twenty years ago. I wouldn't put it past him to have leaked that baby story."

"He wouldn't!"

Dick shrugged. "To be honest, probably not. He wanted her career dead, not her. Anyway, the tattletale could have been anyone. For every secret in this town three people are supposed to know, I assume ten people know and eight of them are going to use it if they can. Anyway, I'm leaving on Wednesday. Get me the address before then."

"I have to go," she said. "We'll be making the announcement in ten minutes."

"Of course. The wonderful announcement." Dick had maneuvered himself so Nina couldn't move from their corner without pushing him aside.

"Lance is the only one who treats me like a human being." Dick looked even less comfortable with his confession than Nina. "Do you think I'm a coward?"

"No more than anyone else."

"Thanks for that much." He stepped out of Nina's way so she could get around him. "You'll get me that address?"

"I'll try," she said.

At 11:00 p.m., Poppa went up to the podium. He cleared his throat and swelled up like a peacock. "Two of my most attractive and talented stars will be joined in matrimony on September 8th. I, as head of Lumina Studios, have asked permission to fund and organize everything, so that the wedding will be the grandest ever seen in Hollywood!" A spotlight trailed across the room. It searched the tables and finally located the couple. Stella and Hollie stood and waved. The crowd broke out in a spontaneous, intoxicated cheer. The intoxication in the room was more than alcohol. It was an intoxication made of romance and glamour and myth. It was a deep drunken infatuation with everything Hollywood stood for. The crowd clapped and whistled with crazed delight. They were falling head over heels once again.

At the very end of the evening, just when Nina thought nothing more could happen, Stella cornered her as the party was breaking up. "I have to talk to you."

"Stella, this isn't the place. We'll be assailed any minute."

"I can't take it anymore," Stella announced.

"Can't take what?" Nina saw a reporter from *Variety* headed their way. "Not now," Nina called to him. "Please, Rudy. I'll call you in the morning."

The reporter tipped his hat and marched away.

"I thought we agreed to be friends," Nina whispered. "Besides, you were the one who..." Nina swallowed hard. "Who pushed *me* away."

"Well, I was wrong."

"It's too late. It's probably always been too late. Or impossible. You know what I mean."

"I can't go through with this wedding without you," Stella said.

Nina's mouth dropped open. "That's it? It's about the wedding?"

"The wedding is a part of the bigger picture. Trust me."

"Trust you." Not a question. Just two words rising from the vacancy where Nina's desires ought to have resided. "I'll do this: I will arrange for you and Hollie to have the most spectacular entry into married life that I can manage."

"And us?" Stella asked, touching Nina's arm.

Nina pulled her arm away. "Let's just get down to business."

"I'm doing this for all of *us*," Stella insisted. "Be fair."

"*You* be fair," Nina said, her voice rising. She glanced around at a few curious eyes. "Think what *I* must feel."

The instant she said it, Nina wished she hadn't. She could feel her protective shell slipping. She could feel the hurt and apprehension where an addled romantic joy like Murray's should have been.

"I know, honey," Stella said. "This is all I can say. We're a great team, the three of us. We can do anything. Let's get this thing done."

And then what? Nina didn't ask. She was exhausted by it all. She nodded her okay. Just in time. Another pushy reporter waving a pen was barreling their way and she didn't have the fortitude to wave him away.

Chapter
Thirty-One

The Nature Of Revision

THAT SUMMER OF 1950, America headed into war in Korea. At home, Reds were everywhere. At Lumina, production of *The Right Man* dragged along, nagged with problems. Cast members caught cold, crewmembers sprained ankles, and May Evans had her breakdowns. The front office kept calling for rewrites.

As things got worse, Dewey Starke adopted the tranquil demeanor of a Zen master. He bore the calamities with an air of detachment, adjusting schedules to meet adversity, reshooting objectionable scenes, placating nervous producers. Shooting wrapped in early June, far behind schedule. With an enormous sigh of relief on everyone's part, the project went into postproduction.

Then, the worst happened. *Red Channels* came out. The index, put out by a group of ex-FBI agents, listed 157 writers, actors, singers, dancers, producers, and radio and television executives with "dubious" political associations. On that list were Ben and Cookie Heller. Poppa was livid. The Hellers had three scripts in development, including a potential sequel to *The Right Man*. Poor Ben and Cookie protested their innocence, but once accused, there seemed to be no possible return to virtue. Redemption came only in the form of repentance, and repentance came in the form of naming collaborators. The Hellers refused.

On June 29th, the remaining eight of the Hollywood Ten who had resisted the House UnAmerican Activities Committee were convicted of contempt of Congress. The Hellers began to hear odd sounds on their phone lines. Men in dark suits followed them to the grocery. Friends suddenly found excuses to not attend their parties.

On July 27th, the Hellers left for London to work on a production of their Broadway hit, *Ain't That The Life?* They wouldn't return to America for twenty-two years.

Chapter
Thirty-Two

Wedding Bells

THE RIGHT MAN was scheduled for premiere on September 20th, twelve days after Hollie and Stella's wedding, two days after they returned from their honeymoon. Postproduction finished in mid-August; they scheduled previews in the latter half of August in Pasadena and Thousand Oaks.

Once editing was nearly complete, Dick and Annabelle were packed off on a Caribbean cruise, conveniently arranged to have them miss the previews. Dick didn't want to miss the previews. At last, audiences would see his fictional evil patriarch brought to justice. But pressure was applied to get Dick out of everyone's hair. The Prestons set sail, reluctantly, on August 15th.

On August 18th, the day before the preview in Thousand Oaks, Elaine came rushing up to Nina's desk, newspaper in hand. She held up the front page. "Oh my God, have you seen this? Julius and Ethel Rosenberg have been indicted for espionage."

"It's terrible," Nina replied.

"It's a tragedy," Elaine wailed. "Do you know what this means for *The Right Man*?"

Nina scanned the newspaper. "Uh oh," she said.

THE RESULTS WERE the same, in Thousand Oaks and Pasadena and Reseda, too. Preview audiences loved the detective team of Hollie and Stella, but they hated the mystery subplot. They despised the son accused of murder. That young man had stolen company papers; his father was the president of the company. The nation's Oedipal doubts were stirred, their fear was rising. Was nothing sacred? Even young couples with children were capable of the darkest acts of spying. Who could sympathize with any form of stealing or espionage? New writers were hustled in to doctor the Hellers' masterpiece. The actors were pulled back, including a fuming and vocal Lawrence Wycoff. When all the reworking was done, the subplot told the story of a weak young man who steals company papers, then murders his accuser despite the attempts of his upstanding father, the company president, to rescue him from ruin.

Poor Dick. In the finished film, the father came out on top once again.

Due to all the changes, the date of the premiere was pushed to November. There seemed to be no reason to postpone the wedding, however. They plunged ahead, knowing they could milk a few months worth of publicity from the early-married-life inventions.

With a troubling volcanic energy, Nina threw herself into the wedding preparations.

One of the team's biggest tasks was to find a new home for the couple. Hollie and Stella wouldn't stand for the usual Mediterranean villa or faux-Colonial or English country estate. They wanted something new, something distinctly modern. The house they discovered sat on a two-acre gated estate not far from the Beverly Hills Hotel, off Crescent Drive. It was a dramatic, two-story curved structure of glass and white cement designed by a student of Richard Neutra for an RKO executive who was selling due to divorce.

Hollie and Stella were ecstatic. With Nina tailing them, they went from one stark but glorious room to another, each lit by windows reaching from floor to ceiling. The entire place evoked a sense of futuristic purity, like a blank slate. Nina was in a bad mood that day. She had been dealing with the realtor, a woman named Annette Sharpe, who had the outer personality of nun and the inner soul of a black widow spider. At present, Annette was waiting out in the car, probably calculating her percentages.

"We want it," Stella said.

"It's perfect," Hollie added.

"It's expensive," Nina replied sulkily.

"Too expensive?" Stella asked.

"No," Nina admitted. "I'm sure Annette Sharpe will suck the blood from the selling realtor if he and his client get too greedy. Besides, the owner has an ugly divorce to settle. He'll be accommodating."

"Then what's the matter?" Stella asked.

Nina didn't reply.

Stella turned to Hollie. "Honey, would you go downstairs to the basement and check the plumbing?"

"What do I know about plumbing?" Hollie took in Stella's expression. "Okay, okay."

When Hollie disappeared, Stella came over to Nina.

"You don't like this house, do you?"

"Well, it's not what I would choose," Nina said. Then she burst out: "But of course it's not my marriage, is it? And I won't be living here!"

"I asked you to be patient," Stella replied.

"I can't do this." Nina sank onto to the plush white carpeting.

Stella sat beside Nina. "This carpet is thicker than a mattress," she said with wonder. "We'll go to the best designers. We'll hire an army of decorators. Everything new. Not one old thing in the place."

"Everything new," Nina echoed. "What about the two of you? What will you bring? Anything of your past?"

Stella shrugged. "Only what can't be helped." She took Nina's hand. "If you don't like this house, we can find another."

"I didn't say I didn't like it. I said I wouldn't choose it."

"Then find us one you would choose."

"But you want this one."

"I want you to enjoy being here. Because you'll be here a lot."

Nina glanced around the light-filled room. It *was* spectacular.

"Just get us through this wedding," Stella said. "Look at me."

Nina looked into Stella's stern face.

"Forget the past. Just help us create this. You have to be a part of it." Stella broke into a smile. "Besides, you're one to talk. Where's your past?"

Now it was Nina's turn to smile, but it was a weak attempt at best. "I guess it's wrapped up in the same Pandora's box as yours and Hollie's."

The negotiations on the house went smoothly, thanks to Annette and her cunning ways. Nina helped select the furniture and the paintings, everything strikingly modern, lots of chrome and black leather, pale blond Danish teak, giant oil canvasses by the latest artists, a home of well-defined edges and triangulated lines and modern statements. All modern, nothing from the past. Their efforts to quell the past extended into family matters along the way. Stella and Hollie had made it clear that, besides Abbie, neither had relatives they wanted to invite for the blessed event.

A week before the wedding, Nina met with Elaine, Hollie, and Stella on an unused sound stage. An assorted group of individuals began to troop into the building. There were short ones, tall ones, young ones and old. Their entire potential cast was brought in from the northern part of the state and sworn to secrecy, under the threat of never working again, anywhere. In truth, they weren't sure anyone would care enough to blow the whistle anyway. It was all too absurd. So absurd that, besides Elaine, the rest of group was rather giddy, including the crowd of hopefuls.

They'd decided on two grandmothers, one grandfather, five aunts, five uncles, some cousins, and a selection of children—

nephews and nieces or whatever. They'd ruled against parents, killing off all the mothers and fathers, including Stella's false adopted parents. They began with a lineup of grandmothers. Tall ones, short ones, fat and thin.

"I want that one," Hollie said, pointing to an endearing matron in an apron.

"No," Stella insisted, "she's mine. She looks like me."

"Thank you, dearie," the grandmother called over. "Now that's a compliment."

"Then let me have the uncle with the toupee. I'll give you a cousin, one of those little buggers over there in the short pants."

"I think the grandma is worth at least two little buggers," Nina joined in.

"Three buggers," the uncle added. "And this is certainly my own hair." He lifted the toupee on and off his head, causing a burst of laughter.

"It sounds like a deal," Nina cried.

"Honestly, Nina, be serious," Elaine protested. "I expect it from those two. But you? You seem a little giddy."

"Sorry," Nina said, still grinning. "It's just been such a whirlwind." She *was* feeling light-headed.

"Nina's a trooper," Hollie offered. "She's been with us at every step of the way. You'd almost think she was the one getting married."

"Yes, well, we all know how devoted she is to her job," Elaine said.

By the end of the afternoon, they'd worked up two sets of family and walked through some practice encounters with guests and the press. Stella and Hollie had charmed all of their accomplices, who departed with big hugs and loving backward glances. Hollie dashed out right after, late for a last-minute tuxedo fitting, followed by Elaine, late for a meeting. And so, there they were, Stella and Nina, alone in the cavernous sound stage. They headed for the door, their footsteps echoing. They were almost out when Stella halted. Nina took a few more steps, moving as though she wasn't going to stop. Then she slowed and turned.

"Very good," Stella said. "Excellent body language. Excellent expression of doubt. Honey, now you really understand dramatizing."

"I learned by watching you," Nina replied.

"I want you to come on the honeymoon," Stella said.

"Are you kidding? The wedding is in a week. Everything's arranged with Sally." They had assigned Sally Mistral, one of Lumina's best press agents, to chaperone and orchestrate the honeymoon.

"Would I kid about this?" Stella said. "Talk to Elaine. Tell her Hollie and I wouldn't go through with the blasted thing unless you come with us."

"Don't do this to me. I've done everything I could to make this perfect. Don't ask me to tag along. It's more than I can handle." Looking around her, Nina realized they were on the soundstage where they'd first met, that first summer during the filming of *The Threat from Within*. "This is where we met."

"I know." Stella put her arms around Nina. "Can I tell you something? Please don't pull away."

"Tell me," Nina said. It felt nice to be in Stella's arms again.

"I can't imagine life without you. I want you with me all the time."

"I wish it wasn't so hard," Nina said.

"It doesn't have to be as hard as it is," Stella said, taking a strand of Nina's hair in her hand and tucking it behind her ear.

"What does that mean?"

"It means what I said."

Stella's face was so close to Nina's that she could feel Stella's breath against her lips. Stella moved in closer. And then they were kissing, this time in a way that promised no return. When Nina felt Stella's hand reaching for her breast through her thin blouse, she moaned, low in her throat. Just then, something crashed behind them. They jumped apart, turning just in time to see a rat's tail disappearing around a mock wall.

"It's not safe here," Nina said, shivering. "It's not safe anywhere."

"That's true," Stella said, smiling her ironic smile. "But I've never let that stop me."

Chapter
Thirty-Three

An Awakening

IT WAS THE biggest wedding Hollywood had ever seen. The previous May, Louie Mayer had orchestrated a monumental matrimonial extravaganza for Liz Taylor and Nicky Hilton and Poppa wanted to top it. He practically brought Beverly Hills to a standstill. Huge crowds of well-wishers blocked Santa Monica Boulevard and North Camden as a cavalcade of limousines drew up outside All Saints Church. Guests poured inside until the place bulged. Every seat was filled, the overflow stood at the back, hungry with anticipation.

Stella appeared at the sacred moment at the back of the church. A collective sigh rose from among the guests, followed by a reverential silence, from which the thrilling burst of the organ welled, playing the traditional "Wedding March." Flower girls tossed red rose petals from baskets as the procession stepped up the aisle. Poppa led Stella, half a head shorter than the bride, but elegant in his British tuxedo. Stella's gown was a white concoction of lace and satin, demure yet sexy, with a scooped neck and a long trail carried by some of the nephews-for-hire.

Nina sat next to Elaine and Murray in the first row of pews, along with Poppa, Aunt Nettie and the "families." Right behind them, Abbie sat with the Snipes.

The entire ensemble strained in their seats, watching Stella. As she passed, Nina saw her head turn to the pews. *Stella, I'm here.* But Nina couldn't see Stella's face through the veil.

When Stella reached the altar, she lifted her veil. As Hollie appeared, several sobs erupted, the loudest from the phony grandmothers. Hollie looked nervous, handsome and eager. As he walked up the aisle, he and Stella had eyes for only one another. The crowd sighed when he reached her. And then the minister began the vows. Nina, like everyone else, had tears rolling down her cheeks. Despite it all, she couldn't help attending to business. She noted that everything was going exactly as planned. Their sham relatives were doing fine. She prayed they could keep it up in the next, more challenging phase.

Poppa had reserved a huge portion of the Bel Air Hotel for the reception. The revelers arrived in waves to the hotel, forming a snaking trail that crawled though the reception line for hours.

Nina stayed alert, watching for trouble in the form of unfortunate interactions—snatching one of the drunken fake uncles, for example, from Dottie Strong's talons. It wasn't an easy job, and it became increasingly difficult as the late afternoon stretched into early evening and the guests grew increasingly Dionysian. Nina spotted May Evans dancing with Tyrone Power, while her husband Jason was gesturing vehemently to a cluster of men that included Jack Warner and Swifty Lazar. There was so much power and star energy on the premises that faces were looking sunburned.

Stella and Hollie traveled on a ceaseless series of rounds, apparently determined to charm every guest present. Their faces were flushed too, and they clutched one another's hands. Nina had asked Sally Mistral to tail them, she couldn't face doing it herself, but she caught glimpses of the couple as they wove though the throngs. Just before the seating for dinner, a seven-course spectacular, Elaine came up to Nina. "I take it you've made all the arrangements for going with them on the honeymoon?"

"Yes," Nina said, trying to sound nonchalantly exasperated. "Aren't they something else? They absolutely insisted, you know."

Elaine was looked intently at Nina. "I know you'll be smart about this." Then she noticed something over Nina's shoulder. "How on earth did he get in?"

Nina turned and felt an unexpected leap of heart at the sight of her old buddy.

"If Aaron or Poppa sees him, there's going to be an ugly scene," Elaine said. "I'll call the guards, if necessary."

"I'll speak to him," Nina said.

Elaine shrugged. "It'd be a shame to make a scene."

"SHANAHAN," NINA SAID.

"Hi, kid, nice to see ya."

Shanahan didn't look well. His eyes were bloodshot, his delicate skin was splotchy and he'd lost weight. "You must know why I came over," she said.

"To tell me you're glad to see me?"

She was glad to see him, but she was equally annoyed that he'd put her in this position and wasn't going to make it easy for her.

"Why don't you finish your drink and let me walk you out?"

"Don't patronize me," Shanahan snapped. "I'd rather your

cousin sent the goons. Besides, I'm just here like everyone else to have a good time, catch up on old times, and maybe find a fresh angle on things."

"I can't believe what that magazine of yours wrote about Montgomery Clift."

Shanahan drained his glass and motioned to a waiter for another. "We went easy on him."

"Shanahan, I do believe you're really drinking tonight, aren't you?"

"Things have been tough lately."

Two thick-necked men in tight tuxedos had appeared from nowhere and were conferring with Elaine. They lumbered their way towards Nina and Shanahan. Just then, divine intervention came in the form of Stella and Hollie, who swooped in from the milling crowd.

"We were looking for you," Stella said. "My poor grandma's overcome. She's bawling her eyes out in a lawn chair by the pool. I was always her favorite." Stella turned to Nina's companion. "Shanahan."

Shanahan tipped his hat. "Congratulations."

The goons were upon them. They surrounded Shanahan, like a pair of gorilla bookends and grabbed both his elbows.

"What's going on?" Stella asked.

"Say," Hollie added, "you fellows shouldn't be disrupting our blessed event like this, you know."

The big guys looked puzzled.

"Let him go," Stella said.

The two goons released Shanahan and let their muscular arms dangle at their sides.

"Go on, now," Stella said. "Take a hike."

The goons stomped away, looking confused. Stella winked at Shanahan. "Now, be good," she said.

Shanahan didn't return her smile. He looked concerned, sad, and very serious.

"You two are the ones who are gonna hafta to be good. There are some folks in this town who'd like to see you crash." He looked meaningfully at Hollie and tapped his temple. "I'm your ears and eyes. Remember that. I'll keep in touch. But it's your job to stay clean."

"Hollie!" Elaine rushed up. "There's an obnoxious man, very tall and very poorly dressed, at the front entry, claiming to be a cousin of yours named Ralph."

"Black hair and bad teeth?" Hollie looked disconcerted.

"Precisely," Elaine said grimly.

"My mother's side of the family," Hollie said. "I wonder how the hell he ever got here from Rochester?"

"It hardly matters at this stage," Elaine said. "We're fending off curious reporters and he's threatening to make a scene."

"Can't we just let him in?" Nina asked. "Put someone in charge of him and let him drink himself silly?"

"Well," Hollie said quietly, "I wouldn't do that. He knows a lot about me."

Shanahan drained his glass. "Can't stay. Gotta go." He started to walk off, then turned around. "Bet I could convince that cousin of Hollie's to forget the whole damned silly wedding and come have some fun with me. You know how convincing I can be."

"You're a lifesaver," Nina said.

Elaine couldn't bring herself to speak, but she nodded as appreciatively as she could at Shanahan.

"Let me give you some money," Hollie spoke up, reaching into his pocket.

"Forget it," Shanahan said. He stalked away, shaking his head.

"DINNER IS SERVED!"

The dinner itself was something of an anticlimax. The entire wedding party was exhausted. Afterwards, the couple ran through a barrage of rice and clambered into a limo headed straight for the airport. Nina followed in another chauffeured studio car. They were off.

The threesome flew to San Diego, then took a flight to Acapulco. A few enterprising newshounds "discovered" them at the Acapulco airport, all arranged by the studio. The press tailed them to the hotel, where Nina allowed the newlyweds to impart a few words of bliss before she whisked them up to the grand honeymoon suite, on the penthouse floor. A gorgeous bellboy in a gold-buttoned red uniform accompanied them to their room. Hollie made small talk in Spanish with the young man, then tipped him more than generously.

It was a suite of gaudy fantasy, three plush pink and white rooms, a living room and two bedrooms, overflowing with heart-shaped knick-knacks. A tropical forest's worth of exotic flowers filled the air with an overwhelming fragrance. Patio doors opened onto a deck that faced the pulsing sea. On the table next to the couch was a champagne bucket cradling a bottle of Dom Perignon, two crystal glasses and two heart-shaped chocolate truffles. Stella collapsed into an armchair with a sigh, and then waved towards the champagne. "We need another glass."

Hollie called down to room service. In no time, they had three crystal glasses and three chocolate truffles. The delivery was made by the same gorgeous bellboy, who seemed by now quite taken with Hollie, batting his eyelashes seductively. Hollie wasted no time in opening the bottle, sending the cork flying across the room. They had a toast, then another, but couldn't make it through the bottle before Hollie yawned dramatically.

"I'm beat. Think I'll hit the hay."

There was an awkward pause.

"I guess I could go down to my room," Nina said.

The absurdity of her words didn't warrant comment from either of the other two.

"Goodnight, ladies," Hollie said. "Happy honeymoon."

As soon as Hollie was gone, Stella stood and came over to where Nina was sitting on the couch. Nina had been lying back against the plush pillows. Stella settled next to her. She ran her hand along Nina's cheek. "Do you know how long I've loved you?"

"How long?"

"From the first time I saw you, on the set of that ridiculous movie, when you came in with your cousin, in your college-girl clothes."

"I was so beastly annoying. I still am."

"You're everything I ever wanted. Tell me when you first started loving me."

"I don't know. Maybe in Ohio. Maybe from the beginning. Probably from the beginning. Don't laugh. When I first saw your picture, in the limo coming from the train station. It was odd. It wasn't just, oh this is a beautiful girl. It was the feeling you get when you're about to make a big turn in your life. Only you don't have the slightest clue yet what it's all about."

Stella got up, went to the patio doors and slid them open. A current of ocean air filled the room, salty and warm. Nina closed her eyes and listened to the pounding crash of the waves along the beach. It was so regular, like the earth's organs. Her eyes were still closed when she felt Stella's lips on hers. When she returned Stella's kiss, when she felt Stella's body covering hers, it had the inevitability of the ocean's unceasing force. Stella was holding her, touching her in ways that she would have dreamed about, if she'd ever allowed herself.

"Does that feel good?"

"Yes." Nina sighed.

Stella stopped what she was doing. An interval passed. Nina opened her eyes and found Stella smiling at her.

"Okay, you were right all along. Don't make me say anything more. I don't care. Right this minute, I don't care about anything else but you."

"Hold me," Stella said. Nina pulled her closer.

"I'm not sure...how..." Nina began.

"It doesn't matter," Stella said.

It didn't matter. It all felt good. Stella arched her neck and groaned. Nina stopped what she was doing. Stella lifted her head and looked questioningly at Nina.

"I don't think you're dramatizing now, are you?" Nina said playfully.

"I'll give you dramatizing, if you don't keep doing what you were just doing."

"Let's go to the bedroom," Nina said. "I want to be in a real bed with you."

JUST AT DAWN, Nina slipped from the tangled sheets and went back to the living room. She stood out on the deck and listened to the surf pounding. A coral-colored light was forming on the edge of the ocean. Her head ached, a little from champagne, a lot from astonishment. A sense of wonder, oddly mixed with loss of self — the sensation of having, for the first time, been with another person. She felt full and empty at the same time. She was weak and strong. She could bring to mind what Stella and she had done together and a wave would hit her, as though it were all happening again, a frightening and delicious pulsing.

Suddenly, Nina heard a crash. She jumped, her heart in her throat. She turned just in time to see a shadowy figure sneaking through the living room and out the door. The emerging light of dawn caught up the gold buttons in a burst of pinpoint lights on the uniform of the exiting bellboy. A moment later, Hollie came out from his bedroom in a thick terrycloth robe. He stood beside Nina on the deck. "Not the honeymoon you might have imagined?" he asked.

"Not in my wildest dreams."

Hollie put a strong arm around Nina's shoulder. Nina leaned her head against his chest. "Now you've got a package deal," he said.

"What will become of us?"

"Who knows? We'll just have to keep inventing and hope for the happy ending."

PART FOUR:

LIFE AS USUAL (1954)
DIR. DEWEY STARKE

"Who Says Life Can't Be Nearly Perfect? "
by Lolly Cooper, *Modern Screen,* **November 1953**

In Tinseltown, we create ideal lives on the screen. But does such perfection exist in our real lives? Hardly. But, you ask, what about Stella Kane and Hollace Carter? All right, they're not perfect. But they are the closest thing—nearly perfect!

Hollywood's most beloved couple invited me to observe the preparations for their third anniversary, an intimate dinner at home. No press, no guests, just the lovebirds celebrating one of the sweetest unions around.

In a town where marriages burst apart like seams in a tight dress, the Carters are still as smitten as on their honeymoon night. They admit to a stormy courtship, full of spats and intrigue, but they have now settled down to a glorious and joyous union, defying the cynics who declare that no Hollywood marriage can last happily ever after.

"The only disagreement we've had in the last year came from trying to choose the menu for this special event," Stella confided to me with a jokester's smile. "Hollie is all meat-and-potatoes, while I like French cuisine."

"You mean you actually argued?" I asked, in the same joking manner.

Stella winked at me. "We finally let our staff surprise us. They brought in a chef to whip up something special, but no one will tell us what. Steak-and-potatoes with a French accent, I suppose. You know, Lolly, I love to cook and would have done it myself, but Hollie insisted I be carefree today."

"My wife can prepare a fabulous meal when she

has the time," Hollace added. "But we're both so busy making pictures, we have to compromise. Even I can fry up an omelet if necessary."

See what I mean by nearly perfect? Hollace is truly the man of the house, but bless the real man who isn't afraid to tackle a domestic task when the going gets tough.

By the time I arrived, Chef Francoise had already barred everyone from the kitchen. But judging from the scrumptious odors wafting from behind closed doors, all would be culinary bliss that evening.

Alfred, the butler, led us out to the breathtaking second-story terrace, where we watched Marie, the French maid, setting the table for two. Later, the loving couple would wine and dine under a starry sky. I couldn't help but notice a Tiffany's jewelry box. My heart began to patter in anticipation, although I would be long banished when the candles were lit and the cherished treasure unveiled.

The Carters graced me with yet another exclusive. They led me to the cottage just built for Stella's sister. Having lived away from Stella in a care situation for too long (Stella's sister is deaf), the Carters are making room in their lives for this "new-old" family member, who will arrive in a couple of months, once the couple has finished shooting their latest joint venture, *Life As Usual*.

We returned to the patio by the pool for a delightful buffet prepared in my honor. While we ate, I hinted at the possibilities of other 'new family members' in the near future. The couple blushed, then Hollace spoke for both of them.

"Of course, we'd like to have children and we certainly will one of these days. But right now, we must concentrate on our careers."

"It's only a matter of time," Stella added.

Was it my imagination or did I see a startled look in Hollace's eyes? Perhaps there are bigger surprises than the dinner menu lurking in this household! Of course all of America has been wondering. I couldn't help fantasizing that I would be the first to announce the impending arrival of a little one...

I could tell by their loving glances that the couple was ready to be alone on this special day. But before I left, I decided to test my theory of near-perfection with a few difficult questions.

As Hollace held my car door open and tried to guide me inside, I asked how he felt about seeing his wife make love to another man in Stella's hit biblical epic of last year, *The Story of Ruth*. Were they disappointed in the reception of their sequel to *The Right Man*? Were the couple's hopes for a revival of popularity as a screen couple resting on their latest venture, *Life As Usual*? How did Hollace feel about the flop of his latest solo effort, *Terror Brigade*?

Did it appear that the couple would have liked to see me drive off into the distance with all my questions unanswered? Who knows? After a pause, they answered at least a few of my queries with good humor.

"I would prefer not to see Stella with another man in any situation," Hollie replied. "But I want my wife to succeed and she must do whatever she has to do." He frowned at me with mock severity. "Within limits, of course."

Stella added: "I always ask him when I have to do certain things for a picture. We talk it over. Most importantly, we're thrilled about working together again on *Life As Usual*. We are sure it will be a big hit."

As I drove off, I glanced in the rear view mirror. The couple waved to me, then rushed into their house. Alone at last.

Chapter
Thirty-Four

September 10, 1953
The *Modern Screen* Interview

IN THE THREE years following their honeymoon night, Nina never needed a clock when she spent the night with Stella. An internal alarm rang at dawn. She'd tear herself from bed, throw on a satin robe and stumble down the hall to "her" room, the room assigned to her when she "had" to spend the night, when it was "too late" to go back to her bungalow at 311 Rose Court in West Hollywood. In those three years, there was not one night that Nina and Stella stayed in bed together after the sun rose, although they spent more nights together than apart. The reason? "Just in case."

Their lives paid perpetual homage to parentheses, and the most important was "just in case." Just in case of nosy reporters and other snoops, just in case of the unexpected. "Just in case" was a demon they kept at bay with their cautionary rituals, which included Nina pretending to awaken in her own bed. It wasn't terribly rational, but what voodoo was?

On the morning of September 10, 1953, Nina woke up extra early, at four-thirty, and was slipping from Stella's bed, when she felt Stella pulling her back. Stella kissed her right ear lobe. "Happy Anniversary."

Nina sighed at Stella's nibbling lips. "Happy Anniversary."

"I love you," Stella murmured into her ear.

"I know." Nina lifted up on her elbow and stared at Stella. And people thought she was something on the screen. They should see her in bed, fresh, without make-up or lacquered hair. Nina felt a welling of something like possessive ego. Only she, Nina, knew what Stella was like here, in bed, naked and exposed. Stella was more beautiful, sexier, than people could know. And yet, trying to imagine her in bed was probably what kept her fans so obsessed.

"Don't look at me like that."

"Can't I take pleasure in how exquisite you are?"

"It's when you look at me exactly like everyone else."

"I hope no one looks at you exactly like this," Nina said lightly. "It's impossible not to be affected by your beauty. You know I love you besides that."

"I know."

"Something else is bothering you."

"Today's interview with Lolly Cooper. I don't know if I can take more badgering about babies."

"Other couples are having them," Nina said, with a mocking smile. She was referring to a couple at MGM in another marriage charade. The two had recently managed to conceive, much to Hollywood's voyeuristic delight.

"Nina, you aren't suggesting Hollie and I..."

"Horrors! I was joking!" Nina interjected. "We'll just have to manufacture more boring excuses. We need Lolly Cooper right now. *Modern Screen* is still putting you two on their cover, which is more than we can say for the rest of the magazines."

The past three years had been a roller-coaster. The film industry was shaken by declining profits, by the threat of television, by the fears that were driving campaigns for conformity. After the success of *The Right Man*, its sequel was rushed out with haphazard editing and met lukewarm reviews and middling box-office. In a burst of alarm, Stella had been assigned to a ridiculous biblical epic and Hollie to an even more ridiculous war movie. Stella, it became apparent, could appear in anything. She was as captivating as ever in the biblical stinker, despite the phony get-ups and silly wig. Hollie, on the other hand, needed security to shine. Both he and his war movie had taken a direct hit from the public. When the *Life As Usual* script was offered to Stella, no mention was made of Hollie. It was Nina who went to Elaine and Elaine who performed her magical manipulations and secured Hollie the part. But Nina didn't want to dwell on situations. Not with Stella stroking her belly, just below her navel. Nina shuddered with pleasure. "I guess I can stay a little longer."

"I like to hear that," Stella whispered, rolling up and over, until she was lying on top of Nina.

And then there was no thinking and no demons. No parentheses. Only something so concentrated and private and extraordinary that all the roller-coaster falls and recoveries were peanuts in comparison. This was, Nina suspected, either an enormous gift or an addiction. Either way, she couldn't imagine life without it.

At five-thirty, she crept from the bed, still wobbly and tingling. She was making her way down the darkened hallway, when a shadowy figure appeared at the stairwell. She jumped and cried, "Oh!"

"It's me," Hollie said, stepping into the dim light of a small lamp that burned on a nightstand in the middle of the hall.

"Just coming in?"

"It was perfectly safe."

"I didn't mean to sound recriminatory," she replied. "I'm just tense about the interview."

"Don't be tense. Lolly needs her exclusive as much as we need her drivel."

"Have fun tonight?" she asked.

"More fun than a barrel of monkeys."

"I'll bet you monkey around with the best of them."

"I'm a monkey king. Watch me swing." As Nina passed him, Hollie laid a hand on her shoulder. "Happy anniversary, my pal."

Nina touched his hand. "Happy anniversary, buddy."

"You know how fond I am of you."

"Ditto."

Nina made her way to her room, a modern landscape of whites and neutral colors. Huge windows opened to a second-story patio. Dawn lit the room with a fiery orange glow. In this room, she made a point of keeping the drapes open. Only birds could see in the top story of their elegant dwelling, but Stella's room was always kept shuttered. Here, at least, Nina could look out onto the sky and imagine freedom from hiding. She fell into bed and dozed until Marie arrived at eight with coffee, scrambled eggs, toast and the trade papers.

"Alfred got here early," Marie said with conspiratorial cheer. "We studied the notes for today. Good scripting, as usual, Miss."

"I love you, Marie. Alfred, too."

Marie grinned. "The feelings are mutual."

After Sybil's death, Alfred had gone to work for a Paramount executive. The executive and his spouse were rabid Anglophiles. Alfred was a proud man, but he had a sick wife and couldn't afford to quit a job, even if it meant working for philistines with nobility complexes. When it came time to hire a staff for the Carter/Kane household, Nina worked out a plan to steal miserable Alfred from the Paramount couple. Marie was even easier. Poppa and Aunt Nettie made a grand show of allowing her to move on to the Carter/Kane household, as a wedding present.

On Alfred and Marie's first day of employment, Nina had awkwardly attempted to outline the need for their discretion, but stopped at their appalled looks.

"Miss Weiss," Alfred said stiffly, "I have only respect and admiration for you, and for Mr. and Mrs. Carter. Your personal lives—" He said those two words with great regret at Nina having forced him to bring up such a topic "—are up to you."

"Same here," Marie affirmed.

THEY WERE STILL making a few last-minute improvements to their plans when Lolly Cooper's black Ford coupe pulled up the driveway.

"The press has arrived," Alfred announced. "Everyone in battle position."

"Let me go out and handle this," Nina said. "Are you two ready?"

Hollie grinned. "Ready as ever. And you, honey?"

Stella stroked his arm. "Couldn't be readier, my love."

"Swell," Nina said. "But, remember not too schmaltzy. Lolly's got the corner on schmaltz. She hates competition." Nina gave Stella and Hollie a mock warning frown and dashed from the house.

Lolly was just wrestling her bulk out of the Ford. Yet another new photographer held the door for her. This one, as always, was very good-looking, with dark blond hair and fine, sculpted features. The lumbering writer headed towards Nina, tailed by the handsome photographer. As they got closer, Nina realized the man was older than he appeared from a distance, possibly in his mid to late thirties. His good looks were a bit effeminate. She wondered fleetingly if he "dropped a hairpin," as Hollie would say.

"This is Teddy Scully, my talented new photographer," Lolly announced. "He used to work for the *Newsweek* bureau in Washington D.C., but he got kicked out of town."

Teddy busied himself with his camera, acting as though Lolly was talking about someone else.

"How is it that every last screw-up in the nation winds up here?" Lolly sighed.

Teddy glanced at Lolly with a look of distaste, which she responded to with a satisfied smirk. She turned to Nina. "He was a heroic war correspondent. You know that picture of the three wounded soldiers in the trench outside of Dresden?"

"Everybody knows that picture."

"Never mind," Teddy spoke up. "That's past history. I'm here now."

"Listen," Lolly said, bringing the subject closer to home, "I hope you have something interesting for me. I don't know how many more features we can squeeze out of all this loving couple pap."

"Look this over," Nina said, handing Lolly a briefing sheet, which Lolly scanned, then handed back to Nina.

"More remodeling? We did that two months ago. And six months before that."

"But this is for her *deaf sister* coming home. And how about the anniversary exclusive we're giving you?" Nina cajoled. "Do you know how many phone calls I received about today? I had a crowd of press all hot under the collar, including a certain female columnist whose relationship to you I won't mention." Nina watched Lolly's face grow ugly.

"I've had a helluva week," Lolly said, jowls quivering. "Making two RKO hussies who don't have one brain between them seem like Einstein's cousins. Making Ava Gardner seem like something besides a tramp. Making some producer's trashy starlet with not enough class to sell hosiery seem like Audrey Hepburn. Do I have to define what I'm trying to make it seem like here?"

"Holy smoke," Teddy Scully breathed out.

As quickly as she boiled, Lolly cooled down. "Look, I *like* you all. Just give me something to work with. You know I'm going to have to nag you about little brats again."

"You know what the answer will be."

Lolly groaned. "I have a migraine."

When they arrived at the house, Stella and Hollie were posing in the foyer, their arms entwined around each other's waists.

"Welcome!" Hollie called.

Lolly rolled her eyes.

Stella squeezed her arm tighter around Hollie's waist. "Sweetheart, I think we should repeat what we were just saying about how happy we are to be giving Lolly the exclusive on our preparations."

"Oh, yes," Hollie said. "We thought only of you."

"I was just telling Nina," Lolly piped up, "how proud I am not only to be here, but how anxious I am for you to tell me every little secret about your marriage."

Just then Teddy Scully, who had gone back to the car for some equipment, appeared in the doorway. Hollie's jaw dropped at least a mile when he caught sight of the photographer.

"Are you all right?" Lolly asked, glancing from Hollie to Teddy, her eyes narrowing.

"Sorry," Hollie said, trying to compose his features.

"This is Teddy Scully, Lolly's new photographer," Nina said.

"Very pleased," Hollie said, with a light in his eyes. "You look almost exactly like someone I used to know. Like his twin."

"Maybe we should get started," Nina said, trying not to sound uneasy.

They started on the terrace, where Marie was setting the table for two. They'd gone all out on that one. The best china, the best crystal. A wrapped Tiffany's jewelry box that contained nothing. Meanwhile, Lolly badgered Hollie and Stella about children, about Hollie's age, about his recent lukewarm reception at the box office in the two films he'd made without Stella, and anything else she could nick at with her journalistic pick ax.

As they headed down the path to the nearly finished cottage, Lolly, Stella and Nina held the lead. Hollie and Teddy hung back, chatting intimately.

"Those two have certainly hit it off, haven't they?" Lolly commented.

"Say," Stella said, taking Lolly's arm, "Nina tells me you'd love some intimate details about the marriage. Let's get at some details while the boys are distracted."

Lolly eyes lit up. "Suit yourself."

"I thought you might like to know who lies on top," Stella announced. "I do. I like to dominate. *Now* does that fry your eggs?"

Nina blanched. Stella grinned.

Lolly's jaw dropped, then she roared: "Ha, ha, ha. Oh, honey, I appreciate you." She took Stella's arm. "What I wouldn't give to lay that line on my little readers. Can I hint at it?"

"Real good way to get your editors and the studio execs all burned up."

Lolly sighed. "Ain't that the ugly truth?"

After a tour of the cottage, they headed back to the pool for brunch. As had been the case all morning, Hollie and Teddy hung back, engrossed in private conversation. Stella, Lolly, and Nina were nearly to the patio by the pool when they realized they'd lost the two men. "Now where could they have gone off to?" Lolly asked coyly.

"Maybe they went to see Hollie's gun collection in the pool house," Stella said.

"Let's not wait," Nina said. "I'm starving."

Nina led Lolly to the buffet. Perhaps ten minutes later, Hollie and the photographer reappeared, looking sheepish.

"Were you showing Teddy your rifles?" Stella called to Hollie.

Nina gave Stella her 'stop-that' look. Lolly was absorbed in a heaping plate of food. She looked up.

"As a matter of fact, Teddy is a gun enthusiast, too," Hollie said.

"I'll bet he is," Lolly snapped. "He's going to have to learn to explore his hobbies on his own time."

"Sorry," Teddy said tonelessly.

Lolly shrugged. "I hope you got some good pictures out of it. Ha ha."

At nearly two o'clock they managed to get rid of Lolly and her photographer. Teddy and Hollie exchanged sweet smiles, while Lolly watched with her eagle eyes. Nina felt a nervous twinge in her stomach as she headed Lolly back to the Ford.

Just as she was about to pull away, Lolly leaned out the

driver's side window. "It's young people the movies are playing to these days. I'm getting letters every day begging for stories on Sandra Dee, Tony Curtis, Debbie Reynolds. Old-timers are fighting an uphill battle. I shouldn't have to be telling you this. Look at Montgomery Clift. Elizabeth Taylor. Robert Mitchum, that's the kicker. A little *scandal* goes a long, long ways in this town. See what you can do, why don't you?"

I am delighted to report that the latest Stella Kane/Hollace Carter pairing restores the magic of their screen presence as a couple. The script of Life As Usual (credited to an unknown named Abraham Persons) is a shameless but delightful theft of a 1945 hit called Christmas in Connecticut. Actually, it's an improvement on the Barbara Stanwyck vehicle, which entranced audiences with the zany complications of Stanwyck pretending to be the perfect wife. In this version, Stella Kane plays the pretender as though she had been pretending all of her life. She's perfect in the role, as is Carter.

Stella plays a supposedly perfect homemaker/ columnist living with ideal husband and infant in a country home in Vermont, while she is in actuality a thoroughly independent single gal reporter living in Manhattan. When the head of the publishing company that runs her magazine invites a handsome Korean War hero to Easter dinner at the nonexistent homestead, the desperate columnist must come up with an instant home life on a hastily rented Vermont estate, complete with fabricated husband (played in an overwrought manner by Brad Black) and borrowed infant. What results are a host of complications, both hilarious and implausible, but the film sets us up to not care. It belongs in the category of romantic absurdist comedy, in which our goodwill is captured and we agree not to question too much. An entertaining piece of sharp-witted whimsy.

—Herbert Maximillian. Review. The New Yorker, May 20, 1954

Chapter
Thirty-Five

Creating Life As Usual

LIFE AS USUAL started shooting in early October and was set to wrap by the end of November. From the first, there were complications. Among other things, Hollie was in love. One Sunday, early into production, he and Nina were having a late breakfast together at the estate. They were both nursing colds. Stella, who was never sick, had gone alone to yet another critical brunch hosted by Aaron Bermann's wife. Alfred and Marie had the day off, so Hollie and Nina cooked together. Buttermilk waffles, ripe raspberries and maple syrup, freshly squeezed grapefruit juice and coffee. Their appetites seemed to be unaffected by their sudden illness.

That morning, Hollie showed Nina a faded photograph of a golden-haired boy on a golf course. She was shocked. Teddy Scully, Lolly's photographer, really could've been the twin of Paul, Hollie's first love.

"Paul's grandfather was an international banker. Teddy's grandfather was a railroad robber baron. Teddy's been around the world three times," Hollie informed Nina. "He's the smartest guy I've ever been around, except Paul."

"You like him a lot, don't you?"

"More than I've allowed myself, since Paul."

"What happened in Washington, D.C.? Why did Teddy leave his last job?"

Hollie shrugged. "Won't tell me. He really doesn't seem to care. Paul was like that, too. He didn't worry about things."

"Things don't seem so catastrophic when you have a trust fund."

"Well, it's not money that prevents fretting," Hollie said. "Look at Dick Preston. Look at you, for that matter." Hollie cleared his throat. "I learned how to impersonate that sitting-on-a-throne attitude. I do a good job."

"A first-rate job."

"It's exhausting." Hollie paused. "I hear rumors."

"It'll be fine," Nina said. But she knew otherwise. Lately, Aaron had been rumbling about Stella going out on her own. He had even made a few "jokes" about divorce.

Hollie seemed to read her mind. "Is there anything I should know? About divorce, for instance?"

"No," she said. Nina silently reviewed Aaron's little jokes. He rarely said anything that didn't carry implications. But his agendas were complicated. Oh, brother. Everything was complicated.

"I know you'll work this out like you always do," Hollie said, a little shakily. "Stella and I can't get a divorce. I'd lose you, too. I'd be doubly heartbroken."

"Don't worry." Nina sipped her coffee. "Perfect."

Hollie took a sip from his coffee cup. "Speaking of matrimonial issues, the gossip-mongers are up in arms about your cousin Elaine and Murray Lasky. Seems as though things are getting serious."

"With Elaine, I don't believe a thing until I've heard it from her lips, and even then—" Nina shrugged. "Elaine will fill me in when Elaine wants to fill me in. No sooner."

Elaine filled Nina in a few days later. Nina arrived at work to find Elaine preparing to flee. "We'll be back in an hour."

"I needed a look-over on some copy from you," Nina protested.

"Shake a leg. We'll go over your masterpiece in the car."

Pampered Paws was on South El Camino. The cousins screeched down Wilshire in Elaine's newest convertible, a red Cadillac. Nina read her press release out loud. She'd prepared a story about Brad Black's return to Hollywood, based as always on wishful thinking. Brad had a major role in *Life As Usual*. She'd tried to get the actor to add some content to the tale, but he had been tight-lipped about his East Coast adventures. "Just make it up like you guys always do."

"Wonderful, as usual," Elaine commented, when Nina finished reading. "Brad took up method acting in New York. I hate when that happens. Now he's back to make money, complete with a terrible attitude."

They finished up their discussion of the Brad Black issue and were briefly silent. Elaine broke the silence with a somewhat cryptic outburst. "Thirty-one years old!"

"You," Nina said.

"Yes, me. Fifty years ago, I'd have been considered a spinster. I'd be knitting booties for other people's brats. Even now, people are funny about unmarried women my age."

Nina couldn't imagine Elaine knitting booties for anyone. Elaine smiled at the look on Nina's face. "I don't even know which end is up on a knitting needle," she said with a mock grimace.

"The pointy side," Nina replied.

"That makes sense." Elaine's expression grew serious. "How would you like to go to New York? Howard Stein, the head of the New York headquarters, is retiring," Elaine said, breaking into Nina's thoughts. "I want you to be my representative at his going-away party."

"What's the catch?" Nina asked.

"You're so suspicious."

"What's the catch?"

"It's only a matter of time for Poppa, we all know that. He's practically a figurehead already and New York has been itching for a change. Who would they choose?"

"Well, there's Aaron, there's Dick Preston, there's maybe someone from the outside, and of course there's Murray." In a surprising move, Murray had recently been promoted to executive producer of the B-division, replacing Sam Saperstein, who had had an unfortunate nervous breakdown and was recuperating at a spa in Palm Springs.

"And if you had to rank them?" Elaine asked.

"Aaron first." An answer neither one of them was particularly pleased with.

"Now Dick Preston, he's a remote possibility," Elaine ruminated. "You know, he's been going off to New York quite a bit lately. I will be just livid if he's playing footsie with the corporate executives."

Nina knew who Dick was playing footsie with, since she had provided Dick with Lance Lewis's address. She turned her head and peered out the window to avoid Elaine's scrutiny.

"In any case, who has absolutely the least chance?" Elaine asked.

"Murray," Nina said.

"I would have to agree," Elaine replied. "Aaron has become a power-hungry nuisance. He knows where he stands in the rankings. Do you know what kind of maneuvers I have to go through to get around him?" Elaine paused abruptly and tightened her lips. Nina suspected that Elaine had just realized she was revealing a deeper level of manipulation than her cousin normally acknowledged.

"What's the point of me going to New York?" Nina asked.

"You're so good at getting people to talk. Sometimes the most valuable tidbits are the rumors floating around."

"What will tidbits buy you?" Nina persisted.

"Time," Elaine replied. "I want a sense of how much time I have."

"Time for what?" Nina asked.

"Ah, here we are. Look, a miracle! A space right in front!" Elaine veered the Cadillac into the vacant spot at the curb, just outside a shop front guarded by two bronze borzoi. "I'll be right out," she said.

Nina was still pondering her situation when Elaine exited the salon holding two silver leashes anchored by Collette and Valentino, the ugly mutt stolen from Kubicek. Hopping jauntily along on three legs, a blue bow on his head, his wiry hair scrubbed to something resembling spun silk, Valentino glowed. "Isn't he gorgeous?" Elaine cooed, as Valentino jumped into the back seat, apparently as pleased as Elaine with his remarkable makeover, completely unashamed of the bow clipped to his scalp. He yapped at Nina proudly, his stumpy tail wagging. He felt beautiful.

"I told Murray that I absolutely could not live with that creature in his sordid condition," Elaine explained.

"So, I take it you're contemplating an end to spinsterdom?" Nina said. "Soon?"

"Soon enough. After some of these ugly studio details are worked out." Elaine put the car into drive and pulled out from the curb. "I'll start making the arrangements for your trip. It's the beginning of November. You can make plans accordingly."

Chapter
Thirty-Six

A Well-placed Boot

BY THE MIDDLE of October, Teddy Scully had become a fixture in the Carter/Kane household. He was not a diplomatic presence. As he came to spend more time in their house, Teddy nagged them about their lifestyles and their elitist philosophies, all the while enjoying the fruits of their "duplicity" and "crassness."

One evening, after a particularly long day's shoot, the trio was poolside, eating a picnic dinner that Alfred had prepared earlier. It was an unusually warm, unsettled night. Even the calls of the night birds in the trees sounded restless. The sun had recently set and the moon was rising very large on the horizon. The pool's submerged lights lit the water with an eerie aqua-colored glow. They had nearly finished eating when Teddy emerged from the shadows.

"How did you get in?" Nina asked.

"Hollie gave me keys." Teddy glanced with exaggerated interest at the picnic spread.

"Are you hungry?" Hollie called over. "Use my plate. Help yourself."

Teddy dug in, filling Hollie's plate. He settled on a lounge chair and announced, "I quit *Modern Screen* today," then took a bite from a fried chicken drumstick.

"Did something happen?" Hollie asked.

"Some moron called me a homo."

The color drained completely from Hollie's face.

Teddy reached over and clapped Hollie on the knee. "Just joking. I just got tired of that witch Lolly and bored with the whole thing. I'll pick up another job."

"Sounds damned easy," Stella commented. She had a certain tone she used with Teddy, an indulgent impatience. Teddy was oblivious to Stella's attractions. Nina wondered if Stella got some odd satisfaction out of this that granted Teddy a little leeway despite his overall arrogance.

"Everything is easy, when you have the right attitude." Teddy pointed an accusing finger at Hollie. "You almost fainted at that little joke about why I got fired. I'm so sick of this crap about homos. Some day we'll be able to be ourselves."

"It will always be this way," Hollie said. "This is one thing people won't accept."

"What do you think?" Teddy inquired, turning in Nina's direction. Teddy liked to needle her, which she didn't appreciate.

"It's probably better to tell the truth. But there are always circumstances..." Nina faltered. She was tired. It had been a long, hard day. The last thing she wanted was to be a new Joan of Arc for societal change.

"A woman of conviction," Teddy drawled with biting wit.

"I don't see you hanging from any crosses in a loincloth," Stella interjected.

"I did that once already." Teddy helped himself to a pickle. "Did you know there's a group called the Mattachine Society, for homosexuals? There's a central headquarters, right here in Los Angeles. And a magazine."

Hollie's face was a sadly funny portrait of studied composure. He stretched and yawned. "I'm beat. Gonna hit the hay. Early call tomorrow." He glanced at Teddy.

"Give me a few minutes to finish eating. I'll be right up," Teddy said.

When Hollie had left, Teddy busied himself finishing off every morsel of remaining picnic. Nina never felt she had much to say to Teddy when Hollie wasn't around and Stella didn't seem inclined to speak, so they sat in the sultry darkness and listened to the crickets and the restless birds.

"I scheduled an interview," Nina said finally. "Dottie Strong has been livid ever since we gave the anniversary exclusive to her sister. Could you and Hollie take some time next Thursday with her?" Nina glanced over at Teddy. "I'll tell you the details later."

"Don't worry about me." Teddy jumped up. "I could care less about your little deceptions." He turned and started towards to the house.

"Teddy?" Stella called.

"Miss Kane?" Teddy turned back and bent down from the hips. It was an elegant and aristocratic bow.

Stella, when she trained all of her energy on a person, was formidable. Even Teddy seemed to waiver in his cockiness.

"Don't rock the boat," Stella said.

Teddy looked at Stella's face. "*D'accord, Mademoiselle*," he said and walked up the path.

Stella glanced at Nina mischievously. "Got to keep those boys in their place."

"You don't think he'd do anything rash?"

"He better not or I'll whip his hide." Stella stood, holding her hand out to Nina. Nina took it and rose. They embraced briefly in the light of the full moon. Just as quickly, Nina pulled away. You never knew who might be watching. "It isn't possible, is it? What Teddy said. That someday we might be able to just be ourselves."

"We're sitting pretty right now, don't you think?" Stella said.

"Yes. But—"

Stella placed a finger on Nina's lips. "This is what our life is."

"I worry."

"Of course you do."

"I get tired of worrying."

"Tired enough to go to New York and not come back?"

Stella's tone was light, but Nina knew her better than anybody did, even if her actress was still a mystery a lot of the time. "I didn't say anything about leaving you."

"It's not the words."

"When I left the first time, you told me I was coming back when I didn't even know. Now I'm telling *you* I *am* coming back."

"It wasn't the words then, it isn't the words now."

"I don't have any secret plans, I'm too exhausted to have any. Let's go to bed."

AFTER HE BECAME unemployed, Teddy didn't jump into another job. Instead, he took to visiting Hollie at the studio. Two or three times a week at first, then sometimes four. He would arrive on the set in the late morning and watch whatever was going on. Afterwards, he and Hollie would indulge in a private little lunch session in Hollie's dressing room. It wasn't uncommon. If you were a big enough star, you could get away with all sorts of hanky-panky on the lot, as long as you remained reasonably discreet.

Up until Teddy's visits, all the crew had always loved Hollie, including the burliest grips, carpenters and teamsters. But Teddy was too pretty. He stood too close to Hollie when they talked. Some felt compelled by this blatant challenge to whisper comments among themselves, smirking. A nerve-wracking day on the set seemed inevitable. Among other things, Dottie Strong was hanging around. She seemed unusually interested in observing the *Life As Usual* set.

Problems on the set, to make matters worse, were not confined to the Hollie/Teddy situation. How about twenty takes of a scene with Brad Black? Before his stint at the Actor's Studio in New York, Brad had been a comedian. Now, he couldn't act without plumbing the depths of his psyche and he was driving Dewey Starke mad.

Take one of scene thirty-seven:

Brad stops the shooting, upset by the sudden revelation of how far-fetched the script is. "I can't *become* this character, knowing how absurd the plot is."

Dewey, patient and calm: "This is a farce. It's supposed to be absurd. Don't analyze. Just be funny!"

Between takes, Nina had to endure Dottie Strong's questions about Brad's recent conversion.

At ten, Teddy arrived. Dottie's eyes lit up. She motioned for Teddy to join them. Nina's heart did a flip-flop. Please let him keep his promise about keeping secrets, she prayed. As it turned out, Dottie was a fan of Teddy's. She quizzed him about his war-correspondent days with perhaps the most respectful tone Nina had ever heard Dottie use. The takes continued. On take eighteen, uncharacteristically, Stella blew her lines before Brad had a chance. On take nineteen, an apprentice electrician knocked over a C-stand. By take twenty, Brad Black appeared to be coming undone. His makeup girl dabbed at the pools of sweat on his face. His eyes were wild. His hands jerked. The actors took their place, the crew readied the equipment.

"Action!" Dewey called.

Brad threw himself into the moment. His frenzy grew wilder. Everyone on the set watched the scene with suppressed laughter. Brad jerked around the set, improvising brilliantly. It was very funny. Then, in a frantic thrust of his fist, Brad Black popped Hollie right in the nose, good and hard. Hollie staggered back. He clutched his face as blood spurted from his nostrils. He sank to the floor.

The entire populace froze. The first to react was Teddy Scully, the man who had climbed into trenches lined with wounded soldiers. He ran onto the set, pulling a handkerchief from his pants pocket. In minutes, Teddy had Hollie on a set couch, head back to stop the bleeding. The studio doctor arrived, but Teddy insisted on staying at Hollie's side. He touched Hollie's cheek. It wasn't a terribly overt gesture, but it was enough. Everyone in that sound stage took note, including Dottie Strong.

NINA HAD LUNCH with Dewey the next day, at his request. They sat along the west wall, served by Irma.

"You know what was wrong with the *Right Man* sequel?" Irma said, handing them the menus.

"A script rewritten by imbeciles. Murdered by imbeciles," Dewey replied. "I wasn't directing. I was embalming."

Irma pointed an accusing finger at Dewey. "I hope you're not losing your fight. I'm seeing too much of that around here. Aleck

Bell making a Roman chariot movie with bleach-blond actresses that look like show girls! Neil Tremon, who directed me in *The American Dream* – that old bum should know better. Directing a musical with no plot!"

"I am not losing one stitch of fight," Dewey said.

"Good," Irma replied.

"I could show you the script I'm doing now," he offered.

"I don't look at scripts," Irma said. "The beef goulash is good today."

"I'll have that," Nina said.

"A salad with Italian dressing and a glass of club soda," Dewey said.

Irma took their menus. "But if someone were to leave a copy behind, I'm sure it could be returned to the person who lost it after a few days. And who knows what kind of comments a person might find written on it." When she had gone, Dewey turned his attention to Nina.

"What am I even fighting for?" He smiled at Nina's startled look. "I shouldn't be asking you that question. You've settled in quite nicely here. Perhaps you think things are just fine."

"Well, yes and no."

Dewey patted Nina's hand. "I've made you uncomfortable."

"It's just that I'm finding things a bit complicated these days. Sometimes I wake up at night and realize I've been hatching schemes in my sleep."

Dewey sighed. "The dreaming mind and its wily ways."

Irma brought a club soda and an iced tea.

"It's the human condition," Dewey announced. "With the ability to perceive time came the curse of scheming. Why?"

Nina took a sip of her tea. "Maybe for its own sake."

"For its own sake, of course!" Dewey's voice rose so loud that the adjoining tables glanced their way. Once the others realized it was a director, however, they turned away, uninterested.

"Is there a reason?" Nina asked. "Aren't we mesmerized by complications for their own sake?"

"Oh, my dear, you are wonderful," Dewey said. "The audience glorifies in absurdity. As long as their passions are aroused! The passions for complications and intrigue. It's just human nature. Oh, my dear, I have it now!"

He jumped up. "I must go and prepare the next scene based on your brilliance."

Irma arrived shortly with the salad and goulash.

"Leave everything," Nina said. "I'll eat some of his." She wound up eating a good deal of what had been delivered. Nothing like intrigue to work up an appetite. When Nina got up to leave, she made sure to leave the script that Dewey had "forgotten" on the table.

At the end of that day, Nina was walking down the sidewalk outside the publicity office when she heard someone clattering up behind her. "You got a minute?"

"As many minutes as you need."

"Let's go sit somewhere quiet," Walter Bermann said. They found a private bench in the little park between the Markham building and the commissary.

"Can I level with you?" Walter Bermann asked. "It's an awful sticky situation."

"So what else is new?"

"You know, I miss going out with you. You've seen me escorting Sally Witherspoon around? The girl is not much of a conversationalist."

"Oh, Walter. It's just—"

"It's just that you don't trust me. I don't blame you. That's why I'm approaching you."

"My ears are open."

"Look, you know everybody wants everybody to be happy, especially if they're doing their jobs and making the studio a lot of money."

"Naturally."

"And people can do what they want. If they're—"

"Discreet?"

"Yeah. After all, I'm discreet. You're discreet. You got me?"

"Understood."

"The word is: Teddy Scully is off the lot. The word is, some guy who wants to keep his big star status, he has to keep his nose clean. That means he drops Teddy Scully. Altogether. That edict is being delivered to Hollie right now. I saw him going into Aaron's office. I'm telling you this when I should be minding my own affairs: Uncle Aaron is itching to get Stella off on her own. He's hoping Hollie will ignore the warnings. So you do what you can. Help smooth things out with all the involved parties."

"Done."

"You're a swell gal."

"You're not so bad yourself."

Nina got up to go, but Walter didn't rise. He looked strangely defeated. "Say, you ever hear from Shanahan?"

"Not lately."

"I miss that old boy."

"Me, too."

"Just because I keep my trap shut around Uncle Aaron doesn't mean—" Walter jumped up. "I'm more like Shanahan than you think. I'll do the right thing. I swear to god, I will."

The next day Teddy was not at Lumina. He also stopped coming to the estate.

A week later, Nina found Hollie lying on his chaise lounge, watching the pool boy scoop bugs with a long-handled net. The muscular kid trailed his net over the water, letting the basket glide, carefully lifting the snared bugs from the water. "Stella and I are making eggs. Want some eggs?"

"I'm not hungry. I'm lonely."

"I'm sorry, Hollie."

"Me, too."

"If there's anything I can do."

"Change the world."

"Wish I could."

"Think it's possible?" he asked.

"I'm not sure," she replied.

"Teddy thinks it's possible."

"I kind of miss his ranting and raving," Nina admitted.

"You can imagine how I feel," Hollie said.

"Come in and have eggs."

Hollie shrugged and raised himself from the lounge. "Well, maybe things will change."

"Maybe."

"Or maybe I'll find some other way."

"Hollie?"

"Don't worry," he said, taking Nina's arm. "I'm the last one to rock the boat."

Nina thought back to the Griffith Park incident, but she didn't think it was a good time to bring that up.

During the next week, Hollie was the consummate professional. He was on time, he knew his lines, he made his marks, he was suave and funny in his scenes. Between takes, he circulated among cast and crew. But there was something so sad in his efforts that even the most toughened of the grips and carpenters took to clapping him on the back sympathetically. They went out of their way to make small talk or bring him a cup of coffee. By the end of the week, everyone was in love with him again and he seemed to brighten up. By Saturday, he was almost himself.

That night, as Nina was stumbling down the hall to her guest room in the early morning hours, she encountered Hollie tiptoeing to his room. "Good morning," he whispered, smiling foolishly.

"You look like the cat that ate the canary," she commented.

"I'm no cat. But I'm discovering that there's more than one way to skin one."

"What does that mean?"

"Well, it means that there's more than one way—"

"I understand the cliché."

Hollie grimaced. "I should keep my mouth shut, but I'm used to blabbing to you."

"Blab to me."

"I meant my life doesn't have to be so empty."

"Hollie, you're being obscure."

"That's the name of the game, isn't it?" Hollie bowed. It was a pretty good imitation of Teddy's classy gesture. Good enough to pass on film, not good enough to hide his inner turmoil. Nina decided not to press him.

Chapter
Thirty-Seven

Return Of The Prodigal Son

THE NEXT SUNDAY, Lance Lewis stepped out of a taxi in the driveway of the Carter/Kane estate, carrying a large valise. Nina, who was already awake, answered the door. "Don't look so horrified," he said, stepping in with his bag. "Where's the blissful couple?"

"Asleep."

"Together?"

"Don't be silly."

"I just read that Estelle and Graham Curtis are having a baby. If that's possible, anything is."

"What are you doing here?"

"I have plans." Lance dropped his bag on the white carpeting and whistled. "Is it a house or a museum? That's a Dunbar chair. Edward Wormley's things are so antiseptic. Don't mean to berate anyone's taste."

"I was making coffee when you rang the bell." It *was* nice to see Lance's puckish face again. He was dressed in an expensive beige cashmere suit and an open-necked white linen shirt. He looked very sophisticated and urbane. But New York had aged him. He had the kind of face that would always look adolescent, but now his cheeks were a bit puffy and lined with tiny wrinkles.

As they made their way to the kitchen, Lance offered a running commentary on the decor. "So *au courant*. I myself am partial to antiques, particularly late nineteenth-century European. Although I suppose I could manage, if a client wanted me to decorate this way. I'd kill for the budget."

"What are you babbling about?"

"Honey, pour me some coffee and tell me what I can make us to eat, then I'll elaborate," Lance said, taking off his cashmere jacket and rolling up the sleeves of his shirt. "Do you have an apron?" He concocted a huge Swiss cheese and ham omelet, toasted English muffins, and squeezed orange juice. They shared the feast in the sunroom.

Between bites, Lance elaborated on his acting stints in New York, about the scramble to survive, how by chance he'd begun helping out a friend, an interior designer named Claude Batiste. "He's an awful queen. But people expect that."

"Let's get to the point. Why are you here?"

"You know Billy Haines."

"The decorator who did Joan Crawford's place."

"And?"

"What do you mean?"

"Come on, Nina. I know you know."

William Haines was a retired actor who'd gone on to become one of the busiest decorators in Los Angeles. That was the bare bones of it, but everybody in Hollywood knew about Billy Haines. "His career was fading in the thirties," she said. "Then he got into a fight with Louie Mayer about giving up his boyfriend, Jimmie Shields. He wound up getting fired from MGM. Now that's he's a decorator, he's making out like a bandit and no one seems to care who he sleeps with."

"Unlike me." Lance made a cutting gesture across his throat. "Bye-bye little Lance."

"What's Billy Haines got to do with your return?" she asked.

"Billy is a pal of Claude Batiste's, when they're not hissing and scratching at one another. Look!" A huge dappled butterfly had settled on a potted geranium just outside the patio doors. The sunlight lit its wings with an iridescent glow. "Oh, my god, I love California! I hated New York. Trapped in lousy plays in theaters that smell like mold, in a city that smells like piss. It's horrid and dirty and noisy and the people think they're so special. I had to come back. And Claude just absolutely raved about me to Billy, so Billy found me a job with a friend of his. *Voila*, I'm a journeyman decorator!"

"Congratulations."

"Thank you. Now I have a profession. And I can be closer to Dick. By the way, thank you for giving him my address."

"What about Annabelle?"

"I told you a long time ago, Annabelle is a fixture. That's all right." Lance paused, looking intently at Nina. "But talk about the pot calling the kettle black. You know about making whoopee with married people, don't you? Dick's been filling me in." Lance winked, but his eyes were serious. "I've always liked you. Now we're kin. I understand about you and Stella. If you ever need me, I'm here."

Nina swallowed a lump in her throat. "Thanks."

Lance glanced around. "Where are those two? Are you sure there isn't some kind of hanky-panky going on?"

"Not anything you could be shocked by," said a voice from the doorway. "What the devil are you doing here?"

Lance ran over to Hollie and threw his arms around him. "Oh, how I've missed you."

Hollie patted Lance on the back, and then extricated himself.

"Lance?" It was Stella, sweeping into the kitchen in a gorgeous powder blue satin robe.

"Oh, my God," Lance cried. "You're getting more ravishing all the time. It's almost enough to make a person change his persuasion."

"What a frightening thought," Stella said.

"Let me make you an omelet," Lance offered.

"Actually, I'd like an explanation first," Hollie said.

"All right, all right."

So Nina, Stella and Hollie sat at the kitchen table and watched Lance beat eggs and grate cheese, while he explained how he'd been seeing Dick Preston in New York for the past three years, whenever Dick could get East. Dick knew Billy Haines and between his influence and Claude Batiste's, Lance was California bound, promised a job with Wilson Tolivar, second most popular decorator in Hollywood.

"My first job when I was a teenager was arranging flower bouquets," Lance said. "What else would a little pansy do in Missouri? I got a few black eyes for it. Naturally, it'd make sense to move on to decorating. Isn't it just so classic?"

"And, now, why don't you fill us in on how we fit in to this?" Hollie asked, trying to sound stern, although he was clearly glad to see Lance.

"I heard about that lovely little cottage for Abbie. Aren't you waiting for shooting to wrap up before bringing her here? Isn't that adorable place empty? It's only for a few weeks, until I can save for a place of my own. I won't be any trouble."

True to his word, Lance was a model guest. Within a week, everyone was getting used to having him around. He and Marie arranged flowers together. He helped Alfred polish silver. He moved around furniture until they made him put it all back where it belonged.

Production of *Life As Usual* was moving along nicely, too. Hollie had stopped talking about Teddy. He seemed so content that Nina was suspicious. She decided to ignore it. Let things be easy. They had all been working hard and were looking forward to the end of production. At least, she thought, I can leave for New York knowing things have finally calmed down.

NINA SPENT THE night before the flight with Stella. It wasn't a peaceful evening. She tossed and turned, her mind filled with anticipation. Any feelings of calm were fading, as she mulled over her impending reunion with her father, not to mention her spying assignment. By four a.m., she was cotton-headed. Just before creeping away, she pressed herself against Stella's back. Just then Stella spoke, in a completely alert voice, as though she'd been up for hours. "I don't want you to go."

"I have to go."

Stella rolled over. "I have a hard scene coming up, I need you to be there, but you won't be. At night, I won't feel you curled up next to me in bed. I won't have you to talk to after a hard day."

"You never say things like that."

"I have a bad feeling. My mama's ghost is whispering to me."

"I'm coming back."

But Nina had doubts. And if they existed at all, Stella would know about them. That was Stella. There wasn't any point in protesting any more. But they both understood there was no point in continuing the discussion, either.

NEW YORK WAS New York. Scarsdale was Scarsdale. And Daddy was Daddy. But he was a shrunken version of himself. He was taking the McCarthy hearings very personally.

Was she doing what was right? Nina wished she had a clear sense of what was justified in her situation. The end result of her reunion with her father was a sense of bereavement. She knew she was loved, but the condition of that love was keeping her love life to herself. She did know one person, however, to whom that truth might be revealed.

"I WAS A little surprised you called me," Sue Edelman said.

"Why?" Nina asked.

"It's only been a few years," Sue replied with an ironic smile.

They were at Tavern on the Green. Light poured in from the many-paned windows. Sue Edelman was, if anything, more regal and mesmerizing than ever.

"I've thought about you," Nina said.

"And I of you." Sue hesitated. Then: "You're living alone?"

"Not exactly."

"I see," Sue said. "And how is your actress? She's married to Hollace Carter now."

"Yes. But we're still very close."

"I understand," Sue said.

"I knew you would."

The waiter arrived to refill their wine glasses with a Macon Villages white burgundy that Sue had selected. They waited in silence until he left.

Nina sipped her wine. It was outstanding, of course. "I've thought about you and New York and everything that's wonderful and progressive here."

"You're thinking of coming back, then?"

"Yes. No. I don't know."

Sue smiled. "That certainly takes in all the possibilities." She took a sip of her wine. "A part of me would like to try and convince you. Seeing you again, I'm reminded how much I'm drawn to you." She set her glass down. "I don't have to be so evasive as I was the first time. You're one of us now."

"I'm not one of anything," Nina protested.

Sue raised an eyebrow.

"Yes," Nina said.

Sue's expression infused with a subtle flirtatiousness. "Should I try to make you stay here? The convincing could be fun. We still have to be careful in New York, but I think you'd find it much easier to be yourself. Especially not being attached to such a celebrity as Stella Kane."

"I appreciate your offer."

"But?"

At every mention of Stella's name, Nina melted. If that mention led to thoughts of Stella in bed, of the two of them together in their private world, that was that. Nothing else seemed to matter. Nina felt ashamed, imposing on Sue Edelman to dispel her doubts.

"Under any other circumstances..."

"Let's stick with the present circumstances," Sue interrupted. She took another sip of wine. "Allow me to be disappointed with graciousness. By the way, I ran into some friends of yours in London last week. Ben and Cookie Heller."

"Poor Ben and Cookie."

"I've heard from good sources they wrote the screenplay for the movie you're currently involved with. Under a pseudonym, of course."

"That's top secret."

"I know a lot of top secrets," Sue said. "For instance, I'm a good friend of Howard Stein's daughter, Elizabeth. Your Howard Stein, who runs the parent corporation of Lumina Pictures. Elizabeth and her father have always had a difficult relationship and she's a gossip. Would it be an accurate supposition to assume you're interested in information about your uncle?"

"That would be a very accurate supposition."

"Elizabeth has always felt compelled to discuss her father's business antics with me, matters I find tiresome and crass. Unfortunately, Elizabeth thinks all her gossip is fascinating. Anyway, I would say your uncle should probably consider how to spend his retirement years in the very near future. The New York office is not, shall we say, in support of him."

"How long does he have?"

Sue shrugged. "A year?"

"You really do know everything."

"Almost," Sue said, nodding at Nina's empty plate. "Did you want anything else?"

"Peace of mind."

Sue burst out laughing. "If I could promise you that, I imagine I'd have a better chance of convincing you to stay in New York."

Nina grimaced. "I'm in love with Stella. You're the first person I've ever told that. I'm sorry I'm saying it. I feel terrible."

Sue bent down and pulled a book from her purse. *Invisible Man* by someone named Ralph Ellison. "Read this. It's about complications and hiding." She took up a pen and wrote something on the inside cover. She handed Nina the book. The inscription read:

> *A gift to help you on your journey. You never know what will happen. With very fond regards, Sue Edelman*

When the lunch was finished and they were about to part, Nina felt an unexpected surge of fear. "You won't tell anyone about this conversation?"

"Not a soul. Go now, before I lose my resolve to let you leave easily."

Chapter
Thirty-Eight

Come Back, Little Nina

NINA KNEW STELLA couldn't meet her at the airport, but she'd hoped at least that Elaine would come. Instead, she found one of the studio drivers waiting for her with a limousine. He dropped her off at her place on Rose Court. Sometimes, Nina had to admit, the little bungalow was a comfort, completely her own. That feeling usually lasted only a few hours, however, before she was missing Stella. After unpacking her bags, she fought off the urge to call Stella. It was nearly 3:00 a.m. and Stella would have to be up in just a few hours to get ready for the studio. Instead, she drank a cup of hot tea and fell into bed.

At 4:00 a.m. the phone rang.

"Bet you thought I'd dropped you."

"I did."

"I thought you had a busy enough personal life without me."

"How could you know about my personal life?" It was a ridiculous question. Shanahan knew every personal life in Hollywood.

"Take it easy. Live and let live. You know I mean that. I was just trying to say it seemed like you were getting out of my league and all."

"I guess we were both making groundless assumptions then, weren't we?"

"I got a scoop for you. Regarding Teddy Scully."

Nina's heart leapt in her chest. "What about Teddy?"

"Guy used to be some journalist. Takes after me, though. Likes to get himself in hot water. But even I got my limits. Say, what was Hollie thinking, taking up with that guy?"

"Love is blind."

"Oh, yeah? Well, this Scully came over to my magazine's office and demanded to speak to Moe. Lucky I'm friends with Moe's secretary, who has big ears. She only overheard a part of the *tête-à-tête*, but Scully spilled the beans about Hollie and himself."

"Oh, no."

"Oh yes. I suggest you hightail it to your cousin and lay the whole thing on the line."

"Tomorrow. Thanks."

"Don't mention it."

"If you find out anything else about what was said—"

"Don't think he mentioned you and Stella, if that's what you mean."

"But you aren't sure. The secretary didn't hear it all."

"This is tough, kid."

It was 4:30 a.m. Nina hesitated briefly. Then she picked up the phone.

Later in the morning, Nina, groggy and sleepless, found Elaine in her office earlier than expected. Nina had arrived thinking she would wait in the secretary's vestibule and stew about her problems, but her cousin was already digging through a thick stack of papers on her desk. Her secretary's desk was empty and Elaine's door was open.

"Welcome back!" Elaine cried, coming around from her desk and giving Nina a big hug. "I can't wait to get the scoop. Come in. Mildred's sick today." Elaine paused and stared. "You look terrible."

"Bad night's sleep. Actually, no sleep."

Elaine's eyes widened. "What did you find out?"

Nina slumped into the seat in front of Elaine's desk. She told Elaine what she'd learned from Sue Edelman.

Elaine shook her head with resignation. "Ah well, then we'll just have to go ahead with—" She stopped abruptly and glanced at Nina. "There's something else, isn't there?"

No use beating around the bush. Nina told her about Shanahan's phone call. While Nina talked, Elaine tapped a red nail rhythmically on her desk. As Nina proceeded with her story, Elaine's tapping increased, until finally she jumped up, went over to her window and peered out. "You'll have to go to Aaron with this."

"I always go to you."

"I can't handle this."

"You've never sent me over your head before."

"I just spoke to Aaron. He's in his office until ten."

"I hate having to tell him anything like this, especially with the way he feels about Hollie."

"Nina, if you're going to get mixed up in sordid lifestyles, you're going to have to develop a thicker skin." It was the only thing Elaine had ever said that rang of condemnation. Without further ado, Nina dragged herself straight to Aaron and told him the problem, omitting the source of her information.

Aaron was strangely subdued about the whole thing. He nodded and stroked his chin. Made some notes on a pad, asking for clarification of some details, including Teddy Scully's previous history. Then he announced, without fanfare, "I'll take care of it," and gestured for Nina to go.

Aaron *would* take care of it, of that much Nina was sure.

Chapter
Thirty-Nine

Days Of Reckoning

ON THANKSGIVING, STELLA and Nina made the trip to the Snipes ranch. Everything was set for Abbie to come back to Beverly Hills and live in the cottage on the Carter/Kane estate. But no one had told her. Each week they discussed telling her, but they were always pressed for time. Now, however, time was pressing in on them. Shooting was scheduled to wrap in less than two weeks and Abbie as of yet had no clue as to how her life was about to change once again.

Thanksgiving morning, Nina and Stella discovered one of the tires was flat on Stella's Oldsmobile. They decided to take Nina's little Mercury, but she'd apparently left the headlights on the previous night and the battery had gone dead. Nina didn't like it. It all seemed like a bad omen. They wound up borrowing Hollie's prized Nash-Healy convertible, a classy green birthday present he'd bought for himself in August.

They finally made it off at around ten-thirty, Stella at the wheel. For fifteen minutes or so, they drove silently.

"I can't do this," Nina said finally.

"Do what, honey?"

"There are the lies we tell to the world for protection. Then there are the lies we're telling ourselves."

"Sometimes we need protection from ourselves, too."

"You know what I'm getting at."

"I know I love you more than anyone else in the world. Except Abbie, and of course that's different."

"I love you too, Stella. But we have to talk about this. There are things we have to do, whether we like to or not. But sometimes I think..."

Stella reached over and took Nina's hand.

"You don't have to explain," she said.

"Yes, I do. That's the difference between us. Nothing is what it seems to be and you seem okay with that."

"Is anything ever what it seems to be?" Stella asked. "That's not my doing. I don't think I have the power to control the world's doings, one way or another."

"You do a good job of trying," Nina said.

"So do you. You are top-notch by now at scheming and plotting." Stella shrugged. "Let's hear it. What's bothering you?"

"We can't go up there and pretend Abbie's coming back."

"Of course not."

"Then why didn't we say something?"

"We're saying something now."

An ancient farm truck passed at that moment, loaded with crates of chickens. As it rattled by, a gust of feathers and dust blew around them in a whirl of poultry odor. They quickly rolled up the windows.

"You knew I'd bring it up, didn't you?" Nina asked.

"I want you to live with me," Stella said.

"What?"

"Live in the cottage. Quit the studio. Become my press agent. My business manager. It doesn't matter what we call it."

Nina slowly let the implications drift in. "You knew Abbie wouldn't come home. You knew the cottage was being built and she'd never live in it."

"Oh, Nina. You knew it, too."

Stella was, as usual, one step ahead of her. It was frustrating. If she, Nina, had really plumbed her soul, she'd have been able to admit she knew about the cottage.

Now it was Stella's turn to fume. "We hide things from ourselves until we're ready to face them. Damn the fancy moralizing. Come live with me. I want you to be a part of my life. Forever."

"I can't just pack up and leave the studio. I'm going to need some time to think about this."

Nina knew what Stella was going to say, of course.

"I'll wait," Stella said. "Take as much time as you need."

THAT THANKSGIVING DAY, they ate a marvelous feast in the roomy dining room of the Snipes' ranch house, at a huge and festive table. There were two roast turkeys with cranberry/orange sauce. For dessert, there was an orange cake. Each guest was presented with a basket of oranges to take with them. Abbie sat next to Tex, the handsome Snipes cousin from Arizona. They conducted intimate side conversations in sign, causing a few knowing glances among the rest of the party. Before Nina and Stella left, Stella and Abbie took a stroll among the orange trees. When they returned, Abbie came running up to Nina and hugged her.

"She knows," Stella said.

"Everything?" Nina asked.

Abbie touched Nina's cheek. She signed something.

Stella smiled. "My sister says she's glad I have someone to love me now that she's not around."

And another person had been told the truth.

SHOOTING OF *LIFE As Usual* wrapped the 5th of December. The cast and crew had a late-evening wrap party five days later in the Playroom at the Players restaurant. Hollie was a good buddy of Preston Sturges and had made arrangements with the genius director and madcap restaurant owner. The general mood was optimistic. In the dailies, Hollie and Stella showed a magnetism that reminded everyone of their earliest films together. But Nina was feeling anxious. As Dottie had predicted, there had been slackening interest in the Carter/Kane couple. Not anything earth-shattering, just a slight drop in phone calls requesting interviews, fewer fan letters, the kind of nagging but nebulous insinuations of the worst kind of trouble: boredom.

To counteract her fears, Nina cooked up a host of plans. She arranged interviews with fan magazines and the major papers, she arranged for whistle-stop tours of fifteen cities, for nightclub outings, for charity balls, and for parties at home. Before they launched into the thick of it all, a veritable storm of exhausting publicity, Stella came up with a startling demand. She and Nina, she insisted, would go away alone together for a weekend. No ifs ands or buts. Stella had made all the arrangements.

Chapter
Forty

Alone At Last

NINA AND STELLA drove to a cabin in the San Bernardino Mountains near Lake Arrowhead. The place, owned by a friend of Hollie's, was on a graveled road a few miles from town, surrounded by ten acres of sloping meadows and trees. It was not, however, a shack by any means. Hollie's pal had raved about how secluded the cabin was, while still equipped with enough modern amenities to suit Hollywood expectations. Nina had presented the weekend to the studio as an intensive planning session. The studio was willing to buy it, with the usual stipulation: Use discretion.

But there would be no studio business.

They had piled into Stella's Oldsmobile, wearing no makeup, in sturdy leather boots, heavy wool slacks and plaid jackets. They brought enough food for a battalion, playing cards, books and a jigsaw puzzle. They brought mittens, wool hats, long underwear and two pairs of borrowed snowshoes, although neither of them had any idea how to use the peculiar contraptions.

When they arrived at the cabin, they found it to be much as described, remote but cozy. Stella checked the electricity and propane, both of which worked fine. There was a huge stone fireplace, a well-equipped kitchen, high wood-beamed ceilings and worn, inviting leather furniture. An unsettling herd of stuffed animal heads hung from the walls. The bedroom featured a huge bed framed in heavy oak, covered with intricately patterned wool Indian blankets. Stella built a roaring fire in the fireplace and unrolled a heavy bearskin rug in front of it. "Ever make love on a bearskin rug?"

Nina blushed. She glanced around the room. It was glowing with fiery intensity from the crackling timbers piled high in the fireplace. The flickering heat came in waves, had a pulsing, sensual quality. One part of her wanted to tear off her clothes and dance wildly over to the soft, bushy rug. Another part felt haunted by an imaginary audience. "I suppose we'd hear if anyone happened to come up the road."

"No one will come."

"But we'd hear if they did?"

"Absolutely," Stella replied. "We're alone."

"For three days."

"That's three days more than we've ever had." Stella sashayed up to Nina and stroked her cheek. "I wish we lived together."

Nina sighed. "I'm not ready to decide about living with you on the estate. I thought we weren't going to discuss anything serious."

Stella nuzzled Nina's neck, letting her lips trail deliciously down Nina's throat. "I don't want to discuss anything."

Nina could feel Stella's quickened breath, warm against her skin. From above the fireplace, a stuffed antelope stared curiously. "You're sure we'd hear someone coming?" Nina closed her eyes.

"I promise," Stella whispered.

"If it's true, we could be as loud as we want, couldn't we?" Nina felt the familiar, wonderful throbbing as Stella pressed against her.

"Mmm," Stella said. "How loud could you be? What would I have to do..." She didn't wait for an answer.

There was no way to measure decibels precisely, but it wasn't necessary to do so.

When they'd finished, they were both damp and deliciously exhausted, throats raw, nerves tingling.

"I'll never feel anything like that again," Nina moaned.

"Think not?" Stella said, stroking Nina's belly. "We have three days to prove you wrong."

In the morning, in the bright sunshine, Stella was beside Nina in the yielding bed, sheltered in wool blankets. It was daylight and they were together and they didn't have to hide. Nina made coffee and brought it back. "Some people can do this every day."

"But do they appreciate it as much as we do right now?"

"I'm getting mad. It's not right. We'll never be able to do this for real."

Stella touched a fingertip to Nina's lips. "Remember? No talking about the outside world."

They read, they trudged in the snow, as far as they could without resorting to the perplexing snowshoes. They ate huge country meals, bacon and eggs, steak and potatoes. They made love on the bearskin rug, in the bed, and once on the squeaking couch. They put together a ridiculously difficult jigsaw puzzle. It portrayed the center panel of Bosch's *Garden of Earthly Delights*. Nina was a jigsaw whiz, but Stella provided worthy competition.

"Damn," Stella commented, placing one of the last pieces. "This is cultured art work? Look at what these people are doing."

"After last night, I feel like one of them."

"After last night, you *are* one of them." Stella pointed to a bacchanalian couple entangled in an amorous and contorted embrace. "Maybe one of these two."

"I never put myself in that position," Nina replied huffily. She placed her hand on Stella's. "But I could try..."

It was wonderful and liberating, and the time rushed by too fast.

On the last morning, Nina woke to find Stella gone from the bed. From outside, she heard a rhythmic chopping sound. She threw on a robe, stuffed her feet into a pair of boots and went out into the frigid air. There was Stella, splitting logs with strong blows. She looked up at Nina, gripping her ax, hair splayed around her face, feet planted firmly in the snow. Her gaze was elemental. She was a mountain goddess. In that moment, Nina was dizzy in love. This, along with the scene of Stella's emotional trouncing at Kubicek's ramshackle place, completed her picture of Stella. She *knew* her now. She knew her at her weakest and at her strongest. Nina turned abruptly and ran into the house.

Stella found her lying face down on the bed, blubbering.

Stella sighed. "What hurts?"

"This weekend. It only makes it worse."

"We always have each other. If we choose to."

"We always have hiding and scheming and being frightened."

"We'll have hiding and scheming. We don't have to be frightened. We can be brave and fierce."

"You can be brave and fierce. I'm not like that."

"I'm not so sure about that. And I'm the one that sees inside you."

"I don't know if I can be whoever you're seeing. I don't know if I can do this."

"What else would you do?"

Nina hid her face in the pillow, leaving just enough air space to make her words intelligible. "Forget it. We promised to ignore the outside world. We only have a few more hours. I'd rather make love to you."

Stella's eyes flashed. "Why, honey, you've never said anything like that out loud before."

"Shhh," Nina replied. "No more words."

Just before they left, however, words did intrude. They were packing to leave. Stella held up a book.

"That's mine," Nina said.

"I saw it in your suitcase. *Invisible Man*. It looked interesting. I was just leafing through it and I saw the inscription."

"That's a friend in New York."

"I'll bet she's smart and sophisticated."

"She is."

"Is she beautiful?"

"Not as much as you."

"Did you tell her about us?"

"It's safe. She understands."

"She likes you, doesn't she?"

"I've never seen you jealous."

"I've never had to be."

"What about me? In love with a universal object of desire?"

"That's different."

"I just get so tired of it all sometimes."

"Tired enough to leave me? Tired enough to take up with the sophisticated lady in New York?"

"No," Nina said hesitantly.

"Nina, you're a lasting part of me. Always, whether you stay or not."

Looking at her, Nina knew Stella was absolutely sincere. More than sincere. She was stating what was, for her, a fact of life. What's more, Nina understood, in a burst of revelation, that the same was true for her. No matter what she did or where she went, Stella would remain a part of her.

IT WAS LATE when they arrived back that night, almost eleven, but the Beverly Hills house was lit up as though a big bash was on the schedule. "Uh oh," Nina said.

Hollie and Lance were in the living room, slumped in two armchairs. Beside each of them was an empty martini glass. "What's happened?" Nina asked, dropping her valise on the carpet.

"It's a long story," Hollie said.

Nina glanced at Stella. Stella shrugged, took off her plaid jacket, and went to the couch. After a moment's hesitation, Nina did the same.

It was a mess, all right. Hollie and Lance took turns narrating, interrupting one another with details and clarifications. The sad story was this:

On the Friday Stella and Nina left on their retreat, Lance had quarreled with Dick Preston. "He promised to go bungalow hunting with me. Then he calls me after I've been waiting two hours, to say it's too risky! I was so hurt and upset!"

"I felt bad for Lance," Hollie added. "I arranged something to cheer him up."

Hollie's consolation was a bachelor gathering for the next night. Two young hopefuls at the studio had been pestering him. Hollie took them up on their advances. Always cautious, he arranged an intimate beach party at a very private rented cottage in Manhattan Beach.

"We were lounging on the patio," Hollie said, "when we heard someone rustling. Who should it turn out to be but Teddy, taking photographs. I guess I lost my temper. I smashed Teddy's camera. We started shouting at each other."

"A neighbor called the sheriff," Lance interjected. "Well, those two young bucks from the studio went tearing down the slope, into the brush, and got away. Hollie, Teddy and I got dragged to the sheriff's office." Lance grimaced at Nina's horrified expression. "Hollie called Elaine, but couldn't reach her. With you gone and no more Shanahan, he called Aaron Bermann. I was going to call Dick, but I knew he'd make a big stink if I did. Turns out Aaron called him instead. Seems like, by some amazing coincidence, the Manhattan Beach sheriff happens to be a personal friend of Dick's father. Dick smoothed things over with the sheriff with a mention of his father and a box of Cuban cigars."

The end result, Hollie and Lance assured the women, was a total cover-up. Teddy Scully was given a firm lecture from the sheriff and threatened with arrest if he breathed a word of the shenanigans to anyone.

"There's no chance of this getting out?" Nina asked. She was thinking about Shanahan's late-night disclosure about Teddy's visit with the *Tinseltown Insider*.

"No chance in hell," Hollie said.

"What about the neighbor who called the sheriff?"

"I rented the cottage under an assumed name. And no one saw us, I'm pretty sure. Only heard the scuffle."

"Oh, brother," Nina said. "Well, let's just keep our fingers crossed."

Chapter
Forty-One

A Little Scandal Goes A Long Way

THE WHOLE THING blew in mid-January, when the *Tinseltown Insider* hit the news stands. The stars of *Life as Usual* had just completed their fifteen-city tour. Stella and Hollie blitzed through endless local interviews, signed autographs, expressed countless words of gratitude to their fans. But the crowds were not as big as Nina would have liked and the local journalists seemed disturbingly blasé at the chance to interview celebrities of the Carter/Kane magnitude. The premiere was scheduled for early spring. The publicity machine seemed to be fighting an uphill battle. Well, they needn't have worried. The *Tinseltown Insider* took care of that particular dilemma:

DOES A HOLLYWOOD LEADING MAN SWING BOTH WAYS?

Teddy Scully's article was a nasty piece of innuendo —

...Everyone knows Hollywood can be a Babylon of Deviate Desires and Odd Appetites. Some of the most 'happy' marriages are actually bedeviled by one member or the other's 'side affairs.' But the most disgusting are those little affairs of the 'queer' kind. Pity the poor wife who has to learn of her beloved hubby's dallying with twisted twerps, queens, and gay pretty boys.
We can't know for certain about one supposedly perfect marriage; however, we did manage to find Hollace Carter, out for a 'bachelor' weekend with an aging 'college boy' type who was featured some time ago in this magazine for his 'lavender' high jinks, plus some young fellows whose identities are unknown. To add to the brouhaha, this reporter was roughed up by the big star, the sheriff was called, and the whole thing was hush-hushed by a producer at

Lumina Pictures, one Dick Preston! Seems the
exec's eminent father is an old buddy of the
aforementioned sheriff...

"DICK'S IN HOT water now, isn't he?" Lance moaned. "At least it's just coercion and not perversion."

"Everyone's in hot water," Nina said.

The next day, the usual gang had the expected meeting. Just as they had settled around the table, Poppa burst in, waving the *Tinseltown Insider*. "I've had enough trouble from New York. They're after me and you all know it." He pointed at Dick Preston. "Well, my only consolation is that you will never run this studio and you've managed to disgrace your very own father once again. But you'll boil in your own oil. Your father still won't allow anyone to fire you. You'll grow old and die here."

Dick Preston sat silently, attempting to look penitent. But there was, Nina thought, an odd, veiled glee beneath the supposed consternation.

"Poppa, why don't you sit?" Elaine said. "Your face is purple."

"Did you know?" Poppa moaned.

Elaine shook her head no.

"How about you?" Poppa said to Murray.

Murray shook his head no.

"And you?" Poppa said to Nina.

Nina shook her head no.

Poppa turned to Aaron. "I'm not going to ask you. I don't want to know. Just fix it." Poppa threw the magazine on the table and stormed out.

Aaron had a look of great satisfaction on his face. *Why not?* His rival, Dick Preston, had just been obliterated from contention for the prize of studio head. "How about that divorce? Let's get rid of Hollace Carter once and for all."

"I think they like being married," Murray said.

"I don't give a good goddamned what they like," Aaron said. "We arranged that marriage and we'll end it if we like."

Elaine spoke up calmly. "I don't think we should hurry into divorce."

Aaron looked as though he was going to protest. Elaine raised an eyebrow at him. He clenched his fists and a vein began to bulge in his forehead. She smiled sweetly. "It's woman's intuition. I just feel like we should wait."

Aaron glowered. "All right, but I at least want her hinting at divorce."

Elaine shook her head. "I have another idea."

"WAIT."

Nina was sliding into her Mercury. Walter Bermann hopped into the passenger seat.

"Drive around the block a few times. No, better yet, drive up to Forest Lawn."

"Walter, I'm exhausted."

"Too exhausted to save your bottom?"

Nina glanced at him.

"Sorry. Just trying to get my point across."

Nina drove to Forest Lawn and parked alongside a row of tall graves in a remote corner of the cemetery. They were, she realized with a start, not far from Sybil Croft's crypt.

"There's something not kosher in this kingdom," Walter said.

"You're not kidding."

"There's a lot of beef baloney getting tossed around here. I swear I saw Teddy Scully and Aaron together one night a couple of months ago. I was walking down a little street in West Hollywood and I saw them together. Now wasn't that an odd coincidence, me seeing them together, us three all in the same vicinity at the same time?"

"When was this?"

"Early October."

"You're sure?"

"Swear on my grandma's grave. I remember thinking it was screwy."

"Extremely screwy."

"I sure as heck can't figure it out."

"Neither can I."

"Now that piece of dope rivals anything Shanahan ever handed you. I'm not such a bad guy, am I?"

"You're a swell guy."

"Thank you. I'll keep my ears to the ground."

"I appreciate it."

"Say, I need a date for that John Huston premiere next month. Tit for tat, right? I need a little intelligent conversation for a change."

"You're on."

Walter Bermann sighed. "Ever get tired of all the camouflage?"

"Very much so."

They watched an elderly man in black setting a bouquet of flowers at a marble gravestone. "From the cradle to the grave," Walter said.

Chapter
Forty-Two

The Final Plan

ON JANUARY 25TH, 1954, Lumina scheduled a press conference at the Beverly Wilshire Hotel. In a ballroom packed with a clamoring press, Hollie poised at the dais with a fierce-looking Stella at his side. Flash bulbs popped and the press hounds yelped, until Hollie held up a stern hand.

"I was framed," he announced to the hushed reporters, "by the *Tinseltown Insider*. The whole mess was a set-up. I'm a happily married guy with a gorgeous wife that *any* man would be crazy to cheat on."

The general press hated Moe Mink and his magazine with intensity reserved for enemies resembling themselves. A relieved gasp was expelled by all. The collected news outlets to the world listened while Hollie explained the innocent get-together he'd arranged since his wife was out of town. The *Tinseltown Insider* and Teddy Scully deliberately twisted his intentions. His release from the sheriff's clutches was due to his actual blamelessness. Blah, blah, blah, as Lolly Cooper would say. The press ate it up. They liked Hollie Carter. They hated Moe Mink.

The next day, Nina arrived in Elaine's office with a stack of newspapers.

"This is a publicist's dream," she exclaimed, dropping her burden on her desk. "Why, you'd almost think the whole thing was planned."

Elaine smiled. "Tell me what you've got."

"I have furious and righteous reports of Hollie's virtue. What a wonderful tale of unwarranted accusations and ultimate vindications. Even Elizabeth Taylor's shenanigans pale in comparison."

"At least until she takes up with a married man," Elaine replied contentedly.

Suddenly, there was enormous interest in the forthcoming *Life As Usual*. TIME and LIFE expressed interest in profiles of Stella and Hollie. Letters in quantities greater than Santa's at Christmas arrived in bulging sacks. The fans were overwhelmingly supportive. The only one who didn't seem pleased was Aaron Bermann. He wore a perpetually distraught look, as though something was slipping away from him. It was odd. On the face of things he was sitting pretty.

On February 8th, Lance and Nina were out shopping. "I feel like a traitor," she said, standing on the sidewalk in front of the window display of Mel's Appliances on Wilshire Boulevard.

"Don't be silly," he replied. "Everyone has one. It's about time you faced the times. Lucille Ball is the funniest woman on earth. And I certainly wouldn't mind spending a little private time with the Lone Ranger. That mask. So sexy. What about Tonto? What do you think those two boys are about? If I was still acting, I would desert the movies for television. It's the wave of the future." He took Nina's arm and pulled her through the door. Once inside, they were accosted by a man who reeked of Burma Shave. He led them down a row of television sets, explaining each model's virtues and shortcomings with a passion that was almost evangelical. The salesman turned out to be Mel himself, owner of the establishment and fanatical television proponent. He led them to a mahogany set with a twelve-inch screen.

"The Tournament of Roses parade on the first of January was broadcast in color. What a historic event. The first coast-to-coast colorcast!" Mel slapped the top of the television. "Because of my connections I was provided with this RCA Model 5 color set, one of only two hundred made. Look at it. It's the future. Someday we'll only have color sets, but for now I can offer you the best of black-and-white."

The rest of the sets in the place were larger, with much more distinct black-and-white images. But the little screen of the color set was ablaze in glorious Technicolor. All of the black-and-white sets were tuned to a single channel, a wall of recurrent images. As Mel blabbered, a show began on the many sets.

Who should appear on the screen but Dottie Strong, in one of her strikingly ugly outfits, complete with ugly hat. Dottie was sitting in a chair next to a coffee table. On the other side of the table was an empty chair. The upcoming premiere of Dottie's show had been the talk of Hollywood in the past few weeks. But knowing it was coming and seeing Dottie on the screen were two different animals, so to speak.

"Isn't that delicious?" Lance crowed. "Now that woman's bad taste can be seen across the nation."

Up until that point, the sound had been muted on the plethora of sets, in order to make room for Mel's sales pitch.

"Can you put on the sound?" Lance asked. "This is going to be good, I guarantee you."

Mel reached over and cranked up the volume on an expensive model made by Zenith. Dottie introduced herself with surprising modesty and grace, then smiled slyly. "Please welcome my very first guest," she announced in her raspy voice. After a brief round of applause from the studio audience, Teddy Scully came marching onto the set and took the empty seat.

"Oh no," Nina breathed out.

"Teddy Scully," Dottie intoned. Television had apparently given her license to adopt the momentous tone of a Roosevelt. "Former brilliant war photographer. Respected political journalist. Disgraced political journalist. Our modern-day Ulysses journeys to Hollywood and encounters Babylon."

Teddy wore a look of ridiculously exaggerated repentance. But Nina knew Teddy. She saw the mockery in his eyes.

"You ratted on a big Hollywood star. He claims you lied. What gives here, Mr. Scully?" Dottie continued. She gave a brief summation of the Hollie Carter scandal. A little of the dirt-gathering edge was creeping back into her voice. "You have an incredible confession to tell us, don't you?" she finished up triumphantly.

"I can't live with the lie," Teddy proclaimed, his voice breaking. "Hollace Carter was framed. By the *Tinseltown Insider*. And by me."

"Incredible," Dottie blurted out. "Fill us in, my friend."

"This is terrible," Teddy began, "I left my job with *Modern Screen* and thought I could blackmail my way into a job at Lumina Studios. I went to *Mr. Aaron Bermann, the head of publicity*," he said with a heavy emphasis. "He promised me work if I would first do some job for the *Tinseltown Insider*. Aaron said he and Moe Mink had a kind of a deal."

"So you went over to the *Tinseltown Insider* and were assigned to frame Hollace Carter?" Dottie prompted.

"It was all arranged," Teddy said. "I don't know what *the head of publicity at Lumina Pictures, Aaron Bermann*," again, he weighted this phrase with heavy emphasis, "has against Hollace Carter, but the whole Manhattan Beach cottage scandal was a sham."

Dottie Strong wagged a finger at the television audience. "Hollywood is an image, an idea. But now you in this vast country will know the real shenanigans, if I have my way. And now a short commercial break before we bring on our next guest, Art Spillane, an animal trainer who brought along one of his most talented chimpanzees."

Oh my god, Nina thought. Television was creating monsters. Dottie was getting out of bed with the studios. What next? What untold nightmares was television going to bring forth? Nina reached over and turned off the sound. "This is getting more and more ridiculous."

Mel stared at the two of them, puzzled. Nina turned to Lance. "Something's up."

"I can't explain," Lance said. "Look what happened to me the last time I said too much."

"Lance..." Nina began threateningly.

"All right," Lance said. "Some of us were involved. But don't ask me any more. Go ask someone else. Please. You have to know, this was a group project. It was too complicated to be anything else."

AUNT NETTIE GREETED Nina when she came barging up to the Villa.

"Where's Elaine?"

"On the back lawn," Aunt Nettie said. "Nina?"

"Yes?"

"Remember. We're family. We love you. We wouldn't ever do anything to hurt you. Sometimes things are done for your benefit that seem hurtful."

There really wasn't anything to say to Aunt Nettie. She was, at best, an informed bystander. Right now, Nina wanted to talk to an actual player. She left Aunt Nettie standing in the hall and marched through the over-decorated house. She stepped down the stone stairs of the veranda and proceeded across the lawn to the pool. Elaine was lying in a chaise lounge, voluptuous and oily. About a hundred feet away, on the back lawn, Murray was engaged in what seemed to be a dog obedience training session. When he caught sight of Nina, he waved. "Hey, watch this!" Murray's voice wafted from the distance. He held up a plastic hoop. Valentino jumped through it, yapping happily.

Elaine was reading a script. Colette lay sleeping on a little doggie bed at her feet. Nina didn't detect an ounce of surprise on her cousin's face when Elaine finally looked up.

"Look at that man," Elaine said fondly. "Murray's teaching circus tricks to that mutt of his. Isn't that cute? Men need their hobbies." She paused. "And some men need guidance," she added.

"I suppose," Nina said, "now that you've eliminated all the competition, Murray has a good shot of running the studio. Do you think he's tough enough? No, you already know he isn't. But, I guess he'll have plenty of *guidance*, won't he?"

"Whatever are you talking about?" Elaine exclaimed. Then she smiled her most dazzling smile.

"Let me see if I can get the story straight," Nina said. "I don't want you to think I'm absolutely witless."

"No one ever thought you were. But, go ahead, tell me what you've come up with."

"This whole thing was a set-up. But it wasn't Aaron who set it up. He got set up."

Elaine sighed. "This plot had so many complications, I myself wondered if we could pull it off."

"Who is 'we'?" Nina asked. Before Elaine could reply, Nina added: "No, let me put it together. The whole thing revolves around Teddy Scully."

"I imagine a person could assume that," Elaine replied.

"That's what Hollie meant about more than one way to skin a cat."

Elaine raised an eyebrow.

"Hollie was sneaking out and seeing Teddy. Teddy came up with a plan and presented it to Hollie."

"Good girl," Elaine said.

"Then Hollie brought the plan to Stella. And Lance brought it to Dick Preston."

"Hmmm," Elaine encouraged, "go on."

"And so they concocted the scandal, then the false cover-up, then Teddy's confession to Dottie Strong. They must have brought it to you. They knew they needed you to pull it off. And of course the whole thing suited *your* needs perfectly. Me, I got sent to New York, I got sent away with Stella. All planned."

"Imagine," Elaine said, "a plan as beautiful as a well-written script. It's complicated, devious, risky, but superb. The good guys win and the bad guys lose. Imagine how thrilled a person would be to get that plan rolling."

"Teddy goes to Aaron. Aaron sends him to the *Tinseltown Insider*. Teddy and Moe Mink arrange to set up Hollie and Lance, only Hollie and Lance are already in on the scheme."

Elaine sighed. "Now I suppose you tell me how you were used and abused."

"Shanahan calls me up with some secret news from Moe's secretary. So I would go to Aaron, on your command. Was that bastard Shanahan in on it, too?"

"Why, Nina, I've never heard you swear."

"I'm sorry."

"Yes, Shanahan was in on it. But, even before Shanahan, we've always had someone helping us at the *Tinseltown Insider*. That doesn't surprise you, does it?"

"Nothing surprises me anymore."

"Shanahan was only a minor player. It's Moe's secretary who's been our biggest resource. She happens to go to the same beauty parlor as your butler Alfred's wife. The secretary hates her job and Moe Mink, so it wasn't hard to enlist her help."

"Alfred knew?"

Elaine nodded.

"Of course," Nina sighed. "The whole world was in on it apparently, except Aaron and Moe Mink and me. Oh, and poor Walter Bermann."

"Poor Walter seemed determined to fill you in, but he wasn't quite smart enough or devious enough to figure out all of what was happening. We arranged for him to gather some information and he probably wondered why it was all so convenient, but he did what we thought he would do. Go to you. I told you, it was risky and complicated. But it worked. Come now, try to appreciate the beauty of it." Before Nina could answer, Colette awoke from her nap and started barking. Murray and Valentino were headed their way, both flushed with excitement.

"Filled you in, huh?" he said to Nina.

"I figured it out myself," Nina replied.

"Smart girl," Murray said, without the slightest trace of concern. He bent down to Collette. "Collette, sit!" Collette bared her teeth and growled. Murray grinned blissfully. "Doesn't listen to a word I say."

"Well," Nina said. "I have to hand it to you all. It looks like you've orchestrated a pretty neat little coup."

"Enjoy it," Elaine said. "With each ending comes a new beginning. Who knows what's next?"

Chapter
Forty-Three

The End

WHEN NINA ARRIVED at the Beverly Hills estate, Stella was in the library. She sat in an armchair in front of the fireplace, reading the copy of Ellison's *Invisible Man* that Sue Edelman had given Nina. "This is one fine story. It's a wonder how much ugliness exists in this world."

Nina went over to the matching armchair and settled in. "I was thinking we should get a bearskin rug. And a big lock on the library door."

"A big rug and a very big lock."

They were interrupted by a knock on the door. Hollie poked his head in. "Is this private?"

"Not from you," Stella said. "Come in."

Hollie stood just inside the door. He turned to Nina. "You knew. When did she tell you?" He wagged a finger at Stella. "When did you tell her?"

"As we were leaving the cabin up at Lake Arrowhead." Stella shrugged. "I could feel her slipping away from me. I knew I was taking a long shot. I wasn't sure Nina could do it. She was going to have to play herself."

Nina laughed. "Okay, okay. I'll admit I was never much of an actress. But I did it. You should have *seen* me in Aaron's office!"

"You deserve an Oscar, at the least," Hollie exclaimed.

"I had two very good role models," Nina said.

"I tip my hat to you, Nina." With that, Hollie stepped back towards the door. "I'll leave you two alone to celebrate. And, girls, thank you." He paused, face struggling. "You won't leave me now, will you?"

"You're stuck with us," they said in unison.

When he was gone, Nina turned to Stella. "I did it, all right. I pulled off a perfect imitation of myself. But what does it mean, really? More deception and lies."

"Take a few minutes and enjoy your triumph. There's plenty of time to fret."

Nina laughed with unrestrained delight. "I was doing it again! I got you. I even got you. This is marvelous. I finally understand acting. I understand Hollywood and I understand..."

Nina went over and positioned herself on Stella's lap. "Am I too heavy?"

"Just right."

"Does this mean we're stuck together too?"

"As far as I'm concerned," Stella said, circling her arms around Nina, "there was never any other ending. The happy ending."

Epilogue

Nina Speaks Out, May 2003

STELLA AND I had planned on being ninety-nine together, two old dames still scheming. Then she went up and died on me. Oh, Stella, this wasn't in the script. At least not the one we created.

I wasn't surprised that she asked me to tell this story. I knew Stella too well. It was because of her passion for story-telling and drama. But, more so, it was a way to honor our relationship.

Her passing was a media event for days.

I wake up shocked sometimes, feeling puzzled at how my life turned out. Now I face what's left of it as a three-ring circus. That's all right. Our life was always something of a circus. I just wish I had Stella here to help me and share a private laugh about all the nonsense.

IN 1985, HOLLIE died of AIDS. Stella and he were still married, although in later years he'd taken to spending four or five months every winter on a remote island in Hawaii with Teddy Scully. Hollie's career faded slowly through the fifties. He worked mostly in television after that, enjoying a little bit of reprieve with a popular detective series called *Whitlock* in the seventies.

When he wasn't with Teddy, Hollie lived with us. In the main house, of course, while I "lived" in the cottage. He was sick for two years before he died. I miss him very much.

Teddy went to work for Dottie Strong. He always managed to land on his feet, which is, I guess, why he was willing to take the most heat in the Final Plan. Dottie loved him and he found her amusing. They worked together happily until Dottie died of cirrhosis in 1959. In the sixties, he went back to Washington and eventually had a hand in uncovering some major political scandals.

Lance died four years ago of AIDS, two years after Dick Preston.

The corporate headquarters in New York ousted Poppa in 1955. Murray was appointed studio chief and acted as Elaine's figurehead. These days, Elaine could run the studio outright, of course. I don't know if she would want to, by now.

Abbie married Tex in 1956. Tex eventually became foreman at the Snipes ranch. Abbie and Tex had three children. The boy is deaf, the two girls are hearing. The boy became an actor in deaf theater, one of the daughters is a pediatrician, and the other a sign interpreter.

Shanahan went back to Chicago, ostensibly because his elderly mother was dying. He never came back. Eventually, I heard, he wound up in a suburb, working for a Catholic weekly, sober and with a wife and two sons from a previous marriage. We never spoke after he left, but I think often of him. I wish he would surprise me with a late-night call.

The *Tinseltown Insider* died in the sixties due to competition from the plethora of scandal outlets that came to be over time. As the many tabloids began to emerge, the poor *Insider* started looking pretty tame. Moe Mink eventually started production on the first of the tabloid-style television shows, *The Hollywood Connection*.

STELLA AND I? From Stella, I learned what love is. The world might not have been perfect, but we were perfect for each other.

And you — now you know the truth.

OR DO YOU?

OTHER REGAL CREST BOOKS YOU MAY ENJOY

Breaking Jaie
by S. Renee Bess

Jaie Baxter, an African-American Ph.D candidate at Philadelphia's Allerton University, is determined to win a prestigious writing grant. In order to win the Adamson Grant, Jaie initially plans to take advantage of one of the competition's judges, Jennifer Renfrew, who is also a University official. Jennifer has spent the past ten years alone following the murder of her lover, Patricia Adamson, in whose honor the grant is named. Jennifer is at first susceptible to Jaie's flirtation, but is later vengeful when she discovers the real reason for Jaie's sudden romantic interest in her. A lunch with an old cop friend reveals that Jaie may very well have ties to Adamson's death.

Jaie is confronted with painful memories as she prepares an autobiographical essay for the grant application. She recalls the emotional trauma of her older brother's death, the murder of a police detective, her dismissal from her "dream" high school, and her victimization at the hands of hateful homophobic students. She remembers her constant struggles with her mother's alcohol-fueled jealousies and physical abuse she had to endure. This wake-up call causes her to look at her life in new ways.

But Jaie is not the only student applying for the grant. Terez Overton, a wealthy Boston woman, is Jaie's chief competitor. Jaie is drawn to the New Englander immediately but is also unnerved by her. She has no clue that Terez is trying to decide whether she wants to accept an opportunity to write an investigative article about an unsolved murder. Writing that article could put her budding relationship with Jaie in jeopardy.

And just when the angst of old memories and the uncertainty of her future with Terez are complicating Jaie's life, her manipulative ex, Seneca Wilson, returns to Philadelphia to reclaim Jaie using emotional blackmail. Senecas actions serve to wound and break Jaie in many ways. Will Seneca drive the final wedge between Jaie and Terez? Who will win the Adamson grant? And what did Jaie have to do with the death of Patricia Adamson?

ISBN: 978-1-932300-84-0

A Question of Integrity
by Megan Magill

Jess Maddocks is a talented business trouble-shooter who has worked hard to win the respect of her colleagues. When her boss assigns her a special case, Jess relishes the opportunity to prove her worth, unaware that her strict professional boundaries would this time fail her.

Rosalind Brannigan captivates people as easily as others smile. Described as charisma personified, she knows the value of her ability and is ruthless in utilising it to her own advantage. Confident in her mastery of the game, Rosalind assumes the rules will never change.

When Jess' assignment brings these two women together, it sparks an unexpected chain of events that proves life changing to both of them. They are forced to deal with mutual attraction and suspicion whilst an increasingly malignant shadow looms over them. As events unfold they must look to their own integrity as the only guide they have.

This is the first book in the Jess Maddocks series.

ISBN: 978-1-935053-12-5

OTHER REGAL CREST TITLES

About the Author:

Linda Morganstein is an award-winning fiction writer who also happens to be the product of a Borscht Belt childhood in the Jewish hotels of the Catskills. In the seventies, she dropped out of Vassar College and drove a VW van to California, where she lived in Sonoma County for many years. She currently resides in the Twin Cities of Minnesota with her understanding partner and intrepid dog, Sherman.

For more information go to: www.lindamorganstein.com